Taking The Lead

Sarah Monk

little
black
dress

First published in Great Britain in 2010 by
LITTLE BLACK DRESS
An imprint of HEADLINE PUBLISHING GROUP

A LITTLE BLACK DRESS paperback

1

Cataloguing in Publication Data is available from the British Library

ISBN 978 0 7553 4514 4

Typeset in Transit511BT by Avon DataSet Ltd,
Bidford-on-Avon, Warwickshire

Printed and bound in Great Britain by
Clays Ltd, St Ives plc

Headline's policy is to use papers that are natural, renewable and
recyclable products and made from wood grown in sustainable forests.
The logging and manufacturing processes are expected to conform to the
environmental regulations of the country of origin.

HEADLINE PUBLISHING GROUP
An Hachette UK Company
338 Euston Road
London NW1 3BH

www.littleblackdressbooks.com
www.headline.co.uk
www.hachette.co.uk

For Louise,
who is so much more than simply my sister

and for TPM,
always

Acknowledgements

Huge thanks to my wonderful editor Claire and all the team at LBD, and to my friend and fantastic agent Amanda Preston at Luigi Bonomi Associates. A very special mention to Hope Rescue Wales, whose dedication to the rescue of abandoned dogs is utterly amazing, and who found my little jewel Ruby for me. Much love and thanks to the fabulous friends and family who I am so lucky to share life with. And to beautiful inspirational Cornwall and the amazing eclectic people who love and live there.

I have been here before,
But when or how I cannot tell:
I know the grass beyond the door,
The sweet keen smell,
The sighing sound, the lights around the shore.

You have been mine before,
How long ago I may not know:
But just when at that swallow's soar
Your neck turn'd so,
Some veil did fall – I knew it all of yore.

Has this been thus before?
And shall not thus time's eddying flight
Still with our lives our love restore
In death's despite,
And day and night yield one delight once more?

Dante Gabriel Rossetti – artist and poet
(12 May 1828–9 April 1882)

Is it true that fates conspire
To find for us our heart's desire?
That we are half and never whole
Until we find our other soul –
The one true love for which we yearn
For which hearts like lights in windows burn?

Is it true that we are not complete
Until that perfect match we meet –
Led to their side by paths unknown
Destined from birth to death to own?
If it is true, then to the fates I plea
With heartfelt cry from bended knee.

Can you find him before I get grey hair
And whilst I still look hot in my underwear . . . ?

Theodora Elizabeth English – artist,
but could never claim to be a poet
(11 April 1985–until the vodka or an empty
King Size finally kills me off)

Afterwards, the thing that struck her the most was that she hadn't cried. Not even a little bit. And creative, artistic Theo was a cryer, a weeper, a wailer, an arm flailer, collapsing on furniture, writing angst-filled poems and painting dramatic canvasses where the paint was splashed like spurts of blood in a rather grisly murder scene. Not that she spent an awful lot of time crying, she wasn't that kind of girl; it was just that to her, crying was like needing a pee – if you really needed to do it, it wasn't good for you to hold it in.

And yet nothing.

Not even as Michael walked out of the door of their rented cottage, carrying his suitcases, not looking back, did she squeeze out one single tear; not a sob, not a snivel.

Nothing at all.

Not that she wasn't upset, of course she was upset. The man she had been with for three years, the man she had left London and her friends for . . . well, actually, she only had one friend, Imelda, but Imelda was as good as twenty friends rolled into the one friend and still she had left her behind . . . the man she had left her life, and her home for, all to follow *his* dream of moving back to Cornwall where he had been born, where *his* friends were, *his* family, *his* home – this man she had quit *everything* for had upped and left her.

Left her in a new and, she had to admit, somewhat strange place – and that was strange as in odd as well as in unfamiliar – with nothing.

Completely on her own.

Now the good thing about having nothing at all to keep you in a place is that you can leave whenever you feel like it, and perhaps the sensible option would have been to go back to London, cancel the so-imminent-it-was-about-to-give-birth-to-sextuplets-sale of her two-bed wonder in Camden and move back into her old flat, her old life, get everything back to how it was before, except with no Michael.

Except for one thing.

As Michael had fallen out of love with her, Theo had fallen *in* love.

First with Cornwall and its wild and wonderful and oh-so-paintable countryside and coastline; then with the weird little village they were living in and the odd people who eyed her paint-splattered person with wary curiosity as she lugged her easel from harbour to cliff top; and then with Otter Cottage, the beautiful quirky three-storey cottage next door to the one they were renting – a cottage that, when suddenly it had gone on the market two weeks earlier, Theo had literally begged Michael to consider as their permanent home.

And, as if by magic, as she had sat there in her stunned and tearless silence, only moments after Michael's car had headed off down the steep little hill towards the harbour and the ferry across the estuary, the telephone had rung.

It was the estate agent, who had been in the business long enough to know when someone had fallen in love with a house and was chomping at the bit to buy it, calling to report that the girl next door had decided she was now desperate to move and was prepared to accept an indecently low offer.

And as Theo sat and tried to listen whilst her emotions were muffling her ears, it suddenly began to filter through into her shell-shocked brain that, despite the fact that Michael no longer loved her, she still loved Cornwall and she still loved the house next door.

A house that had a beautiful secret garden, and a kitchen the size of a squash court which had a skylight made of stained glass so every time the sun hit midday the room was shot through with colour like the inside of a kaleidoscope, and a huge attic room with windows overlooking the ocean, which would make a perfect studio, for when she wasn't so upset she was channelling Goya, she usually painted beautiful watercolours of the sea or the countryside that fortunately sold well enough to provide her with a decent living. A decent enough living that meant she didn't need a bloody man who would leave her with no warning or explanation to help her buy herself a house. A home.

And so she went ahead and bought it anyway.

Completely on her own.

2

Jonas Larsson wasn't a particularly compulsive person. Not that he was Mr-play-it-safe boring, but he usually made decisions with a little bit of rational thought thrown in there.

He had only been this impulsive once before and that had been when he had asked Natalie, his girlfriend of only four months, to marry him and look where that had landed him.

And then there was today.

His second bout of spontaneous action was now sitting next to him in the passenger seat of his car. Well, sitting wasn't quite the right word, he was standing, paws on the arm rest, head hanging out of the part-open window, tongue lolling, ears flapping in the wind.

And smiling. That was the good bit. He was really smiling.

Which made Jonas smile, too. Despite the fact that he was still frowning in puzzlement at his own actions.

He had only gone to the dogs' home in his lunch break to drop off some tins of food and chew toys that had been collected by his charity stalwart grandmother Blix, whose campaign of the month had been Dorset's Destitute Dogs.

Having carried out this promised errand he was sitting

eating a sandwich in his car in the car park, with the door open so as to enjoy the unusually strong September sunshine, when this hairy object literally launched itself into the car, knocking his sandwich out of his hands on to the leather passenger seat, and practically disappearing, which was an amazing feat, considering it wasn't exactly the smallest dog in the world, into the inside left-hand side of Jonas's jacket.

'What the!!!' Jonas had exclaimed as the creature did an 'Alien' in reverse.

An apologetic and thoroughly flustered face appeared at his window.

'I am SO sorry. Out, you! OUT!' the woman commanded.

In response the dog burrowed further in.

She shook her head in frustration.

'They do say dogs have a sixth sense . . .' She glanced up at the dogs' home. 'We were just dropping him off, you see . . . must realise.'

'Oh . . . .' Jonas wasn't sure what to say in response. 'I'm sorry?' was all he could think to offer.

The woman pulled a face.

'So are we, to be honest, although he's not really my dog, he's my mum's. Mum's remarried, new husband's allergic, loves dogs to pieces, they just don't love him, face like an overblown tomato every time he goes near him. Gutted to give him up, to be honest, and I hate the thought of leaving him here, but we can't keep him. Two kids under three' – she gestured to the back seat of the car, where a shrieking toddler was assaulting a bawling baby with a soft toy – 'don't exactly mix, and they're enough of a handful on their own.'

'I can see that.'

'Mum only took him in herself because her next-door neighbour couldn't keep him.' She peered in at the dog glued to Jonas's lap sympathetically. 'Poor little sod, six months old and he's already had four homes.'

'Four?'

'Yeah, well, Mum's neighbour Mrs Powers had him off her friend Mrs Baker because she met a chap and moved to Spain, and he was a pound puppy before Mrs Baker got him. Then Mum had him off Mrs Powers when she went to Australia to live with her daughter Lauren . . . come to think of it, she met a chap out there, too . . . Come on, you, out you come . . .' She waved the lead ineffectually.

Jonas felt the dog move again, but all that popped out was a tail. In fact, the tail only appeared because he was manoeuvring himself deeper inside Jonas's big winter jacket, and he felt the claws sink themselves more firmly into the denim of his jeans.

The only way they were getting him off Jonas's lap was with a crow bar.

'What's his name?'

'Dylan. You know, like in *The Magic Roundabout*.'

At the sound of his name there was another movement and two huge dark eyes blinked out of the darkness of the inside of his jacket and peered up at Jonas.

Apart from the fact that the dog was shaking like a leaf, he was pressed so close Jonas could feel the beat of his heart. It was faster than the beat of the song on his car stereo. And he was listening to the Prodigy.

'Lovely chap he is, too, ever so friendly . . . don't know what he'll make of being here, but hopefully it won't be for too long . . .' she said and sighed heavily.

'It's OK, Dylan.' Jonas looked down at the dog and tried to sound reassuring.

It must have worked, because the tail poking out from under the bottom hem of his jacket, wagged feebly.

And then the words just came tumbling out of his mouth spontaneously, no engagement of brain or rationale or thought process, no consideration of consequence; in fact, the only thing he could say was that they'd come straight from his heart.

'What would you say if I offered to have him?'

She looked decidedly uncertain.

'Well, don't take this the wrong way, but you could be anybody . . . I know this isn't exactly ideal,' she gestured towards the office, 'but at least I know they'll find him a really good home – not that I'm saying that you wouldn't give him a good home, it's just that we don't exactly know each other . . .' She petered off, embarrassed, but Jonas simply nodded his understanding and, managing to lever a hand out from under the superglued dog, offered it to her.

'My name's Jonas Larsson. I've got a big garden, no kids, not yet, anyway, I work from home most of the time, my favourite thing to do when I'm not working is to head down to the beach, and I love dogs.'

She frowned for a moment. 'Jonas Larsson? I don't suppose . . . are you any relation to Blix Larsson?'

Jonas grinned. He always joked that everyone knew his grandmother, maybe he wasn't far off from the truth.

'Grandson.' He smiled his best 'I'm a normal, decent human being and you can totally trust me' smile – 'and if you let me keep Dylan, then I'll make sure home number five is the final one, I promise,' he added.

'Blix does my Auntie Clare's meals on wheels.' The woman smiled and nodded approvingly, and Jonas knew the deal was done.

Dylan had only been persuaded to emerge from Jonas's jacket when she'd loaded a box with basket, bowls and food into the boot of Jonas's car and then driven her two screaming children away.

Jonas could have sworn the expression on the dog's face as her car disappeared down the road and out of view was one of relief.

As he looked in the rear-view mirror he saw that his own was one that was slightly shell-shocked and more than a little bit concerned.

What on earth was Natalie going to say about him coming home with a dog?

He hoped to hell it was 'Hurray.'

To be honest, he didn't actually know her view on pets.

Whilst Jonas had wanted a dog for some time, it wasn't something he'd really discussed with her.

He sometimes wondered how much he did know about his wife to be. They had only been together a few months when he had asked her to marry him, and it had been as much of a surprise to him as it had been to her.

His other 'spontaneous act of idiocy', as his best friend Wilko liked to say.

He had to confess that he had been drunk at the time, but he had also been pretty much in control of all faculties, and filled with this sudden, indefinable sense that he was asking the right question, even though he had originally only opened his mouth to tell her she looked beautiful.

Jonas had met Natalie when her parents had commissioned him to build them a new kitchen. Natalie had called in to have a coffee with her mother and had ended up calling in for coffee every day until the kitchen was finished.

Jonas had never realised that the fact that he was so good-looking usually scared women off; they preferred to drool from a distance, fearing that someone who looked like he did would be dripping with women, and would therefore either be a complete bastard or refuse to date anyone who wasn't on a par on the looks scale with at least Cindy Crawford or Jennifer Aniston, keeping them distant.

Natalie had no such qualms. It was undeniably she who had pursued him. This was new for him, novel – and, he had to confess, flattering. She had been utterly charming, flirty, sexy, funny. And she was different, bright, intense, challenging, and he had always liked a challenge.

They had only been together for a few months when he had actually proposed to her. They had been on a weekend away further down the coast in Devon, at a favourite spot, which Jonas had been to many times before.

They'd had dinner in a little pub right next to the ocean, good food, even better wine, one of those magical evenings you want to go on for ever, and then when the pub closed its doors at midnight, they had staggered outside together to see a full moon shedding shimmering light on to the ocean.

It was the exact same beach where his father had proposed to his mother.

'Shall we take a walk?' he had whispered and she had nodded and smiled, and the smile had bubbled into laughter and she had playfully taken his hand and led him in a laughing, breathless charge down to the ocean's edge, where they had fallen on to the wet sand in a drunken, laughing hug.

And he had kissed her and when he pulled away her eyes had been as bright and shining as the stars in the black sky above them.

And it had just suddenly tumbled out of his mouth.

'Marry me.'

He wasn't even sure himself where it had come from.

Wilko had said some time afterwards that she was probably playing him a subliminal message tape all night in the hotel the night before. 'You will ask me to marry you, you will ask me to marry you,' he had intoned in a stupid and supposedly hypnotic voice, over and over until Jonas had been forced to pin him to the floor of the workshop and stick a large piece of masking tape over his mouth.

'I asked her . . . it was a moment.'

'Yeah, a moment of idiocy that will last a lifetime.'

Since then the whole thing had been like that run down to the sea, a mad, breathless gallop just focussed on that final moment. Jonas had been swept off on a tidal wave of wedding preparation and had decided that the best thing he could do was surf the crest and try to enjoy the ride.

They weren't living together, yet.

That was the one thing that Natalie hadn't pushed for.

Her parents were pretty old fashioned, so he figured it had something to do with this, but she had also been dropping some pretty heavy hints about starting married life in a house that was 'a home for both of them' and from this he gathered that in her head the plan might be that she wouldn't ever move into Jonas's cottage, and that the ideal would be for Jonas to move out.

This might be a sticking point.

Jonas liked his house. It was quirky. There wasn't a single room where you didn't have to go up or down steps to get to it. He could see the sea from his bed. He could walk to the beach. And the local pub was great.

Natalie had an apartment in a 'New build' village, further inland; it was very funky, very loft, and he knew she had a yen for one of the large detached houses in the next road. It didn't appeal to him at all. Perhaps they could be one of those terribly well-adjusted couples who lived in separate houses and found it suited them just perfectly? Jonas liked different, not uniform. In fact, when he really thought about it, Natalie and he were so different in so many different ways that it was sometimes hard to imagine how they were going to fully integrate their lives once they were married.

Natalie liked new; he liked old. Natalie was always impeccably dressed, especially for work, in the latest designer must-haves; Jonas lived in jeans and sweaters. She drove a brand-new, sleek BMW coupe; when he wasn't lugging things round in his work van, he drove an old MG Roadster, one that rattled in places it shouldn't, whose passenger door only opened when it hadn't been raining, and one where a medium-sized, rather scruffy, broadly beaming dog was currently ensconced in the passenger seat with its hairy head hanging out of the window and a great big smile on its face.

A dog that he had just made his own.

He was just hoping against hope that, despite their legion of differences, when it came to inviting furry creatures into their life, he and Natalie finally thought alike.

The suitcases had been explanation enough as to what exactly he was doing. What they didn't explain was why.

He had stood in the doorway for a moment as if about to say something. His mouth opened. Then his mouth closed. His top teeth bit into the soft flesh of his bottom lip. Then they relaxed, leaving the flesh white for a moment before the blood returned.

Theo had stayed where she was, frozen for a moment in just-about-to-relax mode, which meant sitting on the sofa with her feet tucked under her, remote in hand, waiting for the adverts to finish and her favourite programme, *Coronation Street*, to start.

Not able to look at him for a moment longer, her eyes had moved and locked on to the suitcases.

He had followed her gaze, seen her notice them, seen her register their meaning.

And still he had said nothing.

And so they had just stayed there like that for what seemed an eternity.

He saying nothing, she saying nothing, just looking at those bloody suitcases. The ones that only two months previously he had been excitedly packing for his move back home, his move back home with her.

It was completely surreal.

But the weirdest thing of all, the thing that Theo was really struggling to get her head around, was that all she could think was that if he were going, then could he please just hurry up and leave so that she could watch *Coronation Street* in peace.

And then he had finally spoken.

'Theo.'

Just that word. Her name.

Then silence again.

A few more heartbeats later he managed two words.

'Theo, I . . .'

It was on the 'I' that Theo had managed to tear her eyes away from the cases, pointed the remote control at the television and turned the volume up too loud.

He had gone moments later, saved from speech by a blaring theme tune and Theo's stony silence. Once alone, she had pressed pause on Sky Plus and had fetched herself a glass of wine and a large bar of Cadbury's fruit and nut which she had been trying not to eat since Michael had instantly turned his gaze to her arse the moment she had appeared with the familiar packet.

When *Corrie* was finished she fetched the rest of the bottle and put on a chick flick she knew Michael would never have allowed to grace the screen had he been sitting next to her, after which she went to bed, where she had slept like a baby, and woken up star fished with arms and legs akimbo.

Despite what had happened the night before, she kept to her usual routine the following morning. Up, work in the studio until her stomach told her it was way past breakfast, and then walk. She then took her usual walk down to the harbour, thinking that perhaps some fresh air would clear a head that was not so much fuzzy as fuddled, numb.

The village felt different somehow. But Theo was smart enough to realise that the difference was in her. That this morning in Port Ruan everything was probably as it always was – it was just her life that had changed so dramatically.

When she got to the harbour, she sat down on the old stone wall, legs dangling over the edge, feet pointing at the water twenty odd feet below her, and looked out across the estuary to the beautiful old port town of Quinn on the other side of the water.

The usual bustle of boats and wandering tourists taking in the sights and the shops and hoping to spot one of the numerous celebrities who had second homes there, could be seen in the distance.

She and Michael had been planning to go over to Quinn that night for dinner.

'Michael's gone,' she said out loud in the hope that hearing the words instead of just thinking them might trigger some kind of reaction.

She wasn't quite sure how she felt. Disjointed would probably be quite a good word. And slightly numb? Maybe that was why she didn't feel more upset. Perhaps she was in shock, or was that being stupidly melodramatic?

Disbelief was sitting like a soft cloud over a well of upset that would suddenly explode like a volcano erupting lava as soon as disbelief dissipated and reality set in.

'Michael's gone.' She said it again.

The finger poking the sleeping dog.

'Michael's gone.'

The stick in the man trap.

'Michael's gone!' She tried it louder this time.

But both dog and man trap and, indeed, volcano remained dormant.

What was wrong with her?

Why wasn't she more upset?

At the end of the day, he had just upped and walked out on her without a word of explanation.

OK, so she hadn't exactly given him the opportunity to say much, but anyone with even an inch of respect for her wouldn't have waited until they were at the door with their suitcases before just happening to mention that there might be something a little bit wrong.

And then she said it again, only this time it came out slightly different.

'Michael's gone . . . but life goes on.'

And that was it.

That was her answer.

His leaving had only rocked her world a little; it hadn't ended it. And she wasn't sad that he had gone, simply because she wasn't sorry to see him go.

Before Michael, Theo felt that she had done extraordinarily well with men.

Her first boyfriend, Adam, had been amazing.

Theo's parents had split up when she was fifteen.

Her mother, Marianne, ran off with a man who was the total antithesis to Theo's father, William. Peter was as solid as a two-week-old loaf of bread. Fortunately, he was also more agreeable than this analogy might indicate, more chocolate croissant than hard Hovis, but it had still been a difficult thing for the English children to cope with.

Especially as the running away had been literal. Peter was a sailor. His home was a sixty-two-foot Sealine Yacht called *Windswept*, and, quite aptly, he went wherever the wind took him.

Her older sister Augustine had been in her first year at university in Leeds. Her big brother Xavier was in his final year at Edinburgh. They had both offered to quit and come home, but somehow her father and Theo between them had persuaded them to stay put.

Her father had tried, bless him, he really had, but he wasn't the kind of man to play stay-at-home mum and dad to his two youngest children. He was still dancing in the disco at sixty-two, so him in a pinny serving breakfast really wasn't going to work. It really was just like Theo was bringing up her nine-year-old brother Dion on her own.

Her father always made sure that they were provided for financially. In his youth, he had been the drummer in a band who were the biggest thing to hit the music scene since the Stones. For one record and one record only. However, repeat plays of this huge one-hit wonder had made William English a very rich man.

Nowadays he listed his profession as photographer, but actually spent most of his time racketing around the world with his still-best friend and singer of the group, Ian Temple. Ian had since made another fortune in property deals, and lived the dream life, with homes in every port deep enough for his one hundred-and-twenty-foot Azimut Super yacht, and enough shops to amuse the succession of ever decreasing girlfriends – decreasing as in age and dress size and brain cells.

Since Marianne had left him, William's chaos streak,

barely controlled when she was with him, hence their falling out, had got worse, and all he really longed to do instead of playing house with his two youngest children, was hit the high seas and the high life with Ian.

Just days after Theo's sixteenth birthday, he had gone away for the weekend with Ian, and, quite simply, had never come home.

He always said that Theo got her artistic bent from him. If that was the case, it was about the only thing that she had inherited. Where William's instinct was to cut and run, Theo's was to stay and sort out the mess he left behind.

Originally intending to stay on, her dream being to study at St Martins, Theo had quit school just after her O levels and, instead, worked to become a point of stability in Dion's life, determined that he should always have at least one person whom she felt he could rely on, no matter what.

Her friends thought she was the luckiest girl in the world, living with her little brother in a three-storey house in Hampstead, with no parents dictating to them, no school, no rules, no regime. But what they had seen as freedom, Theo had viewed in a totally different light, longing for the days when the whole family had sat down at the kitchen table for a noisy, chaotic Sunday lunch, the days when somebody had told her what time to get home and what time to go to bed.

When she could be the child.

Instead, she had been the mother Dion truly needed. She had cooked, cleaned, ironed, sewn name tags on school kit, attended parents' day, speech day, sports day. It was hard, but it would have been doubly so without Adam.

She had started seeing him when she was fifteen,

about three weeks before her mother had left home. He was only sixteen himself but he had been there for her when she really needed someone. He had been great with Dion, too. He was only nine and pretty clingy since his mother had gone, and most guys of Adam's age would have thought of him as a complete pest, but Adam always went out of his way to spend time with Dion, to play football with him, or whatever computer game was the latest must-have with Dion and his cronies.

He had been sweet, kind, patient and funny. He had also been the first guy she ever went to bed with, and from what her school friends had told her of their first time – shared secrets whispered in corners with shrieks of embarrassment and consternation – she had been pretty lucky on that count. It hadn't been some furtive, forbidden fumble or rushed and soon regretted, it had been romantic and rather wonderful. In fact, she had told her best friend at the time – Lucy, whose own virginity had been lost in the exact same furtive, forbidden fumble Theo had been lucky to avoid – that it had been a bit like school treacle pudding and custard, utterly delicious and left you rather guiltily wanting second helpings.

In fact, Adam Tanyard had been an all-round wonderful guy; he could have been the right guy if she hadn't met him when she was too young . . . but meeting the right man at the wrong time surely makes him the wrong man and not the right man? At least, this is what Theo told herself so that she didn't have any regrets. Regrets were the one thing in life she didn't want.

Things between them had ended when Adam had left London to go to university in Durham. A gentle disconnection that was more to do with geography than feelings. A break-up that would have been harder for Theo to cope with if she hadn't met Felix three months later. Four years older than she was, and fresh from the hippest of London art colleges, Felix Rosenthal was bursting on to the London art scene with all the flash, crash and panache of a firework at the Millennium celebrations. His first exhibition had been held in one of London's big-name galleries, which normally only dealt with established artists, and Theo had to confess that her interest in him was initially motivated by jealousy. His name had been everywhere Theo went. Posters advertising this ingénue had shown big, bold abstract works of strength and colour that exuded such passion she couldn't help but envy his obvious talent, and the recognition of such by so many influential others.

When an invitation for the exhibition found its way to her by roundabout means, her curiosity would not allow her not to attend, and, determined to be aloof and detached, Theo had found to her utter horror that she had fallen completely in love with first the art, and then the man himself.

On Felix's part he had seen her and been inspired.

She had looked to him like a painting come to life: an angelic, theatrical Rossetti, a gold-tinted Titian.

An orphan, who had lived much of his life from hand to mouth, from care to crappy digs, Felix had then been drawn to Theo as much by the way she cared for Dion, as by the usual rules of attraction, such as her big blue eyes, her long copper hair and softly curvaceous figure.

Like Adam before him, he, too, got on really well with Dion, but Theo thought that was probably more because he was just a kid himself, and he used to love doing everything Dion did, not just computer games and football like Adam, but comics and cartoons, and making dens out of old sheets and clothes horses, and dressing up as pirates and raiding the next-door neighbour's greenhouse for a stolen haul of strawberries.

When he wasn't playing games, he was raising hell; he had a bad-boy image to live up to, and he thoroughly enjoyed doing so. In fact, at times his behaviour had been utterly atrocious, more akin to a rockstar trashing hotel rooms than an up-and-coming artist. But of course his people loved it. He was a publicist's dream.

Theo, however, wasn't so keen on the public Felix, and tried to reign him in when he went too far.

He used to call her 'rain' partly as a pun, but also because she was, he had always liked to tell her, the soothing rain to his raging thunderstorm. Something to which Theo liked to retort that she was actually the salt of the earth on the slug of his pretentious posing.

Felix and she had lasted two years, until another fairly amicable parting of the ways left her solo again.

Under no illusion from the start that they would ever be together for ever, Theo had managed this particular ending remarkably well.

She missed him, but in the way one would miss a thrilling ride at a theme park. It was fantastic and heart-stopping and screamingly good whilst you were on it, but if you were honest, you were kind of relieved to get off.

Theo was the first to confess that he had always been too much for her. What she really needed was a balance between bad boy and Mr Reliable, that tightrope between good and evil that men often feared or failed to tread.

After Felix, she had enjoyed a fling with a rather

attractive photographer called Ed, which had been a whirl-wind of meet, mad passion, move in, move rather swiftly into mundane, and then move out when he had decided to escape what they both recognised to be a rather hasty mistake by taking a job for a magazine in Africa.

And that had been it until she met Michael.

Her first three forays into the minefield of relation-ships.

Theo often wondered what they were all up to now-adays. The last she had heard, Adam had been engaged to a girl he had met in his last year of university. He was probably married with eight children by now.

And Felix . . . well, Felix was easier to find. He currently lived in New York and sold his paintings for sums so huge he could buy himself a new Manhattan apartment with every commission. He had been married twice, once to a model who was ten years his senior, and currently to a rock star who was ten years his junior. And apparently she was now pregnant with a baby they planned to call Angel of Harlem – Felix had always loved U2 – regardless of what sex it turned out to be.

Theo had found all of this out in one hit on Google.

Ed . . . well, Ed still e-mailed, so Theo knew that he was on-and-off single and still racketing around the world with his camera.

Everyone she came into contact with always seemed to bugger off abroad.

Even her beloved Dion had left home at seventeen to go into the family business of travelling.

What was wrong with England? That's what Theo wanted to know. And so when Ed had headed off to Cape Town, closely followed by Dion throwing on a backpack and he and his best friend Finn, heading Down Under, Theo had decided that perhaps she should experience some of the world for herself.

This decision was aided and abetted by the fact that after Dion had left, her dad had finally decided it was time to sell the big old sprawling family house in Hampstead to someone who actually had a big old sprawling family who were actually going to live in it.

Being a romantic, and an artist, Theo got out her art books instead of maps and Europe by train was the first thing that came to mind.

Working her way through France, her first stop, of course, the Louvre, on down through Marseille, and then the legion of delights that was Italy, she and her easel had made it as far as the Greek Islands before her longing for soft green grass and refreshing drizzle had her heading for home on the next plane. Her decision to go back to England had been so instantaneous that, as far as she knew, her easel was still in a remote field somewhere in Kefalonia with a half-finished landscape canvas perched upon it.

What was the name of that Kate Bush song? 'Oh England, My Lionheart.'

Maybe she was just a girl who loved home.

And then when she went home, she had met Michael.

Like Felix, she met him at an exhibition, only this time it was of Theo's work. Her very first private view at a small but rather successful gallery in Battersea run by a friend of a friend of Imelda's who owed favours for some rather dodgy reasons.

It had been more than a moderate success, considering the not-so-illustrious start.

Theo had sold eight paintings and had been invited back by the friend of a friend who, feeling rightly pressured to showcase a virtual unknown, had at first greeted her with the air of someone who had just found her upon the bottom of his shoe.

Michael had been there with his boss David Bolt, who was a keen collector, and who actually bought three of Theo's paintings himself. David usually attended such events with his wife Caroline, who enjoyed the social scene far more than she did the artwork, and, like the gallery owner himself, expecting the evening to be more of a *non* event, had suddenly found that she had forgotten a previous engagement she couldn't possibly get out of.

David, hoping that his rather attractive PA Daisy might step in, had complained rather loudly in the office about his lack of companion for that evening, only for Michael to offer his services before anyone else could open their mouths.

His disappointment had been assuaged when he had laid eyes upon Theo. David had seemed to be as much taken with her as he was with her work, likening her first to a Titian (she had dyed her long brown hair flame-red at the time) and then to a prettier version of Rossetti's Mrs Beyer.

Theo had found out afterwards that it had actually been David's idea that Michael ask her out, suggesting that if he were single he'd be asking her himself. She had used to joke that Michael only took her out to please his boss. Now she wasn't so sure that it was such a joke.

Funny how everything that was so familiar, all of her

memories, were painted in such a different light now that she looked back upon them from this different perspective.

Michael was the one person who had never moved in with her.

When they had met, like she did, he had his own place. The total antithesis to Theo's, it was a functional new-build flat in Limehouse Basin.

Even though they had been together for three years, Pound Cottage was their first stab at cohabiting.

And look how that had worked out.

After just eight weeks he was gone.

Sometimes you got hooked into a relationship because of circumstance, and then you got all tied up by shared history . . .

'Penny for them, although by the look on your face I'd probably pay a lot more to hear what you're thinking?'

Theo was so lost in her thoughts she nearly fell off the harbour wall as the dark-haired woman sat down next to her.

'You're the new girl, aren't you.' It was a statement, not a question.

'I am?'

She nodded vigorously.

'Theo, isn't it? The artist who used to live in London and doesn't like Nessa Tregail's curtains?'

'Wha . . . how . . .' Theo stuttered as the other woman repeated a comment Theo had once made to Michael about her new next-door neighbour's choice in soft furnishings, and grinned in amusement.

'A village this small, everyone knows everyone else . . . and everyone else's business.'

'Well, I don't know anybody.' Theo shrugged with a wry laugh.

'Well, you have only been here a couple of months; it normally takes at least three before any one speaks to you. But don't worry, you'll soon know everyone. Whether you want to or not. And trust me, there are some people in this place that you won't want to know . . .'

'Oh . . . it's like that, is it?'

'Well, to give you some idea of what it's like: before you moved here, *I* was the new girl, and I've lived here for years.'

'Whereabouts?'

'The second epicentre of the village.'

'The second?'

'The pub's the first, can't compete with a place that sells alcohol. I run the newsagent's for my sins.'

'Oh, of course. I thought I recognised you.' Theo smiled.

'That'll be from the wanted poster, not the shop.' She grinned back and held out a hand. 'I'm Suzanne, although everyone calls me Suze – well, most people, some people have a few more choice names of their own.'

When she got her hand back, Suze offered her a boiled sweet.

'Thanks. Love these.' Theo took one of the big, hard candy apples with a grateful grin.

'You and me both. See, we already have things in common . . . I had a feeling we might . . . in fact, I did pop up to introduce myself a few weeks ago, but your other half sent me away.'

'He did?' Theo frowned.

'Said you were out tramping the headland, or out on the headland with a tramp . . . not quite sure which.'

'He never told me . . .'

'Probably forgot; he seemed a bit busy at the time –' She paused and popped another sweet in her mouth then offered the bag again to Theo. 'Still, better late than never, so now we've done the pleasantries, do I get to hear the story?'

'Story?'

'The one that made me look at you sitting on this wall, and think now what's happened to make the girl look like she's trying to eat a raw onion?'

'You mean it's not all round the village already?' Theo laughed but there was little humour in it.

'Well, if I'm being honest, then yes, the main morning news is that Michael Trehail is no longer a resident at Pound Cottage.'

'That's a very . . . *tactful* way of putting it.'

'Really . . . I've never been accused of being tactful before. In fact, just in case you're getting the wrong impression of me, I'll ask direct – what happened?'

Theo must have looked at her oddly because Suzanne held up apologetic hands.

'I know, I'm a nosy bitch, but I promise I'm not a gossip with it.'

Theo contemplated her for a moment and then she smiled. Lord knew, she needed to talk to someone, and despite the fact that she was really a stranger, Theo found that she liked this woman; there was something about her that appealed, something honest and real.

And so she told her.

Suze sat and listened quietly without interruption, and then when Theo had finished, she scratched her cheek and frowned in sympathy.

'You know, I hate to say it, but I've always found that the only thing a woman can truly rely on in life is her female friends. Not that I'm still not hopeful there's a man out there who can prove me wrong. I just haven't had the pleasure of meeting him yet.'

'Well, the thing that gets me the most is that I don't understand why. You know. Why bring me all the way down here just to dump me? It doesn't make sense . . .'

'Do you want him back?'

Theo didn't have to think for very long in order to answer.

'No, I just hate it when I don't understand something.' She laughed again, this time more lightly.

Suze cocked her head to one side as if debating whether to say something.

'Sometimes you have to look close to home for the answers.'

'You mean it's me?'

Suze shook her head.

'Nope, I mean that you have to look close to home. I have to go . . .' and she stood up as abruptly as she had sat down – 'delivery coming in . . . but if you ever need someone to talk to, you know where to find me.'

4

It wasn't going so well.

Despite the fact that, as the day progressed, so too did Jonas's feeling that he had made the right decision by offering to bring Dylan home with him.

Dylan had made himself right at home the minute Jonas pulled up on the driveway of Otter Cottage, jumping straight out of the car to sniff and water the flower beds, then galloping up the driveway past the pretty cottage towards the back garden and the huge wooden barn that was home to Blue Closet Joinery, the business Jonas had set up straight after college with his best friend Nick Wilkinson, affectionately known by some as Wilko, his right-hand man.

Dylan had introduced himself very enthusiastically to the long stretch of garden with its apple trees and shrubs and abundance of flowers, even in autumn, and then equally enthusiastically to Wilko, whom he had already charmed the pants off of, and who had been rolling around on the floor with him for most of the afternoon instead of doing any work.

He had shown them his belly, his tricks, and his doggy smile had been on permanent full wattage, like the beam from a lighthouse radiating round the room. He had been utterly charming, totally adorable, and Jonas, to his utter amazement, had found himself falling in love. A strange kind of love he'd never felt before – almost paternal, he supposed.

He was now excitedly certain that Natalie was going to adore him. Rather than being apprehensive, he couldn't wait for her to come home. To see her huge smile.

And then when Natalie arrived Dylan took one look at her through the sitting-room window and hid behind the sofa.

'He must be a man's man,' Wilko announced, wiggling his fingers at him in an attempt to coax him out. 'Either that or they've met before,' he added under his breath, but obviously not under his breath enough, as Jonas took the opportunity of his being on the floor to kick him.

'What on earth are you doing?'

Natalie, who hadn't yet spotted the animal because she was totally distracted by the sight of her arch nemesis prostrate on the floor of Jonas's sitting room, looked down at Nick with the usual finely honed contempt she reserved just for him and a chosen few who dared to try and cross her at work.

'There's something behind the sofa for you,' Wilko replied, waggling his eyebrows at her.

'God, you're disgusting, Nick Wilkinson,' she exclaimed, stepping backwards and wrinkling her nose in distaste.

'Well, it's fabulous that you're imagining it's long enough to actually reach that far, Natalie dearest, but that's *not* what I'm talking about.'

Dylan chose that moment to peer out at them, big brown eyes full of hopeful curiosity.

Natalie screamed.

Not quite the reaction Jonas, who had been watching quietly with an expectant smile on his face, had been hoping for.

Nor Wilko. He clambered to his feet and looked at her in disgust.

'What the hell did you do that for!' he accused her, as Dylan scuttled further behind the heavy sofa. 'You scared him to death.'

'*I* scared *him*!' Natalie roared back. 'What the hell is it?'

Wilko's face was a picture of contempt.

'You're twenty-six and you don't recognise a dog when you see one?'

'Hey, guys, chill out, for heaven's sake.' Jonas, shaking his head, knelt down and held out gentle hands to Dylan, who, after a tentative sniff, licked them and then stepped forward to be lifted out from behind the sofa and presented properly.

'Natalie, this is Dylan; as you can see, he's a dog.'

'A dog,' she repeated.

Jonas nodded, smiling broadly.

'*Our* dog.'

'What!'

It was as if he'd just told her he was seeing someone else, such was the look of shock and disbelief on her face.

He shot Wilko a look as he opened his mouth to interject. Again.

They had been friends for long enough for the words not to be necessary.

'I'm going to make a cup of tea,' Nick said flatly, his lips in a tight, disapproving line, and he headed for the kitchen.

Jonas waited for him to go.

Dylan, still being held on to by Jonas, wagged his lovely plumy tail hopefully at Natalie.

'Natalie, say hello to Dylan.'

Natalie didn't say a word.

She didn't even look at Dylan, she just stared straight at Jonas, big china-doll-blue eyes accusing.

'You got a dog?' she said, as if the evidence alone wasn't enough to convince her.

Jonas bit his lip to stop himself from nodding and saying 'Surprise!' in a joking voice. Natalie was obviously not in the mood for frivolity. Instead, he put Dylan gently down on the floor and, kneeling down next to him, a reassuring hand on the now-shaking dog's flank, said quietly, 'Yes, do you have a problem with that?'

'Do I have a problem with that?' Natalie repeated, and then she rolled her eyes and laughed. 'Do I have a problem with that? Now he asks me.'

And with that she stalked from the room shaking her head.

Jonas let her go.

Sometimes with Natalie it was best just to ignore some of the things she said and did rather than letting them get to you. She didn't mean it half the time. Despite the fact that she was so controlled in most aspects of her life, when it came to her emotions within their relationship, Jonas had come to the conclusion that she was a react-and-then-think kind of girl.

He also wasn't the kind of guy to go running after someone when they spat their dummy out of the pram.

He wasn't a moody kind of guy himself. When Natalie had a face on he usually found something to occupy him until her mood had had time to pass. He used to joke with Nick that she was just like the British weather, a little bit unpredictable, a bit too cloudy at times, but gorgeous when sunny. And it was good to have a bit of rain sometimes, wasn't it? It made things grow.

Nick had, of course, responded with a joke of his own and declared that Natalie was indeed like the British weather: damp, grey and moody and prone to raining on one's parade.

'Why don't you like her?' Jonas had found the courage to ask him, about three months into the relationship. He had only needed courage because he wasn't certain he would like the answer.

To which Wilko had replied with a rather blunt question of his own.

'Why *do* you like her?'

'She's bright, beautiful, funny . . .'

'Yeah, funny as in fucking touchy, Jonas . . .'

But then he had backed out, holding up his hands and shaking his head apologetically.

'Sorry . . . hey, we just rub each other up the wrong way, it happens sometimes, you can't like everyone you meet . . . and you're a better judge of character than I am. I'll have to do what I've done for the past fifteen years and trust your judgement.'

The conversation had kind of ended there, and Nick and Natalie had rubbed along ever since, but it wasn't really a comfortable rub, it was the kind that caused blisters or, sometimes, sparks to fly.

Fortunately, so far, the sparks hadn't ignited into a real explosion, but there was the potential for a major fallout at any moment.

Nick's reaction, therefore, when Jonas had revealed their impromptu engagement, had actually astonished him. Jonas had expected anything from disappointment to anger or, at the very least, a lecture on why he was being an utter idiot, but Nick had simply smiled a little smile that was hard to read and then held out a hand for a shake which turned into a man-hug, and offered him his congratulations.

'I hope you'll be really happy, mate, I really do.' And you could tell that he truly meant it.

Since then he had seemed to try a little harder with Natalie. The tormenting turned to teasing, but Natalie still reacted with the same haughty distaste.

Unlike the two men, Natalie Palmer knew exactly why she didn't get on with Nick Wilkinson.

She was the kind of girl who was used to getting exactly what she wanted.

What she wanted from her fiancé's best friend was a man who secretly wished he could have been so lucky as to get a girl like her himself, someone who flirted with her and fancied her and fed the thought to Jonas that he was the most fortunate man on the planet. Not someone who was so immune to her charms that he called her 'The Gorgon' behind her back.

He thought she didn't know about this nickname but she did.

And as far as Dylan was concerned, Natalie wasn't totally opposed to the idea of getting a dog, but she wanted the same kind of adoration from a dog as she coveted but didn't get from Nick.

She wanted a sweet, groomed little thing whose mistress would be the centre of her world.

Not some medium-sized scruffy mutt who was already so obviously attached to Jonas like a leech on flesh. The only thing in the entire world allowed to do that was Natalie herself.

In the kitchen, after taking a moment to calm down, Natalie had made coffee and gone back into the sitting room with a tray of mugs and biscuits.

Dylan had taken one look at her and shot back behind the sofa.

'He probably just needs a little bit of time to get used to yet another new face,' Jonas had offered, after all attempts to get him to go to her had failed. 'It must be a bit overwhelming for him . . . new place, new people, all the changes he's had recently . . .'

But then Natalie's best friend Clementine had arrived at the cottage with her arms full of wedding magazines, which she had dropped immediately at the sight of Dylan peering out at her, exclaiming how gorgeous he was and throwing herself down on the floor to coax him out with a game of ball.

Dylan was now sitting on Clem's lap, sharing a cheese sandwich.

Wilko was looking distinctly smug.

Natalie was now back in the kitchen making a song and dance of emptying the dishwasher, letting the crashing of cupboard doors and the clashing of china express her displeasure for her.

Jonas was staring out of the French doors into the garden.

He was saying nothing, but if you looked closely enough you could see a tiny muscle twitching in his cheek.

Dylan jumped neatly from Clem's lap and, trotting up to Jonas, raised himself on his hind legs, his front paws landing gently on Jonas's hip, as he stretched, his long back arching, and then sat down next to him, so close that he was leaning against his leg.

Jonas automatically reached a hand down to stroke his head.

'That's so sweet.' Clem, who was watching, commented to Nick, who was sitting next to her on the sofa, working his way through the plate of chocolate biscuits Natalie had fetched.

'He's a great dog, isn't he?'

Clem nodded.

'A sweetheart.'

'So what's Princess Palmer's problem with him?'

Clementine shrugged.

'Maybe he's the wrong colour to go with how she plans to redecorate . . .' she whispered with a wicked smile.

She didn't know what it was but Nick always brought out the bitchy side of her.

She was rewarded with one of Nick's famous laughs.

'Could you have a word, do you think?'

'She doesn't listen to me.'

'No, but you listen to her, Clem, and if we had a clue of what exactly it is she doesn't like, it might help.'

'True. I think I'll just see if she needs a hand in the kitchen.'

It was a good job Jonas had made the kitchen himself; anything less well crafted wouldn't have survived the slamming the kitchen cupboard doors were currently putting up with.

'What is it with you, Nat?' Clem asked, fortifying

herself by leaning against the solid wooden dresser. 'You like dogs, don't you?'

'Sure.'

'Then what is it?'

'He didn't even fucking ask me, Clementine. This is something that we should have done together.'

Clem rolled her eyes.

'It's not like he woke up this morning and thought, I know, I'm going to go and get a dog without asking Natalie . . . it was a spur of the moment thing, Nat, he had to make a quick decision.'

'And he couldn't even pick up his mobile phone and ask me what I thought? It would have taken him two minutes to call me, Clem.'

'And you would have said no?'

'It doesn't matter whether I would have said no or yes, what matters is that he never bothered to find out what my answer would have been, he just assumed.'

Although Clementine didn't agree with Natalie, it was fair to say that she did have a point.

Clementine and Natalie had known each other since the first day of primary school when they had been seated together purely because their names were in alphabetical order on the assembly list. They had grown up together. Sometimes Clementine thought that if she and Natalie had met when they were older, they would never have become friends, they were so different, but the bond between them was long and strong, and although Clementine had learned that life was easier if she just kept her trap shut when Natalie was being a princess, she decided that now was a moment to be brave and say something.

'I think everyone's got the message by now, Nat.'

'What are you on about, Clem?' Natalie snapped, turning to face her, knowing full well what she was on about but in too much of a funk to admit it.

'Well, breaking the kitchen in order to show your disapproval . . . not exactly grown-up, is it?'

'You think I'm overreacting?'

'Actually, I think you're being a cow.'

'Well, say it like you see it, Clementine Peterson,' Natalie retorted archly, her hands on her hips.

'I'm saying it like Jonas is seeing it, Natalie. Just think about that, OK?'

Natalie didn't like being told how to think, particularly by Clementine, but she had to admit that in this instance Clem had a point, and Jonas, easy-going Jonas, had a face that was clouded with frowns.

Her mother had always said to her that the way to a man's heart was most definitely not through his stomach, and that to find the true path a girl should aim a few inches lower.

Failing that, a massage always worked wonders, particularly if the thing that you were massaging was his ego.

Natalie and her mother were so alike people often mistook them for sisters.

But she was far too bright and self-willed to follow this philosophy of acquiescence, and still too annoyed with Jonas to let it go.

Not one to give up at the first hurdle, however, Jonas had tried again later.

'Let's take him out for a walk.'

To his surprise she had agreed without argument or complaint.

It was a beautiful evening. Jonas always called them Rococo days, when everything was frosted with gold.

They walked the path through the woods to the back of Otter Cottage, with the sun filtering through the trees, whilst Dylan galloped back and forth through swathes of fallen leaves.

It really was advert idyllic; they could have filmed the three of them and used it for anything from dog food through to dating sites.

It would also have been extremely romantic.

If Natalie hadn't still been in a mood with him.

Oh, she was trying to hide it, but her mouth gave her away. Set in a thin, tight line that just radiated disapproval.

She had appeared to thaw a little as the walk progressed, and then, unfortunately, without really thinking, he had told Dylan to 'Go to Mum' and she had given him a look that, if it were a weapon, would have been something that could have gutted his liver from his body in two swift movements.

One bright light was the fact that, despite her obvious contempt, it looked like Dylan was prepared to hold out the olive branch.

Well, a stick anyway. Of some indeterminate wooden vintage.

He brought it to her, dropped it at her feet, wagged his tail.

She stepped over it and carried on walking.

Jonas bent and retrieved the stick himself, hurled it into the distance and his frown melted to a smile as Dylan bounded, grinning, after it.

He caught up with Natalie and grabbed her arm.

'You could make an effort with him, Nat . . .'

'Why?'

Her response had him stumped.

Why should she?

It was a perfectly legitimate thing to ask.

In a way she was right. Why should she make an effort? This wasn't something she had chosen, or indeed had any choice in, he had foisted Dylan upon her without warning, without consulting her at all. She had every right to be annoyed, despite the fact that he hadn't thought she would be. In fact, he had thought she would be delighted. But did the fact that his intentions were the best in every respect negate the need for a joint decision to have been made on this?

He thought for a moment.

Relationships, as far as he was concerned, were about being a team, a partnership, but they were also about give and take.

And give and take didn't work when it was one person doing all the giving.

'For me.' Was his final answer. 'Make an effort with him . . . *please* . . . for me.'

5

Jonas was woken from a deep sleep by the sound of Natalie screaming. Jonas thought it was kind of an overreaction to the fact that she had opened her eyes to the sight of Dylan on the pillow next to her rather than him. In fact, he thought it had been rather cute when Dylan had opened one eye at the sound and stretched out a long tongue to lick her on the nose in a reassuring fashion. Naturally, Natalie hadn't felt the same. She was still in the bathroom washing her face. She'd been doing that for ten minutes.

'Think it might be time for your walk,' Jonas had murmured to Dylan who was still stretched out alongside him on the bed. He threw off the covers and pulled on yesterday's clothes, something Nat hated him doing, and crept quietly downstairs. Dylan, at the mention of the W word, stuck like glue to his heel.

They had taken to hopping over the stone wall at the end of the garden – well, Jonas hopped, Dylan had to get a leg up – and walking past the woods down the public footpath that cut through the farmer's land behind the garden, right down to the little sandy bay that was so hard to get to it was usually deserted.

Dylan loved to chase a ball through the surf, bounding

like a jack rabbit in and out of the ocean's edge. With the sun streaming down and the gulls circling above, a gentle breeze running a ruffling hand through Jonas's light gold hair, it was idyllic and peaceful; so much so that he was loathe to leave, especially as he knew the delighted beaming doggy face of Dylan was poles apart from the sour face that was probably waiting for him at home.

It had been just over a week since Dylan had become a Larsson, and Jonas had cemented that fact by making him an appointment at the vet's to get him microchipped, and by buying him a new collar, and an ID disc with his name Dylan on one side and Jonas's phone number engraved on the other, as well as a silver D for Dylan which hung very smartly next to it.

The Indian summer they had been enjoying had hung on with tenacious fingers – unfortunately, so had Natalie's bad mood.

Jonas had tried again a few days after his first entreaty for leniency, when the entente was still far from cordial, but her response to his suggestion that she spend some time alone with Dylan had been less than enthusiastic.

'He doesn't even like me, Jonas,' she had answered him, and flicked her fingers agitatedly through her copper-coloured hair. Jonas knew her well enough by now to know this was not a good sign.

'Don't be daft, Nat. He's a dog, they don't think that way.'

'Oh right, is that so?' she had countered, with an 'I told you so' look as Dylan had trotted into the room with Natalie's brand-new Ballenciaga handbag clamped firmly in his mouth.

He had expected fireworks, especially when told to

'drop', which Dylan had straight away. The bag was found to have two perfect sets of teeth marks now imprinted indelibly in the so-soft leather. But she had simply sighed and shaken her head, and said nothing with words, but volumes with just one look, which in its own way had been far worse than anything verbal she could have thrown at him.

After that Dylan could have been invisible as far as she was concerned.

At least until that morning, when she had woken up to a kiss that tasted of tripe.

She was in the kitchen when they got back from their walk. He fully expected another moan but, to his surprise, she had cooked breakfast. Full English. Even with mushrooms, which Jonas loved but Natalie loathed; she preferred not to even cook them, let alone eat them.

Before he sat down, Jonas fed Dylan, keeping a wary eye on Natalie as he did so.

She was waiting for him at the table, ready with the teapot.

She even managed to smile at him as he sat down opposite her.

He eyed her suspiciously as she poured him a cup, added milk and then got up to fetch a warmed plate from the oven.

Natalie didn't do domestic goddess. She was obviously after something.

At least she waited until he had finished eating before she started.

'What were you thinking, Jonas?' Thankfully, it was a gently said and gently meant approach. He didn't need further explanation, he knew what she was talking about.

'I suppose I wasn't really,' Jonas replied honestly with a shrug, pushing his knife and fork together on the plate and leaning back in his chair. 'It was a spur-of-the-moment decision, Nat, and it was one that needed to be made quickly, too. I didn't think you'd object, I suppose. It's not so awful, is it? Having him here? I genuinely thought you'd be pleased, you know . . .'

She thought for a moment, obviously measuring her response before she gave it.

'You took me by surprise. Something like . . . like . . .' she glanced over at Dylan – 'something like *this*, something that affects us both, well, I thought we were the kind of couple who would have a discussion about getting a dog rather than one of us just coming home with one.'

'So you don't really object to Dylan, just the fact that I didn't talk it through with you first?'

'Well, we are going to be living together after the wedding . . . something like this should have been a choice we made together. And, no, it's not really him' – she looked down at Dylan – 'although I would perhaps have preferred a smaller dog, given the choice . . .' She stopped and bit her lip.

'And there we have the crux.' Jonas nodded at these three last words. 'I didn't give you any choice, did I?'

She shook her head.

'I'm sorry about that, but you should have seen him, Nat. If you'd been there, you'd have done exactly the same as I did.'

'Maybe,' she conceded.

'So can we call a truce?'

'Maybe,' she said again but this time her smile and her eyes were playful. 'If you promise I will be consulted on everything from this moment on?'

'Everything?'

'Absolutely everything,' she stated firmly.

'Even down to the colour of the loo roll?'

'*Absolutely* everything,' she repeated.

'OK . . . although I have to state now, whilst at negotiating stage, that I might not call a prior discussion on certain things – like, say, a surprise . . .'

'Like a gift?'

'Yeah.'

'Or a romantic getaway?'

'Absolutely . . . or, if say I decide to go and get a tattoo . . .' he threw in just to get a reaction.

'As long as it says Natalie,' she replied without missing a beat.

'I was thinking Dylan, actually, with maybe a portrait,' Jonas teased, and knowing that finally, thankfully, he was forgiven, he put his arms around her and placed a kiss on the crown of her head.

Natalie smiled up at him apologetically.

'I'm so sorry, I've been a spoilt brat, haven't I? Truce?' she asked.

In answer Jonas looked at Dylan.

She followed his gaze.

Feeling both pairs of eyes on him, Dylan yawned and rolled over to present a hairy belly; surely one of them would offer to scratch it for him.

To everyone's amazement the person who did so was Natalie.

*

'If he's causing friction he can come and live with me,' had been Wilko's opening line the next morning. No hello, nothing, just that.

Jonas had been amazed at how much the idea of Dylan moving out horrified him.

'He's a great dog, I'd love to have him . . .' Wilko's enthusiasm was impressive but Jonas cut him short.

'Thanks, Wilks, but you see, the thing is, he is a great dog, but he's *my* great dog.'

'I know that, mate, but—'

'No, you don't get what I mean. If you did, there wouldn't be a but tacked on the end of your last sentence.'

Wilko looked at Jonas for a moment and then nodded slowly to show he understood.

'I see. To Natalie he is *that* dog; to you he is *the* dog. Like "The one". When you find them, you know they're for ever.'

'Something like that.' Jonas nodded with a laugh.

'Cool.' Wilko shrugged. 'So long as you know that if you need me I'm there. Or, more to the point, if Dylan needs me . . .'

'She'll get used to him.'

'Sure.' Wilko nodded, but you could tell he wasn't convinced.

'And I made a promise to the woman that his home with me would be his very last home.'

'Better keep Natalie away from the carving knives, then,' Wilko said sombrely and turned back to his work.

'As a matter of fact, we kind of worked a few things out last night.'

'Oh yes?'

'Yep. She admitted she'd been a brat about it and

promised to behave. In fact, she's even taken Dilly boy to the vet's today to get him chipped and vaccinated, so you see, she's already trying.'

'Mmm.' The raised eyebrow denoted disbelief.

'Nicholas!'

'Well, you'd just better hope she gets him chipped and vaccinated and not snipped or exterminated.'

Jonas's eyes popped wide with horror.

'She wouldn't.' It came out sounding more like a question than a statement of fact, but Wilko just laughed.

'Don't be daft, mate, even Natalie couldn't "off" Dylan . . . and actually, even I have to admit that it's great she's giving him a chance . . . maybe the gorgon's not so evil after all . . .' he had said with a wink, then gone back to the kitchen door he was carefully sanding.

6

It was Michael who had found them the cottage to rent, but it was Theo who had fallen in love with the village.

Port Ruan was perched on the end of a headland where the sea thrust inland in a wide estuary and the land curled in like a closed fist to protect the village from the powers of the ocean. Where the land turned its back on the sea and the wind to provide shelter, the village tumbled down the hillside to the tiny harbour, an eclectic mix of cottages, a post office, pub and one village shop which supplied everything from booze to news.

A ferry traversed the estuary several times daily to the antiquated and yet cosmopolitan port town of Quinn, where designer shops vied with Michelin-starred restaurants, and tourists descended in their droves regardless of weather or time of year.

Compared with the glamorous Quinn, Port Ruan was like the quiet, dowdy little sister, who would be so pretty without the dazzle of the elder overshadowing it.

On the other side of the headland to Port Ruan, facing the full brunt of the ocean, were the most dramatic cliffs, and a serrated edge of land that housed beaches only accessible by boat or a steep downward tumble on taut, muscled legs, where gravity made you go faster than safety warranted, and you needed the stamina and agility of a mountain goat to even consider making your way back up again.

Theo was working on a painting of one of these beaches, and so everyday, only hindered by the rain, she went to the edge of the headland and painted.

And every day, as she walked back down the winding path that led to the village, she always made a point of detouring through the tiny memorial park that was set to the highest edge of it.

A tribute to those lost at sea, there was just something magical about the place.

Barely an acre, on a slope facing the ocean, it was amazing that anything grew there at all, but grow it did, in abundance – roses, camellias, and even a magnificent magnolia.

Its focal point was a stone gazebo that had been built by a local ladyship for her captain love, which looked out over a large pond that was a magnet to local water fowl, around which willows wept rather aptly, considering the garden's purpose, and from which you had the most magnificent, omnipresent view of the ocean and the village and everything around, as if you were God looking down from the heavens.

It was here that Theo had met Geoffrey.

At first she had thought he was a walker, one of that hardy gortexed breed who stomped the edges of Cornwall come rain or shine, but when he was there again for the third day in a row, in the same place, sitting on a bench inside the stone gazebo, she looked closer and saw the ragged beard, the layered functional, slightly grubby, clothing, the worn-out hiking boots, the two pairs of gloves, the two hats and the two scarves wound about his thick neck.

Everything about him had an air of grey and grub to it, everything except for the bright blue eyes that glanced up at her as she passed. They were as light and shining and brilliant as the cold-frosted ocean Theo had just been trying to capture on canvas.

He had looked up as she had walked past, and nodded an acknowledgement, one she returned that day and instigated the next. It took her until the fifth occasion, however, to pluck up the courage to speak.

'Good morning.'

'Good morning,' he had replied with a pleasant smile and a remarkably cultivated voice – like Brian Blessed, only not quite so deep and booming.

The day after she managed to get a step further.

Every time she had seen him thus far he had had his nose buried deep in a book. An avid reader herself, who, when she had time, devoured books like they were bars of Dairy Milk to be eaten in one sitting, Theo appreciated a person who appreciated the written word as much as she did.

This time when he said his usual good morning, she paused.

'What are you reading?'

He held the book up so that she could see the cover.

'Any good?'

'Excellent, although I must confess his first is still by far the best.'

'That's exactly what my brother said.'

'Your brother likes him?'

'Loves him. Whereas Michael' – she continued, forgetting that this stranger wouldn't know who on earth Michael was – 'says that Anton Everman is a posingly pretentious, virtually illiterate prat.'

'Really . . .' He smiled, as Theo quoted verbatim. 'I think perhaps that . . . Michael?'

'Michael,' Theo confirmed.

'I think perhaps that Michael might be a bit of a "prat" ' – he used the word like it was something he hadn't said before – 'himself?'

Theo looked at him for a moment and then found herself smiling.

'I think perhaps you might be right.'

The following day he looked up as she walked her usual path through the little park and greeted her with a broad, friendly, open smile, and Theo, encouraged by this and the previous day's exchange, actually felt brave enough to go and sit down next to him with the picnic lunch she normally ate on the headland before walking home.

'Hi . . .'

'Good morning.'

'We never actually did introductions, did we? I'm Theo.'

'Geoffrey,' he had replied, holding out a hand. 'Are you new to the village?'

She nodded.

'Fairly.'

'I didn't think I'd seen you here in previous years.'

'Previous years? Have you . . . um . . . been here long?'

'I've been coming here for the winter every year for the past four years, I think.'

'Here?' Theo indicated the park and he nodded.

'It's the perfect place to winter,' his smile was broad and relaxed, his teeth amazingly white, 'just ask my friends over there in the pond.' He indicated the pair of swans perched on the grass at the water's edge. 'They come back every year too.'

'They're beautiful.'

'And fairly friendly for swans.'

'Especially if I offer to share?' Theo suggested.

Pulling her lunch from her rucksack full of paint and brushes, Theo threw a crust to the magnificent birds and then turned to the man beside her.

'Ham sandwich?'

'Very kind of you, but I don't actually eat meat.'

'You're a vegetarian?'

'Not in the strictest sense, but I prefer not to chew on my fellow creatures.'

'Banana?'

'Thank you, but no, I've eaten lunch already.'

Theo doubted the truth in this, but had the sense and the grace not to press further.

'I see that you're an artist.'

She nodded and touched the easel she had placed down beside her with the toe of her flip-flops.

'This is kind of a giveaway, isn't it? Bit like walking round with a sign on my back.'

'That and the fact that you've got paint in your hair.' He had smiled.

They had both laughed and when she had offered him a home-made chocolate brownie, he had thanked her and taken one.

The following day she had taken him a Dan Brown and

made herself cheese sandwiches. He was delighted with the book, but the cheese sandwiches were politely declined.

The day after, a flask of home-made butternut squash soup made its way up to the memorial park.

And then made its way back to Pound Cottage.

When she arrived the next day with a ginger beer and a salad roll, it was to find that he had picked her the most beautiful bunch of wild flowers and grasses she had ever seen.

'Life shouldn't be all take and no give,' he said, and stemmed her stuttering thanks with a smile and a shrug. 'If you hang them, they'll dry very well and should last for ever. Now, as grateful as I am for everything you have given me—'

'Tried to give you,' Theo had corrected him, and his smile had broadened.

'. . . I am far more grateful for the pleasure of your company and would ask that tomorrow that is the only thing you bring me – assuming you will be coming to the park tomorrow.'

'I will.' Theo nodded.

The next day Theo stopped at the newsagent's on her way up to the headland.

She arrived at the park carrying two large vegetarian pasties in a paper bag, one of which she promptly offered to her new friend.

'It was buy one, get one free.' She shrugged. 'And I couldn't possibly eat two. Although I could always give this one' – she waved the steaming, fragrant bag – 'to the birds . . .'

He had looked at her for a long moment, his piercing eyes hard to read.

And then he had started to laugh.

And then he had eaten the pasty.

This had all been whilst she and Michael were still together, and she had told him about her encounters over dinner that evening. The evening of the pasty.

'I've made a new friend,' she had announced with a pleased smile as he tucked into the casserole she had left stewing in the slow cooker whilst she was out.

He had countered this with a curious look.

'Oh yes?'

'His name's Geoffrey.'

'A man? Should I be jealous?' And he had smiled.

'Hardly, he must be in his sixties at least.'

'Does he live in the village?'

'Well, yeah.'

'Well, yeah?'

'He lives in the park.'

'In the park?'

Theo nodded, grinning, but Michael's smile was no longer there to match hers.

'A tramp?'

'Well, I suppose you could call him that if you wanted, but it doesn't really seem to suit; he's such a—'

But Theo didn't get to finish as Michael dropped his knife and fork with a clatter and, to her amazement, began to bellow at her.

'Of all the people in this village you could spend time with and you make friends with a tramp! What is wrong with you, Theo? You are the only person I know who would make friends with a bloody tramp!'

'What on earth is so wrong with that?' She had been genuinely taken aback.

'What's wrong with it? What's wrong with it?' Michael had a habit of repeating himself when riled. 'He could be a mass murderer, for all you know!'

'He's a kind and decent man,' Theo countered.

'How the hell do you know that?'

'You can just tell.'

'Oh yeah, and you're a great judge of character, aren't you?'

'What do you mean by that?'

'Exactly what I said. Come on, Theo, you live in cloud cuckoo land half the time . . . you probably took one look at him and thought he was "paintagenic", or whatever you call it, and that was it, it doesn't matter what or who he is, he's your new favourite subject . . . you don't think about anything, do you, the consequences of things, you just go ahead in your own merry, thoughtless little arty farty way without a care in the world, not even noticing what's going on around you . . .'

Theo had looked at Michael in open-mouthed astonishment as his rant continued.

Was that really what he thought of her?

Cloud cuckoo land.

Arty farty.

Thoughtless.

Admittedly, she got engrossed when she was painting, she waxed lyrical when she saw something that inspired her, be it scenic, sunset or smelly old tramp, not that Geoffrey was at all smelly or indeed remarkably old, and she liked to look at life and find the shiny things buried in the grime, but was that a bad thing? The way Michael was saying it made it sound so. At least to him. In fact, it sounded like her character was actually pretty offensive to him.

She finally found the voice to say what she was thinking out loud.

'Is that really what you think of me?'

And he had fallen silent and looked disgustingly guilty, and then he had thrown his arms around her and apologised so uncharacteristically and so amazingly profusely that she thought he was having a breakdown.

He had then spirited her upstairs and, for the first time in what was probably weeks, as Imelda would so indelicately put it, shagged her brains out.

It had been the following day that he had packed his bags and gone.

Theo didn't see Geoffrey again until a few days after Michael had left. Not because she had taken any notice whatsoever of his views on befriending strange men in memorial parks – as far as she was concerned, she was a pretty good judge of character, she looked deeper than most people when it came to meeting others; and as far as she was concerned, Geoffrey was a good person – but purely because she did what she always did when she was upset. She holed up in her studio and painted without pausing for breath.

When she did see him, Geoffrey had looked up and smiled at her in genuine delight, as if he had missed her the past few days, and when she had sat down next to him, and he had asked her how she was, Theo had been silent for a moment before suddenly finding herself saying: 'Michael's gone.'

'Michael the prat?' he had responded.

'Michael the prat,' she had replied.

'That's good, then,' he had said nodding firmly.

And Theo had found herself nodding along with him.

7

Jonas got home from delivering a gorgeous cabinet that Wilko had lovingly crafted to find said craftsman had downed tools to entertain his grandmother in the garden of the cottage.

Blix didn't drive any more. Not since she had run over next door's bicycle, twice, on next door's driveway, when she was trying to reverse out of their own. So now she had taken to turning up in a taxi every so often and spending the afternoon in her grandson's bird-filled garden, where she could use the excuse of not driving herself home to indulge in a bottle of her favourite white wine. A pastime that Wilko was all too easily persuaded to join her in.

Dylan had been riding shotgun on the delivery, and leapt out of the van and into the garden to avail himself of a bush. Jonas followed and found Blix and Wilko, sitting at the garden table, a pile of food and a bottle of cold Sancerre in front of them.

'Sonson!' Addressing him in Swedish, Blix squinted up against the sunshine at her grandson. 'How lovely. Do you know, I think you've grown since I last saw you.'

'I'm twenty-eight, Farmor.' Jonas grinned, responding in the same language and bending to kiss her soft, powdery cheek. 'I think I stopped growing quite a few years ago, and, aside from that, I only saw you last week.'

'Then perhaps my perception has shrunk,' she announced happily, waving her wine glass at Wilko in the universal language of empty glass, so that he obliged and filled it for her. 'Did you drop those things at the dog's home for me?'

'Of course.'

'And you picked up something for yourself whilst you were there, I see?' She laughed as Dylan bounded up and placed his paws on her lap, attempting to wash her face with his tongue. 'Nicholas has told me all about you . . . he's lovely, adorable.' She smiled her approval at her grandson, 'I don't know what Princess Tilly will make of him, though.'

'She'll love him. Someone else to reign over.'

Having made Blix's acquaintance, Dylan went off in search of a ball he knew he had left under a bush somewhere and, locating it, he returned and dropped it hopefully at his play buddie Nick's feet.

'*Snygg rumpa!*' Blix rasped appreciatively as Nick bent to pick it up.

'Farmor!' Jonas's voice was full of chastisement.

'What?' Nick queried, looking round.

'She said she wants to open another bottle . . .' Jonas shrugged.

'I did not at all,' Blix reverted to her perfect English. 'I said you have a very nice bottom.'

'Do you guys ever do any work?' It was Natalie, straight back from work, looking foxy in a very fitted suit and expensive court shoes, which looked great until she had to tiptoe across the lawn so as not to sink through the grass and into the mud.

'Not if we can help it.' Wilko smiled at her insolently.

'In fact, the minute you've gone, we normally get out the deckchairs.'

'And crack open the champagne,' Blix murmured, elbowing Nick in the ribs.

Fortunately, she said this too low for Natalie or Jonas to hear, but it was all Wilko could do not to fall over laughing.

And then she turned innocently to Jonas with a beguiling smile.

'Sonson, I have an old blanket box full of books for the children's charity shop in Dorchester. I don't suppose you could throw it in the back of your delivery van for me, could you?'

'Of course, Farmor. I'm going into town on Thursday, anyway. Does that suit?'

'Lovely, thank you. You are a good grandson, *min älskling*, now how about delivering your old farmor another bottle of wine, eh?'

'You know it's rather unfair of your grandmother to expect you to keep running all these errands for her,' Natalie murmured as Jonas opened the fridge in search of a cold bottle of white.

Jonas frowned.

'She only asks me to help out occasionally. Besides, she needs me to be there for her sometimes; she's an old lady, Natalie.'

'Only when it suits her,' Natalie replied pointedly, looking out of the window to where Blix was dancing rather wildly with Wilko to the manic sound of Dizzee Rascal's 'Bonkers', her laughter ringing out into the night air as she shook her funky stuff far too severely for a woman in her seventies.

Jonas followed Natalie's accusing glare and burst out laughing.

Blix and Natalie had never really hit it off.

With her silvery hair and leathery skin, Blix looked like a pretty little Swedish elf, and was a pocket-sized dynamo of mischief and mayhem.

Her sense of humour was too silly for Natalie to appreciate and, in return, Blix found Natalie too dry, too serious, too focussed to have fun.

'Are you really going to take her another bottle?' Natalie frowned as Jonas pulled the cork from a cold bottle of Sancerre. 'You know what she's like when she has too much.'

'Don't worry, Mum's coming to pick her up; she'll keep her in check . . . actually, I asked her if they both wanted to stay for dinner. I thought I'd get the barbecue going, it's a beautiful evening.'

Natalie pouted and went over to him. She slid her arms around his waist and rested her cheek against him.

'But I was going to do us a nice dinner, just the two of us.'

'We've got plenty of time for it to be just the two of us,' he said, squeezing her gently. 'Well, the three of us . . .' he added with a grin as Dylan bounded in from the garden and planted muddy paws on his thighs. 'Oh, and Wilko's stopping too . . . he'll keep Farmor amused,' he added quickly as Natalie pulled away and her slightly petulant frown threatened to turn into a serious snarl. 'Why don't you give Clem a call and see if she wants to come round too, we could turn it into a bit of a party . . .'

'It already looks like your grandmother's doing just

that,' Natalie commented as Blix, still dancing, tried to relieve Wilko of his shirt.

'Mum will be here soon, she'll calm down then.'

As if on queue, his mother's four-by-four pulled into the driveway, her little dog Tilly in the front seat, standing in her usual position, paws on the dashboard.

Jonas's mother Stella was and always had been very beautiful. As dark as Blix was light, she had long thick hair the colour of bitter chocolate that always shone as if someone had just spent several hours lovingly polishing it with a tub of wax and a soft cloth, and luminescent skin that belied her fifty years. Whilst it was his father from whom Jonas had inherited his corn-coloured hair and green eyes, it was she who had given him the cheekbones and the full mouth.

Swedish banker Konrad Larsson had been working in London when he had met her and hadn't stood a chance; he had fallen head over heels in love. Immediately he gave up the work that had brought him there, and he and Stella spent an idyllic summer touring England, with Stella as willing guide, visiting all of the places that Konrad had dreamed of seeing from Lands End to John O'Groats.

When his mother Blix had asked him to bring her something back from the UK that was typically English, she hadn't banked on it being a new wife, but she had been delighted, nonetheless, embracing Stella as the daughter she had always wanted, taking great delight in teaching her how to speak Swedish, how to cook Swedish and, more importantly, the art of how to drink Swedish. An art that Stella had to sideline for a while because, exactly thirteen months after Stella had arrived in Sweden, so had Jonas.

Jonas Dante Larsson, Jonas after his father's father, or his *farfar*, as the Swedish would call him, and Dante after his mother's favourite artist and poet, Dante Gabriel Rossetti.

His childhood had been idyllic; he grew up on the west coast of Sweden, on the Marstrand, where life was full of sunshine and sea and fun and laughter.

And then, when he was thirteen, his life changed dramatically.

His father was killed in a terrible car accident.

Unable to bear being in Sweden without Konrad, his mother had decided to move back to her birthplace, which was a little seaside town on the Dorset coast.

So different to Sweden.

Jonas's grandmother Blix – which, she delighted in telling people, translated as Joy and Cheer in English – had chosen to go with them, and had settled into English life as though she had been born to it herself, her natural eccentricity finding its true home in the English coastal countryside.

It had taken Jonas a little longer to adjust.

He had left many friends back in Sweden, and it was daunting, at the age of fourteen nearly fifteen, to be starting a new school in a new country, with the weight of his grief still heavy upon him.

Thanks to his mother, his English had been good back then, but by no means perfect, and his first day at school had been a blur of new people and new experiences that had been kind of hard to translate.

It didn't help ingratiate him with the boys in his class that the girls were so obviously entranced by this new, decidedly foreign and, to them, used to their awkward, brash English counterparts, incredibly exotic addition to their class, with his blond hair, jade-green eyes and cute accent.

Not one of the boys in his class uttered a word to him all day. Perhaps because they couldn't fight their way through the halo of young girls who constantly seemed to surround him.

And then things had changed.

Dramatically.

On his way home from his first day – he had refused to allow his mother to pick him up – Jonas had come across a group of hooded youths down an alleyway throwing stones at an old upturned bucket. Something about the situation had struck him as odd, their callous laughter perhaps indicating that it wasn't just boredom that was directing those stones, it was malice.

He had paused to watch them for a moment, some kind of sixth sense telling him not to walk on by.

And then he had heard the whimpering.

'Hey, what are you doing?'

His vocal challenge greeted with gales of laughter, Jonas had simply taken matters into his own hands, strode straight through them, lifted the bucket and lifted the tiny puppy he found cowered there gently to his chest, holding it to him until he felt the manic beat of its little heart begin to subside to a normal rhythm.

For a few moments the fury of his gaze had held the older youths distant, but knowing it was only moments before their callous, cruel mischief turned on him, Jonas carefully put the puppy on the floor behind him and prepared himself to defend them both to the best of his ability when it was five against one.

A gang of boys from his new class, the popular good-looking ones, those who had been most irked by his obvious appeal to the girls, had passed by seconds after the gang of hoodies had begun to lay into him.

Jonas got an amazing right hook in on the leader of the gang before they all piled him to the floor.

Nick Wilkinson, smaller and slighter than the others, part of the popular good-looking gang because of his wicked sense of humour, had assessed the situation in seconds and was the only one of the crowd of boys who had roared into the fight to help Jonas without a moment's hesitation.

The puppy, seeing the person who had rescued her from the dark, the fear and the pain, being pounded to a pulp by the person who had put her there, shook her dazed little head, bared her sharp little teeth and joined in the fray, promptly biting the bully hard on the arse.

Eagerly awaiting her son's return from his first day at school, Stella Larsson was horrified to see him coming up the drive to the house with his brand-new blazer ripped and dirty and his face covered in blood from a busted nose.

Accompanied by a tousled-haired ruffian with ripped trousers and a black patch already beginning to shine around his right eye, Stella could not for the life of her work out why both boys were grinning from ear to ear.

'I'm sure you busted Spencer Braithwaites's nose; that was one hell of a hooker you landed him, mate.'

'My dad taught me to box when I was seven.'

'Cool. Do you think he could show me?'

'He died last year.'

'Shit. What a bastard. I ain't got a dad either. Buggered off years ago. She all right?' He peered under Jonas's ruined blazer.

'I think she's OK. Morsa will take care of her.'

'Morsa?'

'It's Swedish for mother.'

'Cool. What's your mum like?'

'She's cool.' English still being a second tongue to him, he automatically copied the other boy's language. 'Yours?'

'She died too.'

Jonas snorted softly in sympathy.

'We are a sorry pair.'

'Too right.'

And the two boys made fists and clashed them together.

Nick's father had done a disappearing act when he was eight. When his mother had died from cancer three years later, Nick had been taken in by his elderly grandmother, who did her best but, to her eternal chagrin, always felt that it was Nick who was taking care of her rather than the other way round.

The day that Jonas and Wilko met, Jonas found a friend for life, and Nick found a new family.

The tiny puppy, christened Tilly by Jonas's mother, had been a much-loved member of their family ever since. Now, thirteen years young, she was his mother's right-hand girl in everything, and she was still as feisty as the day she bared her baby teeth and bit a bullying bastard on the bum.

Tilly had never needed a lead. She had determined straightaway that her heart and her home was with Jonas and Stella and Blix and she never strayed very far away.

She had also been the only thing with a heartbeat that had slept in Stella's bed since Konrad.

Dylan was the first to greet Stella and Tilly as they came into the garden.

Despite the fact that he was a fraction of her age and about ten times her size, the minute his hairy bulk bounded towards her beloved mistress, Tilly was in front of Stella, her hackles up, giving a high-pitched growl, as she rumbled out a warning.

Dylan slammed on the brakes and rolled over to present a belly.

'See? Total submission; the boy knows his place,' Blix laughed gleefully.

Stella smiled at her mother-in-law and bent to rub the presented belly as Tilly, still growling just in case, danced forward on dainty paws to carefully sniff the interloper.

In contrast to Blix, Stella was quiet and elegant with a still, reserved grace that sometimes hid her warm and welcoming nature.

There was something else as well, something that made Jonas very protective of her. Since his father's death there was also an inherent sadness that never seemed to ease with time.

Not that anyone else apart from him and, perhaps, Blix, would ever notice this, but he remembered how she was before his father's accident.

There had been a lightness to her, a sense of fun that had shone like her hair.

His father had called her *'lysande stjarna'*.

His shining star.

His father had kept the girl in her alive. As a single

parent to a grieving child, and support to a distraught mother who had suffered the travesty of watching her own son buried before her, Stella had said goodbye to the star, to the girl, and become Stella the woman.

Unlike Blix, Stella had never asked her son for anything. Determined that he should never be made to feel like he should now be the man of the house, she had fought to make sure that he had a proper childhood and, now that he was a man, that he would feel free to have a life of his own and that their relationship should be based on mutual appreciation and not need.

Unlike Blix, Stella thought that Natalie was a nice enough girl ... just a little too used to getting her own way.

But they had always got on well enough.

Stella's view was that Jonas was an intelligent, rational man who had always been an excellent judge of character, and if he had chosen to be with Natalie, as far as Stella was concerned, that was good enough for her.

Blix's view was that Jonas's head had been turned by a *Snygg rumpa*, and as far as she was concerned, Natalie was the big fat *rumpa* minus the *Snygg*.

Everyone knew that moving was high on the list of the most stressful things to do in life, but you would have thought that moving next door would be a doddle. Especially when someone was as keen as Theo to get away from Pound Cottage and make a fresh start to her new life. Even though that fresh start was only a doorstep away it felt she was moving a million miles.

It had started off fairly well when the removal van with her furniture from the London flat arrived on time, which in itself was a miracle, considering the unpredictability of a journey from London to Cornwall, but the fact that the two men manning the lorry appeared to be sharing a rather small set of brain cells between them kind of scuppered the rest of the day being one of relative ease.

So far they had put her bedroom furniture in the sitting room, her boxes marked bathroom in the small utility area, the small kitchen table in the dining area of the big sitting room, and crammed the long dining table like a size-eight foot in a size-six shoe in the kitchen. They had stacked all of her art equipment in the guest bedroom instead of the attic room, her clothes were in the bathroom, the microwave had somehow ended up in the box room, and yet they had somehow managed to find the kettle and the tea bags without any problems at all.

Theo had also ordered some new chairs. These had arrived just as the removal men had declared a tea break, and the two men delivering them had soon sniffed out the tea bags.

All four of them had then spent an awfully long time sitting at the kitchen table, which they had finally, miraculously, managed to get in the right room, munching on chocolate hobnobs and drinking strong tea loaded with sugar.

Observing them, knackered and stressed from the doorway, Theo contemplated whether to join them or shoot them, and suddenly found herself chuckling at the thought that it was as though long-lost relatives had unexpectedly found each other and were celebrating a reunion. Either that or PG had brought the chimps out of mothballs.

Finally, thankfully, as the autumn day turned to an early dusk, all four had finished unloading and redistributing and trundled off back up the A30 and left Theo in peace, or, rather, in 'pieces'.

There were still boxes everywhere, and everywhere they shouldn't be, but she had a game plan: one room at a time. First on the list was the sitting room. It should really have been the attic, which was going to be her studio, as she had a commission piece that she should really get finished by the deadline, but she had such a clear picture of how she wanted that sitting room with its open fires at both ends and its big sash windows looking out over the village and estuary and the ocean that she couldn't wait to get started on it.

Besides, knowing the removal guys, they had probably put her bed in the garden, and if she got the sitting room sorted at least she could sleep on the sofa.

The hardest part was locating the boxes marked 'sitting room' or 'dining area' which were spread throughout the house like clues in a treasure hunt.

It took her three back-breaking hours, but finally she had her haven, a place where she could sit and pretend that the rest of the house didn't still look like an episode of *Steptoe and Son*.

She had found her duvet in her trawl for books, pictures and rugs, and, as far as she was concerned, a duvet and a sofa equalled a bed for the night, and so the rest of the house could wait until tomorrow.

Pushing closed the door from the sitting room into the corridor of chaos beyond, she sat down on the sofa and looked around at the room she had worked so hard to get right.

It looked great.

With its warm gold walls, and the old gold sofas with the mixture of gold, burgundy and terracotta cushions, her plants, her paintings, the russet rugs. A kaleidoscope of colours that reflected the autumnal tumble of the leaves in the garden outside.

Just how she had imagined it would be when she had dragged a very reluctant Michael round to view it weeks ago.

Although it was empty of one thing that had been very firmly in her picture.

One very major thing.

Michael himself.

Theo laughed softly to herself.

She could just picture him if he were here now, dictating where everything should go, moaning at her for letting the delivery guys have too many cups of tea and the best chocolate biscuits.

It was so odd that she was here now and he wasn't, because it had been Michael who had found them Port Ruan on a fact-finding trip down to Cornwall without her, prior to their own escape to the country. Theo had been exhibiting some of her canvases and couldn't go with him.

They had both sold their own places, but Michael had suggested that it would be silly to buy straight away, that they should rent for a while whilst they decided whereabouts in Cornwall they wanted to be. It had made complete sense and so she had waved him off to try and find them somewhere.

She had been disappointed that they couldn't look together, but he had wanted to tie the trip in with his mother's birthday and, to be honest, Michael was a measurer. Every decision weighed and counted and weighed again before he finally made up his mind. She doubted he would find something without her input.

She had therefore been surprised when he had called to say that he had found them the perfect place, and then even more surprised – and yet delighted – by his choice for them.

Michael's style was totally different to Theo's. Theo liked quirky, not quite cluttered, but lived in.

Michael's style from his clothes to his house was all about modern and minimalist so she had been expecting a brand-new flat somewhere near to his parents, not a quaint little cottage in a village further up the coast, where the only way to join yourself to the rest of the Cornish world was either to drive an awfully long way around the estuary or catch the little ferries that paddled across every day.

But still, seven weeks later, as summer segued slowly into an autumn that was more like summer than summer itself had been, with golden days of sunshine so glorious you would never believe it was nearly October, Theo and Michael left what remained of their lives in London in a large storage unit and turned up at Pound Cottage with their suitcases.

Living with someone else's furniture was kind of weird, a bit like borrowing someone else's clothes after an unplanned sleepover. It didn't quite fit. You didn't feel comfortable enough to really relax. But it was a beautiful cottage. Three-storey, which Theo had always loved in a house, and with amazing views of the estuary and the sea from the top two floors.

The only thing she would have liked, apart from her own furniture, was a garden. Leaving London, escaping to the country so to speak, you would have thought that at the end of that long journey, there would be a garden, even just the tiniest little strip of green, but the house was built on a hill and built in such a way that all it had was a little back yard.

Next door had a garden. Next door was the end house of the higgledy-piggledy little terrace that wound its way uphill as though tiptoeing back from the water's edge. The end house had a garden: where the houses stopped, it carried on, raising itself in terraced steps up the hill, each step a haven of plants and flowers, trees and little bowers – and accessed, Theo knew, because she had peered over the wall in envious curiosity, via French doors from the master bedroom on the first floor. Theo liked this quirk. She could picture herself all warm in bed, peering out of those French doors on to a garden filled with birds and bees and colour, all slowly lit as the sun crept up from behind the headland to wake the village.

And so when she woke one morning in their little rented cottage to see that the house next door had a For Sale sign outside, her first thought was of that very same image.

Michael's reaction when she delightedly told him of this news hadn't been as enthusiastic as she'd hoped.

It was he who had found them Pound Cottage, and he had raved about its delights in an effort to convince Theo that it was the right choice for them. Otter Cottage was so similar to Pound Cottage but so much better in so many ways, how could he not be as passionate about it as she was?

It had the garden, for starters, that was enough to sell it to Theo but, aside from that, it was so much bigger; there were three bedrooms and a huge attic room that would make a perfect studio, the master bedroom had a beautiful en-suite, the sitting room was double the size, as was the kitchen, and there was even a tiny utility room.

But he wasn't to be persuaded.

She managed to get him round to view, complaining and dragging his heels like a dog on the way to the vet's.

As Theo raved, he retreated.

It was weird, really, all of the things he had used as persuasion he now brought out as reasons not to buy: the village was too small, too remote, the house too old and impractical, perhaps they should just continue to rent for a while.

Theo had been gutted. Otter Cottage had been everything she had hoped and more. It had caused a huge argument, probably the worst they had ever had.

Michael had even stormed off and stayed out, overnight. Something he had never done before. Theo had spent a restless night waiting for the sound of his key in the door. He had finally come home just after breakfast, full of apology for storming off but still adamant about his reasons for doing so. They had almost fallen into another row, but had somehow managed to sidestep the knife throwing and name calling and agree, albeit reluctantly, on Theo's side, that any house they bought would have to be one that they *both* fell in love with.

And after all of that she had ended up buying the cottage anyway.

She was fortunate in that she could afford to do this on her own. This was due to how hard she worked, but also thanks in part to her father. To assuage his guilt at selling off the house that had been their family home for twenty years, her father had decided to divide half of his share of the equity between his children.

Using this as a deposit, Theo had somehow persuaded her bank to give her a mortgage and bought the flat in Camden: Apartment 23, Valhalla House, Halcyon Terrace.

It sounded idyllic, but in reality it had been run down, damp, dirty and dismal, but it had a balcony with plants on it that had been enough of an outdoors to sell it to her above the other armpits that were in her price range.

She had worked her socks off to make it first habitable, and then warm and welcoming.

Every so often Dion returned to set up camp in the cupboard-sized spare room.

He would only stay long enough to find a temporary job where he could earn as much money as possible in as short a time as possible, and then he would be off on his travels again.

When Xavier finished university, it was his turn to move into the spare room. These had been happy times. Xavier and Theo were so similar in nature, it was like having a best friend come to stay. They liked the same food, the same movies, the same television programmes, the same books, the same art . . . they were like two peas in a pod.

When Xavier met and fell in love with Jules, despite the fact that it heralded his departure from Apartment 23, there was no one happier for him than Theo.

If Xavier loved her, it was only natural that Theo would love her too, and it was easy to wave one of her favourite people in the whole world off into the arms of someone who was as sweet as Jules.

Augustine's stint in the spare bedroom after gaining her first, had happily been a brief one. She was only there to take some time out to 'consider her options', because her options were so many it was hard for her to choose the best one.

August and Theo were too dissimilar to be anything other than the basest meaning of the word 'sisters'.

Their father had often joked that he wasn't sure they came from the same parentage, something that when their mother was there would always instigate an argument.

They got on fine as long as Theo did as she was told,

and when you're twenty and it's your own home, you don't exactly appreciate being bossed around by your big sister as if you were still twelve, and four years advantage and a 'teen' on the end of her age made her the adult.

Fortunately, August was as ambitious as she was anal, and was promoted through the ranks of the multinational company she finally chose to grace with her presence, faster than the express elevator could reach the penthouse offices of their flagship London building, and Theo had waved a fond, if slightly thankful, farewell at Heathrow airport only three months later.

Dion's returns were getting more and more sporadic, and Theo was tired of London. She had toyed with the idea of moving to the seaside then.

It had always appealed to her, emotionally, aesthetically, artistically, but in her mind, Theo was the lynch pin around which her rambling family moved. Someone had to have a base for them to come back to, even if it was just a tiny two-bedroom flat with hardly enough room to have a cat let alone swing one.

And London was more central than anywhere else.

Especially for Dion.

Imelda had argued that for the amount of time Dion actually spent with her, his needs shouldn't be her first consideration, but Theo had been so used to always putting Dion first that this argument had just washed over her like the distant sea over pebbles on the beach, registering then retracting.

But now, several years later, here she was.

Her own place by the sea.

With her large family in all four corners of the world, this wasn't the first time she'd ever lived alone. It was, however, the first time she'd lived alone when she knew no one within a three-hundred-mile radius except the tramp who lived in the local park.

But she had chosen to stay. She had chosen to make this her home, and make this her home she would. Starting now.

Theo went through to the kitchen, which was currently the centre of operations for unpacking and was as chaotic as the sitting room was tidy. She was looking for two boxes in particular.

One had come from London, the other had come from next door.

It was the one least travelled that she found first – in the downstairs loo, for some strange reason.

Theo had chosen the large attic room to be her studio because it was quite simply perfect for the job: spacious and light with windows to front and rear, and the view of the sea and the estuary was truly inspirational, but wherever she was she always seemed to spill out of her allocated space.

The box she took into the sitting room was full of paints, gouache, water colours, oils and pencils in every shade of colour. Theo pulled them out of the box and spread them haphazardly over the dining table, then returned minutes later with a large sketch pad which she threw open and then an old glass with water with an assortment of paintbrushes in it, which she placed between paint and paper.

The second box was located after a more fervent search, and contained a stack of flat, rectangular objects wrapped carefully in newspaper. Theo unwrapped them carefully, then spent several minutes contemplating the room, before strategically placing numerous photographs of her family on different surfaces.

Next were a couple of art books on the coffee table, and some magazines on the floor next to it.

She stood back and looked around the room again.

There was still something missing.

She went back into the kitchen and emerged with a bottle of red wine, a glass and a half-eaten bar of Dairy Milk, which went down on the coffee table as well.

Then she switched the television on, kicked her Mr Men slippers off under the coffee table, curled her feet underneath her on the sofa and, flicking channels until she found *Coronation Street*, settled back with a satisfied sigh.

She was home.

Jonas had been so busy time had simply flown.

Dylan had been with them for nearly two months now, but already Jonas could not remember how life had been without him.

He was now the official Blue Closet mascot, accompanying him everywhere he went.

He also had his own basket in the workshop and after the first few weeks where every stray piece of wood was a stick to be fetched and played with, he had settled into the routine of Jonas and Wilko's working day, sitting quietly in his basket when their concentration was obviously on their work, knowing that as soon as the kettle hissed to a crescendo it would be time to head into the garden for a break and maybe a game of ball, or hide and seek with Wilko who was daft enough to crawl under bushes to amuse him.

A particular favourite part of his job, however, was to ride shotgun in the van during deliveries, his head hanging out of the window, ears flapping wildly in the wind.

Things were better with the mistress of the household as well, especially since Jonas had blown a huge commission on buying her a new Balenciaga handbag to replace the one that had been turned into a dog chew.

They were still a little wary of each other but Natalie

did seem to be trying harder with him.

She had even come round to Otter Cottage with an assortment of doggie things the other day, some of which were better than others. The balls and bones had been very well received, but personally Jonas thought the poor dog looked a bit of a prat prancing round the garden in a Burberry doggie anorak, although Dill didn't seem to mind too much.

At least that was the impression he gave until Jonas got up the next morning to find the coat had been on the menu for an attack of the midnight munchies.

'You ate that on purpose, didn't you?' he chided him gently, removing tell-tale pieces of check cloth from around his mouth.

Dill thumped his tail in response.

'Did it taste better than it looked?'

'Woof.'

'Better get rid of the evidence before she gets up, eh?' he chuckled, but the laugh stuck in his throat as he turned around with the tattered object to see her leaning in the doorway, arms crossed, fingers drumming against her forearm.

'Er . . . hi.'

'Er . . . hi yourself,' she said archly and then, to his surprise, she burst out laughing. 'He obviously heard that Burberry is *so* last year. Maybe I'll have to get him some Prada for Christmas?'

'Christmas?'

'Yeah, Christmas; you know, the time of turkey and presents, which is galloping towards us faster than Santa in a sleigh full of reindeer and we still haven't sorted out what we're doing?'

Splitting Christmas into two wasn't exactly the easiest thing in the world to do. Last year had been easy, they had only been seeing each other for a couple of weeks and so had been at that stage in their relationship where it's a natural agreement that each of you will spend the day with your own family, and then the rest of the holiday is yours to hole up together in whichever is your chosen way to celebrate, be it bed, beach, or bar.

This year was different.

This year they were an officially engaged couple.

They were expected to spend Christmas Day together.

The problem was, they were expected to spend it in two different places.

For parents who always saw you come home for Christmas Day, it was a natural assumption that this year, like every other year of your entire life, you would be sitting in your pyjamas under their Christmas tree on the morning of the important day itself, waiting to rip open your presents as though you were still eight and believed that Santa had actually squeezed his way down your modern flue to deliver a sackful of joy and excitement.

Natalie had made it quite clear that her parents were expecting them for the day, and although Jonas knew that Stella would never insist that they go to her, it would ruin her day if they didn't.

'I don't know what to do, Wilks . . . Mum and Farmor are on their own; if I don't go there it will just be the two of them and Tilly – that's hardly fair, is it?'

'Just the two of them?' Nick queried in slight umbrage. 'Does that mean for the first time in fifteen years I'm not invited?'

Nick and his grandmother had spent every Christmas

at Stella's and Blix's house since Nick and Jonas first met. Since his grandmother had sadly passed away five years previously, Nick had continued the tradition without fail.

'You'll be at my mum's, then?'

'Of course. *God Jul och ett Gott Nytt Ar* . . . see, I've been practising. Happy Christmas and happy New Year!'

'Cheers, Wilks.'

'You're thanking *me*? Smorgasbord and saffron cake? I wouldn't miss it for the world! I'm just lucky that your mum and Blix take pity on the poor old orphan boy and ask me round but, having said that, if Natalie's parents invite your mum and Blix to theirs I won't be offended if I'm not on the guest list. I'll just crash Declan's Christmas instead.'

'Well, that would be one solution to the whole problem. Unfortunately, it's not even been mentioned.'

Wilko rolled his eyeballs as if to say 'typical'.

'Couldn't Natalie hint?'

'I don't think it's even occurred to *her* that it would be a good idea – well, at least she hasn't said anything.'

'And let me guess, your lovely mum's already suggested inviting the whole clan over to theirs.'

'Exactly. And I know someone else who probably isn't welcome at the Palmer house either . . .' he gestured to Dylan who was curled up asleep in his workshop basket – 'Dilly boy and cream carpets don't exactly mix.'

'What kind of people have cream carpets?'

'The kind of people who don't like you bringing your dog with you when you visit.' Jonas grinned ruefully.

'Miserable gits.'

'You can't choose your in-laws.' Jonas shrugged.

'Well, actually, I think you can.'

'Oh yeah?'

'I'm telling you, mate . . .' Wilko's tongue poked out of the corner of his mouth as he paused to carefully tap the minutest chisel against the last part of his signature acorn – 'there done . . .' he smiled in satisfaction – 'what was I saying, yeah, never get serious with a girl until you've vetted the whole family; they're the people you're gonna be stuck with every Christmas, new year, birthday, and bank holiday for the rest of your life. It's important that you get a bunch of people who aren't going to make you want to stab them every time you see them.'

'They're not that bad, Wilko.'

'That's what the Vatican said about the Borgias,' he replied with a wink.

Jonas bit the bullet and brought the subject up again that night over dinner.

'Maybe we should just do what we did last year; you go to yours, I'll go to mine.'

'No!' Natalie exclaimed. 'I don't want that, I want to spend Christmas Day with you. Can't we do Christmas Eve at your mum's and then Christmas Day at my parents? After all, in Sweden, Christmas Eve is just as big a deal as Christmas Day.'

'Sure. But my mum isn't Swedish, Natalie, is she? To Mum, Christmas Day is really important. Especially without Dad.'

Natalie opened her mouth to say something and then obviously thinking better of it, closed it again.

'We're at a bit of an impasse really, aren't we?' Jonas shrugged, his sigh heavy as she continued to remain silent.

And then she did something that surprised him.

Which every so often Natalie did.

Something to remind him of why he had fallen in love with her in the first place.

'We should do what's best for your mum.' She nodded.

'Are you sure?'

'Absolutely. It's chaos at Mum and Dad's on Christmas Day, anyway, what with Verity and Liberty coming home with kids and husbands, and the eight thousand cousins descending, and three hundred different sets of grandparents . . . they probably won't even notice I'm not there.'

Jonas got up from the table and pulled her out of her seat to hug her.

'Thanks, Nat, you don't know what this means to me.' He gently tilted her face towards him to drop a kiss on her full lips.

'Yes, I do,' she responded, reaching up for another kiss. 'That's why I'm doing it.'

As the Indian summer snuck stealthily away, Christmas came flying towards them like a bumper car on a track, knocking the brief autumn sideways and out of the calendar year with a glancing blow from its tinsel-covered rubber bumper.

Theo had spent most of her time painting, be it in the studio or out on the coast; she had worked most days without pause for thought or *Coronation Street*.

And after this period of self-imposed industry, who would have thought that a trip to the bank would be the definition of a good day out? But in Theo's case a trip to the bank meant that she had been paid. Which was always good when you were self-employed.

The London Gallery who exhibited and sold her work had updated their antiquated banking system and had offered to pay Theo's money straight into her account, but Theo preferred to get a cheque, something tangible, something she could hold in her hands and say, 'I earned that.'

And today she had a rather large cheque to fondle.

She had sold four paintings in the run-up to Christmas, four of her more expensive ones, and had been assured by Livvy, one of the lovely ladies who ran The Fielding

Gallery, that the fabled Denzil Maitland Grainger, art collector extraordinaire, had been so impressed with the two he had bought, she was certain he would be back for more.

Feeling buoyed by the cheque in her pocket, it was time to go and spend far more money than she could really afford on presents and then spend twice as long as she had shopping, and twice as much money, too, in the post office sending them all off to the four corners of the earth in the hope that they would get there for Christmas Day.

There were also quite a few things she needed for Otter Cottage, and today, as her reward for fighting her way through two rolls of brown paper, a whole ball of string, and labels that stuck to everything except the parcels, the kitchen shop was also calling.

Theo loved to cook.

It stemmed from the fact that she also loved to eat properly, and when no one else in the house even knows how to turn the oven on, you learn, and quickly.

When Theo finally left the post office vowing next year to send vouchers, she spent a happy half an hour wandering between the egg beaters and the baking trays, only to emerge with three carrier bags to find it had begun to rain heavily.

A bright sunny day had turned into darkness and the amber lights of a nearby wine bar were far more appealing than the walk to the train station.

She had never had a problem with going into bars on her own. Well, not since she had been friends with Imelda, anyway. Imelda was always late for everything. They often joked that when her halcyon days finally ended she'd be late for her own funeral. Hence Theo had spent an awful lot of time sitting in bars on her own waiting for her friend to arrive, and was practised in the art of not looking uncomfortable whilst doing so. She was also hungry and the idea of a decent glass of wine and a baguette of some sort was far more tempting than a soggy sandwich to chew on en route, and so she only hesitated for a second before ducking into the warmth of the Chy an Dour.

Theo took a seat at the long stretch of mahogany that was the bar, and ordered a glass of wine and, after scanning the menu, a baguette.

It was three in the afternoon so the bar wasn't exactly heaving with people, and, looking about her as she sipped her wine and waited for her food, Theo's eyes were immediately drawn to a couple at the end of the bar.

This was in part to do with the fact that there was something familiar about the pretty girl sitting facing her. There was also something familiar about the man with his back to her, whom the pretty girl was flirting with. The man whose knee she was putting her hand on in such a suggestive way as she laughed and flicked her hair and fluttered her eyelashes.

And then Theo realised why they both looked so familiar.

It was the girl from whom she had bought Otter Cottage.

And Michael.

Together.

In every sense of the word.

She could hear them quite clearly.

'Do you remember the first time we came here?'

'How could I forget? It was our first date . . .'

'Would you believe that was six years ago, now?'

'And now here we are again.'

'Fate works in mysterious ways,' he said softly and then he leaned in and kissed her.

'It sure does,' Theo murmured to herself, taking a swig of her wine, and then, raising the glass slightly, she proposed a toast. 'Thanks, fate, for bringing me here today. I said I wanted answers and you've certainly done your absolute best to give them to me. Cheers.'

It would seem that the stunning beaches weren't the only thing he had wanted to move back for. But why bring Theo with him, if that were the case? With hindsight she knew the answer to that one full well. He was an emotional coward, too scared to let go of her and brave the sea of singledom, until he knew that he had another pair of breasts to float on.

She had wanted an explanation and now she had one.

She was his fall girl.

A mattress at the bottom of the ladder in case he lost his footing whilst making a mad dash for it over the fence to where the grass was greener.

And the grass was so green it was positively radio-active.

When Theo had first met Gemma Whittaker she had immediately thought what a pretty girl she was and how much she looked like Holly Willoughby with her tumble of long blond hair and slim yet curvaceous figure.

She had also thought how nice it was to have someone near her own age living so close and that perhaps they might end up as friends. But she hadn't really spoken to her much, apart from the odd hello whenever their paths crossed. In fact, Gemma had never been particularly friendly towards her. She hadn't been so rude as to ignore Theo's friendly hellos or good mornings, but she had ensured that her responses had been curt enough to curtail any follow-up.

Now Theo knew why.

What made things worse, however, was that Michael had never even mentioned that he knew her.

He would have immediately sunk another few levels in her esteem, but for the fact that he was already so low the level he was at was swamp. Where was there to go down to from there? Rancid pool of scurvy, scummy dead stuff at the bottom of swamp, perhaps? Yes, Theo liked that one; he'd fit in well there.

As for now . . . well, as far as she could see it, she had two options:

The first was to confront them.

Let them know they had been seen and by whom.

The second, and far easier one, as far as Theo was concerned, was to leave.

She had just decided to opt for the second and sneak an escape when her baguette arrived.

Tuna in mayonnaise with red onion and melted cheese. Warm from the oven, it smelt and looked delicious. Theo's empty stomach rolled a protesting growl. It was still raining outside.

Theo looked at the baguette and felt her mouth begin to salivate. Oh, how she longed to sink her teeth into it.

She looked over at Michael. It looked like he was getting stuck into something as well. Not just his teeth but his lips and tongue as well. Hands buried deep in thick corn-gold hair.

The barman who had just brought her food followed her gaze and rolled his eyes.

'Some people, eh? Enough to put you off your food.'

Funny, but it wasn't enough to put Theo off of her food. You'd think, considering the circumstances, it would be, but it wasn't.

The baguette was still calling.

She could always take it with her, but by the time she got to the train station and sat down on the train to eat it, it would be cold. Besides, she hadn't finished her wine yet.

And so, to her own amazement, she stayed and tucked into her sandwich with relish, all the time watching them smooch at the end of the bar and thinking to herself that by rights she should be running from the room weeping and wailing, or taking the lovely crusty baguette and instead of stuffing it in her mouth stuffing it up Michael's lying, cheating arse.

But what a waste that would have been of good food.

Halfway through the baguette, she even ordered another glass of wine. What the heck, she wasn't driving. She had hopped on the foot ferry over to Quinn and then had trained it to Truro from there.

'They still at it?' The barman sighed crossly as he brought her another glass of Pinot Grigio.

'Maybe they're in love,' Theo mused.

'Maybe, but they don't have to inflict it on the rest of us who aren't so lucky.'

Theo found herself hoping that they were in love. Somehow it made her feel better to think that they were, that he had left her, not because he was in like, or in lust, but because he was madly in love with someone else.

It made it all seem far more worthwhile.

Far less scurvy and scummy and all things rancid.

Love had a habit of purifying things that were otherwise deemed sordid.

She therefore really hoped that he had left her the way he did because he had fallen head over heels in love.

'Do you think they're in love?' she asked the still-hovering barman.

Sensing that for some reason this question was in deadly earnest, the barman took a moment to contemplate.

'Well, I'd say it certainly looks that way.' He finally nodded.

'So would I,' said Theo, finishing her wine in record time.

'Would you like another one?' the barman asked, looking at her empty glass.

'I think I would,' Theo mused, looking not at the glass but at Michael, 'but I think perhaps I might have some time out on my own first.'

And she found, to her amazement, that instead of feeling awful as she left that bar, she was actually feeling a little bit better.

11

What was it Suze from the shop had said?

You should look close to home?

Theo had often wondered what she meant, but now she realised she had been talking geographically.

How much closer to home could you get than next door?

She'd received a letter from Xavier that morning, full of news of life in Oz, and asking for the same from her about her new life in Cornwall.

Thus far Theo had told no one other than Geoffrey about her and Michael's parting of the ways. What was the point? Xavier and Dion would worry, her mother and Augustine would lecture, her father would probably need a ten-minute explanation of who exactly Michael was. Imelda would come flying down, literally, with hugs and alcohol and spitting vitriol, not what she wanted right now.

The best way to show them all that she was fine was to get on with her life, and so that was what she had done. This also meant that she hadn't told them about buying Otter Cottage. She knew they would seriously question her decision to stay in Cornwall when life as she knew it had been firmly in London. If she could prove to them that this decision had been a good one and *then* tell them, it would save her an awful lot of angst-filled phone calls.

This hadn't been as hard not to mention as one might think; she just told them she had a new number, which, seeing as she'd only moved next door was just digits away from the previous one, and the elderly postman, a total sweetheart, simply popped her post through the door of Otter Cottage, regardless of which house they were addressed to.

But now, well, now perhaps it was time for the news, now that it was old news, to be imparted to all.

Xavier and his wife Jules had moved to Sydney two years previously. Their little boy Simeon had been born that summer and Theo had yet to meet her new nephew, although copious amounts of photographs had winged their electronic way into her inbox.

Xavier was the best out of all of them at keeping touch, and it was he whom she automatically called first.

Jules answered the phone. Chatted about Simeon for the first ten minutes, so full of news of Theo's nephew that there was no room for anything else, which suited Theo just fine, and then she was passed over to an apparently hovering Xavier.

'Theo, sis, how lovely, how are you?'

'I'm really good – really, really good, Xav.'

'So you're enjoying life in the West Country?'

'Loving it.'

'Painting lots?'

'More than lots.'

'Fabulous, inspiring then, yeah?'

'Very . . . it's gorgeous, you'd like it here.'

'Earning your keep?'

'Of course.'

'Not struggling?'

'I'm doing great, Xav, you don't have to worry about me.'

'Someone has to, Dormouse. Although I'm sure Michael's looking after you . . .'

There was a long silence from Theo's end.

'Look, Xav, I don't want you to worry, but Michael and I . . .' Theo paused, wondering how best to phrase things, but despite the fact that she could have been about to tell him anything, Xavier knew her well enough to tell from the tone and the hesitancy what she was about to say.

'I see . . .' He, too, was silent for a moment, and then he asked, 'Are you OK, love?'

'Yeah, I think so. In fact, it's not a think, it's a yes, I'm fine, amazingly so.'

Xavier exhaled a sigh of relief that was so heavy it almost travelled down the long-distance line and lifted the edges of her hair.

'Thee . . . would you hate me if I told you I'm glad he's gone? I know it's probably not exactly what you want to hear at the moment, but I've never felt that he was quite right for you . . .'

At which point Theo burst out laughing.

At the sound of such genuine laughter Xavier found his smile again.

'I take it I'm not the only one who's said the same thing . . . look, Thee, how about coming out to visit? I know it's an ask, we're not exactly talking hop-on-a-bus territory here, but we'd love to have you and maybe it would do you good, different place, different people . . .'

Theo privately thought that if she wanted to find

different people she didn't have to travel several thousand miles, just step out of her front door, but she didn't say this.

'Well, I'm kind of tied here at the moment . . . work and other stuff. Not that I wouldn't love to see you guys, but I have things here right now that mean it would be a little difficult to get away for so long . . .'

'Are you going to move back to London?'

'Well, actually Xav, that's the other thing I needed to tell you . . .'

He had fallen silent for a moment after she had explained about buying Otter Cottage, and then he had said very carefully, 'That was kind of a spur-of-the-moment thing for such a big decision . . .'

'When I'm not a spur-of-the-moment girl, I know, but it felt right.'

'Don't get me wrong, Theo, I'm happy for you – if it's what you want, then great, but I'm just worried about you being in a new place all on your own.'

'You shouldn't be worried, Xav, I'm happy here, I'm making friends.'

'Really?' Xavier knew how having Dion as her first priority had meant that making friends had gone on the back burner for his sister.

'Yeah, good friends . . .' she insisted, hearing the concern in his voice and wanting to reassure him, but wondering if her blossoming friendship with Geoffrey and the recent acquaintance of Suzanne could really count as this.

'So you're happy and settling in?'

'Absolutely . . .'

He seemed to accept this, and the conversation had turned to news of the rest of the family, and ended on a promise that if she ever felt the urge she would hop straight on a Sydney-bound jet.

It was partly the conversation with Xav that gave her the push to take Suze up on her offer of a friendly ear whenever she needed one.

She had told Xavier she was making friends so she should really put some truth behind this statement. Besides, she had liked Suze. There had been a huge part of her that had wanted to go and see her far sooner than this, but the other part of her, the shy Theo who was convinced that no one would really like her because she was a scruffy paint-obsessed recluse, had held her back.

So it was a very resolute, but rather nervous face that peered around the newsagent's door later that day.

Theo needn't have worried. From Suze's instant smile and friendly, 'Hey, how are you?' it was obvious she was genuinely delighted to see her.

For her part, the intuitive Suze took one look at Theo's face and knew that the news she would not impart herself unless fully aware that it was absolute truth, had finally found its own way to her.

She immediately put the kettle on and offered her a stool by the counter.

'So?' she said simply as Theo took a sip of the hot, strong coffee.

Theo looked up over the rim of her cup.

'I saw Michael today.'

Suze said nothing, just nodded and listened.

'In a bar in Truro . . . he wasn't on his own.'

'Ah yes . . .' Suze bit her lip.

'You knew, didn't you?'

'I'd heard rumours, but like I said before, I'm not a gossip, so I don't pass on rumours, only fact. I promise I would have told you if I knew it for myself to be true.'

Theo nodded her understanding.

'Are you OK? Sorry, that's one of those stupid questions that just make you want to hit the person who's asking rather hard over the head with something heavy, isn't it?'

Theo laughed.

'I'm OK. Thank you. In fact, this might sound weird, but I think it helped.'

'Closure?'

'Mmm, not really that – just reason, you know, reason and purpose.'

'The reason being that he's a two-timing scumbag?'

'I think I prefer to look on it as the reason being that fate had something else in mind for both of us other than each other . . . if that makes sense?'

Suze smiled wryly. 'It not only makes sense, it also reminds me what a bitter, twisted warped kind of woman I am for my theory.'

The shop bell went as a large group of anoraked walkers wandered into the newsagent's in search of sustenance.

Theo put down her coffee.

'You're busy, I should go.'

Suze looked reluctantly at the full shop.

'I could tell them all we've had an outbreak of botulism and they should steer well clear of the pasty cabinet.'

Theo grinned broadly. 'Probably not the best idea . . . maybe you'd fancy a coffee at mine some time?'

'That would be good – actually, tell you what, fancy the pub tonight? Little drinkie? Long chat? I know it looks like the biggest shithole this side of the Tamar, but it's not totally dire, I promise. In fact, it can be pretty good fun when the rowing team turn out for the night . . . if muscles are your thing, of course . . .'

'Um . . .' Theo hedged, shy again, but Suze was having none of it.

'No ums and no excuses. I close at seven tonight, meet me here at seven-thirty and we'll go for a bottle of wine and we could even have some scampi in a basket . . .'

'They do scampi in a basket?'

'And chicken.' Suze nodded smiling. 'Very seventies, since the seventies, in fact, but they're just coming back into trend because the seventies is back in vogue – so, you see, everything comes around, including karma, so Michael needs to watch his arse, before karma sneaks up behind him and takes a great big chewy chunk out of it . . .'

Suze was waiting outside the shop when Theo went back at seven-thirty. She immediately tucked her arm through Theo's.

'Right, are you ready for this?'

'Do I need to be?'

'Well, it is a bit like entering an episode of *Dr Who*.'

'How do you mean?'

'Stepping through time warps, the front door of the Boatman is actually a hole in the space–time continuum, taking you straight back to a different decade.'

Suze wasn't exaggerating.

The Boatman's Arms was a vintage pub with low beams

and mullioned windows, a beautiful roaring fireplace and a long sweep of gorgeous polished mahogany for a bar. Unfortunately, it had been attacked by a seventies swirly patterned red-and-burgundy carpet and brown paisley wallpaper, all clashing wonderfully with Christmas decorations that looked older than Theo.

It was also replete with the clichéd buxom barmaid pulling a pint of dark frothing ale, who looked up as the two women entered the room.

'Alright, Suze?'

'Fine, thanks, Marianne. How are you?'

'All right, Suze.'

'Can I have a bottle of whatever white you've got that doesn't taste like Bevan's been washing his smalls in it?'

'All right, Suze.'

'This is Theo.'

'All right, Theo?'

'My mum's name is Marianne.' Theo smiled at the woman who grinned back.

'Is that so? Perhaps we might be related then, my lover . . .' She winked and, having poured a pint and handed it to the old man perched on a bar stool, whom Theo assumed must be Bevan, she reached under the counter and then popped back up with a bottle of wine.

'This all right, Suze?'

'Great, thanks. Quiet tonight, Marianne?'

'Ah, right, Suze, it is.'

'Any chance of something in a basket to go with the wine?'

'Scampi do you?'

Suze and Theo looked at each other.

'All right, Marianne,' they chorused.

*

By the time the scampi arrived Suze knew the whole story.

'They were only a few feet away from me.'

'And they didn't see you?'

'They were um . . . kind of engrossed.'

'Gross.' Suze pulled a face. 'So what did you do? What did you say to him?'

'Nothing.'

'You didn't say anything?'

'No.'

'Nothing at all?'

'No.'

'So what did you do?'

'I ate my baguette.'

'You ate your baguette?'

'I was hungry.'

Suze burst out laughing.

'Well, that says it all, really.'

'It does, doesn't it?' Theo mused, spearing a piece of scampi. 'How is it that I managed to spend three years with someone who was so obviously completely wrong for me?'

'Well, that's an easy one to answer: no matter what anyone tells you, the first thing any person goes for is looks. And then people put on a front when they first start seeing someone; they try to be everything they think that person will want in a partner rather than being who they actually are. That's why so many relationships fall apart after the honeymoon period, because that's when the real you starts to claw its way back to the surface. I think real love is when you find someone you can truly be yourself with from the very beginning.'

'Michael and I definitely weren't real love, then. It was always the spontaneous things that I did that he didn't like.'

'Such as?'

'Oh, giving to beggars, talking to strangers, painting in the nude . . .'

Suze burst out laughing at the last one.

'Not as mad as it sounds.' Theo grinned back at her. 'I'm ruining my clothes with stray oils, whereas paint just washes straight off of me.'

'Sounds fair enough to me.' Suze nodded. 'So, no regrets that he's gone, then?'

'My only regret is that we lasted too long. I hate the thought that I've wasted so much time on the wrong person . . .' She paused and her head tilted to one side as she contemplated what she had just said. 'But then again, if we hadn't been together, I wouldn't be here now, would I? And I'm glad I am . . .'

Suze nodded thoughtfully. 'That's very true. I suppose that's how I should look at it with me and my ex; if it weren't for him I wouldn't be here, and I'm happy that I am. It may be a bit . . .' she glanced around to make sure no one was listening – 'provincial in Port Ruan, but it's a great place to live. The natives are friendly . . . once you get to know them – well, most of them, anyway; certain people with nasty curtains and even ghastlier manners excepted . . . I think what I'm trying to say is that everything, good or bad, happens for a reason.'

'Fate?' Theo said, thinking back to what Michael had said as he leaned in to kiss Gemma.

'Exactly. Good old fate. To fate,' Suze announced, refilling their glasses and then holding up her own.

'To fate,' Theo echoed, knocking her glass against Suze's so that the chime rang out through the pub.

It hadn't hurt at all as she had thought of that kiss, and she knew that it had put the seal on what she already knew: that she didn't miss Michael.

But what it had made her realise above all else was that she did miss love. She wanted someone, something, anything in her life to make her feel loved.

Even just a little bit.

12

Christmas Eve at the Larsson house belonged to Blix. They always celebrated according to Swedish tradition.

The house was decorated with poinsettias, red tulips and beautiful white amaryllis, and the sweet and itchy scent of ginger hung heavy on the air from the literally hundreds of gingerbread men that Blix and Stella had baked both as gifts for friends and to decorate the tree and the mantelpiece above the fire.

Clementine, whose only family, her dad, was away for Christmas, had been invited to join in the celebrations, and so she, Natalie, Jonas and Nick arrived together in Wilko's Audi – 'shaken, not stirred', as Clementine put it, by Nick's somewhat manic driving on what were slightly icy roads.

They were greeted at the door by Stella and Blix, who was clutching a ladle ready to hand out glasses from a huge bowl of her homemade glogg.

'What's in it?' Natalie sniffed it distrustfully as if Blix were handing her poison.

'It's exactly like mulled wine.'

'Could I just have a dry white instead?'

'I'll try it . . .' Clementine said eagerly, reaching for a

cup. 'Smells gorgeous, like alcoholic fruit cake . . . ooh, *tastes* like alcoholic fruit cake. Nat, sod the wine, have a glass of this – it's gorgeous . . .'

Clementine was equally impressed with the food on offer.

Clementine loved her food. Not a girl for small pants was how she described herself.

The table was heaving with Blix's usual Christmas smorgasbord, or julboard: pies, meatballs, sausages, potatoes, all sorts of herring, salads, ham, broth, potato casserole, all to be washed down with a huge bottle of akvavit.

'What's this?' Natalie queried as Blix, determined to make up for the missed glogg, pushed a glass upon her.

'Akvavit? Literally translates as "water of life".' Blix smiled innocently.

'More like water of death . . .' Jonas warned her as Natalie went to knock it back. 'It's forty per cent proof.'

This whole array was followed by a traditional Swedish pudding.

'Rice pudding?' Natalie queried as Stella handed her a bowl.

'Pretty much, yes; it's called *risgryngot*. The only difference is that there's an almond hidden in there somewhere. It's a Swedish tradition.' Stella smiled at Natalie, who had frowned in puzzlement. 'Whoever gets the almond will be married next year . . .'

'Ah, I see . . .' Natalie winked at Jonas and began raking her spoon through the pudding.

'You're supposed to eat it, not excavate it . . .'

'You're kidding, aren't you? It looks like cement and, besides, I can't do puddings, I've got a wedding dress to fit into in a few months' time.'

'Well, if you don't want yours, I'll have it, it's gorgeous . . .' Clementine offered, and then there was a loud crunch and everyone turned to look as Clementine stopped with her mouth full and then squealed in delight.

'I got the almond!'

'*You* got the almond?'

'Either that or my filling's just come out . . .' Clem put a finger in her mouth and, frowning, pulled out the remains of whatever it was that had crunched.

The frown dissolved back into a smile.

'I got the almond!' she repeated, and began to hum 'Here comes the bride', much to Natalie's chagrin.

'Quick, someone throw a nut in the gorgon's dish before she has a hissy fit,' Wilko whispered to Jonas.

'She'll have a hissy fit if she hears you calling her that,' Jonas whispered, trying and failing not to smile. 'Honestly, Nick, as my best friend and soon-to-be best man, I really think you could come up with a better nickname for my wife-to-be.'

'I suppose you're right.' Nick sighed thoughtfully. 'How about Genghis or Attila?'

He was saved from a beating with a rather huge Swedish sausage by Clementine, pointing out that Blix had disappeared.

'Where's your grandmother gone?'

'Probably fallen head-first into a vat of glogg,' Natalie said with a touch of wishful thinking.

'She's probably gone to get changed.' Jonas grinned, knowing what was coming next.

'Into what?'

'Well, it's not a full moon . . .' Natalie began, but Jonas silenced her with a look and, turning to Clem, he began to explain, 'In Sweden we do presents on Christmas Eve . . .'

'Ooh, I don't know whether that's really good or really bad; it means I don't have to wait until tomorrow, but then, tomorrow I'll wish I still had them to open.'

'Well, that's one of the good things about being half Swedish and half English, because we open presents tonight *and* tomorrow.'

'Double presents? I wish I was half English and half Swedish.' Natalie helped herself to more akvavit.

'Mmm, I've always fancied some Swedish in me, too,' Clem murmured, and then put down her glass of glogg and stared at it accusingly. Had she really just said that out loud? 'Jeez, that stuff must be strong,' she added, looking round fearfully in case she'd been overheard.

Fortunately, a distraction had arrived in the form of Blix, who reappeared at the top of the stairs and struck a pose.

'What is she wearing?' Natalie's eyes were wide.

'Is your grandmother supposed to be Father Christmas?' Clem queried.

'Tomte,' Jonas explained, 'not dissimilar, I suppose, but he's a Christmas gnome instead of Father Christmas. He hands out the presents with a little rhyme for everyone, it's tradition. She usually does them in Swedish but seeing as you and Clem are here, she's worked really hard on English ones this year.'

'Well, that explains the beard and naughty Mrs Santa combination . . . is it me, or do you think she looks like something out of a horror movie . . . or *Gremlins*?' Natalie hissed as Blix pranced down the stairs.

'Shhh . . . Nat,' Clem hissed, frowning. 'She'll hear you . . . and anyway, I think she looks great; she's three times my age and she looks ten times better in that outfit than I ever would. Look at her legs!'

'I'm trying not to, seeing as there's so much of them on show.' Natalie shuddered.

Having heard every word, but totally unperturbed, Blix carried on with the show by reaching into the sack she was carrying and pulling out a gift-wrapped parcel.

'Ah, this one is for you, my lovely daughter-in-law, my gorgeous *Svardotter*:

> Stella, still a shining star,
> The brightest in the sky by far,
> It's a shame you never go out at night,
> So I bought you a subscription to a dating site.'

Stella's hands flew to her mouth as she gasped in horror.

'Svarmor, oh you haven't! Please say you haven't really done that. I don't believe you!'

'I have, *min älskling*.' Blix nodded firmly. 'And I should have done it sooner. You are far too beautiful to waste your life alone. If I were still your age, I would have men falling out of my underwear I have so many of them . . . now,' and she tactically turned her attention to her sack and pulled out another gift before Stella could protest further.

'Who is this one for? Let me see . . . ah yes, this one is for you, beautiful girl.' She turned smiling to Clementine. 'And I have a little poem for you, too . . . ahem . . .' and she cleared her throat.

'*Oh my darling, oh my darling, oh my darling Clementine* . . .'

'I think she might have plagiarised this one,' Jonas whispered with a grin to Wilko, who spluttered his laughter through a mouthful of glogg.

Blix paused and fixed her grandson and Nick with a steely gaze, until silence fell again, at which point she picked up her scroll once more and continued.

'Oh my darling, oh my darling, oh my darling Clementine,
Sweet and juicy little fruit, these will make you more
  divine.
With your arse like two peaches, in sexy, silk breeches,
And those melons, two felons so dangerous they are,
Will be locked up all luscious in a lovely silk bra!'

And she handed a blushing Clementine a package that contained a beautiful set of lingerie.

'Now for my adoptive sonson Nicholas ... ahem ...' she declared, pulling out a large gift-wrapped box and handing it to him.

'So handsome, so funny, but still alone in this world,
  I get you a gift to help you get a girl ...'

Jonas had got the giggles again.

'I thought you were supposed to be Tomte, Farmor, not Cilla Black.'

'Jonas, will you please stop interrupting ... now, where was I? oh yes ...

I myself like to dance bumper to bumper
With a man who has such a *snyg rumpa*,
So I try to think *why* is this gorgeous man single,
And I get you a gift that may help my boy mingle ...'

Nick hurriedly unwrapped his present to reveal an enormous bottle of aftershave.

'Are you trying to tell me that I smell?' he snorted with laughter.

'Don't joke, Nicholas, it is very good *rakvatten* . . . after-shave . . . the man in the advert is running away he has so many women chasing him. Now, who is next, we wonder?' She reached inside her sack again and pulled out another present. 'Aha . . . this is for Tilly and this is for Dylan . . .' she handed Stella and Jonas two hide bones, one small, one huge, and then reached inside the sack again, and pulled out the smallest gift in there – 'and this is for my Jonas.'

And handing it to him, she unrolled her scroll a little further but then, instead of reading her poem out to him, she handed him the scroll.

'My throat is a little dry, will you read this out for me whilst I get some more glogg?'

Jonas frowned in surprise, but took the scroll none-theless.

'*True love is a precious gift indeed It's like the rarest flower* . . .' he read out loud, but then, as his eyes scanned the rest of the poem, he stopped and instead read it silently to himself.

'It shouldn't be a stinking weed
That gets right up your bower,
It should be fragrant, soft and sweet,
Not sometimes sweet, then sour.
And so I buy you something
That will counter any curse
And help you find a woman
Who is for better, not for worse.'

'What does it say, Jonas?' Natalie queried as he fell silent.

'Oh, it's something very soppy indeed about true love, far too embarrassing to read out loud, which is, I am sure, why my farmor gave it to me to do, tell you what why don't you open this for me whilst I get Farmor another drink?'

He handed her the small gift and, her curiosity diverted, Jonas took the opportunity to accidentally drop Blix's scroll in the big punch bowl of glogg.

'Jonas!' Blix cried as both her scroll and her glogg were ruined.

'What is it?' Natalie held up the small leather pouch she had pulled from the wrapping paper.

'It's an Indian medicine bag . . .' Blix turned disappointed eyes away from the sinking scroll. 'It helps you find true love.'

'And keeps it once you've found it, eh Farmor? You are such an old romantic. You just want everyone to be paired up and loved up, don't you?' Jonas slung an arm around his grandmother, and hugged her, *hard*, and she shrugged as if to say 'of course'.

'*Att vara kär*, to be in love, it is such a good thing. Why run away from it, unless, of course, it is the *wrong* love?'

And then, of course, she turned to Natalie.

The two women eyed each other like boxers on opposing sides of a ring.

'I have one gift left . . .'

'Oh lord, it's Nat's turn . . .' Clem bit her bottom lip. 'I don't know if I can watch.'

'And no scroll.' Jonas pretended to sigh. 'Such a shame, Farmor, your poem for Natalie has gone, and I am sure it was as wonderful as the one you wrote for me . . .'

But to his concern, Blix simply smiled.

'Oh, it is OK, sonson, Natalie's poem is very short, so I remember it in my head . . . *Natalie, your poem is simple but true, I saw this and thought straight away of you . . .*'

And, reaching into her tomte sack for the final time, she handed her a strangely shaped parcel.

Natalie looked at Blix, looked at Jonas, her frown puzzled, and then almost as if she didn't want to do it, she slowly took off the paper.

Her gift was an obscenely ugly little carved doll.

A Swedish troll.

Natalie just stared at it.

Silent.

As did everyone else.

And then Wilko began to crack up, until Jonas gave him a warning look and he – not very successfully – turned the laughter into a fake cough.

Natalie looked around the gathered group very slowly, from Stella's apologetic smile, through Clem's fearful face, Jonas's frown, Wilko's smirk, and finally turned her solemn gaze to Blix, who looked back, defiant, challenging, and then, to Jonas's amazement, Natalie smiled, so very sweetly.

'Why, thank you, Farmor,' she said, deliberately using Jonas's familial term for his grandmother. 'Whenever I look at this, it will always remind me SO much of you too, literally. Now I think, perhaps, as you cooked such a huge um . . . "feast" for everyone, it's only fair that I start to clear it all up.' And placing the troll down on the table next to Blix, she looked from one to the other with a sarcastic smile on her face followed by a little snort of derisive laughter.

'*Surpuppa!*' Blix immediately responded.

'Farmor!' Jonas warned her.

Natalie paused.

'What did she say?'

'Nothing.'

'Well, I distinctly heard her say something.'

'It's a toast,' Jonas lied, 'a Swedish drinking toast.' And he held up his own glass mug of Blix's lethal glogg.

'*Surpuppa!*' he announced, knocking it back.

Natalie narrowed her eyes at him, her disbelief obvious, and then Stella raised her own glass and echoed her son.

'*Surpuppa!*' she exclaimed. '*Gut Jul*. Happy Christmas, everyone.'

Natalie seemed satisfied by the usually trustworthy Stella's affirmation of Jonas's translation. But she then, unfortunately, caught him mouthing 'thank you' to his mother, and the storm recommenced.

As soon as she was gone, Jonas caught his grandmother gently by the elbow and talked to her low and hurriedly in Swedish.

'Farmor! Why do you do it? How can you expect the two of you to get along when you are so mean to her?'

'She was very rude to me about my gift.'

'You know you deserved that, Farmor . . .'

She held up a hand.

'I know what you're going to say, and I won't apologise. She is not the right girl for you, Sonson. She has no fun in her, she is too serious, too material, all that matters to her is the outside. You need someone to whom inside is where it counts. Not money, not a big house, but the real things in life.'

'You don't know her, Farmor, you won't get to know her, you only see what you want to see.'

'I could say the same thing to you, Jonas Larsson. Yes, she is beautiful, but not to the core . . . you are *Bergtagna*.'

'You think I'm *Bergtagna*? Is that why you got her the troll? You're saying she's bewitched me?'

Blix nodded emphatically.

For a moment Jonas's face twisted with an emotion that could be read as anger, and then he simply burst out laughing.

'Farmor, you are absolutely crazy.'

'I am not crazy, Sonson, I only want for you to be happy . . .'

'And if I tell you that I am happy with Natalie, will you promise me that you will be kinder to her? Give her a chance?'

Blix huffed, her bottom lip protruding like that of a petulant child.

'I am kind to her, when we first meet. But she is always so uptight. I only try to find out if she ever laughs.'

'She laughs at a lot of things, trust me. Trolls for Christmas, maybe not one of them.'

'I thought it was funny . . .'

'And perhaps a little bit mean?'

'You think so?'

'You mean you didn't?'

Blix shrugged.

'It is not her only gift.'

'What else did you get her? A moustache-removal kit? A device for pulling the poker out of her arse?' His voice was stern but there was no disguising the slight smile on his face.

'You will find out tomorrow morning.'

'I'm not sure that I want to . . . promise me, Farmor, even if it's just for my sake, that you'll try and get along?'

Blix pursed her lips for a moment and then, albeit grudgingly, she nodded.

'OK, for your sake, I promise.'

Unaware of this concession, Natalie was once again banging away her angst in the kitchen.

As Blix took a second telling off from Stella, Clementine smiled an apology at Jonas.

'Want me to go and talk to her?'

Jonas smiled softly at her.

'Thanks, Clem, but I think maybe we should just leave her to cool down in peace. She has every right to be upset. I've had a word with Blix, and she's promised to behave, but you know what Nat's like; give her a bit of time to cool down and she'll be smiling again.'

Privately, Clementine wasn't so sure, but she shrugged and said, 'OK. By the way, thanks for having me here.'

'Hey, you know you're so welcome, don't you? When's your dad coming back?'

'Day after Boxing Day. We're going to have another Christmas Day then, so I'm actually getting *three* this year.'

Also determined to make the most out of Christmas, Blix, undeterred by two tellings off, had put on some music and coaxed Nick to dance with her. Nothing unusual except for the fact that her choice of song was the Prodigy.

'I am the fire starter, twisted fire starter!' she sang.

'Your grandma's utterly insane.' Clementine laughed, watching her.

Jonas nodded.

'You've only just realised?'

'I mean that in the nicest possible way, of course,' she added in a rush.

'Even though she's not always as nice as she possibly could be to some people?'

'She's always been lovely to me.'

'She has, hasn't she?' Jonas pondered as Dylan trotted up to them bone in mouth.

'So are you and Nat OK, now?' Clem asked as the dog assumed his favourite position, leaning against Jonas's leg.

'You mean has she forgiven me for Dylan? I think so, but he's pretty hard to resist, isn't he?'

'Oh yes,' Clem nodded furiously, eyes Bambi wide, 'he's gorgeous.'

'Now I've just got to get her to forgive Blix.'

'Do you mind me asking . . . What *did* Blix say to her? *Surpuppa*? What does that mean, it's not really a toast, is it?'

'She called her a sourpuss, that's all.' He shrugged, and then sighed heavily. 'I hate to say it, but I think that maybe Blix and Natalie are never going to be the best of friends. Farmor is just too wild, and Natalie not so. They are too different. The thing is, if Natalie would just laugh, Farmor would soon stop trying to bait her . . . but it doesn't matter how many times I tell her this, she won't listen to me . . .'

Clementine watched enthralled as Jonas gently stroked Dylan's shaggy head as he spoke.

Unbeknownst to Jonas, he had in Clem exactly what Natalie wished for from Wilko, someone who thought how utterly bloody lucky their friend was to have someone that wonderful.

Clem would never ever confess it to anyone but she had a huge crush on Jonas. In particular, she loved to listen to him talking. She loved the way he had just a hint of an accent there still, despite the fact that he had now spent more of his life in England than in Sweden.

Just a tiny hint, a little lilt to the way he spoke, and it was so sexy.

Then again, everything about him was sexy, from his

gorgeous green eyes and golden hair, down to his feet. He had lovely feet. And he had the nicest thighs she had ever seen, firm, muscular, they filled his jeans so well that just looking at them made her shiver, made her want to reach out and stroke. Bad Clem.

Natalie was one lucky, lucky girl.

Not that you'd think she thought that just by looking at her at the moment.

She was in a stonking mood, convinced – quite rightly, as it happened – that Blix had said something insulting. She was currently doing her usual and taking things out on the kitchen cupboards.

'Why do you put up with her when she's being a moody cow, Jonas?' Clem asked, looking apologetically at Stella as the sound of breaking glass rang out from the room.

'I could ask you the same question.'

'True, but I asked first.'

'OK. Because everyone has their good bits and their bad bits and I think her good bits make it worth putting up with her bad bits. Not very eloquent, I know, but fairly succinct.' He grinned. 'And she also has every right to be angry. However, that's my mother's kitchen she's abusing, so I think it might be best if I had a word.' He winked at Clem and got to his feet.

Natalie's face was as pinched and sour as if she'd just eaten a whole lemon. She knew full well that Jonas had come into the kitchen but she carried on slamming and banging as if she hadn't seen him. He leaned against the door frame, waited until she came close to put something in the fridge, and then caught her arm.

'Don't let her get to you.'

'That's all you have to say about it?'

'Of course not; I told her she should stop being so mean to you. Honestly, Nat, I hate to say this, but you do ask for it by being so uptight with her. You should just play her at her own game. When she baits you, just laugh . . .'

'I did.'

'*With* her, not at her, that just antagonises her further.'

'So I just have to put up with her?'

'Well, I've had a word, so I'm hoping that she'll stop teasing you quite so much, but to be perfectly honest, then the answer to your question is yes, you just have to put up with her. Blix is who she is. She does this to everyone, honestly. It's like she's testing them. Did you know she once bought Wilko an elephant posing pouch for his birthday? He was fifteen.'

Natalie started to laugh.

'There . . . see . . . show her the Natalie you show to me, and she'll soon stop.'

'You think so?'

'I know so. Now can you please stop clearing up . . . I don't want to have to spend Christmas morning reattaching my mother's kitchen cupboards . . .'

The next morning as they sat around the Christmas tree with carols playing in the background, and the lights twinkling merrily, Natalie cautiously opened the small box marked: 'To Natalie, Happy Christmas, Blix', half expecting it to explode as she eased it wide, only to have her jaw drop in amazement as she revealed a pair of utterly beautiful antique pearl earrings.

'They belonged to my mother-in-law, and to her mother-in-law before her,' Blix said softly, smiling as

Natalie gazed in open-mouthed amazement at them. 'I wore them when I married Jonas's *farfar*, his papa's papa . . . Stella would have worn them, too, if she had not of snuck off to marry my son without thought for his *morfa*.' She winked at Stella. 'I thought perhaps you might like to wear them too – at your wedding . . .'

'They're beautiful, Farmor, thank you so much . . .' Jonas offered on Natalie's behalf as she was still too stunned to speak.

Everyone's attention shifted as Clementine pulled a giant vibrating dildo from a package marked: 'To Clem, have a good one, Nick', and screamed with shock and laughter.

'See . . .' Jonas nudged Natalie, who was still staring at the earrings. 'I told you she's not all bad.'

Natalie wasn't so convinced.

'She's just feeling guilty for being so mean to me yesterday,' she whispered.

But Jonas shook his head.

'Hardly, Nat,' he said quietly, smiling fondly at his grandmother. 'I know for a fact that gift has been under the tree for a week.'

Christmas for Theo was usually Christmas with Imelda.

Even when she had been with Michael. He had gone home to Truro. Theo had stayed in London with Mel. Other people had always thought this a little strange – surely couples wanted to spend Christmas together, open lavish gifts in front of a roaring fire in matching pyjamas, but it had never happened that way, and tradition only becomes tradition when it has happened several times before.

Theo's tradition was Christmas with her friend.

And Christmas with Imelda was always amazing.

Statuesque blonde and beautiful in the same kind of way as a thoroughbred horse, Imelda listed her job jokingly as professional girlfriend. In actuality, a hand model and voice-over artist, and doing very nicely at it, thank you, she always seemed to hook up with men who wanted a woman who was all things to them – not just lover, but secretary, accessory, personal adviser and sometimes even stylist.

Not that Imelda was complaining; the kind of man who demanded this kind of woman usually had his compensations, and whilst happy to fulfil numerous other obligations, Imelda drew the line at cook and bottle washer. She did not cook, she did not clean, she did not launder. Fortunately, the kind of man she dated was usually the kind who could afford several different minions to do all of these jobs for the both of them.

She and Theo had met six years ago when wealthy boyfriend number four had purchased one of Theo's paintings, proclaiming that one day Theodora English would be a name to contend with.

Theo had joked that it was already one she struggled to contend with herself, and blamed it on her father, who had christened his children in turn, Xavier, Augustine, and then Theodora, and then had surpassed himself even more when Theo's little brother had arrived six years later, by promptly christening him Dionysus.

Her father was, to say the least, a little unorthodox.

He was not just a rolling stone, he was a skipping rock, one of those flat stones you throw across a lake so fast it simply skims the surface, although when he did impact in her life it usually made a severe dent in something, if only her drinks cabinet.

Whilst Imelda's relationship with number four hadn't made it past Theo's second and equally successful exhibition, she and Theo had been an item ever since.

So very different, they seemed to fit together like two opposing pieces of a jigsaw puzzle.

Imelda, manicure, pedicure, couture.

Theo, a walking paint pallet.

Imelda, glam bam thank you, mam, focussed, organised, immaculate.

Theo, scruffy, scatty, slightly batty, and if Michael was a little bit right and she could be described as thoughtless, it was only when it came to her own life, not that of other people.

'You're an oxymoron,' Imelda had told her not long after they met. 'You'd forget your own boobs if they weren't stuffed into your bra, but you can remember Dion's entire school timetable from Monday morning through to Friday afternoon.'

'It's priorities,' Theo had explained.

'Yeah, and your priority is always other people and never yourself.'

And henceforth Imelda had made Theo her priority.

Imelda loved Christmas, everything had to be advert-cliché correct, from the toes of the goose to the top of the tree. One particularly clement year she had even hired a machine so that she could have snow wafting past the windows on Christmas Day.

'If you ain't got it, fake it,' she had gleefully told a delighted Theo.

This seemed to be a philosophy that Imelda generally lived by, except when it came to diamonds and orgasms. 'They, honey, should both be totally real or they're really not worth having at all.'

This year was the exception to an unwritten rule.

This year Imelda was in Dubai for Christmas with her latest beau, the suave and handsome and, of course, disgustingly rich Sami.

Imelda had been with Sami for nearly a year.

For Imelda this was long term.

When he had asked her to spend Christmas with him, she had turned him down flat, until Theo had persuaded her otherwise.

'Why won't you go?'

'Because Christmas is you and me.'

'A change is as good as a rest, Melly.'

'Are you saying you don't want to spend Christmas with me, Theodora English!'

'Of course not, but I am saying that I want you to spend Christmas with Sami. You need to know what it's like to spend Christmas with a man and this may be your only opportunity. You keep telling me I should never miss out on new experiences.'

'Ha bloody ha,' had been Imelda's response, but eventually she had been persuaded, nonetheless, even though she couldn't then persuade Theo to go with her.

Theo was adamant she was spending Christmas in her new home.

Suze was heading up to family in the Midlands.

Dion was, according to his latest postcard, intending to spend Christmas Day on a beach in Mexico.

Her mother and Peter were in the South of France.

Xav and Jules were in Oz.

Augustine was in New York.

She had been invited over by all of them.

She had made excuses to all of them.

And so, for the first time in twenty-six years of life, Theo was spending Christmas Day alone.

Seeing as she had spent the past couple of months or so pretty much on her own all the time and hadn't been unduly concerned by this fact, it didn't seem too daunting. So Christmas was a time for family, but had the person who coined that sentiment ever met her family? She doubted it.

Rather than contemplating the day with trepidation, she was actually rather looking forward to it.

She had already planned what she was going to do.

She would take a flask full of vegetable casserole to the park, feed Geoffrey, feed the birds, then come home and watch whatever dramatic goings on were happening in soapland at Christmas and consume vast amounts of Quality Street washed down with advocat and lemonade until she felt sick.

It was a good plan.

So good, in fact, that as she sat and shivered on Geoffrey's bench on Christmas morning, watching as he tucked with much appreciation into her casserole, she tried to persuade him to join her, but he simply laughed and stated that the last time he had watched *Coronation Street*, Ken Barlow couldn't have been an awful lot older than Theo, and the shock of how much he had aged since Geoffrey had last set eyes on him would no doubt advance his own demise with the realisation that he had aged as much.

As it was Christmas, he had a gift for her.

The most beautiful little statue of the pair of swans that lived on the lake.

He had carved it himself from driftwood.

'You never told me you were an artist too,' Theo said, admiring the exquisite elegance of their form.

'That's because I'm not.'

'This is art,' she insisted.

'That is a hobby.'

Theo had bought Geoffrey thermal socks, thermal gloves, and a new scarf and hat.

'I can see a theme emerging here ...' Geoffrey laughed, opening each gift with a growing smile.

'Well, it's bloody cold out here, and it's Christmas Day

. . . are you sure you won't come back to mine?'

'And miss all of this for the sake of something on the box?' He laughed and swung an arm across the horizon.

Theo couldn't help but think that he had a point.

It might have been cold but it was a beautiful day.

The frosted blue sky was tinged with an icy pink, and the sea was a crystal-clear froth of lightly churning waves that reflected the same colours.

Across the estuary as dusk began to fall early, the lights of Quinn were twinkling like a thousand stars fallen to earth.

'Well, if you change your mind . . .'

'I know where you are . . .' Geoffrey nodded his thanks. 'Just follow the lane, and don't go near the cottage with the horrible curtains.' He grinned. 'Happy Christmas, Theo.'

'Happy Christmas, Geoffrey.'

When she finally got back to the cottage her answerphone was stuffed with messages. Well, there were five, but that was stuffed for Theo's answerphone, which was usually verging on anorexic.

'Happy Christmas, Doormat!' was the first one, just those three loving words with the sound of a riotous party going on in the background.

There was no need for any other explanation it was so obvious whom it was from. For a start, he was the only one who called her doormat and survived with his life.

Dionysus.

Named after the Greek God of Wine, he was intent on living up to the heritage of his name, despite the fact that he insisted on being called Dion. The last she had heard of him before the postcard from Mexico, he had been skiing in some strange-sounding Iron Curtain country, having made his way there through Europe in alphabetical order as some odd sort of bet with his best friend and travelling buddy Finn.

Even though he had only turned twenty a few months previously, Dion had travelled further than a Virgin Atlantic jet plane.

He took after his father. Although, fortunately, he kept in touch far more frequently, with phone calls sporadic, but postcards aplenty.

The next message was Xavier.

The eldest.

The most sane.

'Hey, sis, hope you're having a good day. It's twenty-eight degrees here and we're having a barbecue on the beach. Jules sends hugs and kisses, Simeon sends a big slobber which is his version of a kiss but leaves you needing a towel. Hope you and smelly Melly are having a great day.'

He had, of course, assumed that she would be spending Christmas with Imelda and Theo had felt it easier to let him keep this assumption rather than correct him. He'd only get an attack of the guilts.

After their mum and dad had split up, Xavier had been the glue that had held the fractured English family together. But now he had Jules and Simeon, he couldn't play Mum and Dad to them all any more. It wasn't fair.

The decision to make the move to Australia had nearly killed him. But he was a geologist, he found gold, and there wasn't an awful lot of gold to be found in England.

In the end, Theo had practically booted him up the bum with the words: 'August's in America, Dion is lord knows where, Dad's probably in hell, for all we know, and we won't know where Mum and Pete are moored until we get their next postcard. Honestly, Xav, the way they all racket around the world, you'll probably end up seeing more of the family by being in Australia than by being in England.'

He had responded to this with a hug and the declaration that he 'didn't want to leave her alone'. To which Theo had said that she wasn't alone, she had Michael, and Xavier had raised an eyebrow but not responded.

She had wondered then at this reaction, although she hadn't had a chance to ask as Michael had come back into the room, but now she knew; he had seen what she had not. Michael was not a keeper. Michael was not the person she would be with for ever.

If Theo had been honest with herself, she would have realised that she knew this too.

She had been happy with him, and she had loved him, she had loved him enough to follow him down here, but if she was honest, he had never been her 'ideal' man. There had been things about him she didn't like, things that irritated, things that if she could have chosen again she would have chosen a man without, or a man with more, such as compassion. Like if she ever gave to charity or beggars in the street he would roll his eyebrows at her 'stupidity' as though she were being gullible or conned.

When she signed up to sponsor a child in Africa she was being 'sucked in by sensationalism' and then when she donated one of her paintings to the local dogs' home for their raffle, he nearly had a heart attack.

When she had told him about Geoffrey the look he

gave her was so withering she could have shrivelled up so badly she would have blown away in the slightest of breezes.

There were other things too. Incompatibilities. Like the way that if he ever came into the sitting room, and she had something on the television that he didn't like, he would switch over, just like that, no by your leave, just a 'harrumph' of contempt and a flick of the remote. Or the way he frowned so severely upon her if she'd had a few drinks, but was happy to lapse into moronic beer monster himself when the mood took him. Or the fact that he didn't like how she dressed, or that she was a little bit overweight (in his view) or that her naturally wavy hair wouldn't sit straight, how he liked it, but preferred to do its own kinky thing, no matter how much you attacked it with a pair of GHDs.

Oh lord, there were so many of them.

She had been shacked up with someone who had been totally wrong for her.

Theo had thought that you had to be realistic and make compromises. She not only thought that the 'perfect man' didn't exist, but also that the 'perfect man for you' wasn't likely to be very easy to find either.

After all, it had been reported recently in the *Daily Telegraph* that a Warwickshire Maths whiz had calculated that the actual chances of you finding your ideal match were one in two hundred and eighty-five thousand. Would she ever meet that many people in her life?

Maybe she had been wrong to compromise.

Maybe now she was free to find her 'ideal' man.

Maybe that was why she hadn't cried when he had left her.

The next message pulled her out of her reverie.

'Theo, it's Gus. Where are you?' Her sister's clipped, efficient tones, with that slight American tone she had picked up since moving to New York with her company four years ago, always made her jump. 'Call me.'

'Maybe next year,' Theo joked to herself, knowing full well that next year was only a week away.

Augustine was as economic with words as she was with everything else in her life. She had rallied against her parents' extravagance and laissez-faire attitude with a need for control and a meanness that was proportionate but not nearly so attractive.

She kept in touch with Theo in a military manner. A phone call every Thursday evening and woe betide Theo if she was out.

August was spending Christmas Day at work.

The next message was from the girls at the London gallery through which Theo sold most of her work.

Well, she said the girls. It was a call from Livvy, who could hardly be called a girl. Livvy and Imogen were mother and daughter respectively. Theoretically, it was Imogen's gallery, but since Imogen had recently married and was honeymooning in the South of France, Olivia was running the gallery on her own at the moment.

'Happy Christmas, Theo. Don't panic, I know you already think I'm a workaholic, so let me reassure you that I'm not actually in the office on Christmas Day, but I just wanted to let you know that Denzil Maitland Grainger came back just before closing last night and bought another two of your beautiful paintings, so there will be a lovely cheque in the post for you first thing on Monday next week.'

The final one was one that made her stop halfway through unscrewing her bottle of advocat.

'Hello, it's your dad, HAPPY CHRISTMAS, POPPET!!!! Hope you're—'

And then the line went dead.

Theo hadn't seen her father for over a year. Not since he had turned up out of the blue at Xavier and Jules's leaving-for-Australia party.

He had sauntered in looking rake-thin, tanned and as wrinkled as wrung-out chamois leather, but with that same smile that Theo always called his red setter smile.

The one you use when you know you've been bad, very, very bad, but you're so fun and gorgeous and utterly charming that even if you've just come in covered in mud and flung yourself on your owner's pure white three-hundred-thread-count Egyptian cotton, they're still going to be dreadfully pleased to see you.

Or, as Xavier put it far more succinctly, 'He could fall in a pile of shit and still come out smelling of Paco Rabanne.'

She got the odd postcard from him, and every so often a wad of foreign currency arrived in an envelope – to her amazement, always intact. Whenever one of his bribery-and-corruption envelopes, as Dion called them, came through, she would always change it into English money and put it straight into an old cigar box of his that she had kept, and leave it there untouched no matter what. She wasn't sure exactly how much was in there now, but it had got to the point where she couldn't close the lid on the box any more, and was thinking of upgrading from cigar box to shoe box.

She knew why her father sent her money; it was his way of taking care of them in the only way he knew how, or was able. Frankly, fortunately, Theo could take care of herself when it came to money; what she craved most from her father was his time. But that was an asset he kept mainly for himself and his own pleasures. She knew, however, that there would come a time when the skimming rock would fall and bounce no more. And that's why she kept the money.

The cigar box had a label on it: Dad's Pension.

It was for when he stopped thinking he was the eternal teenager and accepted that he was old enough for a bus pass and a discount on a stairlift.

She hoped he was having a lovely Christmas.

In fact, she hoped he was having a lovely life.

Whenever she expressed concerns about him to any of her siblings they would have the stock answer that he knew where to come if he needed them.

But Theo knew that sometimes when you stayed away from the people you loved for too long, it was very hard to find your way back.

Even at Christmas.

Especially at Christmas.

She poured out the huge snowball she had promised herself and raised her glass out of the window and towards the vast stretch of sea that she realised, in wonderment, stretched across the entire world and connected every continent on the planet, no matter how far away.

'Happy Christmas, everyone I love. Wherever you may be . . .'

14

He had only popped out for a DVD and a bottle of champagne.

It was the day after Boxing Day, and one of those evenings between Christmas and New Year where things felt a little bit flat, including the alcohol you had in the house. There was nothing on TV but repeats, and nine o'clock seemed too early to go to bed.

He was gone forty-five minutes – an hour at the most.

When he got back things didn't feel right, even before Natalie met him at the door, her face ashen with worry.

'What is it, Nat?'

'He's gone . . .'

'What do you mean?'

'Dylan . . . he's not here.'

'Well, where the hell is he?'

'I don't know,' Natalie burst into tears, 'he was bugging me to go out, so I let him into the garden, when I went to fetch him back in he wasn't there.'

'But how could he not be?' Jonas's mind frantically searched the garden for any possible routes of escape. The wall was secure, he knew that, he'd checked it himself before the first time he'd left Dylan out there unsupervised.

It was too high for him to get over, how many times had he lifted him over himself?

'Did you leave the gate open?'

'No, I swear . . .'

But before she could finish pleading her innocence, Jonas had left the kitchen.

'Dilly?' He stood on the patio and looked out into the darkened garden.

'Dilly?' He called again much louder, expecting at any minute to see a rustling in the bushes that would herald Dylan charging back to him.

But there was nothing.

'Dylan!'

No four paws planted firmly on his thighs, whilst the tail wagged furiously enough to dislodge them and the tongue sought out any unprotected flesh.

'Dylan!' His voice echoed around him, but the only response was Natalie's stricken face at the study window.

He wasn't there.

He was gone.

Jonas ran back inside and grabbed his car keys from the kitchen table.

'He's not there. I'm going out to look for him.'

Natalie nodded, she was already pulling on her coat and boots, her white face clashing horribly with her red puffa jacket.

'I'll check the garden again.'

Jonas drove for hours. He looked everywhere he could think of that he and Dylan had ever been, anywhere he might have gone back to on his own, all the time thinking any minute now, any minute and he would see him. Any minute, any minute now, Natalie would call to say he had come home. Or someone would call to say they had him – after all, he was wearing his collar, he always wore his collar, the one with the little silver D for Dylan and the small disk engraved with Jonas's phone number on it just in case.

But he didn't see him, Natalie didn't call, no one called.

When he got back to the cottage, the back door was open. Natalie was asleep on the sofa, still in her coat and boots.

Jonas looked at the clock. It was three a.m. He had been looking for six hours.

He felt weary, heavy with worry, sick to his stomach.

He sat down in a chair and, pulling out his phone, tapped in a text to Wilko. Just two words: 'Dylan missing.'

He would take ten minutes, make some coffee, and then go out again.

Jonas woke up three hours later with his heart shrunk and hiding in the toes of his left foot. It was a very weird sensation. Almost painful. He didn't even have that moment of grace when you wake up and forget that all is not right with your world, it was straight there in his face.

Dylan was missing.

He shot out of the chair, his body, awkward in upright repose, complaining bitterly as he unfolded mercilessly fast and shot back out into the garden, hoping against hope that just by some miracle he had missed him, that he was out there all along, or that he had found his way home and was sitting in his favourite spot by the pond under the old apple tree, waiting for Jonas to bring him breakfast.

The garden was empty.

Jonas went to the end, stood on the wall and scanned the countryside.

'Dylan!' he called.

'Dylan!!!'

Five times he called for him.

Then five times again.

The only response was a bird shrieking in the hedgerow of the harvested field, and the farmer's collie barking from its perch on the back of the stationary tractor in the yard, a piercing high-pitched bark so unlike Dylan's that it carried the lengthy distance from the farmhouse to Jonas, across the undulating countryside.

His car keys were still in his pocket. He was tempted to head straight out but instead he went to the kitchen. He needed coffee to drive, but he could take it with him.

It wasn't even six-thirty, but Natalie was there, showered and dressed.

It was Saturday morning and she didn't normally get out of bed before nine-thirty at the weekend.

She had made toast and tea, but he ignored them both and, refilling the kettle, put it on to boil before hunting through the cupboards for the flask he usually took on picnics.

'What are you doing, Jonas?'

'I'm making some coffee.'

'I've made tea.'

'I need coffee. I'm going back out to look.'

'Nick texted.' She nodded to his phone which was still on the kitchen table. 'He's already out there. Got your message, went straight out to look.'

Jonas nodded, his heart filled with gratitude for his

friend, but he still filled the flask with coffee and got some of Dilly's favourite biscuits from the cupboard.

'At least have something to eat before you go, Jonas.'

'I don't want to eat, I just want to find my dog.'

There was something so possessive about the way he said 'my dog' instead of 'Dylan' that Natalie's face fell.

She started to cry again.

'I'm so sorry. He was only out there on his own for a little while, ten minutes at most, I truly thought he'd be OK, I didn't think he could get out, I don't know how . . . oh Jonas, I'm so sorry . . .' She was really crying now, devastated, hicupping snotty sobs; he had never seen her like this. In fact, if he was thinking straight he would have realised that this was the first time he had ever seen her lose control.

Instinctively, he went to wrap his arms around her and she pressed her damp face into his chest, clinging to him.

He waited until the sobbing subsided.

'Is there anything . . . anything at all that you can think of that might help me figure out where he's gone? Anything . . .'

She was quiet for a long moment, and then she shook her head.

'I'm so sorry,' she repeated into his shirt.

'I've got to go and look for him.'

Natalie nodded. She was biting her bottom lip so hard it was white.

'Don't worry, I'll find him,' he said, unsure whom he was trying to reassure. 'And I need to get on to the pet tracker people, you know, the chip . . .'

'I'll call them. I'll find out what time they open and call them, I promise. You go look for him.' She ran through to the study and he heard her pull open the desk drawer.

As he got into his car, Nick's Audi pulled up behind him.

Like Jonas he, too, was unshaven and in yesterday's clothes.

'Won't get too close, mate, breath like a badger's arse, didn't clean my teeth.'

He had been out since four searching.

'I've been up to Tanhay Farm and had a word with Bob Stephens – he's not seen him, but he said if he does spot him, he'll call you straight away.'

'Cheers, Wilks.'

'Where are you going to go?'

'Back to the beach.'

'I went down there half an hour ago, no sign.'

'It's his favourite place.'

'I know, buddy, but he wasn't there. Have you called the identification chip people?'

'Natalie's calling them for me as soon as they open.'

'Have you tried the police?'

'Should I do that? You know it's not like he's a missing kid or anything, he's just a dog.'

'But he's not *just* a dog, is he?'

Jonas shook his head, his knuckles on the steering wheel white.

'Anything's worth a try, mate,' Nick urged him. 'Have a word, yeah? Now I'm going to go down to the village – you never know, he could be sitting outside the bakery waiting for his Saturday morning pasty. If not, there's a spaniel in the cottage next door that he seems pretty keen on. You never know, he might have been out all night on a bunk-up.'

'Thanks, Nick.'

'Don't worry, mate, he's out there somewhere, we'll find him . . .'

As Wilko roared back off up the drive, Jonas pulled out his mobile and called Stella.

'Mum, Dylan's missing.'

That was all he had to say for Stella to be galvanised into action.

'Right, I'll get Blix. Don't worry, darling, your grandmother knows someone in practically every single village in Dorset, we'll find him.'

Buoyed by the certainty of both of them, Jonas retraced everywhere he had been the previous night, and then, unable to think of anywhere else that Dylan could possibly have gone, he pulled over in the lay-by and phoned Natalie at the cottage, hoping against hope that she would pick up the phone and tell him that Dill had come home.

But he knew it was a useless hope because if he had she would have called him already.

She answered on the first ring.

'Where are you?'

'About five miles away. What did the chip people say?'

'They said that they alert all the shelters, and wardens and stuff. If he comes in anywhere, they'll know about it. Are you coming home?'

'I've got to keep looking, Nat.'

'Of course.'

The problem was where.

He had been everywhere and anywhere he thought that Dylan might have wandered off to. Several times over. He felt like he was going round in circles. He had taken Nick's advice and phoned the police, who had been as helpful as they could be. He had phoned every single person in his contact list from friends to clients, and each had promised fervently to join in the hunt. What now? *Where* now?

He wasn't quite sure why because it was at least ten miles away, but Jonas found himself driving to the dogs' home he had been to for Blix, when Dylan had come flying through his car door.

Marion Copthorne, who ran the place with military precision, looked out as an unusually sallow-looking Jonas came into the spotless yard.

Big-boned and busty, with a booming voice that could quite clearly be heard across the rows of kennels full of barking dogs, she was dressed in a pair of filthy jodhpurs and a cashmere jumper that was more dog hair than goat hair.

'Ah, Jonas, your grandmother called me. You're still looking, I take it?'

Jonas nodded forlornly.

'Well, I've rung round, put a few of the other rescues on alert for you.'

'Thank you.'

'Is he chipped?'

Jonas nodded.

'Jolly good. In that case, he'll be back with you in next to no time – well, as long as he's handed in, that is.'

Jonas's face fell even further.

'You think there's a chance he might not be? That someone would keep him?'

'Some people would hang on to him, yes, not realising

that there's some poor soul out there hunting till the end of their days to get their buddie back. Then again, there are an awful lot of poor little chaps out there who don't have anyone out there looking for them, so it's swings and roundabouts whether it's a bad thing or not. Take Gary, for instance' – she bent to stroke the lurcher panting next to her – 'been here for eight months and he's only ten months old. I think he'd be absolutely delighted if he wandered off and someone kept him. Still, we'll find him a home one of these days – won't we, Gary? In the meantime, it's Dylan that we need to worry about, now have you contacted the local council, the dog warden?'

Jonas nodded.

'And the police, and Blix has rung everyone she knows.'

'Which is everyone,' she nodded, 'and if he turns up here, we'll be straight on the phone to you, I promise.' She reached out and squeezed his shoulder, a kindness if it weren't for the fact that she had a grip that could crush a tin can.

Afterwards, simply because he could think of nowhere else to look and nowhere else that he could think of that Dylan would rather be, he went back down to his favourite beach.

He could see, even before he'd pulled the car to a halt, that the beach was deserted, but he got out anyway and leaned back against his car, eyes closed against the rain that had begun as dusk began to fall, and the despair that was falling even harder upon him.

'Where are you, Dilly?'

Radio Dorset could still be heard through the open car door.

'. . . And that was the latest offering from Robbie Williams. Now, we've just had a phone call from Nick Wilkinson to say that he's looking for a lost dog, he's a bearded collie cross about nine months old, very friendly, answers to the name of Dylan. If anyone has seen Dylan, then please call the studio and we can put you in touch with the dog's owner, Jonas Larsson, from our very own drivetime weather sponsor Blue Closet Joinery, who is, of course, very keen to get his beloved pet home safe. So if anyone has spotted Dylan, please call in and we'll put you in touch, and in the meantime, this next song is for you, Jonas Blue . . .'

Cat Stevens's 'I Love My Dog' began to play.

And as Jonas stood looking out to sea and listening to the music, he realised that the salt water on his face wasn't simply the spray from the ocean.

15

Boxing Day was a further round of the same as Christmas Day. Up late, lunch with Geoffrey, chocolates and television – very self-indulgent, but Theo had promised herself that she would take some proper time off. That was one of the things about working for yourself and working from home, you could so easily forget that things like weekends and bank holidays actually existed.

Then, the next day, guilty at having spent two days without so much as a sniff of paint, she worked without barely pausing for breath, emerging from her studio only to eat, hit the loo, or collapse in a paint-spattered heap on her bed.

But the day after had been earmarked for some shopping.

She needed new brushes, had run out of some of her oils, and her favourite jeans were so covered with paint that she could have stood them in a corner of a gallery – and they would have stood up on their own they were so thickly crusted – and insisted that they were an art installation.

And so Theo hit the sales with a vengeance.

Art equipment and new jeans were joined by underwear that actually matched – for now – two new jumpers, one for her, one for Geoffrey, a pair of walking boots that would be great for staggering up and down the headland, and a windproof coat for the same reason.

Truro was packed, but after the relative solitude of the last few days, she actually revelled in the manic bustle of it.

She even went back to the same bar where she had discovered Michael's little blonde secret, for a tuna baguette and a couple of very large glasses of cold white wine before hopping on the train for Quinn, where she caught the very last foot ferry back to Port Ruan. They only ran until dusk in winter and she only just managed to hop on board as it set sail, or rather was towed, across the wide estuary mouth.

Knackered, she sat back, closed her eyes and enjoyed the gentle motion and the sounds of the estuary as they crossed the water.

It was beautiful; she listened to the sound of the night birds calling, the soft rush of a slumbering sea, the almost silence of the quiet village.

And then as she staggered up the hill towards home she heard something else.

Something walking up the hill behind her.

Was she being followed?

Theo stopped. Dead.

Listened. Hard.

Nothing. And then, as she started up the hill once more, she heard it again. Footsteps?

And yet every time she stopped to listen, she heard nothing except the echo of her own accelerated heartbeat.

Every time she turned she saw nothing but shadows cast by the lamplight. She reached her front door, unscathed, unaccosted, chastising herself for being so easily spooked and perhaps just a little bit tipsy, put her key in the door, opened it, and then turned to pick up her bags and there he was.

Her stalker.

They stood and stared at each other for a moment, and then he launched himself at her, knocking her off her feet.

And as Theo lay flat on the floor with the weight of him on her chest pinning her down, and his hot breath panting in gales on her face, she began to laugh like a drain.

He had to be the most gorgeous dog she had ever seen. So cute and friendly and cuddly and fluffy – well, he would have been fluffy if he wasn't so dirty. She wasn't sure what type of dog he was. He reminded her a little of a Dulux Dog, but much smaller. A terrier of some kind, perhaps? Or maybe he was a miniature Old English Sheepdog. Could you get a miniature one? Probably. People bred everything to fit into a Louis Vuitton handbag these days.

One thing she had managed to ascertain for definite was that he was a hungry dog. She'd heard his stomach growling whilst he was standing on her chest, and the first thing he did when she took him into the house was head for the kitchen. Maybe he'd followed her home because she still smelt of baguette?

He was obviously well cared for, and, apart from the dirt and a hunger that helped him eat his way through two cans of stewing steak in three minutes flat, he seemed healthy enough. He also seemed quite young, he couldn't be more than a year old, maybe less.

And then Theo spotted a glimpse of leather under the halo of dirty fur that ringed his neck. A collar. Perhaps he had a tag with an address or a phone number.

But all that hung there was a silver D.

16

For the first time in weeks Theo woke up on what had used to be her side of the bed.

This was because there was a snoring dog on the other side.

They had gone to bed not long after she had got home.

Both shattered for their own different reasons. Theo shopped out; the dog, judging by the state of him, walked out.

After she had fed him, she had stuck him in the bath.

He had taken it pretty well, and let her wash the dirt out of his matted fur and then blow dry him. And then she had got a spare duvet, and made him a bed at the side of hers.

Fat lot of good that had been.

He woke up as she was looking at him. Opened huge dark brown eyes, thumped his tail in greeting, stretched and yawned, then reached out a long pink tongue and licked her from chin to hairline.

Theo burst out laughing.

'So, you sloppy kisser, what am I going to do with you, then?'

Totally not expecting an answer, Theo was amazed

when he immediately jumped from the bed and ran down to the French doors.

'You want to go out?'

He barked his response.

'Wow, maybe Lassie wasn't so far fetched after all.'

She pulled on her dressing gown and opened the French doors. Folding her arms against the chill of the winter morning, she stood and watched as he trotted around the garden, nose to the ground, head only lifting when his leg did.

'So what's next on the agenda?' she asked when he trotted back to her, tail wagging.

His face immediately informed her 'feed me'.

'Breakfast? Good idea, come on, then.'

He already knew where the kitchen was, led the way to it, in fact, and sat down by the fridge, his tail thumping.

'Well, there's not a lot of choice, I'm afraid.' Theo peered inside the fridge.

'Eggs, eggs, or eggs?'

He woofed in response.

'Eggs? Great idea.'

'So, do you have a name, then?' she asked him after breakfast, fingering the D on his collar. 'I can't keep calling you "You".'

What did the D stand for?

Well, she supposed there was only one way to find out. She should ask the only person in the room who knew.

Theo fetched a book from the loaded bookshelves.

Baby names.

She had bought it when Jules was expecting Simeon and had thought it might come in handy.

She was, however, going to try the most obvious one first.

D for Dog.

'Deefer?' she called.

He was lounging comfortably on the cushions of the sitting-room window seat next to her, one eye on Theo, the other on the scene outside.

No response.

She tried the book.

Dale. Who the hell would call a dog Dale?

She tried it anyway.

He didn't even bother lifting his head from his paws.

It was the same for Damian – please lord, let it not be Damian the devil dog – and Danny. Darcy? Had she finally found her Darcy? Nope. David, no not that one, who on earth would call a dog David? Dennis? Same. Denzil? Nahah, no way would someone call a dog like that Denzil – or, for that matter, Desmond.

Derek and Dexter both drew a blank.

As did Donald and Dominic.

By the time she'd got to Dudley she was wondering if she was barking up the wrong tree completely.

She closed the book and racked her brain.

What was the name of the dog from the magic roundabout . . . Dougal, that was it.

Or the dog in the film that grew to a hundred feet . . . Digby?

She tried both with no response.

Maybe it wasn't a proper name at all, it could be anything, really, some people liked to call their animals after some very strange things.

She had once lived next door to a girl who had called

her sausage dog Pepperoni, Pepper for short.

Maybe it was something odd like Doughnut or Doodle or Dimples or . . . and then it just popped out of her mouth.

'Dildo.'

Immediately the lounging dog looked up.

Theo's eyes flew wide in consternation.

'Good lord, no, please don't tell me somebody actually called you that?' She laughed in horror, and then she shook her head furiously – 'no, absolutely not; no one would do that, which means that your name sounds like Dildo? So you could be Dill or maybe Dilly . . .' His ears pricked some more and Theo, recognising that she was at last on to something, began to grin.

'Dill?' she called, and was rewarded instantly as he immediately hopped off the cushions and came over to lick her fingers.

Theo grinned with pleasure.

'Fabulous, you're called after a herb, I like it. I like to cook with dill, not that I'd cook you, of course, hot dogs,' she laughed, 'also, do you know that was one of my favourite programmes when I was really, really little? *The Herb Garden* . . . maybe that's what you were called after . . .'

It was so obvious now.

The Herb Garden had been a favourite of her mum's and she had kept videos to show her own children. Theo remembered now that one of the characters had been Dill the Dog.

So perhaps Dill's lost owner was someone the same age as her mum?

'A clue!' Theo felt pleased until she realised that there

were probably several million people the same age as her mum in the country, so this didn't help at all, really.

And she may not have got the right name anyway.

She moved away and called him again.

'Dill?' His tail wagged furiously and he bounded over.

'Well, even if it's not right, you seem to like it, so Dill will do you for now,' Theo said, bending down to hug him.

He stuck his tongue in her ear.

Another opportunity to water the garden was followed by a trip out in the car to the nearest pet shop, where dog food, smart new collar and lead and cosy dog bed that matched her bed linen were on the shopping list.

'Right you, back to the house, and then I think I need to do some work to pay for all of this stuff; we can go up to the headland. I need to do another sketch of Lantic Bay, and you can meet Geoffrey.'

However, with Dill bouncing like a kangaroo on the end of his new lead, it was impossible to carry all her art equipment.

And so she left it at home.

'Fine, this isn't work, this is walk.'

At the mention of the W.A.L.K. word, the dog barked and his tail began to motor even faster.

Knowing that Suze would be back from Birmingham, Theo headed down to the shop first.

Suze was putting fresh pasties in the hot counter.

'Can we come in?' Theo asked, tentatively popping her head around the door.

'Why do you ask, love? Have you done something since I last saw you that means I won't want to talk to you any more?'

Dill was going in anyway, the smell of hot, fresh pasty like a beacon to his flaring nostrils.

'Well,' Theo tugged him back behind her, 'I don't think so, but I might in a minute . . .'

'What on earth has Santa brought you, then?' Suze exclaimed in delight as, lured by the smell of hot food that always slipped alluringly out of the door of the newsagent's every time it opened, Dill slipped around Theo again and thrust a panting, grinning face inside the shop. 'Ooh, I love dogs. Quick, sneak him in, I'm on my own at the moment anyway, what people don't know won't hurt them. Oh, isn't he gorgeous . . .' she bent down to fuss him, 'Is he yours?'

Theo shrugged.

'Followed me home last night.'

'You found him?' Suze frowned.

'Yep.'

'Lucky you, the most exciting thing I ever find is money down the back of the sofa . . . So how was your Christmas?'

'Well, he was the most eventful thing that happened, so an apt description would be quiet but good. You?'

'Bloody awful. It's a bit sad when going home only serves to remind you why you moved so far away in the first place. We still on for New Year's Eve?'

'Karaoke at the Boatman here we come.'

'Fabulous. I've been practising my "I will Survive", but what about him?' She indicated Dill.

'Well, we could put him down for "Hound Dog" or "Puppy Love" . . . or, more aptly, "Who Let the Dogs Out?" '

Suze laughed.

'I actually meant what will you do with him? Will he still be with you, do you think?'

Theo shrugged.

'I really don't know . . . I suppose I should try and find out if someone's looking for him. Do you think I could put a notice up in the shop? You know, try and find out whom he belongs to?'

'Course you can, angel. Although, are you sure you want to?'

Theo grinned.

'Nope.'

'Thought as much.'

'But he is stopping me working today.'

'Sure, and that isn't such a bad thing, what with you working seven days a week most weeks.'

Theo ahemed, raised her eyebrows and pointedly tapped Suzanne's notice of opening times, which quite clearly stated that she was open seven days a week.

Suze grinned gleefully.

'Maybe I should get myself an excuse too.'

'A four-legged friend?'

'Well, I'm actually thinking more of the two-legged variety.' Suzanne winked. 'Or, even better, three- . . .'

'Suze, you're a hussy.'

'Thank you.' Suze beamed in delight.

Armed with pasties, a giant one for Geoffrey, a normal-sized one for Theo, and then a mini one Suze insisted on giving her for Dill, and the last four boxes of mince pies in the shop that Suze insisted she take for Geoffrey, as she was so sick of the sight of anything Christmassy, Theo headed up out of the village on the path that led to the headland. She took the left fork at the top to go to the memorial garden instead of the cliff path, Dill trotting along on whichever side the pasty bag was being held.

Geoffrey was in his usual spot, face hidden behind a book as always.

Theo often thought he devoured novels far more ravenously than any food she ever took him.

He peered over the top of the book at the sound of footsteps and then, seeing that it was Theo, didn't instantly retreat back behind it like a tortoise hiding its shell.

'Hello, stranger. New friend?' Geoffrey's bright blue eyes sparked with interest at the sight of Dill bouncing along beside her.

'New lodger.'

'When did you, and where did you?'

'Well, he followed me home.'

Dilly was having a jolly good sniff of Geoffrey, so intense that Theo began to flush with embarrassment until, thankfully, he decided that Geoffrey smelt fabulous and hopped up on to the bench beside him.

Personally, Theo had always found that Geoffrey smelt of the great outdoors, of sea salt and wood smoke. It was very pleasant, like an expensive aftershave.

She sat down on the other side so Dill was the filling in the sandwich, and passed Geoffrey one of the warm greasy pasty bags.

'You know, you really shouldn't—' Geoffrey began, but Theo interrupted him with a shrug.

'It's two for the price of one again, so I didn't really.'

'Well, thank you Theo, that's very kind.'

'Thank Suze, it's her special offer.'

'Suze?'

'Suzanne, runs the shop.'

'Ah yes, our paths have almost crossed on occasion.'

'Almost?'

'From a distance. She likes to walk, and, of course, so do I, but we always seem to just wave at each other from opposite hillsides. Seems like a pleasant woman, though, from a distance.'

'She is, very, and close up, too; she also sent you these.' Theo produced the mince pies. 'Please don't tell me you can't take them. Suze said if she so much as smells another mince pie she might have to refuse to celebrate another Christmas for at least three years . . .'

But the usually reticent Geoffrey was already reaching out for the boxes.

He laughed self-deprecatingly at Theo's surprise.

'Sorry, but I have to confess you've found one of my weaknesses.'

'*One* of your weaknesses?' Theo probed.

'I have a sweet tooth,' Geoffrey grinned, opening a packet and offering her first take, 'one which is only assuaged by mince pies, treacle tart, and wine gums. My three favourite foodie things in the world. Now, young fellow . . .' He turned his attention to Dill, who had finished his own pasty in one gulp and was totally transfixed with Geoffrey's giant-sized one which had remained untouched whilst he devoured a mince pie. 'Do you have a name?'

Theo pointed to the D on his collar.

'My only clue, so we ran through the whole of the Ds in my name book, and the only name he responded to was Dill.'

'Dill . . .' Geoffrey mused. 'As in Dill the Dog from *The Herb Garden*, perhaps?'

'You know it!' Theo exclaimed in delight.

'One of my favourite childhood programmes.'

'Me too.'

Geoffrey gave Dill a piece of his crust.

'Well, for a waif and stray he looks in good shape.'

'Mmm, you should have seen him *before* the bath.'

'I wonder where you came from, young man?'

'I'm going to print off some posters with a picture of him and put them up, see if we can find his owners.'

But Geoffrey shook his head.

'I wouldn't do that. You might get all sorts of people trying to claim that he belongs to them when he doesn't.'

'You think that would happen?'

He nodded slowly.

'Unfortunately. He's a fine dog. It's more than possible. He's a bearded collie, isn't he?'

'Is he?'

'I would say at least some of him is, yes, at least seventy per cent. Very popular breed, I'm surprised you found one roaming footloose and fancy free . . . You know, I'm sure there are ways of finding out if young Dill here is alone in the world without leaving yourself open to the charlatans. If I were you, I'd place notice with the proper authorities, the local council, dog wardens, and such, and leave it at that.'

'Although,' he added thoughtfully, 'have you had him scanned?'

'Scanned?' Theo suddenly had visions of Dill riding a supermarket checkout conveyor amidst a mound of shopping.

'For an identifying chip.'

'Of course.' She groaned at her own stupidity. 'Do you know, I hadn't even thought of that.'

'Good place to start; any responsible owner would get their animal chipped, and if he isn't chipped, then, well, perhaps whoever had him doesn't deserve to get him back. I know that might sound a little harsh, but I've learned the hard way that when something's precious to you, you take the best care of it – and, Theo my dear, he could do far worse than have you as his caretaker.'

'And his owner? It is possible, even if he isn't chipped, that there is someone out there desperate to find him . . .'

'Well,' Geoffrey nodded thoughtfully, 'I'm a great believer in fate. There is an order to this world, and I truly feel that things will fall into the way they are meant to be as surely as the birds that quit this park in the autumn will be back here by spring.'

17

Suze had called to suggest an evening of wine, food and cards.

Theo had been expecting Sevens, or Kings or perhaps even Cribbage, which she had used to play with her father when she was younger, and so was kind of surprised when Suze turned up on her doorstep with a couple of worn-looking decks of cards and a rack full of poker chips.

'Poker? I don't even know how to play.'

'Fabulous,' Suze grinned, 'I love to win, and if you don't even know how to play the game, then that makes my odds of winning so much better.' She leaned in and pecked Theo on the cheek and handed her the poker set and a huge bottle of wine, before plonking herself on the floor to pull off her boots.

'I meant to ask if you'd heard from Michael over Christmas?' she grunted, struggling with the left boot.

'Who?' Theo bent down to help her, grabbing the heel of the obstinate right boot.

Suze smiled at her. 'Not missing him at all, then.'

'Only in so far as I miss having *someone*. But I have to say, I'm pretty glad my someone isn't Michael, though. How awful is that?'

'You don't need to apologise for not missing him. It's how you feel.'

'I know, but that's not the awful bit. I was with him for three years, Suze, and the day he walks out I don't shed a tear, not one. What does that say about me? I'm willing to waste three years on a man I don't even cry for when he goes? How terrible is that?'

'Don't beat yourself up, Theo. It's easy to get stuck in a relationship and then only see the faults when it's ended. Just count your blessings it was three years and not thirteen . . .'

'Thirteen?'

'Thirteen years, three months and twelve days. The length of time I was married for . . . but I'm not here to talk about that,' she added quickly as Theo's face flooded with interest, 'I'm here to thrash your arse at cards. Grab us a couple of glasses, and I'll diddle . . . er . . . I mean deal' she joked, 'the decks.'

Theo went to the kitchen to fetch glasses and nibbles, whilst Suze said hello to Dill.

'If I can't ask about your marriage,' she said, coming back into the room and sitting down opposite Suze who was already perched at the dining table, 'can I ask you another impertinent question?'

'Ask away.'

'How old are you?'

'Fifty-four,' Suze replied shuffling her cards with an alarmingly professional hand, 'Don't look so worried, we're only playing for your soul . . . are you shocked?'

'That we're playing for my soul?'

'That I'm fifty-four.'

'Oh definitely, I thought you were at least sixty-three.'

Suze's eyebrows shot up her head.

'It's a good job you've already opened the wine or I'd be getting my coat.'

'I actually thought you were about forty-four,' Theo admitted coyly.

'Then you are my new best friend, lady. I tell you what, I am so happy there's finally someone else in this village who realises that life doesn't grind to a halt when the sun goes down and the pub shuts.'

'How long have you lived here for?' Theo asked, watching in admiration as Suze swiftly dealt them each a hand.

'Moved down with my husband in the early nineties, I loved it here, despite the lack of local night life, and stayed; he hated it and went back to where he came from.'

'Where was that?'

'The hell from which all selfish men are spawned.' Suze waggled her eyebrows.

'Probably knows my dad, then,' Theo mused, picking up her cards.

'And Michael?'

Theo shrugged.

'I don't think it's terribly selfish to want to be happy, it's just how you go about finding that happiness.'

'So he's not from hell, then?'

'Coventry, actually.'

'Really? How odd, the Moron was from Coventry . . . I wonder if they're related.' Suze winked.

'The Moron?'

'Ex-husband.'

Dylan jumped up in the empty chair at the end of the table and, resting his chin on the end, flicked his eyes from one to the other.

'He wants to play,' Suze exclaimed in delight.

'Probably be better at it than I am.' Theo sighed, pretending to pass him her cards.

'We could play snap,' Suze teased her, 'if you're not woman enough for the hard stuff.'

'Actually, I think snap is more my level.'

'In your dreams, girlie . . . you're playing poker and liking it.'

'You're going to show me what to do, right?'

'Of course, and if you're a quick learner, I have a cunning plan to ensure that I still win.'

She waved the bottle of wine she had brought with her.

'A few of these and you won't know your Queens from your Bohemian Rhapsodies. It will be like taking candy from a baby . . .'

Suze was wrong.

It was worse.

It was like taking the candy then spanking the baby afterwards and listening to it cry.

An hour later and Theo was still none the wiser.

'You have to count, maths has never been my thing.' She sighed, throwing her hand down on the table in frustration.

'Has art?'

'Always . . . ever since I could crawl.'

'Wish I'd had a calling . . . "Did you always want to be a newsagent?" Not the kind of question anyone ever asks, 'cos the answer is pretty much given as a no.'

'So did you have any dreams?'

'Apart from marry Prince William and be the first cougar on the throne? Well, I did always have this yen to

be a fashion designer, there was just one tiny problem: I
can't sew to save my life. And as you can probably tell,
I don't have an awful lot of fashion sense either . . . can I
see some of your paintings?'

'You really want to?'

'Of course. Do you want to show me some?'

'If it gets me out of playing poker, I'd show you
anything you wanted.'

'Well, that's the best offer I've had in a long time. Lead
the way, Theo baby . . .'

Suze wandered around the attic in silence for at least ten
minutes and then she turned to Theo, her eyes wide.

'Wow. You are actually really good.'

Theo grinned.

'I don't know whether to be delighted by the
compliment or upset that you sound so surprised.'

'Well, I always say when you can't decide have
both.' Suze winked. 'No, seriously, don't be offended, it's
just that so many people down here call themselves
an artist . . . but I didn't know you were an actual *real*
one.'

'Well, I make a living.'

'A good one? No, you don't have to answer that
question . . . that's out of order. Me old mum, God rest her
soul, always used to say you should never discuss sex or
money. I've never adhered to the first one, so I always feel
like I should give her a bit of a nod on the second.'

'I earn enough to live on.' Theo shrugged, uncon-
cerned by the question. 'Sometimes pretty well, sometimes not so well, but I'm good at balancing the times of
cake with the times of dry bread and no butter, and I have

made a vow that I'll always manage to make sure Dill gets his dog biscuits.'

'He's really good in here, isn't he?' Suze looked to Dill, who, the minute they had come into the studio, had gone to a basket by the radiator and settled himself in it, chin on the edge, bright eyes watching them from under hairy eyebrows as they walked about the room. 'The way he is normally, you'd think he'd be running around in a cloud of paint with a brush in his mouth.'

'It's funny. I brought him in here for the first time this morning, and he just settled down and watched me work. Good as gold.'

'Dream dog. Now you just need to find your dream man,' Suze teased, pushing her with an elbow.

'Yeah, you and me both, eh? In the meantime, how does a bit of Patrick Swayze grab you?'

'It grabs me in just the right spot, Theo, just the right spot.'

The pair of them collapsed side by side on the sofa with Theo's DVD of *Dirty Dancing* on the television, but they did as much talking as watching.

'Just look at the body on him.' Suze was practically drooling and it was nothing to do with the huge egg mayonnaise sandwiches Theo had knocked up for them as an antidote to turkey. 'I've always wanted one of those movie moments – you know, where you head out on to a crowded dance floor with this amazing man, and you begin to dance, and slowly the crowd begins to clear as everyone stops to watch because you are just *that* good.'

'Can you dance?'

'With about as much grace as a one-legged sideboard,

and I've never been with a man who could dance either.'

'Felix could dance.'

'Felix?'

'Ex.'

'Oh yes?' Suze's interest was evident.

'You don't want details, Suze, trust me.'

'That bad, eh?'

'Actually, no, it was pretty good while it lasted, but I'm glad it didn't last.'

'Why?'

'He was too much for me back then and, from what I hear, he's got worse.'

'In what way?'

'In every way . . .'

'A bad boy, eh? Sounds interesting . . .'

'More like exhausting!' Theo rolled her eyes, and then, to Suze's surprise, she winked lasciviously. 'But that's not always a bad thing.'

'Ah . . .' Suze nodded. 'Sexual exhaustion. How long has it been since I felt thoroughly and deliciously shagged out . . . so bad boy Felix was not the worst one you had, then?'

'Not the worst, no.'

'So who takes that honour?'

'Last one definitely. Not because he's a terrible person or anything, but I realise now he was just so wrong for me.'

'So what do you want, using Michael as your template for wrong?'

'Well . . .' Theo mused, 'I want someone who's creative too, I think, someone who'll understand that when the muse grabs you by the throat it doesn't matter if it's four in the morning, or you're in the middle of dinner with the in-laws, you have to go and work. And total honesty would be good too . . .'

'Brutal?'

'Total doesn't have to equal brutal. You can be kind and still be truthful.'

'Like buying someone a bottle of mouthwash?' Suze offered.

'I suppose. Yeah.' Theo laughed.

'What about looks? From what I can remember, Michael was pretty tasty . . . tall, dark and handsome?'

'Mmmmmmm. Not necessarily. Tall has never been a requirement. Handsome is all about the way they look . . . which is a bit too external for me, I'd prefer a beautiful soul to a beautiful face. The only thing I would quite like physically is that he's bigger than me, probably, but more in width than height, I think. Would hate to hop into bed with someone thinner than me. That would just be weird. Ah, and most important of all,' she added as Dill hopped on to the sofa and on to her lap, 'they have to love dogs. Now that's my major requirement. Any man that wants to love me has to love my Dill.'

'Love me, love my dog.'

'Exactly.'

'So he's been with you for a day . . .'

'Yep.'

'And he's already "my dog" and dictating what kind of man you're after?'

Theo bit her bottom lip in contrition.

'I know, bit premature, really, considering I've promised myself I'll try and find out if someone's looking for him.' She sighed. 'The thing is, we all have our lists, don't we? But what's a list when it comes to love? At the end of the day, we all want to find someone to love, someone to love us. But in the meantime—'

'You just have to get on with it,' Suze finished for her. 'Or get yourself a dog. By the way, you have cress in your teeth.'

'Thanks . . . great way to pull, eh? Will it gross you out if I get it out with my nail?'

'As long as it's not your toenail,' Suze said, yawning widely. 'I suppose I should really make a move, I've got papers to sort at five in the morning.'

'You poor thing.'

'Hey, it's the highlight of my day, feeling sanctimonious about being up when the rest of Port Ruan are still snoring in their beds . . . it's been a great night, Thee . . .'

'It has,' Theo agreed. 'Fancy doing it again?'

'Absolutely. How about tomorrow?'

'The night before New Year's Eve? Do you think we can manage so much excitement two nights running?'

'Ooooh.' Suze stroked her chin and pretended to ponder. 'Just about, yeah.'

'Girl's night it is, then?'

'As long as Dill doesn't mind being an honorary girl.'

'As long as it's only honorary, eh? Although . . . do you think I *should* get him done?'

Suze's eyes widened and she covered Dill's ears with her hands.

'Theo! Honestly! Not in front of the man himself. How do you think it will make him feel?'

'Gutted.' Theo grinned. 'Except lower.'

'Oh God that's terrible!'

'I know – sorry, Dill.' Theo broke and gave him the last

of the Hob Nobs in contrition. 'Of course I'm not going to . . . why would I want to mess with something so perfect and so gorgeous?'

'She's creeping now, Dill, in case you hadn't worked it out.' Suze lifted one of Dill's ears and whispered to him. 'Although I tell you something, even without your bits, you'd be more of a man than some of the men who've been in my life. And a better kisser,' she added laughing loudly, as Dill, sensing that compliments were flying, rewarded Suze the provider of pasties with a thorough licking, lashing her face with an enthusiastic and incredibly wet tongue.

'Really?' Theo cringed as saliva flew.

'Oh, absolutely, and tons better than the Moron, now he really was a sloppy kisser.'

'Are you ever going to tell me his real name?'

'That is his real name.'

'First or last?'

'Both.' Suze grinned. 'And his middle name is Wanker.'

Suze finally staggered out into the chill night, her breath blowing vaporous clouds as she exclaimed about the cold.

'Are you going to be OK getting back?'

'Are you kidding me? Getting here was the hard bit, that bloody hill, getting back is a doddle, you can just set me off at a roll and I'll spin to a halt on my own doorstep.' She leaned in and gave Theo a kiss on the cheek, 'Night, kiddo, and by the way, you've got paint in your hair.'

After Suze had staggered off down the hill, her knees dancing the salsa as her stiletto-heeled boots fought the gradient and gravity, Theo took Dill out into the garden for his bedtime wander, and as he took his usual sniffing, snuffling route through the bushes and the flower beds, she found herself smiling.

She had always prided herself on being pretty self-sufficient, but it was only as her friendship with Suze had blossomed over the past few weeks that she realised just how much she had missed having someone, or – she looked fondly over at the hairy hound watering her garden – *something* to share things with.

18

Theo was in the kitchen cleaning.

She had left the washing-up in the sink for two days running, because she had been so absorbed in an intricate part of the painting she was doing of Lantic Bay, which seemed to be taking her for ever.

But with Suze coming round she really couldn't justify leaving it any longer, especially when the coffee cups were threatening to stop being simply dirty mugs and become a microbiological experiment instead.

The radio was playing in the background. Theo was just on the last cup when one of her favourite songs came on.

Pink. 'Please Don't Leave Me'.

She had heard it played three times the day after Michael had walked out. Ironic, perhaps, but it was still her favourite song du jour.

With the little mop on a stick she used for washing the inside of mugs and glasses as a microphone, she began to dance around the kitchen singing at the top of her voice, changing the words as she did so.

'MiiiiChael has left me . . .'

And then she heard banging.

Thinking that the objectionable Nessa Tregail was

objecting to her singing by banging on the wall, she cranked it up a volume, at which point Dill decided to join in the singing with the most amazingly melodic howling.

And then as she danced around the kitchen with Dill yowling and prancing alongside her, it suddenly dawned on Theo that she no longer lived next door to Nessa Tregail, she did, in fact, live next door to Pound Cottage which was currently tenantless and therefore empty.

She turned the music back to a level that wasn't deafening. The banging had stopped but someone was trying to break the doorbell by seeing how long they could get it to ring for.

Thinking it was Suze come early, Theo thundered for the door, rubber gloves still on, mug and mop in hand, and flung open the door, ready to wash Suze's face with the mop in revenge for her poor abused doorbell, only to drop both mug and mop on the doorstep when she saw who it actually was who was leaning like crazy on her doorbell.

'Imelda! I thought you were in Dubai!'

Perched on the largest of six suitcases, in a fur coat, stiletto heels and sunglasses, despite the fact that dusk had already fallen, and using a Versace pen to hold down Theo's doorbell, Imelda looked ridiculously glamorous and extraordinarily out of place.

'So did I,' she said, removing her sunglasses, standing up, and glancing disparagingly around herself, 'but look, here I am in what must be the smallest backwater in Cornwall – how many houses are there, exactly, in this place?'

'Forty-two. What are you doing here, Mel?'

'Only forty-two?'

'That's quite a lot for down here, trust me; this may be a backwater, but it is definitely not a small one.'

'You mean we're cosmopolitan?'

Theo nodded. 'Aren't we always, wherever we go?'

And then the two girls grinned and hugged for England, interrupted only by Imelda's exclamation of, 'Who's this?' as Dill, who had, of course, followed Theo to the door, enthusiastically made it a group hug.

'New feller.' Theo grinned.

'Gorgeously handsome devil. I approve,' and then she looked slightly more doubtful, 'not the kind of hound that eats shoes, is he?'

'Which suitcase?'

Imelda pointed to the largest she had with her.

'That one . . .' and then the hand swivelled to the second largest, 'and that one . . .'

Two suitcases full of shoes.

Typical Imelda.

'Well, he'll probably be full after the first four pairs so the rest'll be safe,' Theo teased her, and then, as Imelda's face took on the expression of someone who had just been told by Theo that she was going to eat her first child, she hastened to reassure her that Dill preferred hide to ponyskin, and started to lug the suitcases inside just in case she was wrong.

Used to having other people carry her luggage but not the kind of girl to expect her friends to do the same, Imelda grabbed the two cases closest to her heart, i.e., the ones with the shoes in, and struggled her way after Theo into the warmth of the large cottage.

'You still haven't told me what you're doing here,' Theo puffed as, having dumped the first two cases at the bottom of the stairs, she went back for the ones still in the garden. 'I thought you were wallowing in seven-star luxury on some exotic beach . . .'

'Well, Sami had some big, big, bigwig thing going on tonight and his wife insisted on flying out to go with him and celebrity schmooze – which, of course, left me on my tod on New Year's Eve, so in his guilt I was offered use of the Lear to jet myself off to whichever hot spot could amuse me for the new year. As soon as she was touching down, I was taking off . . .' Imelda laughed raucously.

The fact that she was seeing a married man didn't bother her in the slightest, not because she had no morals, or because she made a habit of it; Sami was the exception, and Imelda's involvement with him was borne purely from the fact that effectively, albeit not technically, he wasn't really a married man. It was known to everyone that Sami and his wife couldn't stand each other. Theirs truly was a marriage of convenience within a culture that dictated no divorce. So Sami had Imelda, and his wife Irane – a handsome firm-thighed cougar in every sense of the word – had a string of younger lovers who all seemed to look like Jesus Luz. Their one unbreakable rule, however, in a marriage that didn't seem to have any rules at all, was that never the twain shall meet, so whenever Irane was in situ, Imelda wasn't.

'Sami suggested to the pilot that he take me to London, so I figured, when you're in a private jet, one UK airport is pretty much the same as another, so I asked him to drop me off at Newquay instead – and hey presto, here I am.'

'How long can you stay?'

'Until Irane goes back to Paris. Sami will let me know and then send someone back to get me.'

Theo burst out laughing at this; it was amazing how Imelda could make a Lear jet from Dubai sound like a taxi journey. She supposed that was a side effect of being with a man as rich as Croesus. She had sometimes wondered in the past if she might enjoy this kind of lifestyle herself. Imelda was always offering to set her up with the rich friends her men always seemed to have floating around single and searching for someone special. She had never taken her up on this offer. She had decided that it really wouldn't suit her. Although she loved to paint, it wasn't her face or her nails, and whilst she would love to have seen some of the sights Imelda had enjoyed on her extensive travels, she would hate it to be at the side of a man who expected her focus to be on him and not the wondrous things the world had to offer.

Not that Sami was so much like that, but some of Imelda's men had been so egocentric you could have launched them off a cliff and they would have floated in their own atmosphere.

Theo liked Sami – despite his situation, he seemed like a genuine and honest person. Theo valued that above most things, certainly above money. The kind of person she always found to be keepers in the friendship area of her life were the ones who were always face value: what you see, is what you get.

Imelda was definitely one of those people, blunt to the point of being rude on occasion. She was always truthful, something Theo really appreciated, despite the occasional dent to her ego this induced.

She was currently making her way around the three floors of Theo's cottage, oohing and ahhing at every room.

'I love it, Theo, you've made it yours.'

'Is that a polite way of dissing my décor?'

'Of course not. I love what you do with houses; not because of how you decorate, but because you always make them feel like a proper home. It's an extra ingredient other than paint, curtains, furniture and ornaments.'

'Clutter?'

'That could be it.' Imelda grinned broadly and hugged her friend. 'Nobody does it quite like you, though, my darling.'

'The shabby chick does shabby chic.' Theo laughed, returning her attention to Imelda's suitcases, which they had lugged up to the spare room between them.

'So, have we actually got to unpack all of these?'

'Not as difficult as you might imagine.' Imelda smiled smugly and, snapping open the first case, revealed all of her clothes neatly hanging as though in a little portable wardrobe. 'See, from case to cupboard in thirty seconds. Simple.'

'It's like watching a magic show,' Theo sighed, impressed, 'although the most amazing thing of all is that someone can think they need six suitcases for a long weekend.'

'Well, you know my motto, be prepared.'

'Thought that was the Girl Guides?'

'Hey, if someone comes up with something good, plagiarise.' Imelda shrugged.

Half an hour later, in casual attire (albeit Ghost), Imelda collapsed with a happy sigh on to one of Theo's lovely squashy sofas.

'Oh Thee . . . It's so nice to just kick back and relax. I do love champagne and caviar, but cava and crisps can be just as good – better, sometimes.'

'Well, cava and crisps I can definitely do, but do you fancy something a little more substantial first?'

'Ate on the plane, thanks, sweetheart.'

'Of course you did.' Theo smiled, imagining that a Lear jet would probably serve up something a little more tempting than the leftover spaghetti Bolognese she had been about to offer.

'So what are the big plans for New Year, then?'

'Suze and I have arranged to go out.'

'Suze?'

'My friend. I've mentioned her to you before . . .'

'Ahh yes, the aging Midlands miss you discovered amidst the newspapers and candy apples. You're still hanging out, then?'

'Quite a bit, actually. We're supposed to be going down to the Boatman.'

'The Boatman?'

'The local pub.'

'The local pub?'

'They're having karaoke.'

'Karaoke?'

'Are you just going to repeat everything I say?'

'I think it's the shock.' Imelda's huge blue eyes widened even further, her long eyelashes fluttering like beating wings. 'I can't quite believe that what I think I'm hearing is what you're actually saying.'

'Don't be such a snob, Imelda!'

'It's my job,' she joked, holding a hand to her chest in mock umbrage. 'Besides, I'm not judging what you're doing, I'm just surprised by it, that's all. I really thought you'd have something more . . . more . . .' she couldn't think of a word that wasn't offensive, 'more . . . planned.

Like last year. Your gallery threw that amazing party, didn't they. Non-stop champagne, living art, that funky jazz band . . . lots and lots of hot, rich men . . .'

'Sure,' Theo nodded and smiled at the memory, 'it was a great party. But things are very different here to how they are in London.'

'Different good?'

Theo nodded. 'I think so.'

'Was that I *think* so or *I* think so?'

'The latter.'

'Well, good then, great, I'm glad you're happy. You are happy, aren't you?'

Theo nodded.

'Great. Well, now I've ascertained that, all that's left to do is for you to point me in the direction of Michael so that I can murder him painfully and slowly and then we can get down to enjoying our weekend.'

Theo laughed.

'Well, I appreciate the fact that you love me enough to spend the rest of your naturals in jail for me, but you honestly don't need to murder him; it was pretty weird at the time, but I can still see he did me a favour by leaving me.'

'Well, I know that, I'm not going to murder him for leaving you, heaven knows if I'd come back and found him still here I might have actually offered him money to go . . .'

'You would?' Theo queried in surprise.

'Oh absolutely.' Imelda nodded earnestly. 'Isn't it awful how your friends only ever tell you they hate your other half after they've gone? They never give you the heads up during, do they . . . anyway, the painful murder offer isn't for him leaving you, it's for the way he did it. He didn't have to behave like that.'

'He fell in love with someone else, Mel.'

'Fair enough. Sometimes you can't fight your emotions. What you can do, however, is play fair with the people who are affected by them. He didn't *have* to sneak around behind your back with someone else, lie to you, make you look a fool. He could have just sat you down and told you the truth. Been honest. It would have cost him nothing to be honest with you.'

'Well, yes, I suppose that's true, but should he pay for it with his life, do you think?'

'A bit extreme?' Imelda queried with a smile.

'Just a touch.'

'So you don't want me to head out into the night with a sub-machine gun and a knife sharp enough to skin a pig?'

Theo laughed and shook her head.

'Not tonight, thanks, Mel. Besides, we have plans already, Suze is coming round tonight, it's girls' night.'

'Face packs, foot spas, French polish . . . ?'

'Actually, it's more like a bottle of Pinot Grigio and a game of poker.' Imelda contemplated for a moment, her bottom lip protruding a touch, and then she nodded. 'Not really my style, but I suppose I can do both of those if I must, although I hope you don't mind if I throw a little duty free Cristal into the mix.'

'You get the Cristal and I'll get Suze a pint glass.' Theo grinned.

'Oh, she's a pint glass kind of girl, is she?' Imelda replied a little sniffily.

'Well, not in the sense that I think you're meaning it . . .'

'No? So what is this Suze like, then? What kind of girl has my girl made friends with in this rusted little corner of England?'

'Don't you mean rustic?'

'I know what I said.'

'Funny, dry, salt of the earth,' Theo said, trying hard to think how best to describe Suze.

Imelda's eyebrows lifted as if she didn't like this description.

'Salt of the earth, eh?'

'Yeah, she's a really decent human being.'

'Dry?'

'You're doing it again, Imelda. Repeating stuff . . .'

'I just wondered what you meant by that? Dry?'

'Sense of humour, irreverent, sarcastic. In fact, now I think of it, she reminds me a little bit of you.'

'Hmmm. Not sure how to take that.'

'Why? You're my friend, aren't you, so it has to be a compliment on both sides.'

'Your *best* friend,' Imelda reminded her somewhat archly.

Theo smiled softly as it suddenly dawned on her why Imelda was being so objectionable.

'Ah, so you're worried you may have a usurper to that title.'

'Hardly,' Imelda sniffed. 'It doesn't matter how wonderful you may think this Suze is . . . I'm irreplaceable.'

It was a great start.

Not.

They eyed each other suspiciously.

Then Imelda said in the snotty-bitch voice she usually

reserved for superior maître d's who even dared to hint that she might not get a table, 'So, you're the aging pint drinker who spends her days selling pasties?'

To which Suze replied without a moment's hesitation: 'So, you're the shopaholic clothes whore . . . I mean horse . . . who's shagging some mega-rich older married bloke for a living?'

Then they both turned accusing gazes on Theo who had imparted this information, albeit in a much more pleasant manner, to each of them.

'Game of cards?' Theo said smiling far too brightly.

Unfortunately, the cards just made it worse.

Theo, out early as always, left Imelda and Suze locked in what Theo could only describe as a fight to the death, with both of them so bizarrely intent on beating the other it was like watching a boxing match, a grudge one, where each opponent would not be satisfied until the other was knocked out of the ring broken and bleeding.

Theo took the opportunity of a loo break to follow Imelda up to the bathroom and corner her as she came out.

'What's going on with you and Suze? Why are you being so mean?'

Imelda shrugged nonchalantly. 'She's just not my kind of person.'

'You've barely even had a chance to get to know her.'

'We just don't have anything in common.'

'You have me . . .' Theo pleaded, 'Be nice, Mel, please.'

Imelda folded her arms across her chest.

'Have you asked her to play nice too?'

'You pulled her hair first.'

Imelda pouted.

'Please, Mel, I really like her. Just give her a chance, I'm sure she'll grow on you too.'

'Yeah, like unwanted facial hair,' Imelda replied, but then she shook her head and sighed. 'OK, OK, I'll try again.'

'And be pleasant this time, yeah?'

'If I must.'

They went back downstairs, and Imelda went back to sit opposite Suze at the table.

Suze looked up warily. Imelda smiled a smile that wouldn't have looked amiss on the face of a crocodile that was about to pounce.

'Sooo . . . Suuuze . . . what's it like being so close to your sixtieth birthday . . . ?'

'Anyone fancy a huge piece of chocolate fudge cake?' Theo said far too brightly, convinced a sweetener was needed, and knowing how much both girls loved a huge chunk of chocolate.

It was a flat refusal on both sides.

'No thanks. In fact,' Imelda leaned back in the chair she had only just sat down in and yawned widely to reveal a row of gleamingly white teeth, 'I think I might hit the hay soon, touch of jet lag.'

'Not for me either, thanks.' Suze pushed out her chair and stood up, 'I think I'd better make a move, it's getting late.'

It was only nine-thirty. Suze had staggered home after midnight the night before.

Theo cast an apologetic smile at Suze and somehow managed to glare at Mel at the same time.

'Oh please don't go, Suze, the night is young.'

'Yeah, please don't go, Suze . . .' Imelda repeated, smiling evilly. 'Even if you're not, the night is young and we've only just begun.'

'Mel!' Theo rounded on her.

'It's OK, Theo,' Suze said calmly. 'I'd rather be heading for my bus pass than be thirty acting thirteen. Don't worry, love, I'll see you tomorrow.'

And then as Suze kissed a mortified Theo on the cheek, went to leave and picked up her boots, Imelda shrieked and pounced upon her, pulling said boots from her and beginning to examine them incredulously like an antiques expert who's just uncovered an undiscovered Gauguin in someone's wood shed.

'These are Claudio Fratenneli.'

From rolling up her sleeves ready for a fight as Imelda tore her footwear from her, Suze's face lit up with a radiant smile at a name that honestly meant nothing to Theo.

'You know Claudio Fratenneli?'

'Do I know Claudio? I shag his brother and take his mother out for tea every Sunday.'

'I don't think she's being literal,' Theo said, not altogether sure that Mel wasn't.

'I have every single pair he's ever produced,' Imelda explained.

'Every pair?' Suze breathed in disbelief.

'All one hundred and three of them.' Imelda nodded firmly.

'You have one hundred and three pairs of shoes?'

'Actually, she has over three hundred pairs of shoes.' Theo shook her head and sighed.

'Oh my word.' Suze's mouth was hanging open.

'Where did you get these?' Imelda was actually stroking Suze's boots as if they were a pet.

To Theo's surprise Suze looked embarrassed.

'Well, my aunt passed away . . .'

'And you inherited them?' Theo frowned.

'Don't be daft, Thee,' Imelda shook her head and actually smiled in admiration at Suzanne, 'she means she used the inheritance.'

'I bought four pairs.' Suze nodded a confirmation, smiling back at Mel.

'What a wonderful way to spend the money! Way to go, girl . . .'

'Um, can I just ask, who's Claudio Fratenneli?'

They both turned wide eyes on her.

'Who's Claudio Fratenneli, she says?' Imelda said, hands on hips.

'Oh Theo.' Suze shook her head in disbelief, as if Theo had just asked who was the Queen, or Elton John, or Kylie Minogue.

'Do you have some of yours with you?' Suze turned back to Imelda, her voice heavy with longing.

'Thirteen pairs.' Imelda nodded.

'Lucky for some,' they both added in synch, and then the pair of them burst out laughing and, grabbing Suze's hand, Imelda thundered her from the room and up the stairs into the guest bedroom, from whence much shrieking of delight and excitement and raised voices could be heard as Imelda proudly unveiled her stash of shoes.

For her part, Theo shook her head in utter amazement, listened to them for a moment to make sure that the shrieks were still of delight and not fight, and then sighed with relief and went into the kitchen to crack open the chocolate fudge cake.

Who would have thought that immaculate Imelda and Suze the slouch would bond over a pair of shoes? But whatever the catalyst, Theo was sending up prayers of grateful thanks.

There was nothing worse than two people you loved not being able to stand the sight of each other.

N ew Year's Eve had been almost as big a bone of
contention as Christmas.

Natalie's parents were throwing a party.

Nick was also throwing a party.

Nick always threw a party on New Year's Eve. It was
his thing. Every year was fancy dress. This year's theme
was Myths and Legends. Nick was going as Dionysus,
Greek god of wine and feasting. His costume consisted of
a pair of gold hot pants, a wreath of gold vine leaves for his
head, and a couple of bunches of grapes that he was
hoping would be eaten off him before midnight.

After Natalie had been so magnanimous about
Christmas, however, Jonas had decided that it was only
fair that they would go to Natalie's parents for New Year.
They could always go to Nick's afterwards. Nick's
party always went on all night, anyway. Nick's party was
also always open house.

Stella and Blix were regular attendees, with Blix's
costumes getting more outrageous the older she got.

This year Blix was dressing as Queen Boadicea,
complete with leather body armour, long blond wig and
broad sword.

Jonas and Natalie had costumes to change into after

they had attended the more formal dinner her parents were throwing.

Natalie was wearing a beautiful shimmering blue and green sequinned dress to her parents', and with the addition of a long blond wig and a necklace made of shells, she was ready to call herself a mermaid.

Jonas was supposed to be Poseidon.

At least, he had a trident and a crown to add to the black James Bond-style DJ he was supposed to be wearing to the Palmers'.

A DJ which was still hanging on the wardrobe door, despite the fact that they were due at the house at seven-thirty and it was already seven o'clock.

Jonas hadn't even showered.

He was standing in the sitting room, staring out into the garden, phone in hand. Racking his brains to try and think if whether there was anyone he hadn't called yet, anyone who might have seen Dilly or at least be able to point him in the direction of someone who could help him find him.

'You should have been ready ten minutes ago, Jonas,' Natalie chided him.

'I don't think I can face it, Nat,' he replied sitting down heavily on the sofa.

She looked at him thoughtfully for a moment.

'We're both worried about Dill, baby, and I don't mean this harshly, but you can't put your whole life on hold—'

'It's only been five days. I should still be out there, looking for him.'

Natalie sighed, and then she sat down next to him and gently took his hands.

'We won't get drunk, we won't be late and we'll spend

the whole day tomorrow out there looking for him together, I promise. And when we go to Dad's tonight you can give everyone there one of the posters you made yesterday; he's got people coming from all over the county – friends, work colleagues – we can spread the word, and I'll ask Daddy to take them into work, too. He can send them out round all of his building sites, that's the whole of Dorset, Wiltshire, and Somerset, too – we're talking hundreds of people looking for Dylan, Jonas, so you see, we'll probably do more good towards finding him by going than by not . . .'

Jonas listened, digested, and finally nodded.

'Good. Now have a shower, put your suit on, and if we hurry, we can call down to the beach on the way just to make sure he hasn't finally found his way back there. You know how he loves it down there so much . . .'

'What if he comes home whilst we're out and finds the doors locked and bolted?'

'All in hand. Lucy's coming round just in case.'

'Your sister's nanny?'

'Yeah, Lib is taking the kids to Mum and Dad's tonight, so I've arranged for Lucy to come round here instead. I hope you don't mind, but she asked if she could bring her boyfriend, seeing as it's New Year's—'

'She could bring her whole fucking family if she wanted . . .' He leaned his golden head against her bare shoulder, 'Thanks, Nat, I don't know what I'd do without you.'

'Well, it's a good job you'll never have to find that out, isn't it? Come on, Poseidon, get washed and grab your trident . . .'

*

At eleven-thirty, Nick's two-up-two-down in Dorchester town was filled with so many people that by rights it should have burst at its brick seams.

Gods and monsters, strange mythical creatures, fairies and folklore abounded, wandered, disco-danced, drank, debauched, discussed, sang, swayed and staggered their way between the four large rooms and the long garden like a constantly moving sea of colour and weirdness.

A good time was being had by all, except the neighbours.

Nick as Dionysus, god of wine and feasting, was necking a beer and feasting his eyes on the gaggle of gorgeous girls who had been parading past him all night.

Even if he said so himself, it had been one of the best New Year's Eve parties he had ever thrown.

He'd almost cancelled, even right at the last minute, as it somehow didn't seem right to be partying when his little mate Dilly was still missing, and then the first guests had turned up early bearing champagne, and it had seemed churlish to turn people away, especially when the invites had gone out so long ago.

He'd hardly been the host with the most, though. Normally the life, soul, feet, mouth, arse, belly and heart of a party, he had spent most of the earlier part of the evening sitting on the sofa in the living room. The whole thing had been saved, however, by one of the guests – a short, fat, bald guy dressed as Cupid.

The strange thing was that Nick didn't have a clue who he was, but he had been amazing so far, getting people to dance, mixing cocktails, leading the way on the karaoke Nick had set up.

He wasn't a gatecrasher.

He was actually kind of familiar.

It was one of those things where they knew you, and you knew you should know them too, but could you dredge up whom they were from the deep dark recesses of a slightly drunk and somewhat depressed brain? No, of course you couldn't.

And then as midnight neared Clem had arrived.

The short, fat, bald guy dressed as Cupid was dancing on the buffet table.

'I'm so sorry,' Clem puffed as he kicked a tray of sausage rolls flying.

'Why are you sorry?'

'That's my dad.'

'That's your dad!'

Clem nodded.

'Do you want me to take him home?'

'Lord, no. He's been the life and soul of the party all evening. I love him. If your dad was a woman, I'd ask him to marry me.'

'Does that mean you like your women short and fat?' Clem grinned.

'Yeah, and bald,' Nick grinned back at her.

'Nick Wilkinson, you are SO rude.'

'Well, actually, Clementine Peterson, that wasn't what I meant, but now that you've mentioned it, if a girl is stupid enough to take me to bed, then I'm not that fussy whether they're bald, Brazilian or David Bellamy, just as long as they don't kick me out again the minute I get my kit off.'

Clem, blushing at the thought of Nick perhaps checking out how she was styled down under, privately thought that for a girl to take Nick Wilkinson to bed, she wouldn't be stupid, but rather lucky.

And then she did a mental double take.

Had she really just thought that?

'You just come from the Palmers'?'

Clementine crossed her eyes, crossed her legs and nodded, thankful for the change of subject.

'How's Jonas?'

'Trying to put on a brave face. He asked me to say sorry to you for him. I don't think they'll be coming here after, he's far too upset. It was all Natalie could do to get him over to her mum and dad's. He's spent the whole evening handing out posters, and asking people to keep a look-out for Dilly. It's awful, isn't it? Natalie's absolutely gutted.'

'Yeah, I bet she is,' Nick said – so bitterly that Clementine found herself asking a question she had often thought but never voiced.

'Why do you hate her so much?'

'I don't hate her.'

'But you don't like her.'

'I don't see much to like.'

'She has her good points.'

'I've never seen much evidence of any.'

'Yeah, you seem to be the only one, though; most people love her.'

'Blix doesn't like her.'

'Don't get me wrong, 'cos I love Blix to pieces, but she probably wouldn't think *anyone* was good enough for Jonas.'

'Don't agree. I know for a fact she can't wait to see him settled and married; she just doesn't think that Natalie's the right woman for the job.'

'Well, it's a bloody good job that Jonas doesn't agree with either of you, then, isn't it?' she said tartly.

Nick narrowed his eyes in surprise as the usually sweet Clementine riled up and roared at him and found himself smiling at her.

'Are you getting arsy with me, Clementine?'

'She's my friend.'

'And for that I think she's a very lucky girl,' he replied with the most sincere look that Natalie had ever seen on his usually smiling face.

'Thank you.' Clem found herself blushing, not from the compliment but because of the way he was suddenly looking at her.

'You're welcome.'

And then they realised that the room had fallen silent, and Clem's dad, still on the buffet table, was looking at his watch.

'Ten seconds, everybody!' he yelled, waving at his daughter, and then someone turned on the radio and the chimes of Big Ben rang out through the room.

And as midnight struck, Nick looked about him as the room seemed to fall instantly into a plethora of kissing couples and wondered how it was that at twenty-eight he had managed to avoid ever being in a relationship that had made him want to take it long term.

And then he realised that Clem was looking about the room with much the same expression of questioning angst.

And then, to his surprise, he noticed for the first time that her eyes were the same beautiful colour as his favourite blue shirt. He wondered that he had never seen this before, and then told himself with a surprised and yet delighted inner laugh, that it was probably because he had never been this close to her ... nose to nose ... and kissing.

20

Suze and Imelda had hogged the karaoke, snogged the rowing team, downed copious amounts of cocktails and, as the countdown to midnight began, found themselves racing down to the harbour along with the fifty or so others who had been celebrating New Year's Eve in the Boatman.

'What on earth's going on?' Theo panted as she ran alongside them simply because she had got swept up in the tide of people.

'It's the New Year's Streak!!' Suze yelled back happily.

'It's what?'

'It's Port Ruan tradition. Everyone runs to the harbour then hurls themselves naked into the sea!'

'You're kidding me,' Theo gasped, but learned the truth of Suze's words seconds later as a pair of abandoned underpants were thrown over a shoulder and landed on her head.

Theo screamed and stopped; Imelda carried on running and stripping.

'Look, no clothes, I'm New Year's Eve!' Imelda yelled as she reached the harbour wall and total nakedness. 'Anyone got a fig leaf?' Suze grinned, and then, hand in hand, they hurled themselves into the sea where they landed with a huge splash and a massive gasp as the freezing water enveloped their naked bodies.

Louise Bickerstaff, owner, manager, receptionist, handyman and official pooper scooper of Dorset Hope for Dogs, a small independently run shelter-cum-rescue centre, had had a trying morning.

The phrase 'A dog is for life, not just for Christmas' had been haunting her all day.

People, festive cheer fading as the new year began, offloading their poor animals for reasons heartbreakingly valid or infuriatingly insipid, leaving them confused and bewildered, homeless, until she could with luck, perseverance, and a great deal of tenacity, hopefully find them new ones . . . well, it made her want to weep twenty-four hours of the day – but, of course, she couldn't do that; she had to put on a brave face and when you did so for too long, it stuck and you became a hard-nosed cow instead.

So when Jonas Larsson came into her office at the end of a long day where she had taken in five more unwanted dogs she really didn't have room for and had found homes for none of the ones she already had, she was at the end of what had once been a mile-long tether, and was now only a couple of inches.

'What can I do for you?' Please God, this handsome

young man had come to find himself a new best friend, or perhaps two; two would be wonderful.

'I've lost my dog.'

'Well, that's incredibly careless of you, young man,' she had snapped, and then watched in horror as those big green eyes flooded with tears, which he furiously blinked away, whilst pretending to rub a weary hand across his forehead.

'I'm sorry, bad day. Every day is a bad day here at the moment. You've lost your dog, and every other man in the world is throwing theirs away . . .' Louise sighed and then painted a brittle smile back on her face. 'So, you're looking for your dog and wondered if he or she has ended up here?'

'It's a he, Dylan, he's a bearded collie cross. I have a picture . . .' Jonas hurriedly pulled one of the posters from his pocket and passed it to her. 'He's been missing for a week now. I've looked everywhere, I keep thinking any minute that he's going to come strolling home . . .' he trailed off and began to blink again. 'There's been no sign of him locally, so now I'm widening the search. I've already e-mailed his picture to so many different dog rescue centres, but, like you said, you guys are so busy at the moment, if I don't come and look for him myself, then it's just another message in your in-box . . .' As his voice trailed off in bleak despair, Louise felt her own eyes well a little, noticed the shadows under his eyes, sighed in sympathy.

'Look, why don't we go and take a look around? We can see if Dylan is here.'

She already knew they didn't have his dog. They might have had forty-two dogs in at the moment, but she knew every single one of them by name . . . but Louise was a desperate woman.

You never knew, if she got him to take a walk around the kennels, he might fall in love with one of the other homeless little chaps she so desperately fought to find a better life for.

They all deserved a chance.

Jonas followed her along the rows of kennels where hopeful faces peered out through wire walls, and tails wagged nineteen to the dozen.

'This must be such a hard job to do,' Jonas murmured, his heart falling with each footstep, with each new little face.

Louise shrugged.

'I keep telling myself that if I don't do it, who will? And I love my job, I really do, but I truly wish that circumstances were such that I was completely redundant.'

And then she realised that Jonas wasn't listening, he was looking ahead of them to a run a few runs up, to the shaggy, hairy, smiling face that was thrust up against the wire eagerly awaiting them.

'Dill?'

For a moment he felt a wave of hope run upwards through him like a rolling tide, only for it to burst into bubbles of disappointment as he realised that it wasn't actually Dylan. Oh so similar, but not him.

He still went up to the kennel.

'This is Poppy . . .' Louise was behind him.

'She's gorgeous.' Jonas hunched down and pushed his fingers through the wire door to stroke her.

'She's one of the lucky ones.'

'She has a new home already?'

To his surprise, Louise shook her head.

'No. But like you say, she's gorgeous, and because she's such a pretty girl, she won't be here for very long . . . whereas this little chap, or rather chappess' – she walked on a little and then waited for him to join her at the kennel next door – 'this is Wilma. Wilma is what my delightful granddaughter calls a mingrel. A "minging", I believe was the word that she used, mongrel. So, *not* blessed in the looks department which means that she will probably be with us for a very long time, which is such a shame as she's only a baby and such a sweet little girl.'

With her short legs and her barrel body, she looked not unlike a little wriggling piglet. But as far as Jonas was concerned, she was so beyond ugly as to be totally adorable. She had a ginger coat, huge amber eyes and a tail that wagged faster than a humming bird's wings could keep it on a hover.

As Jonas bent to say hi, Wilma, so keen for human company that she was prepared to try and squeeze through chicken wire, hurled herself bodily at the door to her run. To her utter delight, as she did so, something broke and the door came flying open. She almost made it to Jonas before Louise scooped up the little puppy and sighed heavily.

'God give me strength. Everything's falling to bits. You no sooner look at something and it drops off.'

Imagining the inappropriate retorts to that one that Wilko would come up with, Jonas found his smile again for the first time in days. This was also due to the fact that, after feeling so utterly useless for so long, he could now do something, no matter how tiny, to help, if not himself, someone else.

'Do you have a set of tools?'

'If you call a hammer, one wrench and a screwdriver a set, then yes, I do.'

'It'll do. I can fix that for you. If you'd like.'

Desperate for help, Louise didn't need asking twice. She didn't even have time to nod properly, she put the puppy down at Jonas's feet and was off at a trot back to her office to get what she'had.

Jonas bent down to take a look at the broken wooden door.

As soon as his bent knees were in reach, Wilma immediately climbed on to his lap and curled up with a sigh that was as much a mix of relief as it was content-ment.

Jonas's heart broke a little bit more.

'Just so you know, little girl, you are not ugly. So don't take any notice, OK?' he said gently stroking her silky head.

The way she automatically sought refuge with him, gave him her trust, reminded him of the day that Dylan had come flying through the car door and into his life and his heart.

Dylan wasn't just a dog, a pet, Dylan was family.

And somewhere out there.

Perhaps in a place like this, waiting for Jonas to come and find him.

And he wouldn't stop looking until he had.

He cuddled Wilma closer to him, taking comfort from the smell of her.

'Who would have thought I'd miss smelling like a dog?' he whispered with a broken laugh into her fur.

*

'Thank you so much . . .' Louise watched Jonas finish fixing the broken latch and smiled her appreciation, then she paused and frowned, her face apologetic. 'I'm so sorry, you've come to our rescue and I don't even know your name.'

Jonas stood up, wiped his hands on the front of his jeans, and held one out to Louise.

'Jonas, Jonas Larsson.'

And her smile became even broader.

'Oh goodness,' she trilled happily, 'you're Blix Larsson's grandson, aren't you?'

He did not go home, back to the cottage. Instead, he drove to Dorchester and the neat detached house that his mother and grandmother shared on the edge of the town.

Eager for news, his mother was at the front door before he'd even pulled the car to a halt.

'Any luck?' she asked, ushering him into the house.

He forlornly shook his head and Stella's own face crumpled in upset.

'Oh darling, I'm so sorry, but don't you worry, we'll find him. Your grandmother's been on the telephone again all morning. She's already called everyone she knows and asked them to keep a look out for Dylan for you, so now she's working her way through the phone book. Total strangers were woken up at six this morning and asked if they'd seen a lost dog . . . she won't rest until we find him . . .' she repeated.

'It's been a week, Mum.'

'That means nothing . . . you need to stay positive.'

'I know, but it's difficult after a day like today. Do you know how many dogs there are out there who don't have someone looking for them? The last place I went to . . . they had one who looked just like him, a little girl, she was lovely . . . it was all I could do not to bring her home with me . . .' he paused for a moment, looked down at the floor, and then back up at his mother, with an expression which even she found hard to read, 'which brings me to this . . .'

He paused again and Stella looked at her son in concern.

'What is it, Jonas?'

Jonas bit his lip.

'Um . . . well . . . do you remember my first day at school after we moved here from Sweden, and I came home with more than just a bag full of homework?'

'Well, if I remember correctly, there was also a brand-new blazer, shredded, a scruffy little cake hoover called Nick, and the Princess . . .'

'Yes, well . . . today is a little bit like that day. I came home with less than I wanted, but with more than expected.' And, without further explanation, from beneath his jacket, where she had been tucked, snoring, he pulled out a very sleepy ginger puppy.

'Mum, this is Wilma. She wants to know if she can come and stay . . .'

His mother hadn't even blinked. She had simply reached out for the puppy and cradled her to her chest like a baby.

'Oh Jonas, she's gorgeous,' she breathed as Wilma, soporific from attention, affection, body heat and the beat of Jonas's heart, curled a kiss to Stella's chin before closing her eyes again and beginning to snore.

Jonas suddenly found himself weighed down with a kind of exquisite sadness. He had known that his mother wouldn't call Wilma a mingrel. He knew his mother would see that she was beautiful. That she would instantly find a place in her heart and her home for her. But how many people were like his mother?

Wilma and her plight had touched his heart, but he now knew that she would be loved and cared for wonderfully for the rest of her life. What about the other dogs he had seen today, what about Dylan?

'The shelter let you just take her? No checks or anything?' Stella asked after Jonas had explained about Louise. She looked about her warily as if someone might pop up and snatch the sleeping puppy from her.

'They're desperate for space . . . but not only that, I kind of . . . um . . . volunteered. I am now Dorset Hope for Dogs's new handyman, on an ad hoc basis, of course . . . but I promised to come when called, if I can – and what really swung it was that Louise Bickerstaff, the lady who runs it, well . . .' his smile appeared again and his mother's own grew broader at the sight of something usually so present, but recently so missed – 'she's like every other good cause in this county . . .'

'She knows your grandmother?' His mother nodded in amusement.

'She knows Farmor, yes.' And Jonas laughed.

Despite promising Natalie that he would be home on time for once today, he stayed with his mother and Blix for an hour. Watching as she introduced Wilma to the boss of the house, Princess Tilly.

To his amazement, the usually wary Tilly took one look at Wilma and began to wag her tiny tail.

Within seconds they were playing like old friends.

There was one hairy moment where puppy-boisterous Wilma knocked Tilly flying in a game that was a touch too energetic for her advancing years, but Tilly simply got to her feet, shook herself out from top to tail, and barked out a brief yet shrill reprimand, at which Wilma bowed her apology and then rolled over on to her back in submission.

Authority imprinted, pecking order sorted, Tilly allowed the game to resume, allowed Wilma to eat side by side with her at supper time, and then, bellies full, allowed Wilma to climb in and fall asleep, side by side, in Tilly's basket.

Jonas watched this whole procedure with a smile tinged with such unhappiness that the usually indestructibly happy Blix turned to her daughter-in-law with tears in her eyes after he had driven away.

'Poor Sonson, he is so sad. I hate to see him so unhappy. I cannot believe there is still no sign of Dylan. I really don't understand how he can just disappear off the face of the planet like this. *Här ligger en hund begraven . . .*'

'You do know that the literal translation of that is "Here is a dog buried"!'

Blix rolled her silvery-blue eyes. 'Of course, of course, how thoughtless of me, but you also know the Swedish meaning and I do, Stella, I smell a rat.'

'What do you mean, Blix?'

'I am not so sure, *Svardotter*, and it could be the ramblings of a superstitious, cynical old lady, but there is something not quite right about all of this. I think I might call my little friend Clementine . . .'

22

Suze made a surprise announcement at their next girlie evening.

'I miss Imelda . . .'

Theo looked up from what was, frankly, the world's worst poker hand and grinned.

'It's funny you should say that . . . you've just reminded me.' And putting down her cards, Theo trotted off into the kitchen, returning moments later with a beautifully gift-wrapped box.

'For me?' Suze queried in surprise as Theo set it down on the table in front of her.

'From Imelda. There's a note.'

Suze pulled the beautifully scripted note from its envelope.

'If you must, then at least do it in style . . .' she read, frowning in puzzlement.

'Open the box,' Theo urged her.

Suze opened the box. And pulled out a solid crystal pint glass.

The two women burst out laughing.

'She makes life a little less mundane, doesn't she?' Suze grinned.

'You can say that again.'

'Do you know, I don't think I've ever met someone with that many pairs of shoes.'

'Yeah, and talking of shoes . . . what about you, you little closet collector? I didn't think you were really into clothes.'

'Well, I'm not, that's pretty obvious, isn't it?' Suze smiled self-deprecatingly and indicated her usual jeans-and-jumper ensemble. 'But shoes are a bit different. Who's your favourite artist?'

'Oh, Rossetti, definitely, closely followed by Titian, Tintoretto, Canaletto, and Michelangelo.'

'Well, I'm the same with Claudio Fratenneli. To me his shoes – well, they're works of art. Beautiful. I have four pairs, nothing like Imelda, though . . . oh my word, her wardrobe must be the equivalent of the Louvre . . .'

'And about the same size.' Theo grinned.

'But out of my four pairs the only ones I wear are the boots. The other ones just sit in Perspex boxes on their own shelf where they can be seen and admired.'

'In Perspex boxes?'

Suze nodded.

'To be seen and not touched.'

'Won't you ever wear them?'

'Maybe, on a *really* special occasion.'

'Seems odd to buy shoes that you'll never wear.'

'Despite my art analogy?'

'Afraid so. You buy art to hang on the wall or put in a corner; you buy shoes to put on your feet. But hey . . . I do understand what you're saying . . . I just think you might get even more pleasure from actually wearing them once in a while.'

'Oh, I will wear them at least once.'

'Yeah?'

'Yeah, I'm going to be buried with them, wearing one pair, clutching the other two.'

T heo woke up to a bright white light shining through
 her window.

Confused, she rolled out of bed and pulled open the
curtains covering the windows.

'Snow!' she exclaimed as she realised the glare was
from a pure blanket of white that was covering the garden.

'Have you ever seen snow before, baby?' she asked as
Dill, jumping from the bed and following her to the
window, thrust a nose against the glass.

Quickly she pulled on some warm clothes and her
wellies and took Dill outside.

He was certainly acting like he hadn't seen snow
before, a joyous kind of lunacy overtaking him as he
plunged straight in and frolicked madly as if he were in
the sea, and then ploughed through with his nose as if
trying to clear a path, and then began to roll until he stood
up and shook like crazy but still looked like a giant
snowman.

When she finally persuaded him back inside and had
used three towels to get him clean and dry and then
showered herself, Theo's thoughts turned to Geoffrey. If it
was cold enough to snow, then how must he be feeling
sitting in his little folly, open to the elements? She

shivered at the thought and, hurrying into the kitchen, shunned her own breakfast, quickly fed Dylan, and began to cook.

The layer of snow covering the ground was thick enough to roll up and build a snowman with. Geoffrey looked like a snowman himself, the end of his nose tinged a rather pretty shade of blue.

Theo had bought two flasks today. One hot soup, the other a steaming vegetable stew with mini dumplings.

He did not refuse the food today, although he simply sat with one flask between his knees and the other one cupped in his hands for some time before actually eating.

'Why don't you come and stay at mine for a few days?' Theo finally ventured to ask after he had drunk the soup.

As soon as she had sat down on the bench, Dill, who usually thundered off to do his round of the little park, had jumped on to her lap and pushed his way inside her coat, nose peering out to watch Geoffrey eat, hairy body pushed against Theo to share heat.

'See, even Dill says it's too cold to be out at the moment.'

Geoffrey looked at her with such apology in those bright blue eyes that there was no doubt his answer would be a polite no.

'Theo, you are such a kind girl and a wonderful friend, but I wouldn't dream of imposing upon you like that.'

'You wouldn't be imposing at all . . .' she began to protest, but he gave her the look he always gave her when he was determined not to be swayed and, knowing him well enough by now not to pursue it, Theo didn't press him any further.

She obviously looked decidedly unhappy, however, about leaving him there as, just as she decided that her toes were going to drop off if she stayed any longer and stood up to leave, he reached out and squeezed her hand reassuringly.

'I've weathered worse than a small snow shower, I promise you. I was part of a party trekking across Nepal when I was younger, and the temperatures there at night dropped to considerably below freezing. This is a summer's day in comparison. Please don't think I'm being rude, Theo, and I am truly grateful for your kindness, but there really is no need to worry about me. Now will you please go home before Dill turns into a dogsicle . . . please.'

She hung her head, and bit her lip.

'I'll see you tomorrow, though . . .'

'I shall look forward to it.'

Theo looked out of the window for the hundredth time that day.

It was still snowing, and she was almost certain it was getting heavier.

Michael's mother had told her that it never snows in Cornwall. At least not very often.

'It must be so cold out there,' she said out loud. 'It's no good, Dill. I don't care what Geoffrey says; he's not staying up there in weather like this. I'm going to go and get him.'

Dill barked as if in approval.

'You stay here though, eh? No use both of us freezing our socks off whilst I try and persuade him . . .' she pulled on her wellies and her big waterproof and, grabbing a flashlight, set out into the dusk.

She didn't need her torch for very long.

The whole lane was lit up by the flashing blue lights at the bottom.

Theo's mouth fell open, a wave of panic rising like bile from her stomach.

Pushing her way past the ambulance, she ran breathlessly up the hill, her rubber-clad feet slipping as the path inclined.

A small group were gathered in the folly.

Two paramedics and a shivering Nessa Tregail clutching on to a struggling snow covered Percy, her giant over-indulged cat who was almost as objectionable and antisocial as his aging mistress.

The two paramedics were strapping Geoffrey on to a stretcher, ready to carry him down the lane to the ambulance.

'Where are you taking him, please?' Theo rushed up breathlessly.

'Treliske.'

'I'll follow you up there.'

'Are you a relative?'

Theo, never one to lie, didn't miss a heartbeat. 'He's my uncle.'

'Well, your uncle has hypothermia. You shouldn't have let him stay out here in this weather.'

'Absolutely not.' Theo, who didn't think this chastisement was at all unfair, nodded her agreement.

She wanted to run all the way back home, but was hindered by Nessa who, usually struggling to say two civil words to her, insisted on holding on to Theo's arm and telling the story of how she had found him, as she picked her way gingerly down the hill.

Fighting the urge to shake her off, Theo somehow managed to hold her angst until they were in sight of the cottages. Dill was waiting in the window of the sitting room, his tail beginning to motor like crazy as soon as he caught sight of her.

Posting Nessa speedily through her own front door, Theo charged two doors up to Otter Cottage. Sensing her urgency, for once Dill stayed stock still whilst she put on his collar and lead. She paused only to grab her bag and car keys before setting back out into the snow again.

The first stop was the newsagent's.

The lights were on in Suze's apartment above, and Theo could hear the theme tune to *Coronation Street* coming from the sitting room as she sprinted up the snow-clad steps and hammered on the flat door.

Suze responded to the urgency of her knock by flinging open the door, eyes wide with surprise and concern. At the sight of Theo's stricken face she immediately pulled her into a hug before she even knew what was wrong.

'What's the matter, Thee? What's up, what's happened?' She let her go as Dylan jumped up to join in.

'Will you take Dill for me?'

'Of course, but what's wrong?'

'It's Geoffrey.'

'Geoffrey?'

'My Geoffrey from the park.'

Suze's face lit with recognition.

'What's happened?'

'Well, I tried to get him to come home with me when it started snowing and he just wouldn't . . .'

'He stayed out in this?' Suze exclaimed in disbelief.

Theo nodded.

'When I went up earlier I begged him to come back, even if it was just for one night, and he refused as always, said he'd be fine, he was used to it, but he looked so grey, Suze, I couldn't get him out of my mind, and so I went back up . . . Nessa Tregail had found him passed out on his bench –' Theo swallowed a sob, and took a breath, steadying her voice. 'Nessa called an ambulance. I'm on my way to the hospital now, I was hoping you'd—' She didn't have to finish the sentence, Suze reached out and took Dill's lead.

'Go, I'll take care of him, ring me when you know what's happening, OK?'

Theo nodded. 'Thank you.'

'No problem at all . . . and come back whenever you want, it doesn't matter what the time is, OK? I don't care if it's three in the morning and I'm dreaming that I'm the filling in a Brad Pitt and Tim Roth sandwich, just hammer until I hear you, all right?'

Theo reached out and hugged her.

'You're such a good person. I'm so glad I met you, Suze.'

'You won't be if you make me cry!' Suze warned her, blinking furiously. 'Suzanne Lord does not do tears, and does not appreciate people who make her go back on this rule! Now go, scoot, and call me when you know how he is, OK?'

The roads were treacherous, but thankfully because of this they were practically empty. Reaching the hospital, however, was actually easier than finding Geoffrey when she got there.

At first she was sent to A & E, but he had already gone

from there, and so she went back to reception, who said that his notes hadn't been updated with a new location, but if he'd gone from A & E, he'd probably be on a general medicine ward, of which there were four.

Right on the other side of the hospital campus.

Theo walked the entire length of the hospital street which must have been over a mile, tried all four gen med wards only to be told that he was actually still up near A & E getting a chest X-ray.

The duty nurse who had decided that a fearful Theo reminded her of her daughter, took pity on her and sent her to a nearby all-night McDonald's for coffee with the promise that she would text as soon as Geoffrey surfaced somewhere more permanent.

It was gone eleven when her phone finally bleeped and Theo rushed back to the right ward only to be told by a harassed-looking nurse that it was far too late for ward visits.

'But—'

'You'll have to come back in the morning.'

'But—' Theo began again and then almost crumpled with relief as Liz Maitland, the kindly duty nurse, reappeared at the nurses' station.

'It's OK, Sandra. I was expecting Miss English . . .'

'Theo, please,' Theo urged her with a nervous smile, 'How is he?'

'Well, he's rather poorly at the moment, but I promise you, with a little TLC he's going to be just fine. You can come and say hello, but, like Nurse Havers said, it is somewhat after visiting hours, so you need to be as quiet as a mouse and it would probably be best if you only stay a little while . . .'

Theo wouldn't have recognised him if it wasn't for the beard. What struck her the most was how thin he was. He had always looked such a big man, swaddled in a thousand layers of clothing, but lying in bed in a pair of borrowed pyjamas he looked so utterly frail, as if even the weight of the beard would make him topple if he tried to stand up. Despite the mound of blankets covering him, he was shivering uncontrollably.

He managed a smile when he saw Theo, however.

'Geoffrey . . .'

'Hello, my little artist friend.'

'Hi, you. How do you feel?'

'Like an ice cream that's just been defrosted. I think if I stand up I might collapse into a pool of chilled mush on the floor . . .' He smiled weakly. 'Do I have you to thank for rescuing me?'

'Actually, no, you can thank Nessa Tregail for that, or rather Percy. Nessa was out looking for him. He'd found you. Apparently, he was sitting on your chest and licking your face. Nessa thought he was trying to keep you warm.'

'Do you know, that explains an awful lot, I was dreaming I was kissing Joanna Lumley and was so surprised to find that instead of strawberries and cream, she tasted of tuna-flavoured cat food.'

Theo and Liz Maitland both burst out laughing, and then smothered their mouths to suppress the noise, glancing guiltily at each other and the dormant people around them.

'Please will you pass on my thanks to both Nessa and Percy?'

'Of course.'

'And my apologies to everyone involved in my rescue?

As they say, there's no fool like an old fool . . .'

He turned his face away and started to cough, and Liz Maitland indicated silently that perhaps it was time for Theo to leave.

She waited until Geoffrey had stopped coughing and put a gentle hand on his shoulder.

'I'll see you in the morning, OK?'

'You don't have to, you know . . .'

'I know.' Theo nodded. 'But I'll still see you in the morning . . .'

Theo got back to Port Ruan at half past one and, reluctant to knock on Suze's door no matter what she had said, was relieved to see that the light in her sitting-room window was on and that Suze could clearly be seen waiting there, looking out for her.

The door was opened before she was even up the stone steps that led to it.

'How is he?'

'Severe hypothermia.'

'But he's going to be all right, isn't he?'

Theo nodded and Suze broke into a smile of relief.

The next morning, Theo got up half an hour earlier than usual to walk Dill. As usual, Dill charged up the path towards the headland.

It was so odd to Theo not to see Geoffrey in his usual seat, even though she knew he wouldn't be there. Dill, who didn't have a clue that Geoffrey wouldn't be in his usual spot, ran straight into the folly and then came back out to Theo with such a surprised look on his little hairy face that despite her melancholy she burst out laughing.

'Don't worry, honey, Uncle Geoffrey's fine, in fact,

Mummy's going to see him as soon as we get home, OK?'

Back at the cottage, she threw a new toothbrush, toothpaste, soap and shampoo into a spare washbag, grabbed some grapes and bananas from the fruit bowl, and unearthed one of Dion's clean dressing gowns and a pair of practically new PJs from a suitcase in the spare-room wardrobe.

Everything in an overnight bag, she headed for the door with Dill in tow.

'Come on, Dill, you're helping Auntie Suze in the shop for a few hours.'

Dill's tail began to wag furiously as they pulled up outside the newsagent's.

Spending time with Suze meant being fed too many delicious treats, and then a guilt-driven trip to the beach with a ball to burn off the calories. Fabulous. He was smiling. Suze used to laugh at Theo when she pointed out that Dill was smiling.

Dogs don't smile, people told her. But she knew that wasn't true. She'd seen Dill do it often enough in the past couple of weeks to know that for a fact.

Suze was waiting on the doorstep of the shop for them, holding a huge paper bag.

'Wine gums,' she explained, holding them out to Theo.

'Oh Suze, thanks, he'll love you for ever . . .'

'Most men do,' Suze nodded matter-of-factly, 'but it's not usually for my wine gums. See you later, yeah? And don't worry, Geoffrey's as tough as old boots; he'll be fine.'

He didn't look fine.

He looked better than he had the night before, but fine

was most definitely not a word Theo would have used to describe him.

Grey was one of them, shaking, cold as ice when she touched his hand.

Theo tried not to tell him off but she couldn't help it.

'Oh Geoffrey, why didn't you come to me when I asked you?'

'That wouldn't have been fair, Theo. I value our friendship too much to ask any more of you than your company.'

'Hogswash,' Theo said not unkindly, 'you were just too bloody proud.'

Geoffrey bit his lip, desperately wanting to contradict her but unable to do so.

To soften what she had just said, Theo reached for the bag of things she had brought him.

'Now these are just a few bits I thought might be useful . . . and Suze sent you something too.'

She hefted the huge bag of wine gums on to his bed.

He cringed at the thought of even more 'charity', but when he saw what it was that Suze had sent, his embarrassment was now tinged with utter pleasure.

'Maybe I should get hypothermia more often . . .'

'Don't you bloody dare!' Theo cried, and begun a tirade that had the other people on the ward look in astonishment at the young girl telling off the older man as though he were a naughty child. But all Geoffrey could do as Theo ranted at him about pride and stubbornness and idiocy, was to think with a wry smile that it had been many years since someone had cared enough about him to tell him off.

*

He was there for five days in all, and he was like a bird in a cage. Well, maybe 'bird' wasn't the best way to describe Geoffrey; Theo would have said 'bear', before all of the layers of clothes had come off, although he was now so tall and thin she supposed he could be a stork, but whatever type of winged creature he was, he was ready to peck his way out of Templer Ward.

Oh he had borne his confinement with impeccable manners.

He had charmed all of the nurses, discussed literature with the old gentleman in the bed next door, classical music with his consultant, and wildlife with Liz Maitland, and thoroughly enjoyed every single conversation with the delight of savouring good gourmet food.

But you could see he was itching to fly.

His eyes would wander to the window and the bright blue sky beyond with the same kind of longing that Theo had noticed in Dill's big dark brown eyes when he looked at his lead hanging by the front door of the cottage.

Finally, thankfully, Geoffrey's consultant gave the nod for him to go and Liz Maitland chose to impart the good news during one of Theo's regular visits.

'Well, I'm delighted to say that you're well enough for us to be kicking you out tomorrow morning; now, we've found you a bed at a hostel in Camborne . . . and you can take that look off your face, Geoffrey DeCourcey, because you either go there or stay here . . . it's your choice.'

Theo had been thinking how best to broach the subject, but at the sight of Geoffrey's face when he heard those words, her hesitance ended.

'That won't be necessary,' Theo interrupted her with an apologetic but firm smile. 'He's coming home with me.'

Geoffrey opened his mouth to protest.

'You're coming home with me,' she repeated firmly and it was obvious to all that her intent brooked no question.

'A hospital ward, a hostel, or Theo's . . . I know which I'd choose,' Liz said, and cocked an eyebrow at him.

In preparation, Theo had already moved the bed in the guest room so that the first thing Geoffrey would see when he opened his eyes was the view from the window. She had found another box full of books that she had yet to unpack and loaded his shelves and the bedside tables, she even left him a sketch pad and pencils in case he felt inclined to draw. The thing she worried about most was that he would take flight before he was well enough to do so, but short of locking him in, there was little she could do about it other than try to make his confinement as pleasurable as possible.

Suze came up just before Theo left to collect him, to see if there was anything she could do to help. She had bought one of those big plastic shop tubs full of wine gums for Geoffrey and a stack of wildlife magazines.

Theo added them gratefully to the growing heap of diversions in the guest room which now included the portable television from her own room.

'Thank you so much, Suze. If anything will persuade him to stay put for a while it's them.'

'You think he might do a runner?'

'Well, he hates being cooped up, and he SO hates thinking that he's beholden to anyone, or the subject of pity or charity, or that he's taking things from anyone other than companionship. So yes, I wouldn't be surprised if he makes a break for it as soon as possible.'

'I could always lend you my handcuffs.'

'You have handcuffs?'

'Pink fluffy ones.' Suze nodded happily. 'Not terribly effective, the last chap I locked in them managed to escape in five minutes flat, but if Geoffrey threatens to do a Steve McQueen we could always slap him in them . . .'

24

Natalie looked out of the window at the fifth day of snow and shuddered.

It was freezing out there, and Jonas was out yet again, searching everywhere he'd already looked several times over, extending the search even further afield each time.

He had barely done any work since Christmas.

When he was at the cottage he spent most of the time on the Internet scouring the rescue sites, or on the telephone, ringing round anyone, anywhere that might help him find Dylan.

It was painful to watch. It upset her to see him hurting so much.

The snow was falling again. Heavier this time.

For a moment she allowed herself to wonder where Dylan might be. Was he out in the snow somewhere, cold, hungry, hurt?

And then she shook her head.

It was absolutely no good thinking like that.

The best thing she could do was to try not to contemplate but to stay calm and focussed and to help Jonas through this as best she could.

Never one to usually play housewife, she went into the kitchen and began to make dinner. A casserole, something hot and satisfying to thaw him out, to fill him up.

One thing she had determined, no matter what it took: once he finally came home, she would persuade Jonas to stay there. No one should be outside on a night like this, not beast, nor man.

G eoffrey was in bed for a week.
The first step was getting him outside again on a decent day.

The snow had not lasted for very long after that first six-day flurry and the cold snap had segued into a mild January.

He seemed to sigh as she settled him into a seat in the sunshine, a long exhalation of breath that was pure ecstasy just to be outside in the fresh air, as if finally basking in the arms of a love that has been gone too long.

He had needed both Suze and Theo to help him back inside, however, a fact that mortified him.

'Why do you waste your time with me?' he had asked dejectedly as he sat back down on his bed, exhausted from such a small journey.

'Why do you think that time spent with you is a waste of time?' Suze had countered with a look.

As time went by they inevitably found out more about him.

Little bits of information seeping through the veneer like sweet sap from the heart of a sturdy tree.

His current situation was so far from how he had started off in life.

He had grown up in a house called Hallows in Hampshire.

Theo and Suze gradually learned that Hallows was not just some minor country house, but a major country pile.

When his father had passed away, Geoffrey, as the only child, had not only inherited the forty-room mansion and three hundred acres, but also his father's substantial debts as well.

After three long years of fighting to pay back every penny owed, Geoffrey had then given the stately pile – lock, stock and pre-Raphaelite paintings – to the National Trust.

'To be honest, I'd spent so long fighting to keep it, it was actually a relief to let it go,' he had confessed to Suze one afternoon. 'My father always used to joke that I was the offspring of the gamekeeper instead of him, a cuckoo in the nest, he used to call me, and I was always happiest when I was out stomping through the grounds. After Hallows went, well, one day I just started walking and didn't stop . . .'

When he felt better, he insisted on earning his keep.

At first with odd jobs around the house and then, as he got better and stronger, an actual job. At Suze's suggestion he joined her for a few days a week down at the news-agent's, something that to everyone's surprise he came to enjoy immensely.

Girls' night had now gone from once a week to three times. Tuesdays, Fridays and, although not technically 'night', Sunday afternoon.

Although they still played cards every time, the activities had become slightly more diverse, with Friday night's session usually starting in the village pub, the Boatman, and Sunday's always following a large lunch, where a proper English pudding was always on the agenda.

With Geoffrey in situ, 'girls' night' still endured, just at home.

At first Suze and Theo played cards whilst Geoffrey and Dill reclined upon the sofa sharing a duvet and watching nature programmes.

Then one evening, when Geoffrey was a little stronger, and his interest was so obviously divided between the television screen and the raucous game going on at the dining table, Suze and Theo relaxed the rules on girls and Dill only and invited him to join them. Soon after which, Theo retired to recline on the sofa with Dill and a duvet.

Rather than it being like taking candy from a baby, it was like trying to wrestle a salmon from the jaws of a very hungry grizzly bear.

Geoffrey was even better at poker than Suze – although ever the gentleman, he usually let her beat him, but it was only by a whisker.

Theo was so out of their league that it wasn't even worth sitting down with them and so she headed into the kitchen to make coffee and see if there was anything sweet to have with it that she hadn't already lost to Suze, who, when Geoffrey had joined them, had been hoarding a pile of booty straight out of Cadbury World.

When she returned to the room with three coffees and nothing more exciting than some digestive biscuits, because that was all she had left, the game was in full swing, and by the look of determined concentration on each of their faces, she could see that this game was in deadly earnest.

'What are you betting on? Cake? Wine? Chocolate?' And then, knowing Geoffrey's fondness for his favourite sweets, 'Not Geoffrey's supply of wine gums?'

Suze looked up at her and grinned evilly.

'Ooh no, Theo my darling girl, we're playing for something far more important.'

'More important than wine gums?'

Suze nodded gleefully.

'If I win this game, you're going to see a brand-new Geoffrey standing before you.'

Theo frowned in puzzlement.

'What exactly are you planning, Suze?'

Suzanne looked from Theo to Geoffrey and back again.

'Geoffrey has promised to shave off his beard.'

'Seriously?' Theo burst out laughing. 'Won't it be a bit like Dill without fur?'

'Chilly.' Geoffrey nodded, with a slightly scared smile. 'It's been a bit of a necessity recently . . . but a wager is a wager.'

'And if you lose?' Theo asked Suze.

'Oh,' Suze frowned too, 'we hadn't settled on that one. What do you think, Geoffrey? What if I lose? What's your choice?'

'You could shave off your moustache?' Theo teased her.

'Cheers, Thee. Geoffrey, want to add your own twist? Or twist of the knife, perhaps?' She winked at Theo and pretended to twirl her non-existent moustache.

Geoffrey mused.

He mused for so long, that Suze started to do the clock music from *Countdown*, and then he beamed.

'I think if I win, then perhaps I would like to see you out of your jeans,' he replied with a nod.

'Geoffrey!' Suze exclaimed. 'And I thought you were such a gentleman . . .'

'Oh no! No, no, that's not what I meant . . .' he stuttered.

Was Geoffrey actually blushing?

'I just thought that it might be nice to see you in a dress for once. Not that you don't always look lovely, because you do, but if we're talking makeovers here, then . . .' he trailed off, thoroughly embarrassed.

'A dress it is, then. I'll even leave off the boots and put on a pair of heels . . .' Suze reassured him that she'd only been teasing with a squeeze to the arm. 'But it's irrelevant, really,' she picked up the pack and began to shuffle with frightening skill, 'because I have absolutely no intention of losing . . .'

At nine o'clock that evening, Suze and Theo were perched on the top few steps of the stairs, waiting outside the main bathroom. Dylan was perched on Theo's lap, his tail wagging in Suze's face as she sat a few steps lower.

'He's been in there for nearly half an hour,' Theo exclaimed, looking at her watch.

'Well, there was rather a lot of hair to come off.'

'I can't believe you're actually making him honour the bet.'

'He wouldn't have it any other way; you know what Geoffrey's like.'

'Honourable.' Theo nodded with a roll of her eyes. 'Unlike someone else I know . . .'

'I don't know what you mean . . .' Suze pursed her lips and pretended to look angelic.

'Well, put it this way, I've never seen a pack of cards with nine aces in it.'

Suze spluttered with guilty laughter. 'I'm doing him a favour, Thee. That beard makes him look like Charles Manson.'

'Perhaps you are, which is why I haven't already knocked on the bathroom door and told him to leave his facial hair on his face because someone didn't win fair and square . . . perhaps,' Theo mused, 'to make it fairer, the next girls' night, someone should turn up in a dress?'

Suze wrinkled her nose. 'Nah, I don't think a dress would suit him.'

'Ha ha ha . . .' Theo trilled dryly, pushing Suze with her toe so that she fell down on to the step below.

Suze was just about to retaliate by stealing Theo's stripy socks right off her feet, when they were distracted from their mock fight by the sound of the bathroom door finally opening.

They paused mid-scrap like Tom and Jerry in cartoon carnage and looked up expectantly.

A very nervous and very different face peered out cautiously.

Suze couldn't help herself.

She screamed. 'Oh my word, it's Sean Connery!'

The nervous face turned blush-red and, for a moment, Theo thought he would dart back in the bathroom and lock the door again, but Suze was up on her feet before he could move and had pulled him out of the room.

'Let's take a proper look at you, then . . .' She beamed, pulling him gently but firmly on to the middle landing. 'Oh my word, look at you . . .' She led him into a very self-conscious twirl and then wolf-whistled. 'It's like someone's hidden a masterpiece behind that picture of dogs playing cards . . .'

'Suzanne Lord, you are such a tease,' he chastised her, but it was hard to hide the pleased smile flickering at the corners of his mouth.

Her genuine amazement at how good he looked could have been insulting, but fortunately, it was obvious that she meant to flatter, and Geoffrey was astute enough to realise this and accept the compliment rather than feel the negative.

And a stream of them kept coming for the next half an hour until Suze finally pulled on her coat and headed back down the hill.

As soon as Suze was gone, however, the insecurity reappeared.

'Theo, I know you'll tell me the truth . . .'

'You look absolutely fantastic, Geoffrey,' Theo hastened to reassure him.

'You don't think I should grow it back?'

'If you really want to, if you feel dreadfully uncomfortable, but why don't you give yourself time to get used to the new you?'

'It is a bit like giving up a security blanket,' he mused, rubbing a hand over his unfamiliarly smooth chin. 'Maybe I could give it a few days . . . at least until I head back home . . .'

Theo, who was silently praying that the still-feeble Geoffrey would give it a lot more than a few days before he headed back out into the still-frozen landscape he called 'home', nodded encouragingly.

'This could be your indoor persona . . . and you do look remarkably like Sean Connery, you know.'

'Well, that's very sweet of you, Theo, but I'd say I'm more like Shaun the Sheep,' Geoffrey joked with a smile, 'after shearing time.'

The following evening, she was just cooking a huge wok of vegetarian chilli when the doorbell rang.

Although she wasn't due to see Suze again until the following day, Tuesday night's girls' night, it was definitely her face mixed-up, Chagal-style, by the glazed glass panel.

Before she even opened the door, Theo could see that there was something markedly different about her

Gone were the jeans and the boots and the ever-present baggy neck jumper.

Suze was wearing a dress.

And high heels.

'Oh my word, you have legs!'

'Is that all you have to say?'

'They're very sexy legs.'

Suze grinned.

'Not bad for an old bird, eh?'

'You're not old.'

'It's all relative, Thee.'

'Well, I wish we were related, 'cos then I'd have your genes. You look amazing, Suze. Like an older version of Catherine Zeta Jones.'

'Love the comparison, not sure about the "older version" bit.'

And then as Suze grinned, Theo noticed something else; she was wearing make-up, not an awful lot, just mascara, a touch of blusher and a lipstick in a soft pink, but it made such a difference to her, and there was something else, Theo peered closer, had she curled her hair a touch?

'I knew I might have tugged on a trailing thread of conscience when I suggested the dress might be appropriate due to the um . . . *nature* of your card win, but don't you think this' – Theo reached out a hand and cupped and bounced a curl – 'is above and beyond the call of contrition?'

'Well . . . may as well be hung for a sheep as a lamb. You spend so long in jeans, when you put on a dress it doesn't feel right without a touch of war paint and a bit of hairspray.'

'Nothing to do with the fact that Geoffrey minus beard is a bit of a FFOF.'

'A bit of a what?' Suze smiled, confused.

'A Fabulously Fit Older Feller.' Theo laughed.

Suze grinned broadly. 'You know me, Theo, personality is my thing, just 'cos Geoffrey's suddenly morphed into an . . .'

'FFOF,' Theo reminded her, pronouncing it as one would when not so politely telling a person to go away.

'You just made that up, didn't you?'

'Yes, do you like it?'

'Oh, definitely, but anyway, just because Geoffrey is now revealed to be an absolutely gorgeous FFOF, it doesn't mean that I'm viewing him any differently than I did before.'

'Well, before he morphed into an FFOF, you already thought he was great.'

'True. But attractive doesn't always lead to attraction, so stop stirring.'

'I'm not stirring, just asking.'

'Well, stop blooming asking, then – unless, of course, what you're asking is me inside. Another thing about wearing stupid dresses is that they don't keep you as warm and snug as jeans and boots.'

'Yeah, of course.' Theo smiled apologetically and stood aside so that Suze could step into the warmth of her hallway. She stopped in front of the hall mirror, smoothed down the skirt of her dress, smacked her lips together to revive the lipstick.

'OK, Thee. Grand entrance time.'

'Do you think I should prepare him? He's been so weak recently that the shock of your knobbly knees might just finish him off?'

'Just shut it and do a drum roll,' Suze winked, 'and if you could fling open the door with just the *right* level of drama please . . .'

The impact of Suze's grand entrance was kind of lost as they hurled open the sitting-room door to see that Geoffrey was so fast asleep on the sofa a bomb could have gone off and it wouldn't have woken him.

'Well, Dill thinks you look amazing,' Theo offered as Dill jumped from where he was curled up with Geoffrey's feet as a pillow, to come and sniff at Suze's exposed legs.

'Dill loves everyone regardless of whether they look like Elle or Hell,' Suze sniffed, bending to stroke his hairy head.

'Actually, that's not entirely true; he's not so keen on Nessa . . .'

'Who is?' Suze crossed her eyes. 'Well, I don't want to wake him up, heaven knows he needs his sleep, bless him, but I'm damned if I'm dressing up like Lady GaGa at fifty-four again so you'll just have to vouch for me.'

'He might not believe me.'

'Of course he will, you're the soul of integrity.'

'Tell you what, why don't I take a picture? Then I have evidence.'

'If you must.' Suze waited for Theo to fetch her camera from the attic studio and then struck a pose against the door frame.

'Hang on a minute,' Suze urged her as Theo was about to click and, running to the sideboard in the dining area, picked up the pint glass that Imelda had sent her and struck her pose again.

'There you go,' she said with a wink, holding the pint glass high as Theo began snapping away, 'this way he'll know it's actually me and not Catherine Zeta Jones dropped by to have her portrait painted.'

I t had been nearly two months since Dylan had gone missing, but Jonas's heart still stopped every time the phone rang or the door opened.

Dylan's bed was still in the workshop, and there was another in the kitchen; the one in the bedroom had been surreptitiously moved out by Natalie on the pretext of washing it, so that it would be nice and clean for when he came home, but it had been washed weeks ago now and still not returned to its place in the corner of the room on Jonas's side of the bed.

Despite the fact that he kept telling himself he had to accept the fact that his chances of finding Dylan were getting slimmer, he still searched for him every chance he got.

Natalie had been utterly amazing. She had searched everywhere, made countless phone calls, hadn't complained once when he came home late yet again from another fruitless search and, every week, scoured the Internet religiously and phoned the tracking company to see if anyone had found him and scanned him, but every time she called, the response was always the same: 'if they had any news, they'd call her'.

Jonas spent his days, when not working, looking, and

his nights when he couldn't sleep, surfing the many dog-rehoming sites on the Internet, scouring the hundreds of pictures for a familiar hairy, smiling face.

But it was as though Dylan had vanished into thin air.

It seemed like every time Jonas went down to help out Louise Bickerstaff, he would come home with another dog that had been a long-term resident at Dorset Hope for Dogs.

So far, his mum and Blix's next-door neighbours had been tempted into taking a West Highland white with three legs, who had spent eighteen unflourishing months in Louise's care and was now king of the house and as well cared for and loved as any dog could wish to be.

His friend Declan and his girlfriend Abby were now proud parents of a little whippet called Maggie who had been a bag of bones when she first came to the home, and was now a sleek and shining sprint of joy, who was a blur on the beach and a bag of cuddles at home.

After the last visit, he had managed to marry some clients, a sweet couple for whom he had been building some wardrobes in their dressing room, with the sweetest-natured, cross-eyed, bow-legged German shepherd that had been at the home for an incredible – and incredibly sad – two years.

Louise had started to call him the Cilla Black of the dog world.

Something which made him laugh but also made him sad, as it reminded him of his comments about Blix on Christmas Day, when Dylan was still safe at home with them.

Despite Louise's predictions that Poppy wouldn't be with them for very long, she had been found to have a form of canine epilepsy, albeit mild, and had yet, therefore, to find anyone willing to take her on.

Every time Jonas went into the kennels, she would run to him.

Jonas knew that one day he would bring her home.

But not quite yet.

Although he knew that she would not be replacing Dylan, it still felt to him that if he did take her home, that was what it would seem like to others, and he didn't want anyone to ever give up on the hope of finding him.

And there was the task of persuading Natalie, too. Although, deep down, he knew that he would just take Poppy home, the same as he had with Dylan, and that would be that, regardless of whether Natalie wanted it or not.

Was that so very wrong of him? Perhaps. But every time he saw Poppy, she reminded him so much of Dilly, and to his surprise, expecting only to feel pain at this reminder of his loss, he found it also to be a good thing.

A very good thing.

27

Geoffrey had been with Theo for nearly nine weeks, in which time their friendship had been cemented for life. Theo had decided that she never actually wanted him to leave, but she knew that it was inevitable that he would.

It was, therefore, with some foreboding that she took up his offer to sit with him in the garden one girls' night, whilst Suze, freshly trounced at poker, took her forfeit for this by making coffee and dessert in the kitchen.

She knew he had been building up to saying something important to her for a few days now, and she also knew that the only thing he would have to tell her was that he was moving out, moving on and, if she were perfectly honest, she had to confess that she hadn't made it easy for him, but she knew she couldn't avoid the subject for ever; it wasn't fair on him, for starters.

When he patted the seat next to him on the garden bench and smiled, Theo vowed to give him time to talk instead of running away on some excuse like she had done previously every time he tried to talk.

'You've completely changed my life, Theo,' was his opening line. 'I am so glad that I met you. As you know, I've been somewhat of a recluse for far too many years and you have completely restored my faith in human kind, and my awareness of the value of being with other people . . .'

Theo smiled and blushed, embarrassed and yet pleased by such a huge compliment.

'Which brings me to the point I've been stumbling around for the past few days.' He reached out, took her hands. 'It's time for me to move out.'

The pleasure fell away from Theo's face as swiftly as it had arrived there.

'Geoffrey, you can't . . .'

'I can't stay for ever, Theo . . . and I'm sure you wouldn't want me to, either . . .'

Her face said otherwise, and when Suze came out bearing a tray of cake and coffee, she tried to enlist her help to persuade him that leaving was a bad idea.

'Suze, Geoffrey says he's leaving, but he's not ready yet, he's been too ill. Tell him, please. He can't go yet . . .'

'I'm sorry, Thee, I can't tell him not to – you see, I think it's an excellent idea.'

Theo's mouth fell open in surprise, her big blue eyes liquid with hurt that Suze, her friend, was not backing her up on something that to her was so dreadfully important. Any idiot could see that whilst Geoffrey was definitely on his way to mending, he was far from well enough to be living a feral lifestyle again. He was still rake-thin, for starters. His handsome face had sharper cheekbones than Brad Pitt. And whilst the weather was undeniably getting much warmer, it wasn't warm enough for him to even contemplate spending his nights outdoors again.

Theo turned her worry on to Suze.

'I can't believe you think it's a good idea for Geoffrey to go back to where he was . . .'

'Oh, I didn't say that.'

Why was Suze still grinning like a Cheshire cat when Theo was obviously so angry with her? The logical part of Theo's brain pointed this fact out to her and suggested she stop talking and listen for a moment.

'Then what?'

Suze and Geoffrey looked at each other, and then they smiled, and then Suze turned the same smile back upon her friend.

'He's not going back to the park, Thee ... you see, Geoffrey's moving in with me.'

Theo looked from one to the other, mouth open as though waiting for someone to throw something in it.

Suze and Geoffrey?

Her Suze and her Geoffrey?

Not only were they together, but they were at the point where they wanted to live with each other?

And she hadn't even seen it?

Was she really that blinkered to the things that were going on around her? That a whirlwind of a romance was taking place right in front of her and she hadn't even felt the slightest breeze from it?

Had Michael been right? Was she so egocentric and wrapped up in her own thoughts and feelings that she took no notice of the people in her life. People who were important to her. People who had just announced that they were more than just the good friends she had thought them to be.

As if sensing her distress, Dill jumped up on to her lap and slurped a lick up her cheek. Her arms instinctively went around him to hug him close.

'Are you OK?' they both enquired in unison, and the look of concern and affection on both faces was enough to make her feel doubly as bad. They'd just told her their own amazing news and now all they were worried about was that she was OK with it.

'I'm really happy for you,' Theo squeaked, her bottom lip wobbling. 'No, honestly I am. I'm utterly over the moon, I just feel a–a–a awful for not even noticing that you guys were . . .'

'A lot more than friends?' Suze offered, filling in the gap. 'Well, don't feel bad . . . we weren't exactly advertising it.'

Geoffrey nodded his agreement. 'We thought it best to keep it to ourselves, see how things went before we made any announcements . . . even to you, Theo. It rather took us both by surprise too . . . sort of crept up on us and—'

'Hit us over the head with a baseball bat,' Suze finished for him, her smile laden with affection. 'Although, you know that picture you took of me in my posh frock?'

Theo nodded and Geoffrey coyly pulled it, very dog-eared, from his shirt pocket.

'It's been close to my heart for a long time,' he said, smiling.

'So, all the time down at the shop . . .'

'It's not just my shelves he's been filling,' Suze laughed.

'Suze, you're so rude sometimes!' Geoffrey flushed.

'Only sometimes.' Suze grinned happily. 'And I'm only kidding – you see, it's not just sex and shopkeeping, my fabulous little friend . . .' she grinned, squeezing between Geoffrey and Theo on the garden seat and throwing an arm around each of them – 'it's bloody love.'

28

Jonas and Wilko were in the works van.

They had been out finishing a job together and were on their way back to the workshop with their lunch, when Louise called.

'Jonas, so sorry to bother you, feel awful, but I've had a lady here desperate for someone to take in two collies; their owner's passed away, and we're oversubscribed as usual and I've figured the only way to fit everyone in is to split the big pen at the end into two with a temporary wall . . . given it a go myself, but not having much joy getting something safe up, joinery skills sadly lacking . . . I don't suppose this is something you can help me with?'

'I would have thought so. We're not far from you, actually, just hold on a sec . . .' he lowered the phone – 'Wilko, do you mind if we take a detour? Louise needs a hand.'

Nick shrugged his agreement.

'Yeah, no worries.'

Louise was waiting for them in the yard, hands on her voluminous hips, her handsome, lined face a frown of worry.

'I've had another one in since I called you,' she tutted loudly, as she led them around the back into the long row of pens that were the kennels. 'Honestly, I don't know what I'm going to do for room, but I just can't bear to turn them away.'

She paused at the pen she needed adjusting.

'Right, this is the one. It's basically double the size of the others. Usually use it for a mother and litter, but seeing as we don't have any of those at the moment, may as well be split, needs must . . . what do you think, Jonas – a job for you?'

'I think we can knock something up for you.'

'In the meantime, I might put the new one in with one of the others. She's a little girl and she seems friendly enough, so I might just pop her in with Eddie, he likes the ladies.'

'He's me in dog form,' Nick joked, as Louise gestured to a Jack Russell with stubby legs and one eye in the next pen.

'Yeah, he looks like you, too.' Jonas grinned.

'Of course. He's a handsome little feller.' Nick bent down to wiggle his fingers through the cage then thought better of it. 'Doesn't bite, does he?'

'No.' Jonas shook his head. 'He's got better manners than you.'

'You can let him out, if you like,' Louise threw over her shoulder as she went to put the kettle on, 'he likes to stretch his legs.'

'So would I, if mine were that short,' Nick quipped, bending down to stroke the little piebald dog who shot out of his pen the minute Jonas drew the latch.

'How long has he been here for?'

Having spent several afternoons and many a Saturday afternoon when Natalie was otherwise occupied with wedding or shopping or nails, Jonas now knew all the dogs by name, age, and length of service.

'Eddie's been here for six months,' he replied, bending to stroke him.

'Poor little sod. Why hasn't anybody had him?'

'Same reason as the others that are long-termers. They all have their own little quirks.'

'Like one eye and legs shorter than a kid's dressing table? Well, I think the fact that Eddie here has only got one eye suits him; makes him look like he's winking all the time . . . winking at the ladies, eh, Eddie? Where's this Poppy you've been telling me about, then?'

'She's further up a touch, come and meet her.'

As they moved off, Eddie followed. He sat down beside Wilko as he bent to say hello to a delighted Poppy, and then trotted back up the row of kennels at his ankle as Louise returned with tea, and they returned their attention to the job in hand.

'I think he likes you.' Jonas grinned.

'Of course he likes me, everyone likes me.'

'He was very fond of young Wilma,' Louise commented as Eddie turned his attention to sniff excitedly at the bottom of Jonas's jeans. 'How is she getting on at your mother's, Jonas?'

'Well, Tilly has finally been promoted, which means she is now Queen to Wilma's princess . . .'

'Don't suppose your mother wants to add a lady-in-waiting to the entourage . . . ?' Louise said slyly, knowing full well Jonas's preference for Poppy.

'If I could get away with taking another one, I would, Lou, you know that . . . and not to my mum's, but not yet, eh?'

'I wouldn't wait too long, young man . . . someone will take her soon, I'm sure of it . . .'

It didn't take the two men long to finish the work that Louise needed. Afterwards, they sat in the weak winter sunshine and ate their lunch surrounded by dogs. Well, *tried* to eat their lunch was probably more apt; they got about one bite of sandwich each before giving in to the big eyes boring into them and sharing it out.

It didn't go very far.

'So is this place a charity?' Wilko asked, looking at the row of eager faces and feeling a strange sensation tug at his usually fairly well-muffled heart.

Jonas shook his head and pulled a pasty out of its bag. 'Nope.'

'How do they survive?'

'Donations, help where they can get it, fundraising, but everyone's in dire straights at the moment; a bunch of ratty dogs is last on the list when you have your own family to worry about feeding – in fact, they've really been struggling recently . . . although . . .' Jonas gave up trying to even get a crumb of his pasty and split it between the drooling hounds – 'I've put Louise in touch with Farmor, Queen of fundraising, so hopefully that will help.'

'Good idea.' Wilko nodded thoughtfully. 'You know, by rights your grandmother should be added to the Queen's Honours list thingy, the amount of money she must have raised for good causes over the years, she deserves an OBE at least . . . and for someone her age as well . . .'

'Old But Effective,' Jonas joked, screwing up the paper bag that had housed the lunch he had hardly even got a sniff at. 'We'd better get back to work, the Palminters' dining table and chairs are due to be delivered tomorrow.'

Louise followed them out as they left, smiling her gratitude.

'Thank you so much; I really don't know how we managed without you . . . well, yes, I do, we didn't manage at all. Your friend' – she turned beaming to Nick – 'has been an absolute godsend, sent from heaven.'

Nick paused for a moment, wiped his pasty-greasy hands on his frayed work jeans.

'Well, if you can cope with something sent from the other side, you can sign me up too.'

'Do you mean that?'

'Yeah, I do.'

'Wonderful! You'll put your number down on our list of helpers?' Louise clapped her hands in delight.

'As long as it's not picking up poo, then I'm your man.' Nick nodded.

He was quiet as they drove away.

'Gets to you, doesn't it?' Jonas smiled apologetically.

Nick didn't reply but nodded emphatically.

Half a mile away he began to drum his fingers on the dashboard.

Two miles down the road and he finally spoke.

'Turn back.'

'What?'

'Turn back, mate, please.'

'What's up?'

'I've left something behind at Louise's.'

'What are you like?' Jonas shook his head good-naturedly and began to indicate so that he could turn around. 'You'd forget your arse if it wasn't in your jeans.'

As soon as they got back to the shelter, Nick jumped out of the cab of the van and ran back into Louise's office.

He was gone for so long that Jonas was just about to get out and go and look for him, when the door to the office swung open and Wilko came back out again, Louise just behind him with a strange smile on her face.

Jonas looked from Louise to Nick and then he suddenly realised that what he was carrying as he strode so purposefully and swiftly back to the van wasn't his tool kit, or his lunch box.

It was Eddie.

Nick got back into the van and settled back into his seat, Eddie on his lap, and exhaled heavily.

Jonas simply looked at him, a smile curving one corner of his mouth.

'I had to sign for him in blood and she's coming to visit tomorrow and taking him straight back if my garden is even one foot less than I've told her it is,' Nick said, still staring through the window at Louise as if at any minute she might come galloping after him.

'What are you like . . .'

'Couldn't leave him there, could I? Now put your foot down before she changes her mind.'

He said nothing more until they were at least five miles distant from the dog's home and then, his arms still protectively cradling the small dog, he turned to Jonas and began to laugh.

'What have you done to me, mate?'

'Wasn't me.'

'Oh no? Not the first time you've made me go all bleeding hearts over a dog.'

'If I recall correctly, the first time you just bled, everywhere.'

'That's what happens when you get a busted nose, Joan Arse . . . Well, all I'll say is thank fuck it wasn't a bloody orphanage you took me to, I'm far too immature to be a dad.'

When they got back to Otter Cottage and the barn that was the headquarters of Blue Closet Joinery, Eddie had delightedly galloped the length and breadth of Jonas's long cottage garden and then followed his new master into the joinery, where he had had a good sniff from corner to corner, and then jumped straight into Dylan's bed, which was still in the workshop, and settled down with a happy sigh.

Nick had immediately rushed to move him out.

'I'm so sorry . . .' he began, his eyes full of sympathy and apology.

But Jonas shook his head.

'No, it's OK, let him stay there. Dilly wouldn't mind, he'd have been happy to share.'

And then Nick's heart had gone out to his friend as the smile Jonas had been wearing the whole time he'd watched a deliriously happy Eddie explore slipped slowly from his face, and he covered his eyes with his hand and sighed heavily. Scrubbing the same hand back through his hair he looked at Nick and shrugged in despair.

'He's not coming back, is he?'

And to his utter chagrin, Nick found that he couldn't answer because the first response that sprang to mind was 'no'.

'Dill English, room three please.' Theo got up thankfully from her chair in the crowded vet's waiting room.

It had taken her a while but she had finally taken Geoffrey's advice and had booked Dill in to get him scanned for a chip and just checked out in general.

It had been a long wait. The waiting room was amazingly crowded, full of women in bright lipstick, chattering like budgerigars, clutching an assortment of animals on their laps and in carriers at their feet.

Theo had shut herself off from the hubbub into her own little world of worry. In just a few minutes' time she would find out if someone had a very undeniable claim on Dill, a creature who, in the short time he had been with her, had wormed his way so firmly into her heart, that it would take some painful levering with a crowbar to get him out again.

But her inherent good nature had finally overruled the selfish being who refused to book him into the local vet's. If this was how she felt about Dill now, imagine how the poor soul who had lost him, if there was such a person, might be feeling.

It was only fair and right that she find out if someone

loved him enough to get him chipped, if someone was out there now, desperately hunting for him.

And so it was with some trepidation that she got to her feet and went to room three when Dill's name was called. All fingers and thumbs and with an overexcited Dill, thoroughly carried away by the smell of at least thirty other creatures in such close proximity, dragging her there all the way on his lead, she got into the small room and promptly dropped her handbag on the floor.

And then her mouth nearly dropped on the floor as well when the man in the white coat turned to face her.

No wonder the waiting room was full to bursting with women in freshly applied make-up.

He was gorgeous. Stunningly, outstandingly handsome.

She bent to pick up her handbag and almost dropped it again as he smiled at her and said, 'Good morning. And what's the problem with . . .' he consulted his notes – 'Dill?'

'Dill . . . yes . . . well, there's no problem, per se . . .' Theo blustered, regaining control of her fingers and her Fiorelli. 'The thing is, I found him – well, he found me, if truth be known – but I thought I'd better get him checked out, scanned for a chip, that kind of thing, just in case there's someone out there desperately looking for him, and also just to get him checked out, vaccinated, if he needs it, you know, that kind of thing . . . not knowing where he's from and if it's been done . . .'

'Very sensible.' The vet bent down and ruffled the fur on Dill's head and was rewarded with a Dill special of a lick that went from chin to forehead.

Watching, Theo found herself thinking that most of the

women in the waiting room would have loved to have done that to him. They'd have started lower than his chin, though.

'Where exactly did he find you?' he carefully lifted Dill on to the table.

'Well, I don't really know, because he followed me home.'

'He followed you home?'

Theo nodded enthusiastically. 'I would imagine you get that kind of thing all the time . . . did I really just say that? Oh lord, so sorry . . .'

And then to her relief she saw that he had the ends of a stethoscope pushed firmly in each ear, and was listening to Dill's chest and not her ramblings.

'Well, he certainly seems to be in good health.' The vet straightened up and removed the stethoscope. 'I'll just get him scanned and then we'll let you know if he's chipped.'

They were gone from the room for five minutes.

By the time he came back, Theo had no fingernails left. Even though they tasted of turps she had still chewed them all to a stump.

Fortunately, he didn't keep her waiting any longer.

'No chip,' he announced as Dill tugged away from him to pounce upon Theo as if he hadn't seen her for five years.

'No chip?' She needed him to repeat it.

'No chip.' The vet shook his head.

'So no home?'

'Doesn't necessarily follow. He's obviously been very well looked after. Not everyone thinks to chip their dog. Just because he hasn't been done doesn't mean that there isn't someone out there who's missing him very much. The problem is, with no chip, it would be rather difficult for us to trace them. Now there are lots of organisations who can help you find him a new home. I'd be tempted to take him myself, he's a gorgeous feller and my wife's a bit of a sucker for strays; we started with one and we've got four now.'

'Four!' Theo exclaimed, all the while thinking, sod it, he has a wife, well, of course he has a wife, some lucky and probably equally gorgeous woman has pounced and very firmly staked her claim.

'I know, a lot of dogs for one household, but I think we might have to stop there.' He grinned and his gorgeous gold-green eyes positively sparked with delight, 'We're having a baby.'

He was obviously bursting with the news, at that point where you had to tell total strangers because your happiness was brimming so high it was spilling out of you.

'Congratulations.'

He looked happily sheepish.

'We passed the three-month mark yesterday and I've told every single person I've spoken to today.'

Theo grinned back at him. Her disappointment was fleeting – after all, she didn't even know the man, and his delight was deliciously infectious. How wonderful to have a man who was so obviously over the moon at the start of a new family. She had met a few fathers-to-be, and most of them had been utterly terrified. His obvious ecstasy was lovely, and inspiring. She made a mental note to tell Suze to add it to her list of wants: a man who is deliriously happy at the thought of being a father.

'So no more dogs, I'm afraid, not for a while, any way.

However, I can get on to the local RSPCA, if you'd like me to, and find him a space at a local rescue centre . . .'

Theo shook her head vehemently.

'There's no need for that.'

He smiled as if he had already anticipated this would be her answer.

'Somehow I didn't think there would be.'

She pulled a contrite face.

'Well, I have to confess, I'm already in love. In fact, if I'm completely honest, I have tried to find out whom he belongs to, but if I'd actually managed it I'd have been completely gutted.'

He nodded his complete understanding.

'Maybe he's actually meant to be with you.'

'I hope so. But I hate the thought of someone out there missing him, the way I know that I would if he wasn't with me.'

He ran a hand through his silken flop of conker-shiny hair and nodded.

'Well, there is that, true . . . but my wife Liesel, well, she always says that fate has a way of making things right in the end, and she usually turns out to be right.'

So he wasn't chipped.

At least, he hadn't been. He was now.

It had seemed to Theo a logical thing to do, and the vet didn't seem to think it odd when she suggested it.

'If you do find his original owners, they can always get the details changed with the tracking company. And at least he'll have someone to come home to if he does go on walkabout again. He seems very happy with you,' he had said.

And Theo had been amazed how delighted she had been by this last comment.

Dill did seem happy.

Right now he had inched his way very slowly and surreptitiously from the passenger seat of the car, across to her side, so that his head was on her lap.

Theo drove the winding road home, enjoying the warmth and weight of him there, and laughing as every time she glanced down he would be staring doe eyed back up at her. If only a man could ever be as quietly and unsickeningly devoted as a dog.

'We're home, kiddo,' she said as they arrived back at Port Ruan. And as far as she was concerned, that was it. She had done her best to find his previous owners, and failed. And now Dill was home where he belonged.

April the fourth, Easter Sunday, and also Jonas's twenty-ninth birthday.

Lunch at Natalie's parents' house wasn't exactly what Jonas had been expecting when Natalie had told him she was organising something special for him.

But there they were, the whole family sitting around the huge table on the terrace whilst the caterers worked diligently on the food.

He was really trying very hard not to yawn.

The problem with trying hard not to do something was that it made you far more likely to go ahead and do it because that was all you could think of.

They had arrived early, to be greeted by Natalie's entire family: her mother and father and her sisters Verity and Liberty, with their husbands and an assortment of children between the ages of five and thirteen.

Liberty he loved; she was dry, smart, funny and real.

Verity he could easily have put on the spit roast instead of the pig that was currently rotating there, earmarked for lunch.

She was snotty and pretentious, and they were two of the nicest things he could think of to say about her.

It was just lucky she lived the furthest away.

Fortunately, the day seemed to be as much about wedding talk as birthday party, and therefore, as best man, Nick had been included on the guest list, so Jonas didn't have to suffer alone.

Unfortunately, it was the first time Nick had ever been to Natalie's parents' house and it had had the effect upon him of primary school boy on first day at big school.

'This place is huge!' had been the first thing he had said as he stepped out of the car.

And that was the only thing he said for about half an hour as he was given the guided tour of 'Chez Palmer' by Natalie's cigar-toting father Edward, who showed him around the seven-bedroom, seven-bathroom mansion; eight-acre garden with indoor and outdoor swimming pools; lawns more manicured than Lady GaGa's nails; grounds with room for several ponies and perhaps a few elephants, if you felt so inclined; and eight-car garage that actually had eight cars in it, with a very deserved air of enormous pride.

Nick hadn't been able to speak because his mouth had been hanging open so far his lips wouldn't meet.

After a glass of champagne he had finally managed another sentence.

'Now I can see why you want to marry her. Kill off the folks, inherit the mansion.'

'Hey,' Jonas shrugged, 'you know me, I'm not a material boy. The best things in life are free . . .'

'Well, this place is the best, and I bet you it cost a damn sight more than free.'

Edward Palmer, Natalie's father, was a nice enough guy, blunt to the point of being a bit like someone hitting you in the face with a rusty shovel, but down-to-earth and good hearted with it. He had built his business up from nothing and was still the kind of person who appreciated his good fortune.

Sybil Palmer, Natalie's mother, was a different kettle of fish entirely.

A faded, jaded beauty held up by nip and tuck and embittered by Botox, Jonas was never quite sure whether she loved her daughters as much as she was jealous of them.

From finding her quite charming the very first time they had met, Jonas had come to the increasing conclusion that he couldn't actually stand the sight of her.

Fortunately, as their acquaintance deepened, so his initial observation that Natalie and her mother were very much alike, had decreased. Sybil was a spoilt, vain creature, who lived for the material things in life. Whilst Natalie liked her shoes and her handbags and her manicures as much as the rest of the women in her family, since Dylan had disappeared, he had also found in her so much more than that – a calm, dependable, compassionate friend. Even Nick had seen this in her, accepted that she had been a rock. Despite the occasional sniping and sarcastic comment, he was almost certain that the two of them were at the point of a friendship.

Stella and Blix had also been invited for lunch but Blix had had some charity thing first, a fundraiser she had organised for Louise at Dorset Hope for Dogs, and therefore arrived several hours after lunch, when most of the party were replete with roast pig and champagne and intent on lying in the glorious April sunshine to roast their full bellies.

Blix, whose idea of a good party was not one where

most of the guests were sleeping on rugs in the sunshine, was carrying a huge basket full of chocolate eggs.

'I have the *paskagg*!' she called happily, rousing the snoozers. 'We will have a hunt! And so now, who will help me hide them? You,' she pointed to Edward, 'you will help me. You look strong and fast.' She reached out and felt a muscle on the surprised man's arm.

'An Easter egg hunt?' Natalie queried as Blix led her father away into the garden.

'It's a family tradition.' Jonas smiled. 'Which means that it looks like Blix is finally accepting that our two families will soon become one.'

'Hallelujah!' Natalie grinned, and she called out to Blix, 'Hold up a second, I'll come and help you too . . .'

Clementine would never have confessed it to anyone, but her overwhelming love of chocolate had made her competitive for the very first time in her life.

As soon as Blix, Edward and Natalie had returned from laying the trail, she was out there searching.

Her diligence as opposed to most other people's apathy had rewarded her with three slightly melted cream eggs, and a chocolate rabbit.

And then, tiptoeing through the rose garden, she saw it. The biggest egg of all.

'Ooh, come to Mama,' Clementine husked, picking up speed.

But someone else had seen it too.

Nick was heading down the same path in the other direction.

'It's mine!' he called out possessively.

'Not if I get it first!'

And they both dived for it.

They ended up with one end of the box each, about to commence a slightly drunken tug of war, when Nick paused and smiled at her wickedly.

'How about a deal?'

'A deal?'

'I have something better than chocolate.'

'What can be better than chocolate?'

Nick fumbled in his pocket and pulled out a bottle of akvavit.

'What do you say to a little drinking competition? Winner gets the egg.'

'Winner gets the egg?'

'Absolutely.'

'Then pass me the bloody bottle.' Clem grinned.

Half an hour later, the bottle was empty.

And so was the Easter egg box.

Clem had won the drinking competition.

But she had still shared the egg.

Collapsed in the shade of a nearby tree, Nick looked across at her as the sun filtered through, patterning her peachy skin, and announced, 'I'm drunk.'

'So am I,' she replied with a giggle.

'That's OK, then. So long as we're both pissed, it's not a problem.'

They spent several more minutes in silent camaraderie and then Nick asked her, 'How's your dad getting on?'

'Loving it living in Spain, wishes he'd moved there years ago.'

'You must miss him.'

She nodded wistfully.

'Sure do, he's not like a lot of parents, he's fun to have around.'

'You can say that again. Do you remember New Year's Eve?'

Clementine did indeed remember New Year's Eve. *Everything* about it.

'It was a pretty memorable night.' She nodded.

'Any bits in particular stand out?'

'Several bits,' she said, somehow plucking up the courage to turn and look him in the eye. 'You?'

'One bit in particular.' He smiled softly at her.

Oh how she had longed to hear him say that he, too, remembered that long, sweet, soul-searching kiss.

She had spent over a year yearning so badly for Jonas that she had never even looked at Nick Wilkinson, not properly. Two minutes after midnight had struck, when she had finally opened her eyes, it had been like seeing him for the very first time.

As for Nick, to him Clementine had just been an extension of Natalie. Not an auspicious start. He only ever saw Clementine because she had come round with the gorgon. He had never been able to see past the haze of vitriolic fumes to the sweet person standing just beyond them.

He reached out a tentative hand and touched her face.

For a second Clem closed her eyes and relished just the feel of his touch, then, unable not to look at him for a second longer, opened them again.

'Natalie said I should stay away from you because you're an idiot,' she whispered almost breathless.

'Do you do everything Natalie tells you?'

Clem shrugged.

'Makes my life easier to comply, most of the time.'

'Do you want an easy life?'

'No,' she said simply, 'I want you.'

And her honesty was rewarded with a kiss.

Natalie and Jonas were driving home.

Natalie, slightly drunk from champagne, leaned across and rested her head on Jonas's shoulder.

'Did you have a good day?'

'Great,' he lied.

'Did you like your present?'

Natalie had bought him clothes: new designer jeans and a smart jacket.

'Great,' he repeated.

'You don't sound too sure . . . if you don't like them, you can exchange them. I kept the receipt just in case.'

'I do like them,' he said, this time truthfully, and, looking across, he added carefully, 'but it was just that there was something else that I really wanted . . .'

'Oh yes?'

Jonas bit his bottom lip and wondered if this truly was the right moment to mention it again. The first time he had tried she hadn't been at all keen.

'Poppy . . .' he murmured.

She sat upright again, turned to look at him.

'I don't think it feels right, Jonas, not with the chance that we might still find Dylan . . .'

He nodded his understanding. 'I felt that way for a while, but then it suddenly occurred to me . . . I'm never going to stop looking for Dilly, never, but if we find him . . . *when* we find him, then what does it matter if, in the meantime, we give a home to another dog? Why not have *two* dogs . . .' He paused for a moment, but Natalie remained silent.

He tried again. 'She's lovely, Nat, a total sweetheart. I'm sure you'll like her, and I just know that Dilly would too . . .'

And then once again she surprised him.

'OK, I'll meet her.'

'I'm sorry?' he had to ask her to repeat it.

'Let's go and meet her.'

'You mean that?'

'Sure. In fact, there's no time like the present. I just need you to promise me, Jonas, that if we don't click . . .'

'Oh, you'll click . . . you wait and see.'

It was like losing Dylan all over again.

Poppy was gone.

Louise was apologetic but adamant.

'I did try to call you, Jonas, but your mobile's been switched off all day. I know how fond of her you were, but I had to think of Poppy first. She's been here for so long, she couldn't wait for ever. And they were such a lovely couple, absolutely super. They all bonded straight away, Poppy adored them from the outset, and I know they'll give her a fantastic home . . .'

'But still, you let her go without a home check first?' Jonas asked, his heart sinking.

Louise nodded.

'Well, as you know yourself, I do occasionally waive the usual rights of passage when I'm certain about someone, and also, you see, the gentleman, well, it's the oddest thing' – she pointed to one of Blix's fundraising posters – 'but he knew your grandmother . . .'

31

Theo was in St Ives.

Theo didn't want to be in St Ives, but running a house the size of Otter Cottage on your own meant that she needed to be earning a little bit more than just exhibiting at one gallery was getting her.

She had always meant to try and get some work in Cornwall, but as she had never been one to put herself out there, it had been something she had been putting off for a while.

Her winter electricity bill put paid to any further prevarication and so, loading up her portfolio and Dill into her car, she headed off down West to what was really the artistic centre of Cornwall.

The day had started well when she had managed to find a parking space right outside the gallery she was visiting. She told herself this was a good sign as she mentally girded her quivering loins to go in. What she really should have done was ask Imogen and Olivia at the gallery in London if they knew anyone down in Cornwall who was open to taking on new artists. Instead, what she had done was Google for galleries in St Ives and chosen the one that appealed to her the most.

The Eve and Adam Gallery had caught Theo's interest

because its website had been a work of art in itself, each page a riot of poetic words and animated birds and flowers that flew and unfurled and scrolled around the pages as you moved your mouse.

There must literally be hundreds of art galleries in Cornwall, over forty of those in St Ives itself, but Theo knew that even if the Eve and Adam turned her down, she wouldn't be trying any of the others.

'I am a wimp,' she announced to herself, and Dill, who was riding shotgun, responded by climbing on to her lap and sticking his tongue in her ear.

'Thanks, Dill. Moral support much appreciated. Tongue in ear not so much.'

Dill licked her face instead.

'I really must stop giving you fish-flavoured dog food for breakfast. Your breath smells worse than one of the harbour boats before they clean it . . . right, you wait here,' she instructed him, 'Mum's got to go and earn us some dog-biscuit money. I'll be as quick as I can, OK? In fact, I'll probably be super speedy 'cos I'll come flying back out when they grab me by the back of my jeans and eject me . . .'

This was the bit that Theo hated doing, but it was a necessary fact of life, sometimes you had to push yourself forward.

'Right, stop that, Theo English. Positivity, that's what you need. They will love me. There isn't only one gallery owner in the entire country who has faith in my work . . .'

Dill wagged his tail enthusiastically.

As far as he was concerned it was impossible not to love Theo, but perhaps she needed some help. He turned and thrust his nose down the back of his seat and pulling out a biscuit he had been saving for later, offered it to her.

'Bribery?' She smiled. 'You think that might work? Well, thanks for the thought, honey, but knowing girls who work in galleries, chocolate might be a better bet than a dog biscuit. Why don't you munch on that whilst you're waiting, won't be long, OK . . .' Reaching across him, she wound down his window a bit, kissed him on his nose, and gathered up her big leather portfolio and her courage.

Despite the fact that it was still out of season, the gallery was busy with people browsing.

Long and narrow, every wall was crammed with work, which was great, as it was obviously a popular place to get your canvasses hung, but not so great as they looked like they were kind of full already.

A pretty girl with long straight hair the colour and shine of olive oil, was standing behind a long curved desk to the centre side of the room. She was flicking through a pile of prints whilst talking on the telephone, the cordless handset tucked under her chin as she multi-tasked.

When she saw Theo approach the desk, her eyes flicked up and she smiled and mouthed, 'With you in a moment . . .'

She seemed typical of the attractive, polite, efficient and intelligent girls who manned gallery desks in their absent owner's honour and Theo's heart sank, as, nice as they were, they were also thoroughly adept at getting rid of the stream of wannabe artists who made their way through the gallery doors, portfolio in hand.

Theo was proven right.

As soon as she had tentatively explained why she was there, the girl smiled.

The smile was kind, but Theo instantly knew it was dismissive.

'I'm so sorry, but we don't have wall space for any new artists at the moment . . .'

'Sure, of course . . .' Theo stuttered, but then as she began to back off and away from the desk, she realised that she was not alone.

Dill, fed up with waiting in the car for Theo to come back, had decided that if she wasn't coming to him, then he would just have to go to her, and posting himself like a letter through the open part of the car window that Theo had been certain was far too small for a dog of his size to get out of, he trotted into the gallery after her, pushing his way through the people until he could plonk himself down at her side.

Happy he'd found her again, he began to wag his tail.

'I'm so sorry, he must have Houdini'd his way out of my car . . .' she began, turning to take his collar.

But the girl was already round from behind her big barrier of a reception desk, on her knees and stroking Dill's head with both hands, the smile on her face transformed from automatic to genuine.

'Is he yours? I love bearded collies, he's lovely, my mum used to have one just like him . . . his name was Norman and he used to follow her everywhere, too.'

'His name's Dill.' Theo smiled as Dill, the tart, rolled over and offered his belly.

'Hey, Dill . . . who's a gorgeous boy, then? Yes, he is, he's gorgeous . . .' the assistant renewed her attentions to her new hairy friend, slipping into that voice that everyone seems to use when addressing a cute dog. 'I love you, yes I do, you're bootiful . . . just bootiful.'

Dill's tail was going nineteen to the dozen at the attention, which he returned by washing the delighted girl's face with a warm, wet tongue. She was obviously a major dog lover who didn't mind the thought of where that tongue could have been that morning before connecting with her.

'I know someone else who'd love you too . . . yes, I do . . .' She grinned up at Theo. 'Coral just adores dogs. Coral Matthews, she's the owner, she has six dogs, *six*, can you imagine? I'm Laura by the way.' She straightened up and held out a hand, and as Theo took it, she looked about herself as if checking to make sure no one was listening. 'Did you say that you had your portfolio with you?'

'I do, but I thought you weren't exhibiting any more artists at the moment?'

The girl smiled softly, conspiratorially.

'That's what Coral always tells us to say, because we get so many people who come in here claiming to be artists and you end up having to look through such utter dross . . . and, to be honest, she has her own stable of favourites who keep her just as busy as she wants to be. But if you promise me I'm not going to be flicking through another pile of painting by numbers, I'm sure I could take a few minutes to have a look . . .'

Theo said nothing but simply held out the large leather portfolio she had leant against the desk when she had first come into the gallery.

It was really disconcerting when someone was so quiet as they looked through your work. A face reader, Theo watched her intently for the slightest twitch that might betray what Laura was thinking as she flicked through the prints in Theo's portfolio, but there was nothing, until she got to the middle and looked up, and then her expression was undeniably apologetic.

'I am SO sorry ... it's just that we get so many wannabees, there's something about this place that makes someone who couldn't even draw curtains think they could be the next Jean Michel Basquiat ... but these are absolutely amazing ... just the kind of work we like to have. I must show these to Coral, I'm sure if she saw them she'd like them. Strike that, she'll love them.' She continued flicking through. 'These are so good ... just lovely ... Look, are you going to be around this morning? Coral will be in at eleven. I can get her to take a look for herself and I'm positive she'll find some space for you.'

Theo nodded hopefully.

'We can hang around, can't we, Dill? We'll go down to the beach for a walk and come back. If you're positive she'll want to see me?'

Theo's uncertainty was quashed by the girl's adamant nod of the head.

'Oh, absolutely. In fact, I think she'd kill me if I let you go without her seeing you.'

'I'll be back at eleven, then.' Theo allowed herself a smile.

'Fabulous. Although, actually, on second thoughts, do you mind leaving this with me? I promise to take great care of it, it's just Coral's time-keeping's pretty erratic, so if she decides to come in at ten-thirty and then buggers off twenty minutes later, I can still make sure she has a look ...'

Theo took Dill to the beach. If she hadn't had Dill with her, she would have headed straight for the Tate, and wandered through the exhibits dreaming of the time when perhaps her own work might hang in somewhere with such a famous name.

As it was, she took her inspiration from the scenery that had moved so many before her from Marianne Stokes through Barbara Hepworth to Sandra Blow to the current artists who lived and worked in the area.

Theo had always wondered if the tales about the quality of light in St Ives were just a myth to lure the holidaymakers, but she now knew them to be completely true. It truly was extraordinary. A certain Mediterranean sparkle she had never seen anywhere else in England. It made her itch to sit down at her easel. Dylan, however, had other ideas. For him the beach meant balls to chase and waves to chase and seagulls to chase and then, hopefully, an ice cream.

He was smiling like the Cheshire Cat as they headed down on to the sand. She had never known a dog to actually smile before. She knew enamoured people claimed all sorts of weird and wonderful things about their beloved pets, cats who could juggle, llamas who could knit jumpers from their own wool, parrots who whistled the whole of Beethoven's fifth, but, in Dill's case, that was a definite smile, all teeth and curling lip.

He was happy. A day out, a run on the beach, enough to make life worth smiling about. How simple and satisfying life must be as a well-cared for, well-loved dog.

And Dill really was well loved.

At eleven, covered in sand and with the freckles on her nose tempted out by the April sunshine, she made her way back to the Eve and Adam.

She really hoped that the gallery liked her work

enough to show her. It would be something else to make her feel settled, like she belonged here, that she wasn't just here because she'd followed Michael, that it was her home too.

She needn't have worried so much.

As she walked through the door she was swooped upon by a vision with dark marmalade-coloured hair piled high on her head like the vanilla ice cream in the cone Theo and Dill had just devoured between them, huge marmalade eyes to match, fringed with the longest thickest eyelashes Theo had ever seen. Her smile was broad and lipsticked bright fuchsia, and she had the whitest teeth Theo had ever seen.

'You must be Theodora.' The lady that Theo could only presume was Coral Matthews, the gallery owner, flung her arms around her and pressed a lipstick-sticky kiss on each cheek. 'Laura tells me she nearly turned you away – how people in St Ives would have laughed at the Eve and Adam if we'd turned down the chance to show Theodora English . . . I would imagine it would be a little bit like those poor agents and publishers who turned down Harry Potter . . .'

'Are you saying that you've heard of me?'

'Oh, of course, absolutely; you deal with the lovely Imogen Fielding, don't you? We have artists in common, another Laura, actually, not my Laura, well, I suppose in a way she is my Laura, but not my lovely Laura here, but yes, gorgeous Imogen has mentioned you, actually, told me you were moving to Cornwall and to think about you, said you do very well at the Fielding . . . although, thinking about it, she's Imogen Avery now. I wonder if she'll change the name of the gallery, now she's married; what do you think, my lovely Laura?'

Laura shrugged and smiled at Theo.

'So, what I'm going to do is I'm going to squeeze together some Martha Baileys, Laura, and that gorgeous Gareth Greene is going to its new home tomorrow morning, so that will leave room for something of Theo's. A little taster, a tempter, to see how our clients like her. Does that suit you, Theo darling? Does it?'

'That would be fantastic, thank you so much.' Theo, still a little dazed and dazzled, managed a grateful smile.

'Marvellous, lovely, so happy to have you with us, Theo,' and she reached across and wrapped her in that gorgeously scented hug again. 'Well, I have to rush, doggy doctors for poor little Humbug at twelve, you must know what it's like being a doggy mummy yourself, Theo, darling . . . I'll leave you with Laura to run through the dirty details – you know, the necessary evil that is commission, et cetera et cetera . . .'

And with that she was gone in a whirling scented flap of chiffon and silk, sailing through the doors and out into the sunshine.

'It's like being hit in the face with a hippy, isn't it?'

'Sorry?'

'Meeting Coral. Don't worry, you'll get used to her. And she's very good to her artists. Of which you are now one. Welcome to the Eve and Adam, Theo.'

'Thank you. Thank you so much. But can I just ask, why's it called the Eve and Adam and not the other way round?'

Laura laughed, her pretty face lighting up with mirth.

'Well, apparently Coral chose the name and twisted it, because the Bible says that man came first, and Coral's philosophy was that the bloody man always comes first, so it was about time that woman had a chance . . .'

32

April the eleventh. Theo's birthday.

She had spent the morning delivering her first painting to the Eve and Adam, where she and Dill had watched, both smiling, as her painting had been hung, and then still both smiling had shared a huge birthday ice cream down on the beach, revelling in the beautiful spring sunshine, and in the realisation that life was really rather lovely. That she was now twenty-seven, which was scarily close to thirty, and she was single, and her family were still a million miles away, but she was happy.

They returned to Otter Cottage to a pile of birthday cards with foreign stamps on the doormat and a plethora of phone calls, tuneless choruses of 'Happy Birthday' being repeatedly sung down the telephone as first her mother, then Xavier, then Dion, followed by Imelda, then August, who didn't sing, and then even her father, who had by some miracle managed to get through and even stay on line long enough to sing and wish her a good day.

'Happy birthday, poppet, are you having a lovely day? I've sent you some money . . .'

'Thanks, Dad, but I wish you wouldn't.'

'Well, what are dads for, eh?'

'Actually, dads are for far more important things than

sending cash at odd intervals, like . . . like . . .' Theo stumbled to a halt. What were dads for? When you didn't have one around for a lot of the time, you kind of forgot the purpose of them. 'Ooh, I know, they're for vetting dodgy boyfriends and for telling you that you were too good for them anyway when they dump you . . . they're for calling you princess, and treating you like one, and then walking you down the aisle when you finally find a man who doesn't drive you so round the bend with his bad habits and double standards that you'd actually consider marrying him. They're for calling you more than twice a year, and popping round to help you put up shelves at the weekend, and for hugging and . . .'

Theo stopped as she realised that most of the last breathless rush of words had been said to the dial tone.

'Damn. Gone again. Bloody typical!'

And full of angst she had stormed upstairs and painted a speedy recreation of a Bruegel with her father as a little devil with horns and a pitchfork.

Painting soothed as always, enough even to have her laughing at her new, rather bizarre, creation which she resolved to hang in the downstairs loo. Theo then got ready to go down to Suze and Geoffrey's where a birthday tea was being held in her honour, and where they were now singing 'Happy Birthday' at her too.

Geoffrey had made her the hugest chocolate fudge cake, the size of a car wheel, which was presented with twenty-seven candles flickering whilst they sang.

'Make a wish!' Suze demanded as she blew them out.

Theo closed her eyes and wished. Opened them again and peered at her arse in her jeans.

'Nope, didn't come true, still not a size ten . . .'

Then came presents.

Dill had apparently sent Suze out to buy her new slippers on his behalf, seeing as he had stolen her old ones and buried them in the garden, and a beautiful silk shirt that was such a riot of colour, Suze explained, because then she could spill paint on it and no one would even notice.

And then Suze handed her a gift-wrapped box which contained the most beautiful antique pearl earrings Theo had ever seen.

'Oh my goodness, they're absolutely gorgeous!' she had exclaimed, rushing to put them on and check them out in the hall mirror.

'I saw them and thought of you. Well, actually, Geoffrey saw them first, but we both agreed they were perfect . . . are they? Do you like them?'

'Love them, thank you so much. Where on earth did you find them?'

'In a jewellery shop in Dorset.'

'In Dorset?' Theo stopped looking at a reflection of her ears, and looked curiously at her friend instead. 'When were you in Dorset?'

'Yesterday.'

'But I thought you guys had the day off to walk the Saints' Way yesterday?' She frowned.

'We lied,' Suze replied cheerfully.

'Why? What were you doing in Dorset?'

'Well, that's the next surprise. You see, Geoffrey was surfing the net . . .'

'Really?' Theo's eyes flew wide in pleased amazement.

'I know, two months ago and a net to me was something you either knocked a tennis ball over or caught a fish with.' Geoffrey shrugged self-deprecatingly.

'And whilst we were on the net we found something pretty amazing. And it was in Dorset, so that's why we were there,' Suze continued the story, her eyes shining.

'Amazing?'

Suze nodded.

'Well, it was something we'd been thinking about for a little while, and then we spotted . . .' she trailed off and looked at Geoffrey with raised eyebrows. 'Shall we just let her see for herself?'

'Oh, I think so. Besides, she's still not too keen on being left on her own, and she's been out in the garden since Theo got here . . .'

'She? Will someone please tell me what's going on?' Theo smiled at their delighted faces in utter puzzlement, so Suze just took her hand and led her to the back door.

'Theo, ooh, and Dill too, come here, Dill, because it was you that really inspired us, my gorgeous hairy friend . . .' She opened the back door as Dill trotted over. 'This, my lovely ones, is our new baby . . .'

And there in the garden, peering out from behind the garden bench, uncertainly wagging a plumy tail, was Dill's mirror image.

'Theo, Dill . . . meet Poppy.'

33

Theo hadn't gone to bed until two.

She had stayed at Suze and Geoffrey's until ten, eating far too much cake and trying to persuade Poppy, who was decidedly unsure about an extremely over-enthusiastic Dill, that he was friend and not foe, and wanted to play, and not devour her with one bite.

When she had finally returned to Otter Cottage, she had then stayed up late finishing a commission that was due in. A rare request through her gallery in London for a portrait. A chap who had purchased several of her London-based landscapes, and now wanted a painting of his wife. His very fat wife. Theo could have sworn it would have taken her half the time to do if someone had only introduced Mrs Dudley Anstell, size twenty and the proud possessor of at least six chins, to the delights of Slimming World.

She had finally finished and taken it, still tacky, to put it in the boot of her car for an early morning trip down to Suze, who had promised to help her pack it to post, only to impale it on a piece of driftwood she had forgotten she'd picked up last time she'd walked Dill.

Theo contemplated the stick poking through the middle of her freshly finished canvas and wondered whether it was too inconsiderate towards the neighbours to scream. Deciding that it probably was, she stuck the painting in the hall, threw the driftwood back in the direction of the ocean, and poured herself a large vodka.

By the time she had fallen into bed, she had also fallen into a deep sleep born of utter exhaustion.

At first she thought she was dreaming. She was, for some bizarre dream-fuelled reason, on stage about to sing an aria in front of Simon Cowell and the incessant knocking sound was her knees, but then Theo's brain dragged her groggily from sleep and she realised that the noise was actually someone hammering on her front door. Theo looked in concern at her alarm clock. It was two fifty-five a.m.!

'Who on earth? . . .' she murmured to Dill, who had only just emerged from slumber himself, knackered from running twenty miles round Suze's tiny garden after what was now his new best friend, even if she didn't realise it herself yet.

They both heaved themselves reluctantly from the bed, and went through into the guest room where the bedroom window overlooked the little front garden. Theo opened the window and called out softly.

'Hello? Who is it?'

'Special Delivery,' came a prompt reply.

At three in the morning? That would make it a very special delivery. It wasn't a voice she recognised. And then she heard laughter. The laughter sounded so very familiar. There was only one person it could be, but it couldn't be, could it? Theo peered so far out of the window that she was in danger of falling out, but she still couldn't make out the figure standing in the darkened doorway.

There was only one way to find out.

She pulled on her dressing gown, and hurried down the stairs, feeling comforted by the fact that Dill was silently at her side.

The warm night air flooded the hallway with the scent of sea and summer flowers as she cautiously pulled open the front door and peered out into the darkness. And then she shrieked and Dill barked as a tall figure jumped out from behind the lilac bush to the side of the front door and shouted.

'Boo!'

It *was* him.

Six foot two, eyes of blue, face of a fallen cherub, and heart the size of Africa.

'Dionysus!' Theo rasped and realised that for the first time in months she was finally crying.

His grinning face fell into a frown and, reaching for her, he pulled her into a hug.

'Hey, Dormouse. Thought you'd be *happy* to see me.'

'Oh, you don't know how much, little brother,' Theo sobbed.

And he was pleased to see that her eyes were shining not just with tears, but with delight.

'Happy birthday, sis! Well, I know technically speaking I'm a day late, but the aim was to get here for your birthday, so I'm hoping it's the thought that counts.'

'Best birthday present ever,' Theo replied. 'Let me look at you . . . I swear you've grown!'

'An inch and a half . . .' he nodded happily, 'and feel these biceps,' he made a fist and clenched the muscles in his forearm, 'been working ten-hour days on a cactus farm in Mexico just to earn enough money for a flight home to see my favourite sister . . . by the way, I brought you a present. I hope you like it . . .'

Theo jumped as another man stepped out from behind the lilac.

'Hi, Theo,' said the voice she thought she hadn't recognised, which suddenly sounded scarily familiar. Theo's bottom jaw fell so hard to the floor it should by rights have dropped off and begun rolling down the road to the harbour.

She opened her mouth to speak but all that managed to tumble out of it was, 'What . . . what . . . what . . .'

His mouth quirked in amusement.

'I think you're trying to ask what am I doing here?'

She nodded vigorously.

'Well, muscles weren't the only thing I found in Mexico.' Dion grinned, clapping a hand around the other guy's shoulders. 'I found old Felix here too, propping up the bar of the dingiest little cantina south of the border. When I told him where I was headed next he insisted on tagging along.'

'But I thought you were in New York, wife number two, baby number one?'

Felix shook his head.

'You shouldn't believe everything you read in the papers, Theo; you should know that by now.'

'So you're single?'

'Footloose and fancy free.' He nodded.

'No baby?'

'Can you imagine me as a father?' He pulled a face.

'Are you going to ask us in?' Dion demanded. 'I have gifts,' he added with a grin as if she needed an incentive to let them off the doorstep and into the house. Nessa Tregail's nasty curtains were twitching furiously.

This was incentive enough.

Under the kitchen lights she could see that they were both brown as berries.

And so bloody good-looking, the pair of them, it made you sick with envy.

The last time she had seen them together, Dion had been a child, and Felix had been one too, albeit mentally not physically. They had both grown in different ways. Matured. Dion upwards, Felix outwards, not that he had run to fat – it was rather that he had lost the lithe boy body and become a more muscled man. You could have said the same about Dion. It was a good transformation, for both of them.

Albeit physical.

Theo just hoped that it wasn't only the body that had matured.

The pair of them were exhausted from their journey, but they still had enough energy to eat their way through the entire contents of her fridge, before falling into the sleep of the dead in the spare room.

Despite being woken at three, Theo still got up to her alarm at seven, took Dill for his walk, and then was back in her attic studio by eight to start work. Dion was still snoring in the spare room; Felix she could hear in the bathroom, singing in the shower. For some reason she shivered at the sound of something that had once been so familiar. It was strange, not altogether comfortable. And so she lost herself in the familiar comfort of work.

Twenty minutes later, however, Felix wandered in

behind her, didn't say a word, just walked around the room looking at the canvases on the walls.

She turned to face him, looked at him properly for the first time in such a very long time. Observing him as he observed her work.

Apart from the muscles, he hadn't changed very much at all. His hair was slightly longer than she remembered, maybe a few more lines around the eyes, the clothes expensive, still the same Breitling around his wrist. The tan suited him, it brought out the blue of his eyes, the gold in his hair.

He turned to face her. Said nothing for a moment, simply looked at her, as she had been looking at him, but far more blatantly, and then he smiled, a long and languid smile.

'These are good, Theo. You've got better. Don't take that the wrong way, you were always good, but I could see the potential; now that potential has come to fruition.'

'Thank you,' she replied, her discomfort at his searching gaze making her polite. 'And how are things going for you? I understand you're doing remarkably well.' Goodness, she sounded like Geoffrey now. 'I mean I hear you sell really well, rockstars, royalty, that kind of thing.'

He shrugged.

'That's how it was. Unfortunately, I haven't touched a paintbrush for nine months . . .' he said, picking up a sable and stroking the soft bristles with his thumb. 'This is the first time I've even held one in my hand . . .'

'But why?' Theo asked, her mouth falling in horror at such a thought.

He shrugged.

'I'm burned out, Theodora . . . Done too much, much too young,' he sang.

'Married with a kid when you should be having fun?' Theo said the next line back at him.

He took it as a question.

'Like I said, don't believe everything you read. When they can't find out any real stories they make up what the hell they like. People always have an agenda.'

He was right, especially people like himself.

Felix had always had an agenda. A game plan.

'And what's yours, Felix?' she asked warily. 'Why are you here?'

'Get my mojo back.'

'And you think you might find it in Cornwall?' she asked, her surprise evident.

He looked at her, a long, slow, appraising look again that had her wriggling in her seat like a schoolgirl being told off in class.

'Perhaps.'

And then Dion had loped upstairs in his boxer shorts, his dark curls wild from sleep.

'Morning, Peeps. What's for breakfast, Dor? I'm starving!'

Theo had made pancakes.

And then Felix had announced he was going out to take in the sights.

Dion had rough-and-tumbled in the garden with a delighted Dill, and then, when he was covered in mud and grass, remembered that he did indeed have presents, and rushed to fetch his rucksack.

He had birthday presents from her family, but the most precious gifts were photographs.

He had seen everybody.

'These are from Sav and Jules . . .' he said, handing her a beautiful set of watercolours. 'And this . . .'

It was a painting, a child's painting, with blobs of paint that could have been anything from cow to cookie.

'Simeon made it. He is the cutest baby, but he's going to be, isn't he? He's got the same genes as me and look how gorgeous I turned out. Talking of which, are there any fit women in this place?'

'None under fifty.'

'Shit. I won't be staying long, then . . .' he joked.

'How long can you stay?' Theo replied hopefully.

His face twisted into one of apology.

'Only a couple of days. Promised to meet Finn in Cuba yesterday, I figured I can get away with being a few days late, but you know what Finn's like; if I'm not there to keep an eye on him, he'll be stealing drug barons' girlfriends and getting himself laid to rest under brand-new sky rises . . . only kidding . . .' he chirped happily as Theo's mouth dropped in horror, 'but I am supposed to be meeting him, just couldn't resist the chance to see you when Felix offered it—'

'Felix offered it?'

'Yeah, said he had a friend with a plane who owed him a favour, did I fancy a quick detour for your birthday, and here I am. Anyway, Xavier and Jules want to come and see you, but Xav's too tied up with work to leave Oz at the moment, although they were talking about a family reunion here next summer, you up for that? The whole lot descending?'

Theo couldn't think of anything nicer.

'Now this is from your big sister.'

He had stayed with August in New York?

'She has a new man. A married one . . .' he told her with a grin and raised eyebrows.

'A married man! Augustine? Never, she wouldn't.'

'She is. She also sent you this.' He handed her what looked like a rag, but when Theo shook it out it was actually a dress. Taken out of its protective box and screwed up and stuffed into the corner of Dion's stinking rucksack, but still beautiful, nonetheless.

'August sent me this?' Theo breathed incredulously, spotting that the label read Versace.

'Yeah, birthday present.'

'Is there something wrong with her? Has she been hit on the head by something?'

Dion burst out laughing.

'Yeah, well, I can understand the scepticism, but she really does seem to have changed. You think a married man would be bad for her, but I actually think it's doing her some good. You know, making her connect with emotions that most human beings normally have and she hasn't. Oh, and this is for you from Dad.'

He handed her another screwed-up bundle pulled from one of the rucksack pockets.

More money.

'You saw Dad?'

'Yeah, it was the funniest thing. Mum and Peter were ported up in Cancun. When we found out how close we were to each other they invited me down to stay and Dad was holed up in the cabin next door.'

'He was staying with Mum and Peter?'

Dion nodded. 'Weird, isn't it?'

'Maybe they're mellowing with age.'

'Maybe they've got a dodgy geriatric threesome thing going on.'

'Oh D, no, don't make me think about things like that . . .'

'No, seriously, I think they were just catching up; it was kind of nice. This is from Mum and Peter.' He pulled a silver charm bracelet from his pocket.

'Pretty!' Theo cried, examining the tiny silver shells that adorned it. 'Did you bring me a birthday present?' she teased him, knowing full well that Dion as the baby of the family and permanently broke, was more used to being bought for by others, than buying for other people.

'Sure did.' He grinned and, as if on cue, he looked to the door where Felix was just coming back in.

34

So Felix was her birthday present.

An intriguing and rather disturbing thought, Theo mused as she showered and dressed to go out.

The thing was, despite the fact that she had been relieved when she and Felix had ended their relationship, there were certain bits about him that she had always missed.

Very particular *bits*.

The sex had always been amazing.

She missed amazing sex.

She hadn't had much amazing sex with Michael. It had been decent sex, then methodical sex, then habitual sex, segueing into occasional sex, then no sex at all. But never amazing.

When she thought about it, which she tried not to very often, she hadn't had amazing sex for years and years.

When she went downstairs in a dress, Dion whistled at her in amazement.

'What, no jeans? Is this for Felix's benefit?'

'As if, we're going out, remember? Jazz band playing at the Boatman.'

'Ah yes, the local pub. Meeting Suze and Geoffrey.' He repeated what Theo had told them at breakfast, 'Why not? Get a bit of local culture.'

'Well, I'd hardly call the Boatman culture,' Theo grinned, 'but you might enjoy yourself. Is Felix coming?'

'I think that's his intention . . .' Dion grinned wickedly.

'To the pub, D, to the bloody pub.'

Dion nodded. 'Yeah, but he's only just got in the shower, said he'd join us down there later.'

Dion and Theo were at the bar, Theo buying drinks, Dion trying, albeit not very hard, to stop himself from falling into Marianne's cleavage.

'Have you ever', he asked her with one of his most disarming smiles, 'considered getting yourself a toy boy?'

'Is that like one of them rampant rabbit thingies?' she had replied in her lovely West Country burr. 'Does it need batteries? 'Cos I can't be doing with something you can't plug into the mains . . .' and as Dion had almost fallen off his chair, she had winked at Theo and escaped to the other end of the bar to serve the rowing team, who had just turned in in high spirits, having finally beaten their arch enemies at Polporth.

Suze and Geoffrey arrived just after them, and there was just time for swift introductions before the jazz band took their seats on the other side of the room.

They were actually really good.

They were also really old.

They played a fantastic set of old classics for an hour before needing a break, at the end of which the pianist and the drummer were asleep in a corner propped against each other like bookends, with Marianne trying to wake them up for the second half.

'Do you think they're actually still alive?' Suze queried, fighting the urge to hold a mirror over their mouths.

Theo laughed guiltily.

'Just. Not sure they'll survive for an encore, though.'

Marianne had managed to rouse the drummer, the pianist snored on regardless.

'We can't carry on without our piano player.' The trumpeter shook his wizened head.

'You've got another hour to play, I've paid you already.' Marianne crossed her arms over her magnificent bosom.

The rowing team, full of cider and getting restless, began to slow clap and chant.

'Why are we waiting?' they chorused.

'We can't keep time without Ernie,' the trumpeter insisted. 'Even old Eric on the drums as to follow im since he had is grommits done.'

'Well, we're gonna av chaos in ere if you don't get back up and play,' Marianne insisted.

They stared at each other.

An impasse.

'Maybe if the rowing team do riot it'll wake the pianist back up.' Suze, who was also a little too high on cider, couldn't control her laughter.

'Or kill him off completely,' Theo snorted and fell on Suze's shoulder.

Geoffrey stood up, the calm in a stormy beer mug.

'Well, if it would help get everyone out of a pickle, I do play a little piano myself,' he offered quietly.

The trumpeter looked at him hopefully.

'Do you know Count Basie?' he asked.

'Is he any relation to Count Dracula?' Suze replied and the pair of them finally exploded with laughter.

*

'Well, I've always known he's good with his hands, but I never knew how good!' Suze exclaimed in amazement as Geoffrey once again proved that when he said he knew a little of something, he always turned out to be an absolute virtuoso.

'He's amazing.' Theo nodded, awestruck as his fingers flew skilfully across the keyboard.

'Just amazing . . .' Suze sighed. 'I could watch him all night.'

All night, however, turned out to be another five seconds, as her attention was torn from the sight of her beloved Geoffrey with the fingers of fire, to the man who had just strolled into the pub.

'Who', was all she managed to force out of her open mouth, 'is that?'

'Felix,' Theo replied with a wry smile.

'*That*'s Felix? I could almost be struck speechless at the sight of him, and you know me, Theo, Suze is never, ever lost for words. Oh my word, Thee, he's almost as good-looking as Geoffrey, and half the age.'

'Close your mouth, Suze, you're drooling, and you're practically married to a man who is practically my adopted dad.'

'True. Doesn't stop me looking.'

'True again, I suppose.'

'And it also doesn't stop me sizing him up for *you*.'

'Oh no, I don't think I want to go back there, Suze. He's not exactly relationship material.'

'Do you want a relationship at the moment?'

'Oh yes.' Theo nodded emphatically. 'I may not miss Michael, but I do miss having someone to cuddle up with.'

'You have Dill.'

'I know . . .' Theo beamed and then hiccupped loudly. 'I'm so lucky, I love Dill, he's gorgeous, if he was a man, I'd marry him, if that doesn't sound weird. I think I want to make myself puke . . .'

'Don't worry, I know what you mean . . .'

'So glad, I actually think "adopt" him would be a better word. He's my baby. My son. My son Dill the dog,' she added, and they both started to giggle.

'Do you think we've had a little bit too much to drink?'

'Probably.'

'Should we make this our last?'

They both looked down at their glasses and then back up at each other.

'Nah!' they chorused together, and then fell on each other's shoulders again.

'So OK, you want a relationship, but there's nothing to stop you just "cuddling up" with Felix in the meantime,' Suze whispered in her ear, as he waved and motioned with his hands that he was in the chair for drinks.

'I think what I'm trying to say is "why not?". Life's not always about waiting for Mr Right, Theo. Why not have a bit of fun with Mr Fuckable, you're single and sexy, he's single and so hot he could burn asbestos; who says that a relationship can't start with the sex and then work its way into the rest of it . . .'

'Because I know him, I know what he's like . . . even if it did somehow segue from sex to serious, I couldn't be with him again full time, it's too exhausting.'

'You haven't seen him for years, Thee, he might have changed.'

'Yeah, he's probably got worse . . . anyway, why are you so keen . . .'

Suze pulled a 'duh stupid' face.

'Just look at him, Theo. He's gorgeous, actually, change that to delicious. He is *deeeelicious*. Every woman in here from fourteen to eighty-four is watching him instead of the band, fantasising about taking him home and . . .' Suze stopped talking and did a very good impression of Hannibal Lector verbalising an overwhelming desire for fava beans and Chianti. '. . . have a fling,' she finally managed to say. 'That's it, my little sex-starved friend, have a fling.'

'Have a fling?'

'Yeah, get some good old-fashioned, no-strings sex.'

'But he thinks he's God's gift to women.'

'That's because he probably is. Look at him, Thee. If that isn't a sweet little present from the man upstairs, then I don't know what is.'

The two old ladies at the next table, one of whom was a very lipsticked Nessa Tregail, had stopped listening to the band and were listening to them instead.

Suze gave them a look and leaned in closer.

'Tell me truthfully, is Felix a . . . um . . . a good *musician*?'

'He has a very fine . . . um . . . instrument' Theo grinned.

'And does he know how to play it?'

'He is a veritable virtuoso.'

'And do you have an unfinished symphony?'

'Not so much that, but my strings are getting a bit rusty from disuse.'

'They could do with a good pluck?'

'A jolly good pluck, yes. In fact, I think perhaps if he offered it to me on a plate, then I might not be able to resist . . .'

At that moment Felix arrived at the table with their drinks, eyeing their flushed faces suspiciously, a curious smile curling at the corner of his mouth.

'What are you two talking about? I could see you in cahoots from the bar.'

'Music,' Suze rushed a response, holding out her hand. 'I'm Suzanne, by the way, *enchantée* . . .'

'Delighted to meet you, Suzanne.' Felix took her hand, bending to kiss it, much to Suze's laughing delight, then raised eyebrows at Theo.

'Music, eh?'

'Yes, music.' Theo nodded quickly, her face as red as her jumper.

'Making sweet, sweet music,' Suze growled in Theo's ear, and they both collapsed under the table in drunken laughter.

'Oh no . . .' Theo moaned to Suze as Felix returned to the bar to fetch the rest of the drinks and Dion, who was still stuck to Marianne like a magnet. 'Do you think he heard us?'

Suze shrugged.

'I don't know. But if you're worried about it, the best thing you can do is pretend to yourself that he didn't. And then deny everything if he says he did.'

Felix didn't say a word when he got back to the table – at least, not about the conversation he may or may not have overheard. Instead, he seemed to be on a mission to charm everyone, with drinks and jokes and tales of life in the fast lane in New York.

But when Theo went to bed that night, or rather that morning, at one a.m., merry and still dancing, to find Felix lounging unabashedly stark naked on her bed, his rather large cock balanced atop one of her best bone china dinner plates, she knew for definite that he had heard every single word.

Theo awoke with a yawn and, stretching sybaritically, found herself alone in the bed.

No Dill, was her first thought.

And then, as the memories came flooding back: no Felix.

'I can't believe you did that,' she chastised herself gently.

Her first thought had been to turf him out, plate and all, and then he had smiled at her, a self-deprecating, wicked little smile that had turned her knees to jelly.

And that had been it.

Seduced by a smile and a dinner plate and a sense of humour she had forgotten was so appealing.

It was five a.m.

Theo got out of bed, pulled on her dressing gown, and went in search.

He was upstairs in her studio.

They both were.

Dill was in his basket, chin on paws, watching Felix – slightly warily, Theo thought – as if he were a guard and Felix a wayward prisoner.

Felix, well, he was stark naked.

And painting.

He must have been there for hours, he was so covered in paint, like a tribal warrior ceremoniously prepared for war.

And she remembered that look on his face so well.

A focussed absorption as his brush flew as fast as Geoffrey's fingers had lovingly caressed the keys of the piano the night before.

And then he stopped, set the brush down at his side and smiled. A smile of pure triumph. And he looked over at Theo, and the smile widened, and without saying a word, he turned the canvas towards her.

It was a portrait of Theo.

Naked, and vulnerable, and so very, very beautiful it made her want to cry out with pleasure again.

35

Theo was woken again two hours later by a strange rumbling noise, a little like a bumble bee trapped against a window.

And then she realised that Dill was growling.

Theo had never heard Dill growl before.

For a moment she couldn't work out what the low rumbling noise actually was, and then as her eyes adjusted to the dim morning light that was filtering through the gauze curtains, she realised that it was him, nose pushed through the gap in the middle, complaining quietly yet persistently about something that he could see through the glass that he obviously didn't like.

'I think there might be something out there . . .'

Theo poked Felix, who was hogging most of the bed and ninety per cent of the duvet, but he simply groaned and rolled over, taking the final ten per cent with him, and so she slid out of bed and pulled on her dressing gown. She went over to the window and peered through the same gap in the curtains that Dill was.

'I can't see anything, Dill.' Running a reassuring hand along his back she yawned. 'Back to bed, baby . . .'

Dill eyed the bed distrustfully.

As far as he was concerned, he wasn't so sure it was big

enough for the three of them.

And then he turned back to the window and growled again. A short, sharp, warning gruff.

This time Theo saw it too.

At least, she thought she did.

It was such an odd thing to see that for a moment she thought she might have imagined it, especially as for several minutes afterwards there was nothing . . . but then, just as she was about to give up and go back to what little part of the bed she could reclaim, there it was again. A head, bobbing up above the wall like a meerkat looking out for danger.

And there again.

Hurriedly Theo pulled on yesterday's jeans and jumper and with Dill treading quietly at her heels, crept downstairs, out through the kitchen and the backyard, and quietly opened the door from the little yard into the back lane and peered up it.

There was a man standing precariously on tiptoes on an old crate, no doubt 'borrowed' from the backyard of the Boatman, looking over her garden wall.

The man had a camera slung about his neck.

He was so focussed with trying to get enough height to see into Theo's back garden that he didn't notice her and Dill tread silently up behind him.

'Good morning,' Theo said in a loud voice.

The man gave an incredibly girlie shriek, jumped, and fell backwards off the crate into the gorse hedge that marked the boundary of the lane.

Theo peered down through the undergrowth at him.

'Can I help you?' she enquired archly.

And then, to her amazement, the man, still prostrate

in the prickly hedge, lifted his camera and took a photo-
graph of her and then, rummaging in his pocket, pulled
out a dictaphone, pressed a button, and thrust it towards
her.

'As a matter of fact, you can . . . I was just wondering if
you had any comment about the fact that you're having a
very cosy bunk-up with Felix Rosenthal when his new
wife is stuck at home alone in New York with a ten-week-
old baby?'

It was all true. Everything he had denied. Everything he
had said was all press lies, rumour, speculation . . . fact.

Theo stood at the end of the bed and looked down at
the splendid sleeping form of Felix Rosenthal. In her
absence he had kicked off the duvet completely and the
entire nakedness of him was spread across her king size in
all its glorious, cheating, lying, stinking rat perfection.

As if suddenly aware of being watched, Felix opened
his eyes, stretched, yawned, saw her, smiled.

'Morning, beautiful,' he murmured.

'Fuck face,' Theo responded.

The sybaritic smile fled from his face and, grabbing the
duvet, he quickly and instinctively covered his crown
jewels.

'Theo?' he queried nervously.

'Get up, get dressed and get out of my house and out
of my life,' Theo said quietly, but each word fired like a
bullet and then, turning, she stalked from the room.

He was hopping his way into his trousers and following
her before she hit the bottom of the stairs.

'Theo?'

Theo continued through the sitting room, stopped in

the hallway, paused for a moment, unclenched her balled fists.

'Theo,' he said again, still following, now conciliatory.

She turned around to face him.

'You've been lying your arse off to me, you bastard.'

At least he had the grace not to try and deny it. To look guilty and then look down at his feet because he couldn't look her in the face.

'I haven't painted for months. I did my best work when I was with you . . . You know me, Theo.'

'No, I don't. I don't know you, Felix, I don't know you at all. I haven't seen you in lord knows how many years and you turn up on my doorstep in the middle of the night with your suitcase full of lies and—'

'Six,' he said.

'What!?' she snapped, blinking rapidly at him, interrupted mid-rant.

'Six years; we haven't seen each other for six years, six long drought-filled years. I know what I did might seem wrong to you, but can't you see I had to do it, Thee, for the sake of my career, for the sake of my sanity? You've saved my life, Theodora English, you were my only hope and it worked, the painting I did of you is the best thing I've ever done . . . I'm back, Theo, I'm back.'

Theo looked at him in astonishment.

'Do you know, I was totally wrong, Felix, I do know you . . .'

Sensing a reprieve, he nodded a furious agreement and attempted a smile, a smile that was wiped from his face as her brow knitted into an even deeper frown. 'And the reason I know you is because you haven't bloody changed. When we were together it was all about you, and it still is.

Did you ever stop to think about how what you were doing would affect me? No, of course you bloody didn't. Or your wife, yeah, how about her? What about your wife, Felix!'

He didn't have an answer.

Of course he didn't have an answer because he hadn't thought about her, and he hadn't thought about his wife; he'd just thought about himself and what he thought he needed to make his life better, regardless of what it would do to anyone else.

He was like the damaged painting still leaning against the hall wall behind her.

Beautiful, full of talent, but essentially flawed.

Theo felt herself fill with a white-hot anger, not so much for herself but for the poor woman sitting at home in New York with a newborn and her husband's infidelities making headlines.

'What are you like? Artist's block? Can't paint? I know, let's go back to England for a bunk-up with Theo, a bloody good retro shag will shift that bloody artistic block, knock it down like a bulldozer through bricks! You're a selfish, no-good, lying, scheming two-timing prick!'

And with that she picked up the damaged painting and brought it down very firmly over his head.

For a moment he just stood there.

And then he burst out laughing.

'I've been framed, your honour,' he said in mockney, and then his long eyelashes fluttered downwards as he stared at the floor in contrition.

'I'm an arsehole, aren't I?'

'You said it,' Theo responded sourly, arms crossed.

'Does this mean I'm not staying the night?'

'Out.'

'You don't mean it.'

'Get out, Felix.'

And with that she pulled open the front door and pushed him through it. For a moment, Felix stood on the doorstep, still imprisoned in the painting. And then the flashbulbs began to pop. It wasn't just the back garden that had been invaded by paparazzi. The tiny front garden was full of them clambering at him.

'Felix! Felix! Felix!'

But still he didn't budge.

'Piss off, Felix,' Theo shrieked as he jammed his foot in the door the moment she tried to close it against the rain of intrusion.

'Not without my painting.'

'What!'

'I want my painting. If you don't let me take my painting, I'm going to stay here and—'

Nobody found out what Felix would do if she didn't let him have the painting, because Theo finally managed to get his foot out of the door and slammed it hard.

Two minutes later, Felix heard a window open above his head. He looked up just in time to see a furious Theo hurl the painting out.

His arms were still pinned by the wooden frame over which was stretched the ruined canvas of Dudley Anstell's fat wife.

'A grand to whoever catches that!' he yelled.

Miraculously, one of the paps did a flying tackle and caught the sides of the canvas just before it hit the ground.

He brought it over to a just-escaped Felix, and handed it over with an expectant grin.

Felix looked at him scathingly.

'In your dreams, moron.'

And clutching the painting of *Theodora in the Nude*, Felix set off at a run down the hill towards the ferry, the whole flock of them running after him, flashbulbs popping like fireworks on bonfire night.

This time Theo really thought she might cry.

Not because she was upset that Felix had turned out to be a bastard after all, but because she had given him the chance not to be when she knew full well what he was like. She had been an idiot. A trusting idiot.

She also felt inordinately guilty. Albeit unwittingly, she was now, or at least had been for one night, the 'other' woman. Theo didn't do that. Other women's men. It wasn't her style. But she didn't cry.

Instead, she did her usual and lost her guilt in a frenzy of work, trying to paint a replacement of the painting last seen being worn by Fuck Face Felix.

It was hard work. Theo tended not to revisit the same painting twice, but that was the thing with commission work; if someone wanted something specific, then they weren't going to be fobbed off with something else. Dudley Anstell had asked for a painting of his wife, so he wasn't going to be fobbed off with one of Dill on the beach, or Geoffrey asleep in a deck chair in the garden.

It was here that Geoffrey, Suze and Poppy found her in the garden, feverishly daubing away at Mrs Anstell's fourth chin whilst Dill lay at her feet with his chin on a bone and watched her.

'You busy?' Suze asked, hopping from foot to foot. 'Only Geoffrey has something for you.'

Theo put down her paintbrush and looked at her friends.

Suze was grinning from ear to ear as Geoffrey stepped forward somewhat coyly. He was carrying something large, currently hidden under an old flowered sheet.

As a proud Suze did a game show girl-style flourish, he placed it in front of Theo, and pulled the sheet off to reveal a polished wooden structure.

Exceptionally well made, beautifully finished.

The only problem, and not really a minor one, when you're trying to think of the right words to thank someone, was that Theo really didn't know, exactly, what she was supposed to be thanking Geoffrey for.

'It's beautiful . . .' Theo said truthfully, but there was no missing the confused expression on her face.

'She hasn't got a clue what it is!' Suze grinned.

'That's true,' Theo smiled apologetically, 'but it *is* beautiful, whatever it may be.'

'An explanation or a demonstration?' Geoffrey said cryptically to Suze.

'Oh, demonstration, I think.' Suze nodded eagerly. 'And then she'll be able to see the true beauty of it.'

It was obviously far lighter than it looked as Geoffrey lifted it with ease and began to walk away, but to her surprise Geoffrey bypassed the cottage and, going straight to her car instead, opened the boot.

Dill immediately jumped in.

'Out of the way, Dilly boy, Uncle Geoffrey can hardly demonstrate to Mum with you in the way, young man.' With kind hands Geoffrey gently shooed Dill out of the car, and placed the wooden structure inside instead. It fitted Theo's boot almost perfectly. Geoffrey stepped back and, unusually for him, did the same kind of 'ta da' flourish with his hands that Suze had done.

Theo still looked so pleased and yet so confused that Suze burst out laughing again.

'She's still none the wiser,' Suze cackled with laughter.

'I'm still none the wiser.' Theo nodded self-deprecatingly.

'It's a rack for your paintings – see, you open this up and slot them in lengthways, the bars move across to hold them in place no matter what size they are. Ergo, no more damaged canvasses.'

'Oh wow, that's amazing.' Theo hugged him in delight, 'Geoffrey, you are so clever, thank you so much.'

'See, he's not just a pretty face,' Suze said proudly, squeezing his arm.

'And if you want me to take a look at the damaged painting I might be able to do something to save it? I was an art history major when I was at Cambridge, spent one summer working in a restorer's, might be able to help, you never know.'

Theo's face was a picture in itself, not simply because Geoffrey had just casually dropped in another piece of amazing information about his previous life, but because of how damaged that particular painting now was.

'It's a lovely offer, G,' she replied, biting her bottom lip, 'but it's just, well, I really think the painting's beyond repair now . . .'

'But it was only a little tear . . .' Suze frowned in puzzlement.

'*Was* being the operative word.'

'What's happened to it, Thee?'

'Last seen being worn as a necklace by Felix Rosenthal.' Theo shrugged.

Suze's eyes widened in concern.

'That painting was worth a thousand pounds to you, Theo.'

'It was worth it,' Theo responded emphatically.

'And what exactly did he do to deserve that?' Her face had gone from loved-up to livid.

'Well, it's a sordid story. Fancy a cup of coffee and cream cake to go with it?'

The cream cake was not sweetener enough; if possible, Suze was even crosser at the news than Theo had been.

'I'm going to murder him.'

'You know, I really do think you and Imelda are non-identical twins separated at birth.' Theo laughed and shook her head. 'Thanks for the thought, Suze, but you don't need to murder him, it's my own fault; I know exactly what he's like and I still . . . well, you know . . .'

'Sure, but I encouraged you, I feel partly to blame.'

'And so you should.' Theo was glad that she now felt strong enough to tease Suze about it. 'I only sleep with people on your say so, you know . . .'

'Oh God, why on earth did I egg you on to shag the little shit?' Suze wailed, dropping her head in her hands.

'Suze, if you told me to go and throw myself in the harbour, do you think I would?'

'Maybe if you were Imelda, or on fire . . .' Suze smiled weakly up at her through splayed fingers.

'Exactly; I'd have to have my own good reasons for doing it, as well. Yes, you may have pointed out that Felix was so fit that I should get my fix while I could, but it was I who decided to go ahead and do just that. What you've forgotten is that you also very sensibly told me to go into anything with my eyes well and truly open, and my heart ready for the inevitable fall . . .'

'Yeah, a fall, not a bloody great boot up the backside.'

'I'll survive, Suze.'

'You sure . . . ?' Suze asked her, her voice heavy with concern.

'Of course. You see, someone can only break your heart if you actually give it to them to play with in the first place . . .'

36

There was a little courtyard garden to the rear of the flat above the newsagent's, on the same level as the flat, as the entire property was built on a slope.

It was a beautiful Sunday afternoon and with the shop closed, Geoffrey, Suze and Poppy were making the most of the spring sunshine.

Geoffrey had been up since six stock-taking – a job the anticipation of which would once have had him running for the hills, but today it had given him a quiet satisfaction to complete. He had his feet up in a deckchair with Poppy stretched out upon his lap and legs.

Suze was gardening.

Geoffrey watched her tending the marigolds in her flower boxes.

She was dressed in denim shorts, a mud-smeared T-shirt and red wellington boots, her hair tied back into a haphazard ponytail, tendrils escaping on to her face so that she kept having to pause and push them out of her eyes.

Suze the utter scruff-pot.

It was amazing, he thought, how much his life had changed in just a few short months. He had shunned convention for much of his adult life. But just because he chose to live with nothing did not mean that he had nothing. But everything that he did have was nothing in comparison to what he had found, here in this quirky little village.

Fate had brought him here.

First to Port Ruan, and then to Theo. Lovely Theo, oh how he wanted to catch that philandering ratbag Felix by the scruff of the neck and boot him into the harbour.

He shook his head. Theo had insisted she was fine, and he should let it lie. It had just been such a long time since he had cared enough about anyone to worry so much about them. And Theo was like a daughter to him now. Lovely Theo who had brought him to Suze.

He had often pondered the meaning of life. The life that he had led had given him much time for thought and contemplation. He had decided eventually that the meaning of life was different for every person on the planet, and that rather than looking for the meaning of life in its entirety, he should be asking what was the meaning of life for him.

And now, looking at Suze, he realised that perhaps he had found his answer.

'Feeling his eyes upon her, Suze looked across at him and smiled, a tender smile, full of love that flooded her eyes as well as her face.

How lucky am I, Geoffrey thought, so strongly that for a moment he almost thought that he had said it out loud.

And then Suze turned back to her boxes, and he realised that he hadn't . . . but perhaps he should have done.

'Suzanne?' he called softly.

'Yes?' She looked up and as she did so the golden rays of the evening sun lit her face.

He thought she had never looked so beautiful.

For a moment he caught his breath and then as he exhaled again the words came tumbling out so easily.

'Will you marry me?'

'Theo, you need to let go now.'

Theo didn't let go. If anything, she clung on harder.

'Theo, my train's here. If I miss my train, I miss my flight.'

Theo still hung on to her little brother. Even Dill had his front paws on Dion's feet and his hairy arse on Dion's rucksack. He had fallen in love with Dion, his new bestest play buddie other than Poppy, who still hid from him, but hey, hide and seek was fun, and he was as reluctant to see Dion leave as Theo was.

'I would have thought you'd be glad to see the back of me after what happened,' Dio said, gently disentangling himself from his sister's marathon hug.

'It wasn't your fault.'

'I'm the one that brought Felix back with me.'

'You hitched a lift, he did the bringing, and the bright side is, if he hadn't, I wouldn't have got the best birthday present ever.'

Dion laughed softly.

'You always look on the bright side, don't you? I love you, sis. You're the best, you know that. Oh, and thanks for the ticket back too; I'm really sorry about that – you know me, pockets always empty. Hope I haven't left you short.'

'Yeah, well, don't worry about that, I dipped into Dad's pension fund.'

'His what?'

'Never mind. Just don't worry about it, OK? I can afford it. In fact, any time you want to come back and see me, let me know; I think the pension fund can manage another flight or two, as long as you don't mind flying cargo.'

It had taken her two seconds to decide to finally put the money in the cigar box to good use once they realised that Felix's mad dash for Heathrow had left Dion without his lift back to America. She had been saving the money for a reason. Dion had reported that her father was doing just fine. He had sent her the money to make her happy . . . and what could make her happier than seeing her family?

'You take care of yourself, OK?' He dropped a kiss on the crown of her head.

'Yeah, and you,' she called after him as he shifted his rucksack from under Dill and sprinted for the train. 'And if you just happen to bump into Felix again . . .'

'I know, I'll make sure I bump a damn sight harder.' Dion grinned.

Jonas emerged from a long day in the workshop to see tiny Blix staggering up his driveway carrying something huge.

He rushed to help her but she waved him away.

'No, no, I can manage it myself, I don't want you to see it yet. Just open the door for your poor old Farmor, there's a good boy, Jonas.'

He knew Blix well enough not to argue, so he simply opened the door and watched as she carried the large sheet-covered object into his sitting room, where Natalie was on the sofa flicking through a wedding magazine.

'What is that?' she asked, looking first at Blix and then at the thing she had deposited on the carpet.

Blix turned to Jonas, her bright blue eyes shining with excitement.

'I know it is a few weeks too early, but it came today and I could not wait . . . it is your wedding present, Jonas. I am so excited for you to see it, I have to give it to you now.'

'A wedding present.'

'*Ja.* Yes. I say to myself what can I get for Jonas that is as much an investment as a marriage should be? Savings, pah too boring, antiques, no, you make better things yourself than I ever see in an antiques shop, and then I think, ah yes, my sonson is just like his father, he appreciates good art. And so I bought you a painting by a famous artist everyone is talking about. You can look at it and love it, and it will be like your own little bank vault hanging on the wall. A nest egg for your future, if you ever need it. A joy to own, if you don't. And it is a very rare piece. I've had my ear to the ground for so long that I've been looking for something by this man, but nothing, for many months, and then suddenly this turns up at a gallery near to Heathrow, such a strange place for it to be, but it is run by someone I know . . .'

'Of course it is.' Jonas smiled, his mouth turning up at one corner.

'. . . and he called me this morning and said, "Blix, I have one for you, and it is such a strange tale, the man himself dropped it here on his way back to America, said he couldn't fit "the fucking thing" in the plane's overhead locker, and to forward him a cheque . . . so odd, but so good, because finally I have a superb Felix Rosenthal. And so I rushed to see . . . and it could not be more perfect, like it was meant to be for you, you'll see why in a minute. And so I snapped it up for you, for my Jonas. Happy Wedding, Sonson.' And she pulled off the sheet.

'It's a naked woman,' Natalie stated the obvious.

Blix turned her bright blue-eyed gaze to her soon-to-be daughter-in-law.

'I think I bought it also because it actually reminded me a little of you, Natalie, only far more, now what is the English word for "*vek*", Jonas?'

Jonas knew that it had many different meanings.

But looking at the painting he knew the meaning that his grandmother was searching for.

She did indeed look a little like Natalie, the same silken shining hair with a hint of red in the dark tresses, the same creamy complexion and fine turn of features, but her beauty was infinitely softer, gentler, sweeter, somehow.

It was truly a stunning painting, but its true beauty lay not only in the skill of its creator but also in the look captured in those eyes, a look that was wistful, vulnerable, haunting, almost.

'It's simply beautiful, Farmor, thank you so much.'

'I knew you would like it,' Blix gently squeezed his arm as he bent to place a gentle kiss on her downy cheek, 'because your father would have done.' She reached up and patted his cheek. 'And you are so much like your father . . . such a good man, I am very proud of you, and I so hope that you are going to make a happy marriage, a happy life together . . . I really—'

Natalie, who had been staring at the painting transfixed ever since Blix had mentioned a comparison, suddenly butted in.

'Fatter,' she announced. 'It looks like me, but fatter.'

N atalie's hen night had been a sedate affair.
   Dinner with her sisters, some friends from work,
and Clementine, at one of the best restaurants in
Dorchester.

They had drunk little, eaten even less, and spent the
whole evening discussing all things wedding day, from
flowers and favours to seating and eating.

She didn't even have a hangover the following
morning.

Which left her with a clear mind to quiz Nick about his
plans for the stag weekend he was organising for Jonas
when he called in with the Sunday papers for breakfast
the following morning.

'Where are you taking him?'

'Um . . . Natalie, this is Jonas's stag do.'

'Yes, and?'

'*And* . . .' Wilko emphasised the same word that
she had, just as belligerently, 'the word *stag* denotes
male . . .'

She continued to stare at him, hands on hips.

'. . . and groom . . .'

The stare remained.

'. . . not *fe*male and bride. So really, you have no right

to ask that question. And I certainly have no intention of answering it.'

They stared at each other for a moment, and then Natalie shrugged, a dismissive gesture.

'Well, if you want to be like that about it. So ... *childish*. Then again, I probably shouldn't expect anything less from you really, Nicholas.'

'I'm glad you don't expect anything from me, Natalie. Because that's about as much as you deserve to get.' And he infuriated her even more by smiling sweetly at her.

Unbeknownst to them, Jonas had watched this exchange from the kitchen doorway.

Honestly, they were like bickering children.

So much for his view that maybe, just maybe, they were turning a corner.

He really wished that they could get on, but it had been like this from when they first met.

He had never had a girlfriend before whom Wilko had been so inordinately *un*fond of. But when he had tried to tackle the situation by a heart-to-heart with both individually it had got him nowhere.

Natalie had just raved on about what an immature, ignorant, insensitive idiot he was, and Wilko's only response had been a blunt 'she doesn't deserve you', a statement upon which he wouldn't elaborate.

Sometimes he caught them both giving each other severe evils.

Sometimes he caught them both chatting and laughing like drains.

Although, when he thought about it, it was usually when they'd had a few drinks.

To be honest, when they'd had a few drinks, Natalie

took the stick out of her arse, and Wilko didn't try and beat her with it.

Natalie had been horrified when she found out that he was organising the stag do. To be honest, even Jonas was a little concerned, but as Wilko was best man it came with the territory. Still, visions of strip clubs and worse had been haunting him, too, for the last few weeks, so much so that, despite Natalie's aborted attempt at infiltration, he felt the need to ask him the same question.

'Where are we going, Wilks?' he asked when they were back in the workshop the following morning.

'It's a surprise.'

'I know.'

'So why ask? Surely surprise says it all. Surprise . . . i.e., you don't know until we get there.'

'I'm not going to end up tied naked to the back of a polar bear in the middle of the Antarctic, am I?'

'Are there polar bears in the Antarctic?'

'Haven't got a clue.'

'Me neither.'

'Guess I'm safe from the polar bears, then.'

'Guess you are.'

'Camel in the Gobi?'

'Are there camels in the Gobi?'

'Would have thought so.'

Wilko mused for a moment.

'Nope. Not naked on a camel.'

'Naked somewhere?'

'Well, the somewhere is a definite.'

'And the naked?'

'Well, the way you're going on about it, it sounds to me like that's how you want to be, so I'm happy to oblige.'

Jonas narrowed his eyes and shook his head, but couldn't help smiling.

'Take my word for it, Nicholas . . .'

'Oooh, it's Nicholas now, I'm in trouble . . . quick, help me, Eds.' Wilko grinned, pretending to step backwards away from him, and holding up Eddie in front of him in self-defence.

'Take my word for it, Nicholas . . .' Jonas repeated firmly, as Eddie did nothing fiercer than lick Jonas on the chin. 'It is most definitely NOT what I want. No tied to anything, no naked unless I'm in a bathroom, alone, and stepping into the shower, ready to get washed and dressed to go somewhere decent and fun, that isn't full of drunken idiots and half-naked women, OK?'

His friend pretended to think about this request for a while.

'What do you think, Ready Steady Eddie?' he asked the tail-wagging dog.

And then he grinned and nodded.

'Sure, thing Joan Arse. Whatever you want.'

'Whatever I want? I want to know where we're going.'

'And I want to get naked with Scarlett Johansson. We can't always get everything we want in life, can we?'

Jonas sighed and shook his head, but his eyes were still full of mirth.

'Then I guess I'll have to wait and see.'

'I guess you will, my friend, I guess you will.'

Jonas woke to find that he was wearing something decidedly weird. Tight fitting. Restrictive. *Rubber*. What the hell had they done to him?

He also couldn't see.

Something was tied around his eyes.

He put a hand up, amazed that his arm actually squeaked when he did so, and realised that what was tied around his eyes was his own scarf.

The minibus jerked to a halt just as another hand reached out and stopped him pulling the scarf down.

'Two minutes,' said Wilko's voice, bubbling with laughter. 'Trust me, OK?'

And with that, he pulled him to his feet and guided him out of the minibus and into the fresh air. And then he pulled down the scarf.

Jonas inhaled and then exhaled in sheer amazement.

'This is absolutely bloody amazing!' he roared in delight.

He was standing on the edge of a wide sweep of beach with the wind in his hair and the salt on his lips. The sun was making the crests of the ocean sparkle like frost. The sky and the sea were equal parts of blue that melted to jade where they clashed together.

It was beautiful.

It was also most definitely not a strip club.

'This is not what I was expecting.' Jonas grinned at his friend.

'I know. Told you it was a surprise.'

'Well, you were right, this is a genuine surprise . . .'

'A good one?'

'A bloody brilliant one!' Jonas grinned as ten of his friends went roaring past him towards the sea. Grabbing the surfboard Wilko was holding out to him, he pulled up the zip on his wetsuit and joined the charge down to the ocean.

*

The weekend hadn't actually started out so wonderfully.

Twelve men and a minibus was the launching point to the long weekend that had been allocated for Jonas's stag do. Thursday night through to Monday morning. Four long days of beer and debauchery, as Wilko had put it when the minibus pulled up outside Otter Cottage, and everyone had fallen out clutching cans of beer and wearing Elvis outfits.

'Not fancy dress,' Jonas had groaned.

'Yes, fancy dress.' Declan had nodded, smiling evilly. 'You're Priscilla to our Elvis.'

'Priscilla?' Jonas groaned, images of being stuffed into a little sixties dress and knee-high boots running screaming through his head.

'Yeah . . .' and with a flourish, they produced a feathered headdress, a sequinned leotard, and the highest glittery heels Jonas had ever seen – 'Priscilla, Queen of the Desert!'

Fortunately, it had just been a joke.

He had been allowed to stay in the moleskin jeans and Paul Smith shirt that he had originally dressed in.

Unfortunately, the visions of strip clubs weren't nightmares, they were premonitions.

At midnight, rather the worse for wear, he found himself propped up outside Divalution, a lap-dancing club in Dorchester where, if rumours circulating were true, you could get everything from a bottle of Bolly to a blow job if you had enough fifties in your wallet.

And then, just as he was trying to get his drink-fuddled brain to think of an excuse not to go into what was quite possibly the tackiest bar in England, Declan, who, he only just realised, had disappeared earlier in the evening, had screeched to a halt beside them in a minibus, and with a cheer he had been picked up and bundled inside of it.

Full of beer, he had slept all the way to wherever it was they were going, until he woke up and there they were.

Surf up turned to surf over.

Breakfast on the beach was the next order of the day.

Damp and happy, dressed but dishevelled and hair full of sticky salt, Jonas lay back on a tartan rug and smiled up at the sunshine.

It was so early in the morning, he had expected that they would be the only ones here, but the water was full of other surfers enjoying the rip.

He heard the sound of a dog barking.

As he always did now, he looked around.

There was a girl walking some way in the distance. The dog was with her, bounding through the waves like a kangaroo, running away and then back to her, away and then back to her, just as Dylan used to do when Jonas took him to the beach.

Dylan would have loved it here.

For the thousandth time, Jonas wondered where he was, was he safe, was he happy, would he ever find him?

'Are those tears in his eyes?' Declan, who had abstained from the beer the previous night so that he could drive them, and was now making up for it by having a Bud with his bacon sandwiches, turned to him teasingly.

Jonas quickly wiped his eyes on the edge of his scarf and turned to face them with a smile.

'It's just sunk in that he's getting married in two weeks.' Wilko, who had also seen the dog in the distance, laughed along with the others, but the warm grip of his hand on Jonas's arm belied the joke.

'Yeah, I'd be crying, too, if it were me.' Woody grinned.

'It's the wind, guys,' Jonas lied, 'making my eyes water.'

'Getting in the marital grip of Natalie Palmer, that would make my eyes bloody water!'

'There's only one thing to do to alleviate the pain.'

'Pub!!!'

The cry was mutual, and Jonas was lifted up by several pairs of hands and carried like a surfboard back to the car park.

'Er guuuysss . . .' Jonas asked, his voice vibrating as they manhandled him back into the minibus, 'pub . . . great . . . but can I just ask one question? Where the *hell* are we?'

'Right, now you've had your walk, I've just got to deliver my paintings to Coral, and then we can go home. That's if she's open yet . . .' Theo looked at her watch; it was eight-thirty. The Eve and Adam Gallery was due to open at nine, but she knew that Laura, the only reliable person in there, was on holiday, and Coral's hours could be pretty erratic, depending on how she had spent her evening the night before.

'Do you fancy some breakfast, first, Dilly baby? Give Auntie Coral time to stagger in?'

Dill's tail thumped in response.

She had come prepared. St Ives was thirty odd miles from Port Ruan and so Theo had determined to make it into a day out.

She had made a picnic and took the basket and a rug from the boot of her car and carried them out on to the sand. Familiar with the ritual of 'the picnic', Dill waited patiently until Theo had spread the rug and opened the basket, and took his place on the tartan expectantly.

'Pork pie, pasty, or let me see . . . some nice healthy grilled chicken?' Theo asked him with a grin, waving the grilled chicken option at him temptingly, but he still swerved it and went for the pasty.

'OK, just for a treat, don't want you getting as porkie as your mum now, do we?'

After they had eaten, Theo lay back in the sunshine, eyes only half-closed so that she could keep a watch on Dill as he burnt off the pasty by galloping down to the water's edge and back so many times he should by rights have made himself thoroughly dizzy.

After about ten minutes of mad running, she felt him thump back down on the rug beside her, tail wagging so hard it was smacking her in the face.

She opened her eyes to see that he had something in his mouth.

'What have you got there, Dill?'

It was a scarf.

Someone had dropped it on the beach.

'Oh Dill, you don't know where it's been; leave it, Dill . . . leave it . . .'

Dill sat with the scarf clamped firmly in his mouth. Leave it was obviously his last intention.

'We've got to go, Dill, you don't really want to take that with you, do you?'

His answer was to sit and watch Theo clear up the picnic and fold up the rug, with the scarf still firmly in his mouth, and then to follow her to the car with it.

Theo tried again when they got there.

'Drop, Dill. Leave it.'

He wagged his tail as if in apology, but drop it he didn't.

She peered closer.

It was clean, and it smelt pretty good, to be honest, better than Dill, who was so covered in sand she could have rubbed down the skirting boards of Otter Cottage with him.

'Oh, OK, if you like it that much, bring it with you.'

Dill hopped straight into the back seat of the car.

Today Coral's hair was brighter than the sunshine. She had gone from marmalade to a brilliant orange that clashed violently but fabulously with her fuchsia kaftan and bright-red lipstick. She also smelt of oranges, oranges and cinnamon. If Theo hadn't already had breakfast it would have made her hungry.

'Oh, Theo, they're great. Absolutely great,' she exclaimed as she worked her way through the rack that Geoffrey had made. 'Oh, and look at this; we have Lantic Bay finished at last . . . well, it was worth the wait, Theo, it's gorgeous, and who's this on the beach? Is that Dill? Oh yes, it's Dill on the beach. How precious!' She beamed up at Theo. 'We really must get this one hung straightaway. Come and see, I have a little area here just for you now, your own corner, a Theo corner in the Eve and Adam.'

She excitedly lead Theo to a prominent position near the door.

'This is you,' she announced, pointing to the biog on the wall in the middle of the empty space that awaited the paintings she had just delivered.

'Theo English is twenty-seven and lives on the south coast of Cornwall. She is establishing an excellent reputation as a landscape artist and also produces some rarer portraiture pieces. She exhibits in London and we are proud and delighted to show her exquisite oils and watercolours at the Eve and Adam.'

Theo flushed with embarrassment.

'That's so nice, Coral, thank you.'

'No more than you deserve, darling. Now where's my

favourite boy? My little ones have sent him a present.' She
went back to the reception desk and rummaged behind it
then presented Dylan with a huge hide bone. 'Now do you
have to rush back, or do you fancy hanging around to keep
old Coral company today whilst little Laura's not here?'

Theo smiled apologetically.

'I'd love to, Coral, honestly, but I promised I'd help out
a very dear friend today, and I really can't let him down.
Another time, though . . .'

'Oh definitely. We can have a party.'

'A party?'

'Oh yes. We can celebrate your painting selling.' She
pointed to Lantic Bay, 'It's so wonderful, Theo, someone's
bound to snap it up straight away.'

I t had been a mad day, followed by a mad night, and the pub was followed by a mad dash to find the large cottage near the beach that Wilko had rented for them. The cottage was followed by the pub, which was followed by a bar, by a bar, by a bar, by some food, lord knew what, none of them could remember, then another bar, then a club, and then Jonas somehow managed to slip away as Declan demanded tequila. He had joined the guys on tequila before; it had not been a pretty sight, and the pain the following morning had been enough for him to make the vow of 'never again'; a vow that he would actually keep.

Despite the night before, Jonas was up early the following morning woken by the sun streaming through the window and stroking his face.

He was the only one.

Everyone else was dead to the world, all sleeping off their hangovers, in various states of undress, disarray, and decomposition, from the smell of them.

He showered and pulled on some clean clothes.

The door to Wilko's room was open a couple of inches. As he passed on his way downstairs, Jonas could see his friend, splayed face down, butt naked, on top of the duvet, dead to the world, the only sign of life his long slumbering slightly snoring breaths slightly rippling the fabric.

Smiling to himself, about to move on, the lure of what was obviously a gorgeous day calling him outside, Jonas stepped forward, only for his eyes to catch sight of something that made him instantly step back and look inside the room again.

Naked Wilko (and Jonas had seen naked Wilko far more times than he would really have liked) suddenly looked slightly different.

Was that a tattoo?

Feeling a little weird for getting in close to peer at his best friend's arse, Jonas took a couple of steps nearer to get a better look.

'Bloody hell, Wilks,' he rasped in hushed tones so as not to wake him, 'what have you done?'

It was indeed a tattoo.

One word and one word only, emblazoned in bold black, but with that sore-looking red halo that usually came with needle-assaulted flesh. It was long enough to cut across the entirety of his left arse cheek, and big enough, Jonas suspected, to join the ranks of the Great Wall of China in being one of the few earthly objects that could be seen from space.

'Who would have thought it?' Jonas, reading the word again to make sure he hadn't got it wrong, began to chuckle to himself, then backing out of the room, he quietly closed the door.

He just hoped Wilko's head ached enough for him not to notice the pain in the arse. That way he might not realise what he had done for a very long time.

There were slightly more signs of life downstairs.

Declan was in the kitchen. More nakedness assaulting Jonas's eyes, as he had chosen to head for the fridge and some much-needed orange juice in nothing but a pair of socks.

Declan was the only one who almost managed to go with him, only to get to the point where, when he bent to pull on his shoes, he turned an amazing shade of Incredible Hulk green, and thundered for the bathroom.

And so it was that Jonas ventured out into a Saturday morning St Ives on his own.

The Dorset coast was stunning, but he'd always had a soft spot for Cornwall because that's where his maternal family were originally from. The summer after they'd moved to England, his mother had taken him to Cornwall for two weeks on a tour of his family history.

She had shown him the house where she had grown up as a child, an old rectory on the Roseland Peninsula, sited so close to the shore that she could hear the waves breaking from her bedroom.

She took them everywhere she had taken Konrad the summer they had met.

Blix had come with them, of course, as had Tilly.

It had been one of those family times that you remember always.

A time full of many tears but also much laughter, like opening up a wound and pouring in salt, but strangely cathartic.

They had been back a couple of times since, but it was somewhere that Jonas always felt he should visit more often.

Maybe he would come back next year, with all the

women in his life, Natalie, Stella and Blix. What would that be like?

Mayhem, responded a voice in his head that sounded remarkably like Wilko's.

He had never been to St Ives before, and was struck by how beautiful it was.

He was also excited by the number of art galleries.

His father had been a keen art collector. He had several of the earlier works of Anders Zorn, a well-known Swedish artist who had painted gorgeously luminescent watercolours at the beginning of his career, and he had also been very fond of the later works of a German artist called Erich Heckel; indeed, it was Heckel's woodcuts that had first interested and inspired Jonas in working with wood himself.

As far as paintings were concerned, Jonas usually liked scenic – countryside, seascapes. And realism, he wasn't very much into abstract, although he joked with Stella that Impressionism often impressed him.

Blix's inordinately generous gift had wetted his appetite again, and he couldn't have found himself in a better place to have that appetite sated.

Gallery followed gallery. Some paintings good, some devastatingly bad. There was one painting only that made him pause. It was a watercolour of a beautiful stretch of beach.

He glanced at the biog that was attached to the wall next to the painting. '*Lantic Bay* by Theodora English'.

'Wow,' Jonas heard himself saying almost involuntarily.

'Wow,' he said it again.

The painting was beautiful, the colours so vibrant and so real you almost felt as if you could fall head first into it and you would be there, walking that beach, listening to the roll of the waves, feeling the sun beat a warm tattoo on the back of your neck.

He looked at the price tag.

It was eight hundred pounds.

A lot of money, but for something so good it felt like a bargain.

Natalie would murder him if he bought it.

They were supposed to be saving, what for, he wasn't quite sure, a plethora of things quite possibly from bread makers to BMWs, but his father had always taught him, and Blix had reminded him, that buying good art was as good as putting money in a high-interest savings account. It was an investment worth making.

He turned towards the reception desk, where a woman with bright marmalade hair, looked up, caught his enquiring gaze, and smiled broadly.

'Can I help, young man?'

His response even surprised himself.

'I want to buy one of your paintings. This one. *Lantic Bay* . . .'

'Oh goodness!' the woman with the amazing hair clapped her hands together with excitement, 'Theo will be pleased, she only dropped it off to us yesterday morning. Such a lovely girl. She's been selling steadily for the past seven years, you know, I really do think that some day soon she's going to start getting noticed by the bigwigs and our little gallery won't get a look in . . . Laura, Laura, I'm so glad you're back, my darling girl,' she cried happily as a young girl with long blond hair came through the door, 'can you take this lovely man's nasty money. He's buying Theo's *Lantic Bay*, clever boy.'

Laura came behind the desk, took off her jacket and stowed her handbag under the long curved counter. She smiled up at Jonas as he handed over his credit card.

'Are you taking it with you now or would you prefer to arrange another time to collect . . . ?'

For a moment he imagined trying to get it home safely in the chaos that was the minibus.

'Or we can send it to you, if that would suit you better,' she added as he hesitated.

'That would be better.' He nodded thankfully.

'No problem at all, we'll just need your address . . .'

The orange-haired lady was still hovering.

'I think you're making a jolly good investment, young man. I guarantee you in a year's time that painting will be worth twice what you're paying for it today, but I'm sure that's not why you're buying it?'

Jonas shook his head.

If he was honest, he knew exactly what had made him buy the painting.

It was the dog.

It was a beautiful painting, just the kind of thing that would appeal to him anyway, but the little portrait of the dog running on the beach reminded him so much of Dylan that he couldn't bear to walk away without knowing that it would be coming home to him.

Dylan, where are you? It was a question he had asked a thousand times, and still sought to answer.

It was funny how something could make its way so firmly into your heart in such a short space of time. Not having Dylan was so hard. It was like an ache that wouldn't go away. He missed him. And, what was worse, he not only missed him, but he was also truly worried about him. He could be anywhere, cold, hungry, hurt . . . or worse. But that didn't bear thinking about. He would have given anything he had to have him home and safe, but at the moment the best that he could hope for was that he was with someone who would give him everything he needed.

Natalie didn't even seem to notice that he was gone any more.

He supposed she was pretty preoccupied with plans for the wedding – or, as he had overheard Blix say to Wilko, 'The wedding express, a bridal train that's thundering down the tracks towards the black hole of the big day, with no brakes and terrified passengers screaming for mercy.'

Despite this, Natalie had been his rock since Dill had gone missing. So much so, that he now understood why he'd asked her to marry him.

Which was a bloody good job, considering the big day itself was only two weeks away.

If he was pushed he would have to confess that he had for a time begun to wonder if he had rushed into it all too quickly, blown away by the girl he had thought she was – bright, quirky, funny, creative – only to find that this wonderful sunny side was tainted with a spoilt, petulant, moody Natalie, a person he was sometimes pushed to even like. He had begun to worry that he had been carried away by heaven knew what, a wave of romance, perhaps – appropriate, considering he had been on the beach where his father proposed to his mother after their own whirlwind romance, and it had been a mistake.

But how she had been since Dylan went missing . .

well, it had proven that deep down she was the great girl he had first fallen in love with.

Wilko said it was so deep down you needed a pit helmet and a shovel to get there, but Wilko was biased.

Natalie just wasn't Wilko's kind of girl.

Nick liked his women how Blix liked her wine: sweet and full bodied.

He also knew that she wasn't Jonas's usual type, either, and Jonas thought that this worried his friend.

She was ambitious, she was driven. There was nothing wrong with that, was there? Knowing what you wanted in life and working to achieve it?

She was also clever, and beautiful.

If he was completely honest with himself then he would admit that Natalie was not the kind of woman he had ever pictured himself marrying, but how often did a person end up getting together with someone who fitted the ideals on a list? Love didn't work that way, love had its own agenda that more often than not took absolutely no notice of hopes and dreams and preconceived ideals. But that was one of the fun things about it. You asked for a chocolate éclair and life gave you a vanilla slice. You took a bite and discovered that you really loved vanilla slices.

Simple.

Wasn't it?

When he got back to the cottage, Wilko was up and in the kitchen making himself a cup of coffee.

Declan, looking putty-coloured instead of pistachio, was sitting at the table gingerly poking a bacon sandwich as he debated whether it would make him feel better or worse.

They both glanced up as he walked in, his sun-licked, windswept health a marked contrast to their drooping hungover pallor.

'See, told you we hadn't posted him to the outer Hebrides,' Declan said to Wilko.

'Where have you been, mate?'

'Just taking a walk.'

'All day?'

'How long have you guys been up?'

'About twenty minutes.' Declan's voice was muffled by his coffee cup.

'Well, there you go, I wasn't going to sit around here on my tod until' – Jonas looked at his watch – 'four in the afternoon.'

'How come you're looking so bloody healthy?'

'A distinct lack of tequila in my bloodstream.' Jonas

grinned. 'But I'm not going to say I told you so. How do you feel?'

Declan's response was a simple but very eloquent groan.

Wilko tried to roll his eyes but found that simple gesture too painful.

'I feel like I've been run over by the entire cast of *Riverdance*. My head's banging.' He pushed his temple with his finger and winced.

'Just your head?'

'I think so . . .'

'Not your arse?'

Wilko frowned. 'Why, did I fall over or something?'

'Yeah,' Jonas said, wrestling to keep his smile in check. 'Twice.' He rolled his eyes.

'Oh Lord. Was I embarrassing?'

'Aren't you always?'

His friend snorted with laughter.

'Yeah. Pretty much so. You know, now you mention it, my arse is a bit sore.'

'Yeah, probably 'cos you ended up in a gay bar at the end of the night,' Declan teased him, and winked at Jonas to show that he knew exactly what he was hinting at.

'That gay bar was the best time of the night,' Wilko protested. 'Those guys really know how to party . . .'

'So what's on your agenda for this evening?' Jonas grinned. 'More pink party?'

But Nick shook his head.

'Variety is the spice of life and we've done the drunken moron thing, so tonight we are going to show our sophisticated side . . .'

'Do we have one?'

'Well, if we don't, we'd better get one and quick, because young Declan here has pulled a few strings.'

'A few strings?,' Declan interjected, finally giving up on the thought of eating the sandwich. 'More like a whole bloody orchestra. Do you know how many favours I had to promise . . .'

'OK, Declan has sold his soul . . .' Nick offered.

'And yours too . . .' Declan pointed at him

'Couldn't have done,' Jonas interjected. 'Wilks bartered that away years ago.'

'. . . to get us a table at one of the best restaurants Cornwall has to offer,' Nick finished.

'Champagne, sea view, celebrity chef, the works,' Declan added, the large belch that followed this sentence negating the initial anticipation it induced. 'It's mega posh, so best behaviour, chaps. My second cousin's the maître d' there, so I have some influence, but it doesn't mean he won't get us evicted for bad behaviour, brawling, belching and bottom baring.'

'Are you sure you can manage dinner in a restaurant?' Jonas said, indicating Declan's abandoned sandwich with a nod of his head.

'Sure,' Declan nodded firmly, 'all I need is a nice big hair of the dog.'

'You serious?'

'Yeah, but I'm talking Rottweiler big here, chaps, so no chihuahuas OK?'

'*Dra mig baklänges!*' Jonas rolled his eyebrows, as Declan then produced the remains of an enormous bottle of tequila.

'You're talking Swedish, aren't you?' Declan crossed his eyes in confusion.

'Yeah, and you're talking crap, so we're even,' Jonas said, firmly taking the bottle from him. 'Now drink your bloody coffee.'

Restaurant Sam Mendoza was in an old fish warehouse right on the edge of the harbour of the port town of Quinn.

'This place is amazing,' Jonas said as they walked down from the car park just outside of the town, through the old narrow streets, with their ancient buildings tall and eclectic. 'Beautiful.'

'Lots of shops.' Nick pulled a face.

'Safely interspersed with bars,' Jonas pointed out. 'Mum and Blix would love it here.'

'And Natalie?'

'Of course.'

The restaurant itself was pretty unprepossessing from a distance, a three-storey building of old stone, with big, unevenly sized and shaped windows. But when you got up close, the big black double doors, closed to keep out the wandering tourists, with two perfectly manicured bay trees standing sentry either side, were the perfect understated accompaniment to the discreet neon sign that simply said Sam Mendoza and nothing else. Such was the fame of the name it needed no further explanation

'You were right about it being posh, are you sure they're going to let us in?' Nick eyed the place suspiciously.

'Did you look in a mirror before we came out? Do you not realise how fabulous we look?'

They were suited and booted to a man.

'We look like a hit squad.'

'We look great.'

'Reservoir dogs.'

'More like pond puppies.' Wilko grinned. 'We're not hard enough to be reservoir dogs.'

Declan's cousin Seamus was waiting for them.

Despite the fact that he was actually a second cousin, they looked so alike they could easily have been mistaken for brothers.

After some ribbing and manly hugging, he showed them to a large round table towards the back of the room, where the whole wall was made of glass and overlooked the estuary and out to sea.

'I've kept you one of our best tables, though Lord knows why, 'cos you won't appreciate it, you heathen. We don't serve big Macs in here – you do know that, don't you?'

'Oh, don't you worry about that, Seamus; a fillet of fish'll do me just fine.'

They were handed the menus, and for the first time that weekend, apart from when they had been passed out the night before they fell silent as they studied the vast array of gastronomical delights on offer.

As usual, though, when they were together, the silence didn't last for long.

Menu negotiated, dinner served, they discussed everything from politics to piano concertos, girls to Gorbachev, negative thinking to negative equity.

Jonas looked at his friends deep in discussion about the state of the world economy, and joked to Wilko that who would have known the pissheads from last night were this sophisticated group of intellectuals.

Nick had nodded sagely.

'My beloved gran, God rest her soul, always used to

say to me that a man should not only have an arse like a peach to attract a woman, but he should also be like a peach too . . . well rounded.'

'Your gran was a star.'

'She still is . . .' Nick said, pointing out of the window at the night sky like velvet above the ocean. 'That one . . . I think . . . I named a star after her, my Christmas present to myself. Sad git, aren't I . . . ?'

'Nope.' Jonas shook his head and slung an arm around his friend's neck to briefly hug him. 'That's not sad. Not sad at all.'

'I'd never have confessed that in front of this lot if you hadn't just poured three glasses of extremely good wine down my neck.'

'Of course not, mate.' Jonas grinned and looked about the table at his friends.

His closest friends.

They each had their own commitments, jobs and, some of them, families, but Nick had told him that none of them had even hesitated when the call had come out for them to sign up for the stag do.

They were part of a huge social crowd, but the guys that were there with them on this weekend to mark the end of Jonas's life as a single man, were Jonas's and Nick's 'brothers'.

Declan had been the second boy to follow Wilko into the fight the day that Jonas had rescued Tilly from the gang of youths intent on tormenting her. Rick and Tony, brothers, and Chris, affectionately and unimaginatively known as Woody, because his surname was Woods, all sitting in a semi-circular row just beyond Declan, had been the rearguard that day, piling in after them.

All three of them were now over six foot tall and, Tony in particular, as broad as tree trunks, but at the time they had been skinny little things with no meat to their bones or muscle to their punches, but they had come to his rescue, nonetheless.

With the fight then even, if only in numbers, the others of the large group had just watched until, bloody, bruised and battered, the school boys had emerged, not quite triumphant, as the teenage gang had literally beaten them to a bloody pulp, but victorious, as the puppy was safe in Jonas's gentle hands, and the mission was accomplished.

The leader of the gorgeous gang had looked them up and down and shaken his head, and then he'd turned to Jonas.

'You're mad, you are.'

There had been a moment of silence, and then they had all burst out laughing. Jonas had been accepted.

And the desperados had been a tight-knit bunch ever since.

The five other guys with them at the dinner table were friends who had been gathered on the path of life thus far: Rob and Alexander were mates from college, and Liam, James and Ed were long-term drinking, hiking, climbing and sailing buddies.

Not the kind of guys you would normally find altogether in a restaurant like this; maybe with wives and girlfriends, or perhaps with family, but not just the group of them. Their style en masse was more pasta or madras, but they had thought that Jonas, the foodie, would love this place and therefore they were here for him.

They had been right. He liked everything about this place. He would definitely be coming back to Quinn.

And he would absolutely be coming back to this restaurant, he thought as a smiling waiter took away the empty dessert plates.

It had been amazing. Four courses of perfectly prepared food. Jonas often wondered, with the many restaurants that housed that increasing breed the celebrity chef, whether their popularity was more down to hype than substance. Sam Mendoza had proven him wrong.

The place was packed full of people, but this really was a testament to the food rather than the kudos of being there.

And as he looked around at the full restaurant his glance was caught by a man sitting alone at a nearby table. There was something about the back of his head that looked remarkably familiar.

Weird. Now why would the *back* of someone's head be recognisable? he mused, and then the answer hit him. If, during the time that you had known them, they had spent much of their time facing away from you . . .

Whilst drawing on a blackboard! Suddenly it came back to him.

'Professor?' he called.

The older man at the next table turned, and Jonas's unsure smile turned into a full-on beam.

'It *is* you! I thought it might be, but it's been such a long time . . .'

'Jonas? Jonas Larsson?' the man replied, getting up from his seat.

Jonas stood up and held out a hand.

'How are you, sir?'

The man's face broke into the broadest of beams as he reached out to shake Jonas's outstretched hand.

'Well, goodness me, fantastic, how wonderful to see you, and please don't tell me this is young Nicholas Wilkinson?'

'The one and only.' Nick was on his feet holding out his hand in delight.

'Still joined at the hip, then?'

'He can't get rid of me.' Wilko beamed, taking his turn to shake the older man's hand vigorously.

'Robert Vaughan.' Rob stood too, and held out his hand.

'Of course. Robert, I remember you well, how are you? And Alexander Duncan . . . well, this is a turn up for the books.'

'Are you still teaching, sir?'

'Goodness, you don't have to call me sir any more, Jonas – and no, I'm not, that was more a sojourn on life's journey rather than life's journey itself.'

'Shame.' Wilko shook his head in genuine regret. 'You were a great teacher. Yours was the only class I didn't fall asleep in halfway through.'

'Only because if you had you would have ended up with fewer digits than the required ten. I clearly remember how much you used to like to get your hands on the class jigsaw, young man.'

'And I'm still a dab hand . . .'

'So what are you doing now?'

'We've set up a business together,' Jonas replied.

'Well, if truth be known, Jonas set up a business and I begged him for a job, 'cos no one else was stupid enough to employ me.' Nick grinned.

'And is it going well?'

'Really good, yes, thank you.' Jonas nodded.

'He's being modest,' Nick burst in with a proud smile at his friend, 'which of course is an alien word to me, so I can boast about the fact that Blue Closet Joinery is one of Dorset's premier names when it comes to joinery.'

'Blue Closet? Unless I'm very much mistaken, that's a rather beautiful painting by Dante Gabriel Rossetti?'

'My mother's favourite artist and poet.' Jonas nodded.

'And you're still living in Dorset? So does that mean you're down here on holiday?'

'Stag weekend.' Nick nodded. 'Jonas here is tying the knot.'

'I'm getting married in two weeks' time,' Jonas confirmed.

'Well, goodness,' the handsome man's grin stretched even further, 'what a wonderful coincidence, because I'm here celebrating my engagement. In fact, here is the very unlucky lady herself.' He beamed as a good-looking dark-haired woman, weaved her through the tables towards them. 'Darling, come and meet Nicholas and Jonas, Robert and Alexander. Gentlemen, this is my beautiful fiancée . . . Suzanne.'

42

As the ferry from Port Ruan to Quinn stopped running at dusk, Geoffrey had arranged, with a lot of help from Theo, to borrow a small boat from an acquaintance in Port Ruan harbour to get them back home.

It was basically just a large rowing boat with an outboard motor, but the way Suze beamed with delight when she saw how Geoffrey had organised for them to get back across the water, it could have been the *QE2*.

This could have been something to do with the fact that as he held out a hand to help her on board, she realised that the entire boat was filled with tulips. Her favourite flower. It was like stepping into a field in Holland. And then, as the little vessel began to motor her way towards the lights of Port Ruan, Geoffrey pressed the button on the tape recorder he had hidden under the seat and suddenly Suze was not only surrounded by her favourite flowers but was also being serenaded by Michael Bublé.

'I hope this is dreadfully romantic and not just horribly clichéd . . .' Geoffrey had asked in concern as he put his arm around her.

Suze's delighted response had rocked the little boat and Geoffrey's world at the same time.

Back at Port Ruan they walked up the hill to fetch

Poppy from Theo who had been dog-sitting for them.

Poppy, still very wary of Dill's rather too enthusiastic attempts at friendship, had been playing peekaboo with him for most of the evening from various different hiding places, and she shot out from under the dining table and plonked herself on Suze's lap the minute she sat down.

Suze, in her best frock, simply grinned and put her arms around the shaking dog.

'Did you miss your mummy, Popsy baby? Did you . . . ?'

'Well, that's the understatement of the decade. I think she thought she'd been abandoned for life.' Theo laughed.

'Well, apparently it can take them a while to settle. You know, once they've been in the pound and stuff . . .'

'Well, hopefully now she's had an evening without you and survived and been reunited with you, she'll realise that you're always going to come back for her . . . so what was the restaurant like? Did you have a good time?'

'Oh, it was amazing, you should have come, Theo.'

'A romantic meal for three? Not quite the same, is it?'

'You wouldn't have been a gooseberry . . . you'd have enjoyed it, Thee . . . the food was wonderful . . . we had this disgustwotsit menu.'

'Degustation?' Theo offered with a grin.

'That's the one – well, they match a wine to each course, and we had six courses. I'm surprised I'm not comatose by now. Oh, and Geoffrey bumped into some old students of his who were at a table nearby . . .'

'Students?' Theo mouthed in puzzlement.

Suze nodded, her own smile one of amused confusion.

'Apparently my husband-to-be was once a woodwork professor at a rather exclusive college in Dorset.'

'I settled there the summer after leaving Hallows,

stayed for a couple of years.' Geoffrey shrugged, as Theo's questioning look demanded an explanation. 'It's not a big deal, honestly. I'd kind of forgotten about it myself . . . lovely to see the boys again, though, really nice bunch, they were . . .'

'Well, I'd hardly call them boys, Geoffrey. Definitely men,' Suze interjected, winking at Theo.

'Lovely chaps,' Geoffrey continued. 'Really enjoyed teaching them. Very gratifying to know that something I taught to them has stood them in good stead for life in the real world.'

'A professor?' Theo queried, as Suze settled on Theo's sofa and Geoffrey headed into her kitchen to make them all a cup of coffee.

'I'm learning new stuff about him all the time.' Suze shrugged. 'Every so often these amazing little facts pop out. It's got to the point where I wouldn't be surprised if he suddenly announced he was Santa Claus.'

'And you'd believe him.' Theo nodded firmly.

'Well, if you want a walking personification of honesty, he's your man.'

'Well, actually he's *your* man.' Theo grinned, still dizzy from the news of their engagement.

'I know, and I'm one very lucky girl.'

'Let me see that rock on your finger again.'

Suze stuck out her hand and Poppy, fearful of being dislodged from her already beloved mistress's lap, dug claws firmly into Suze's thighs.

'Ouch! Pops!'

'That's not a rock, it's a bloody great boulder.'

'Apparently it was Geoffrey's mum's.'

'Geoffrey's mother must have been a weightlifter;

look at the size of that thing.'

As soon as she got her hand back from Theo, Suze disengaged Poppy's claws from her leg.

'How did the kids get on?'

'Well, Dill is still trying to win her over, but Poppy's playing coy.'

'She's just shy.'

'She hid behind the sofa for most of the evening. Only managed to coax her out at supper time and walk time.'

Suze stroked the head of the dog crammed on to her lap and smiled as big lash-fringed eyes blinked adoringly up at her.

'She's not like her mummy. She doesn't want to play with the boys . . .' Suze affectionately twirled the hair on Poppy's head between her fingers. 'And talking of boys, Theo English, you *really* should have come with us tonight. Geoffrey's students are now absolutely strapping young men.' She leaned in conspiratorially. 'There were eleven of them . . .'

'You counted?'

'I counted and measured and read them more times than the menu . . . not for me, of course – on your behalf – and I'm telling you, lady, they were as delicious as the food . . . I almost asked the Maître d' to pop one in a doggy bag for you and bring him home.'

'Any one in particular?'

'Well, I actually picked out three, one for the starter, one for main course, and one for dessert . . .'

'I've never had three courses of men before.'

'Me neither.' Suze sighed as if genuinely regretful. 'Although I did once have a disgustingly delicious man sandwich.'

43

It was the weekend before the wedding.

A weekend with a full schedule.

Saturday night was an American-style pre-wedding dinner for family and friends.

On Friday night, Jonas and Wilko were heading out on the town.

The stag weekend had been for the select few; tonight they were going out for a few drinks with the whole crowd.

Clem and Natalie henceforth were having a girlie night in at Jonas's place.

A girlie night in. Clem couldn't remember the last time they'd done this.

And she'd waited for so long to spend some time alone with Natalie.

She had come armed, DVDs, face packs, necessary items to manicure and pedicure and, of course, a bottle of champagne, as it was such a special occasion, plus wine and chocolate and other edible, drinkable treats, including a beautiful chocolate cake, with 'Congratulations, Natalie' scrolled on top, which she had lovingly made herself.

'But first,' she had announced to Natalie as she unloaded everything on to the coffee table, 'we're playing truth or dare.'

'You're kidding, aren't you?'

'Oh come on, Nat, it'll be fun.'

'If we were ten.'

Clementine poured her a huge glass of the very cold champagne she had brought with her, then poured another for herself.

'Cheers. To next weekend,' she toasted.

'Next weekend,' Natalie echoed, clinking her own glass against Clementine's, 'when I shall become Mrs Jonas Larsson.' She said it again as if savouring the taste of the words.

'Mrs Jonas Larsson . . . Natalie Larsson. I was going to suggest double barrelled, but it makes me sound like an Italian cheese . . .'

Clementine, who would happily have changed her name to Mrs Feta Gouda Parmesan Stinking-Bishop if it meant that she were marrying someone like Jonas, watched as Natalie drained her glass and immediately topped it up again.

'Right, we're off.'

It was Jonas and Wilko.

If she wasn't sitting down, Clem would have kicked herself for instantly blushing as the two men came into the room to say goodbye.

She and Nick had hardly spoken in the weeks since Easter and Jonas's birthday.

As it had been for New Year, Nick had said nothing afterwards about their encounter amidst the camellias and Clem was too bloody shy and unsure of herself and his feelings to mention what had happened, even though it played constantly on her mind.

She looked up at Nick, or at least halfway up, at that fit

arse in a pair of grey jeans that were the same colour as his eyes and tried hard not to sigh with unrequited lust.

She couldn't believe how she had never noticed him before. He was a brilliant moon that had been eclipsed by the radiant sun of Jonas's beauty. OK, so maybe she was getting poetic, but that's what those kisses had been. Blooming poetry. Oh how she longed for a repeat of that sonnet of a snog in the Palmers' garden.

But since then, it had been back to the normal Nick and Clementine: the odd bit of banter and a shared joke, as though each tantalising, tingling time had never actually happened.

And maybe, Clementine thought, Nick had said nothing about it because that's what he wished, that nothing *had* happened.

And so she simply lusted from afar.

And smacked herself repeatedly on the forehead with her handbag after every meeting and missed opportunity.

However, tonight was not about Clementine, tonight was more important than her own pathetic longings; tonight was about Natalie. And so she waved goodbye to them both with good grace and a big smile and returned her attention to her friend, waiting five minutes whilst Natalie sipped her second glass of champagne and banged on about her wedding dress and the flowers and what colour to have her nails so that it tied the two together, and then she tried again.

'Come on, Nat, truth or dare.'

Wilko, who had left his jacket slung over the back of a chair in the kitchen and had left Jonas waiting at the end of the drive for the taxi whilst he ran back to get it, stopped as he heard two words that really caught his attention.

'Truth or dare?' Natalie repeated with a disdainful curl of her nostril.

'Truth or dare, Nat!' Clem insisted as Natalie poured herself another glass of champagne but didn't answer.

'Oh, OK, truth,' replied Natalie as she couldn't be bothered to move for a dare.

Clem rolled her eyes and bit her lip as she thought of her first question.

'OK . . . where do you see yourself in five years' time?'

'That old chestnut!' Natalie humphed.

'Yep,' Clem grinned pouring more wine, 'don't you just love old chestnuts?'

'No, not really.'

'Oh Nat, don't be a spoilsport . . . come on, this is your last weekend as a single woman. If we can't succumb to a few clichés now . . . look, I'll start, OK? If that helps. In five years' time,' she began, ignoring the fact that Natalie's eyes immediately glazed over, 'I'll be living in a gorgeous cottage near the sea, old stone, garden full of flowers, big country kitchen, with the man of my dreams, tall, brown haired, grey eyed and handsome, sweet, kind and funny. We'll be married, of course, big white wedding with horse and carriage, quaint church, six bridesmaids . . . we'll have two kids, one of each, perfect . . . a boy first, Harry James, then a year or two after, a little girl, Emily Rose. I'll be a stay-at-home wife and mother, but I might have my own little business too, maybe something crafty, like making quirky cushions or baking cupcakes, and my husband will have his own business . . .'

She had obviously given this an awful lot of thought; her eyes shone as she visualised the whole fantasy scenario becoming her reality. It was so detailed and lovingly crafted that Wilko, who had been about to leave, had stopped to listen, an indulgent smile upon his face. It was also almost inspiring to Natalie, who cut in just as Clem was describing the fact that her husband would work with his hands, as she had always liked a man who was good with his hands.

'Well, OK ... if I must play this game ... if you insist ...'

Wilko, who had begun to feel bad for eavesdropping as Clem's dialogue had become more intimate, and had just recommenced the sneaking out, couldn't stop himself from pausing mid-step, and he waited silently, ears cocked.

Not at all phased by the interruption, Clem, too, fell silent and nodded eagerly.

'In five years' time ...' Natalie mused, her eyes rolling to the right as she thought, 'well, I definitely want to be regional manager instead of area manager, and we will definitely have moved to one of the biggest houses in Kipling Close, that one with the triple garage would be nice – do you know, it has five bedrooms and four of them have en-suites? The master bedroom is absolutely huge, but I still think I'd need to turn the bedroom next to it into a walk-in closet, and I'd have to get the kitchen redone, too; the one they have was expensive when they got it, but it's white, and isn't white so eighties?'

'Oh, and Jonas and Nick do gorgeous kitchens ...' Clementine nodded enthusiastically.

'Oh no, I wouldn't get Jonas to do it; his kitchens are nice, but I'd want something really decent, maybe a Christian's ... oh, and I'll definitely have a new car too, a Porsche or a newer BMW, I think ...'

'A four-by-four?'

'Oh no, probably a convertible, a black one . . .'

'A convertible? Not very practical.'

'Who wants practical?'

'You don't think you'll have had kids by then?'

'Oh goodness, no – well, at least not unless we can afford a nanny . . .'

'Are you being serious?'

'Semi . . . if we had the kind of money to pay a nanny's wages, I think I'd rather spend it on handbags.' Natalie laughed. 'No, I really don't think kids are on the agenda any time soon . . . if at all.'

Clementine's mouth dropped open.

'But Jonas wants them, Nat. You know that.'

'I know.' Natalie poured herself more wine. 'But we can't always have everything we want, can we? Unless, of course, you're me . . .'

Nick had heard enough.

He had a choice: either he stormed in there and confronted her, or he took a hold of himself and walked out.

If he went in there, he'd probably want to take her smug face and push it straight into the beautiful cake that Clementine had baked for her. And he wouldn't let himself do something like that. It would be so wrong. After Clementine had worked so hard on it.

Nick walked.

Moments later, an equally mortified Clementine melted with relief as Natalie started to laugh.

'Don't look so horrified, Clem, I'm only kidding. I do want kids at some point, but we're talking a good few years yet . . . I'm only twenty-eight, women have children now right up until their forties; I want to concentrate on my career, is that so very wrong?'

'Of course not. I just thought for a moment from what you said that you didn't want them at all.'

'Of course I do; can you imagine how gorgeous our kids would be? But I want a few years of having my man all to myself first, just him and me – in the meantime, we can practise making babies as much as he wants . . .' she said, and as she started to laugh lasciviously into her rapidly emptying glass, Clementine knew that Natalie was well on her way to being drunk.

Twenty miles away in a pub in Dorchester town centre, Jonas and Wilko were far from being drunk, despite being surrounded by a horde of their friends who were. Extremely.

But whilst everyone else necked pints and progressed to shots, the two of them sat side by side on the sidelines watching, but not partaking.

Nick, Jonas thought had been in a strange mood all evening, and as he had refrained from getting bladdered, so had Jonas kept pace and watched, until eventually he had to ask.

'Are you OK?'

Wilko had nodded slowly.

'Sure?'

'Yep.'

'Eddie, all right?'

'Little star . . .' For a moment he had smiled at the thought of his canine friend who, having been sent to stay at Stella and Blix's whilst they were in Cornwall, had greeted Wilko's return with an explosion of relieved delight that had been an utter privilege to have inspired.

And then he had turned to face Jonas and asked him a rather odd question.

'What do you want from life, Jonas?'

Jonas frowned at his friend in surprise.

'That's a very general question, Nick.'

'So give me a general answer.'

'Well, actually, I can give you quite a specific answer at the moment.'

'Fire away.'

'Find Dylan.'

Nick nodded sadly. 'Sorry, mate.'

'Yeah . . . well . . . aside from that, do you really want to know?'

'Wouldn't have asked if I didn't.'

'And haven't we already covered this subject a million times already over the years?'

'Maybe, but humour me.'

'OK . . .' Jonas shrugged, leaning back in his chair as he contemplated. 'I suppose I'd like to travel some more, see some more of the world, but having said that, I'd also like to expand the business, so that means staying put and working my arse off.'

'Anything else?'

'Like what?'

'Do you want to have kids?'

His surprised frown deepened, but he answered, nonetheless.

'Oh yeah. Definitely.'

'How many?'

'I don't know . . . how many do you want?'

Totally not expecting Nick to have an answer, Jonas blinked with surprise when he immediately responded.

'Two.'

'Two?'

'One of each. Boy then a girl. Perfect.'

Jonas frowned at his friend in total puzzlement.

They had been friends for years and of course they had always shared their hopes and dreams and aspirations, but this was one step further for Nick.

'This is all a bit deep for you, isn't it?'

'I do have my philosophical moments sometimes – strange though, it's normally when I'm watching your life unfold rather than my own.'

'You mean you see what a wonderful life I'm making for myself and you start to covet and emulate?' Jonas winked at him.

'More like I learn from your mistakes.' Nick grinned.

'I never make mistakes,' Jonas countered, mock arrogant.

To his amazement, Nick nodded.

'That's almost true. Never isn't quite right, though. If you'd said "almost never", then I would have agreed with you . . .'

There was something about the tone of his voice as he said this that worried Jonas.

'Will you just get to the point, Nick, please. If there *is* a point to this . . .'

Nick sighed heavily.

'That's the thing, I made a vow to myself that I never would . . . get to the point, that is . . .'

He suddenly looked so down, all of the humour gone from his voice and his face.

'What is it?' Jonas demanded and then, tilting his head so that he could look into Wilko's downturned face, added quietly, 'You're actually scaring me, Nick.'

Nick closed his eyes for a moment. Exhaled slowly and heavily. And then finally he looked up at Jonas.

'I really thought that keeping my mouth shut was being a good friend, but I've decided that I've been totally wrong, for me to be a good friend to you is for me to tell you the truth, and the truth is . . .' he paused, gathering the courage to say it, 'the truth is that if you go ahead and marry Natalie, I think you'll be making the biggest mistake of your life.'

Natalie was just upending the last of the wine into her own glass, and wondering hazily what Clem was going to dare her next, when a light rap on the sitting-room door heralded the arrival of Blix, looking foxy in leather trousers and a silver cashmere jumper to match her silver hair.

'Hi, girls.'

'Blix!' Clementine cried in delight.

'Jonas told me you were having a little party . . .'

'Hey, grandmother-in-law-to-be . . .' Natalie waved her almost-empty glass at Blix. 'Come in and park your broomstick . . .'

Blix and Clem exchanged a look.

'Don't worry, I'm not gate crashing, I just wanted to give you this.'

She held out a huge bottle of akvavit.

'It's a Swedish tradition that the bride and her maid of honour drink this together before the wedding. It is good luck for a happy marriage.'

'It is?' queried Natalie who had done a little reading up on Swedish traditions in preparation for the big day.

'Oh, absolutely; especially in the Larsson family . . . so . . . enjoy, and I'll see you tomorrow for the dinner . . .'

Putting the bottle down on the coffee table next to the empty champagne and wine bottles, she blew a kiss to Natalie, winked at Clem, and left.

'Akvavit!' Clem cried, taking hold of the bottle.

'Akvavit,' Natalie repeated, not sounding so keen.

Clem narrowed her eyes, unscrewed the top, and held the bottle over Natalie's empty glass.

'Dare you . . .' she said.

'Oh you dare me, do you?' Natalie replied, holding out her glass. 'Well, you better be careful; I might just dare you back.'

'Feel free . . . I once won a drinking competition downing this stuff.'

'Do you know, I never knew that about you, Clementine Peterson.'

'I think perhaps there are lots of things you don't know about me,' Clem mused. 'Whereas . . . on the other hand . . . I know you inside and out, Natalie Palmer.'

'Ah, that's what you think.' Natalie pointed at her, rotating her finger as it got closer to Clementine's face until it came to rest in a fingernailed point against the centre of her forehead between her eyes. 'That's what you think.'

'That isn't what I think,' Clementine gently batted the finger away, 'that is what I *know*. In fact . . .' she paused and licked her lips, 'sometimes I think I know you better than you know yourself.'

'Impossible!' Natalie cried, 'We all have our little secrets . . .'

'Not from me.'

'Even . . . from . . . you,' Natalie slurred, waving her glass at Clem for more akvavit. 'There are lots of things that you don't know . . .'

'Like what?' Clem said, laughing to show her disbelief.

'You want to know?'

'I want to know.'

'Then I'll show you something.' She swept back her curtain of thick hair to reveal the diamonds in her ears. 'These are new.'

'Very pretty.' Clem nodded, frowning. 'But new earrings? Hardly a secret.'

'It is when I swapped Blix's awful pearl earrings for them . . .' Natalie hiccupped.

'You didn't!' Clem's mouth fell open, as Natalie nodded furiously and cackled with laughter.

'Did so . . . stupid old witch, like I'd want to wear her cast-offs to my wedding.'

'I can't believe you did that.'

'I know.' Natalie smiled triumphantly. 'See . . . told you there are things about me you don't know . . .'

'You mean there's more?'

'Oh yes . . . and this is the biggy, the doozy.'

'Oh yes?' Clementine poured some more akvavit, then cupped her chin in her hand and leaned forward conspiratorially. 'Tell me about it . . .'

44

Jonas had been so surprised by what Nick had said that for a moment he had been unable to answer, and then before he could, Nick had told him what he had overheard Natalie saying, apologised profusely for being the one to do this, hugged him hard and briefly, and then just left.

Walked out of the pub where all of their friends were singing and drinking and celebrating, leaving Jonas to watch him leave with a stunned look on his face, then make his own excuses to quit his own stag do and go home. Where he found Natalie had drunk so much that she had passed out face down and fully clothed on the floor of the bedroom.

They were back in work the following morning.

Wilko would be running Blue Closet on his own whilst they were away on their honeymoon and it had already been pretty manic getting everything up to speed so that he could do this without having major heart failure from the pressure of doing it all alone.

Hence the reason they were both in the workshop on a Saturday.

They had both arrived, nodded a greeting, and picked up their tools.

And then Jonas had waited for Wilko to say something.

And Wilko had waited for Jonas.

And they had both stayed silent.

With regard to the conversation Nick had repeated to Jonas, there had been only one thing Jonas could do, and that was to ask Natalie, but not outright.

He had casually brought it up in conversation over breakfast where Natalie clutched a cup of coffee as if she were drowning and it was a life raft, and her reply, after she had paused to belch in a very un-Natalie-like fashion, had been that of course she wanted kids, just not quite yet, there was plenty of time for that a few years down the line.

Which is what he had thought all along.

He had tried to tell Nick this as they sat silently side by side sharing their lunchtime sandwiches with Eddie. But Nick had simply shrugged and said, 'Of course that's what she'd say to you ...' and giving the surprised and yet delighted Eddie a whole cheese and ham roll, had returned prematurely to a bookcase he was finishing, where for the first time in eight years of trading, he had finished a piece and forgotten to add his acorn.

'I can't be a hypocrite any more, Jonas,' had been his response when Jonas had said to him, 'See you later?' as they locked up the workshop.

'Is it hypocritical to compromise?' Jonas had fired back, made angry by the utter disappointment he felt that Nick would not be joining them for dinner.

'Maybe you should ask yourself that question,' Nick had said, then shrugged sadly and, whistling for Eddie, had left.

And now, Saturday night, one week before the day he was due to get married, Jonas was taking his leave of a restaurant full of his nearest and dearest and one of the nearest and dearest had been glaringly missing.

And as he said goodbye to the people who had sat with them and shared in their celebratory meal, who had proposed toasts and told stories and proffered hopes and wishes for their future, he pondered the fact that despite being surrounded by such love and good will, the absence of just one person could throw such a shadow.

And it wasn't just him.

Clementine and Blix had been unusually sombre.

Both, he thought for reasons very different, missing the little ray of sunshine that had suddenly turned into a storm cloud.

They were together now, whispering in a corner.

Clem was such a sweet girl, he really wished that Blix could get on as well with Natalie as she did with her.

Blix, who made a friend of everyone she met. She really didn't like Natalie.

That was two of the people he cared about most in the world who hated the woman he was marrying in only one week's time.

He looked over at Natalie and sighed.

He wasn't naïve, or stupid, or an idiot, he just always took people as he found them, how they treated him.

She felt him watching her, looked over and smiled as she made her way out of the room.

She was so beautiful.

So sweet and affectionate.

And such a fucking bitch sometimes.

And yes, if he were totally honest, for a while he had started to ask himself if he had rushed into things before he really knew her properly. And then Dylan had gone missing, and she had been a different person again; she had been amazing, buoying him up when he was down, helping him in so many ways from practical to emotional. He really didn't know how he would have handled it all without her.

And Nick had seen all of this, but still he questioned.

Someone who he knew loved him and wanted only the best for him was so adamant that he was doing the wrong thing.

He felt a warm hand slip through the crook of his elbow, take his arm, and he looked down to see Stella, smiling up at him.

His mother had always got on fine with Natalie.

But was that just because his mother was the kind of person who would make anyone from girlfriends to Genghis Khan feel welcome in her home.

'Hey, you,' she said gently, sensing something from him that he might need comfort. 'Penny for them?'

Jonas laughed softly, a dry snort of derision for himself.

'What is it? Is it something to do with Nick, with why he's not here?'

He didn't answer her. Instead, he asked a question of his own.

'Can I ask you something?'

'Anything, you know that.'

'Do you think I'm doing the right thing?'

His mother actually groaned. A low audible sound of foreboding.

'Oh Jonas, I really wish you hadn't asked me that . . .'

'Why, because you don't think I am, and you don't want to say it?'

'No, because I think you're doing the right thing only

if *you* think you are, and I know you, Jonas, and if you truly thought that you were, then you would never have asked me what I thought . . .'

She fell silent as they were joined by Blix and Clementine.

'Sonson?'

Jonas turned to ask his grandmother for a moment alone with his mother, but the words fell away from his lips when he saw her face.

She looked grey, worried, and every inch her seventy-two years.

'What is it, Farmor?' he asked in concern. 'Are you ill?'

'Sick to my stomach.' She nodded, but talking more to herself than him, and then she visibly appeared to pull herself upright and lifted her bright blue eyes to his.

'It's Clementine . . . well . . . myself and Clementine. I shared a worry with her, you see, and Clementine promised to help me with it . . . and, well, now she has something she needs to tell you . . .'

'Clem?'

Clementine could barely meet his eyes.

'Not here, eh?'

She looked like she was about to tell him someone that he loved had died.

'Clem, you're worrying me . . .'

'Please, Jonas, can we just . . . can we talk outside? Please . . .'

And as she hurriedly scrubbed away the tears that began to tumble from her eyes, he nodded, and took the hand that she offered to him.

He was quiet on the way home, but Natalie was talking enough for both of them not to notice.

'That restaurant has definitely gone down hill since we last went, I think they've changed the chef . . . perhaps we should give the place a miss for a while . . . do you know, I really think that Stella should have consulted my mother before she bought her outfit. There is a theme to this wedding, and that colour just clashes with everything . . . will you have a word with her, or do you think I should? I know we're getting close to the day itself, but do you think she'd get something else if I asked her? And I tell you what I really think, Clementine's been looking a bit porky, recently; if she's put on weight, she won't fit in her bridesmaid dress . . .'

She only realised that he had been totally silent throughout the entire journey when the car pulled up outside Jonas's house.

'Jonas, have you actually been listening to a word I've been saying?' she demanded.

Ignoring her, Jonas got out of the car and went into the house and, taking the stairs two at a time, went to his bedroom.

*

It was there, exactly where Clem had said, in the inside zip pocket of the chewed-up Balenciaga handbag that had sat, abandoned on the floor in a corner of the wardrobe ever since Dylan had taken a few chunks out of it.

Natalie had kept it like some trophy.

A visible sign of her own deceitful triumph.

He held it in his hand, so tight he could feel the metal cut into the flesh of his palm.

She caught up with him moments after he had found it.

'Jonas, what the hell's going on . . . ?'

But he turned to her, a quiet fury resonating from him that made her fall silent.

'Why did you do it?' His voice was so low, so obviously controlled, some inner instinct made her stop in her tracks by the doorway, a few feet away from him.

'What are you talking about?'

'You know full well what I'm talking about.'

'Oh for goodness' sake, Jonas, if you've got something to say, then say it, stop playing games.'

'Playing games! Playing games!' he thundered in a voice that she had never heard before, a voice that made her take a step backwards. '*Me*, playing games? Why would I do that, Natalie, when you're such a fucking expert at it?'

'What are you talking about, Jonas?' She said it again, only this time all hint of belligerence had gone from her voice.

And then she trailed off as he opened his clenched fist, palm out towards her to reveal the shining silver disk engraved on the side facing her with one word.

'Dylan.'

'Dylan?'

She said it like she didn't even know who he was talking about, like she had already forgotten he even existed.

'Dylan . . .' Jonas repeated, his voice catching on the word. 'The Dylan you didn't take to the vet's, the Dylan you didn't get chipped, the Dylan you took to the station and put on a bloody train to God knows where, for heaven's sake, you twisted—' He shook his head as if to shake out the image of it. '. . . Is that succinct enough for you?'

She opened her mouth but nothing came out, just a pout, like she was blowing bubbles.

'Why, Natalie, why would you even do something like that?'

'Clementine told you.' It wasn't a question, it was a statement of disbelief. And then the edge of her nose curled, like a petulant teenager. 'It was only a stupid dog, Jonas . . .'

Only a stupid dog? How well did she know him?

And then she tried a beguiling smile.

'Don't let a dog come between us.'

'It was you that did that, Natalie . . .' he said quietly. 'Where is he?'

The smile went. She shrugged as if she really didn't care.

'I don't know.'

'What did you do with him?'

'I thought Clementine already told you everything,' she growled and he was amazed at the bitterness in her voice.

Who was this woman?

Who was this person standing in front of him, her face suddenly a hard, unreadable mask.

'I don't even know who the hell you are.' He sighed, but the anger was gone from him, replaced by an indescribable sorrow.

Natalie returned her gaze to his.

'I'm your fiancée, Jonas, your wife a week today. For better or for worse, remember . . . ?'

But Jonas stepped back and away from her, shaking his head.

'No,' he said, and then more firmly. 'No. *This* is not what that means . . . for better or for worse means riding the waves with the person that you love, side by side with someone who keeps your back no matter what . . . not being with someone who stabs you in it the minute you turn away . . . I don't know who you are, Natalie Palmer, but I sure as hell know one thing . . . you are not the person I want to spend the rest of my life with . . .'

46

When Jonas left Natalie, left Otter Cottage, he had gone straight to Nick's.

Nick had opened the door and as Jonas had started to stutter an apology, had shaken his head, and then just hugged him.

'You know?' Jonas asked as they let go.

Nick nodded and led Jonas into the sitting room, where Clementine was perched on the sofa, clutching Eddie on her lap, red eyed and shaking like a leaf.

'She came straight here from the restaurant, told me everything. Natalie just called her. You should have heard her, language worse than Sharon Osbourne with tourettes.'

'I'm so sorry, Clem.'

Jonas sat down next to her, took her cold hands. Tried to smile reassuringly but found that his face just cracked into a lopsided frown.

'And thank you. For telling me the truth. I know it must have been really hard for you.'

Clem shrugged, rolled her eyes, sniffed loudly.

'I know she's been my friend for a long time, but what she did was just so . . . so . . . so . . .' Clem stopped as she realised she just couldn't find the words.

'I know.' Jonas closed his eyes for a moment.

'So what now?' Nick asked.

Jonas shrugged despairingly.

'I don't know where to start, to be honest.'

'Cup of tea,' Nick said.

Jonas laughed.

'The Englishman's solution to every dilemma . . . sure, a cup of tea would be great.'

Nick headed for the kitchen. Racked by the guilt that had somehow evaded Natalie, Clementine went with him, unable to sit alone with Jonas when it was someone that she knew and cared about who had deceived him so badly, who had made his handsome face so drawn and defeated.

It was as if Nick could read her mind.

'It's not your fault, you know,' he said softly as they stood and waited for the kettle to boil.

'Then why does it feel like it is?'

'Because you're a good person, Clem. But you're not guilty by association, remember that. It was Natalie, not you . . .'

When they came back into the room, Jonas was fast asleep on the sofa.

Nick fetched a spare duvet, covered him over, looked at Clem, shook his head and sighed.

'I never wanted to be right about her, you know.'

Clem nodded.

'But you were . . . if only the rest of us hadn't been so blinkered . . . I'd better go.'

But as she reached for her coat and her bag, he stayed her with a hand to the wrist.

'What if I said that I don't want you to?' he whispered.

His kiss was as sweet and delicious as she

remembered, and oh so longed for, but as he slid his hand from her wrist to gently take her hand and lead her upstairs to his bedroom, she felt not only the stomach-twisting fluttering of desire, but the hollow ache of uncertainty. She had wanted this for so long, but it had to be that he felt the same way. It had been one hell of a night. Was this just him in search of temporary comfort? Would it be months of nothing afterwards?

'I can't do one-night stands . . .' she stuttered, as he kissed her again, and then drew her towards the bed.

Nick stopped, let go, moved away.

And then he turned around, sheepishly lowered one side of his jeans, and as she read the word emblazoned across the taut muscle of his arse cheek, began to laugh softly.

'You don't know how glad I am to hear that . . . because I have every intention of keeping this . . . *Clementine.*'

Downstairs, wide awake on the sofa, Jonas lifted the duvet to let Eddie hop under as well and, listening to the sounds of soft sighs and low laughter from above, found a genuine smile of pleasure that his unhappy ending had at least been the beginning of something good for someone else.

When Jonas went back to Otter Cottage the next day, it was to find the front door wide open. Natalie had gone but not before she had taken her displeasure out on his house.

It was as if a tornado had hit, rampaging through the rooms, dislodging anything that wasn't fixed. Cushions were thrown from the sofa, a glass vase shattered, kitchen cupboards thrown open, their contents emptied on the slate floor, his clothes pulled from the wardrobe.

It was all an utter, utter mess.

Not just the cottage.

Everything.

It would take him hours to sort it out, but it would have to wait. Everything would have to wait.

There was one thing that came first, above the broken plates, and the ruined carpets, the phone calls, the things to cancel, like wedding cars and churches and matching waistcoats.

Dylan.

He had to find Dylan.

Poor, betrayed Dylan.

But where to start?

Jonas turned with a start at the sound of a knock on the front door.

Half expecting his mother and Blix, who had not been at all placated by a phone call first thing, he was surprised to find that Bob Stevens's muddy Land Rover was on his driveway, and the man himself was standing on his front doorstep holding up a large wooden crate.

'Delivery for you, Jonas. Came yesterday. Couldn't get you, so I was asked if I'd take it in . . .'

As Jonas offered his thanks, Bob peered over his shoulder into the chaos beyond.

'You been turned over?' he asked in friendly concern.

'Something like that, yes,' Jonas replied nodding flatly.

He carried the crate through into the sitting room, swept the remaining debris from the coffee table and set it down there. He fetched a screwdriver and unscrewed the lid lifting it to reveal what was inside.

It was the painting he had bought in St Ives.

He had forgotten all about it.

With everything that had happened, it had slipped his mind completely.

It was more beautiful than he remembered, heightened by a poignancy that was piercing. All blue sky, soft sand, smooth pebbles and a sea that sparkled with light . . . and, of course, the dog running joyously up the sand.

Jonas sighed heavily.

Oh how he wished that he could just fall head first into that beautiful day.

Oh how he longed to be on that beach with Dylan safe and happy and running beside him.

And then he saw it.

It was so tiny that it was no surprise he hadn't noticed it before, but now that he did see it, it was like someone had struck him in the face with a fist.

The dog in the painting, his painting, was wearing a collar.

And from that collar hung a tiny silver D.

47

It was a beautiful sunny day, the kind of Sunday where the whole world and his wife and thirteen children are tempted out to visit relatives or garden centres, or pretty pubs for long liquid lunches under the hanging baskets.

It felt like it took him for ever to get there, constantly being thwarted by Sunday drivers meandering along with all the time in the world, no sense of urgency, nothing to make them overtake on bends and speed where they shouldn't.

Frustrated by the slow-moving stream of traffic that had made his journey there unbelievably, unbearably slow, he practically ran across the fields to the edge of the cliff.

He had been here before, many years ago. With his mother and Blix.

Lantic Bay.

A beautiful curve of sand and pebble beach cut into the cliffs on the south coast of Cornwall. He remembered it well; they had made their way down the steep, steep path and picnicked in the sunshine, and then had laughed as they'd had to climb back up again, with an exhausted and complaining Blix threatening to call the coast guard to come and rescue her in their helicopter as he and Stella had towed her up between them.

And here he was again on that same path, running down it, despite the idiocy. Several times the gravity caught his feet, made him stumble, nearly fall, but still he kept running downwards, following the twists and turns until finally he could see the beautiful curve of the beach before him.

And it was completely empty.

Jonas slowed his pace, walked the last few feet, stepped down on to level ground, and sighed, exhaling his disappointment into the wind.

What had he been expecting, he chided himself, to find Dylan sitting waiting for him?

It was a beach, for heaven's sake, people visited beaches from far and wide.

He rubbed a hand across his forehead and tried to think rationally.

He could call the gallery tomorrow, find out everything he could from them, and start the search again.

And then as he turned to leave, he heard it.

Laughter.

Melodic, sweet laughter.

Followed by the sound of a dog barking joyously.

He had often wondered if he would recognise Dylan again. That bark that had become so familiar to him.

And now he knew. It was like the sound of a much-loved voice. Never forgotten.

'Dylan?' he called.

'Dylan!' he called again, shouting this time so that his voice echoed against the rock face.

Theo laughed as Geoffrey missed his footing and plunged his leg straight into a rockpool, and then her laughter turned to contrition, as Suze, stifling giggles, bent forward to offer him a hand to haul himself out again, Dylan barking as if he were laughing too, Poppy thrusting her nose in concern into her master's hand.

'You OK, G?' Theo asked him.

Geoffrey smiled up at her.

'I was fine until you horrible pair started laughing at me.'

'Sure?'

'Nothing worse than a soggy shoe to contend with. Although I will have to walk all the way back to Port Ruan squelching . . .'

'You'll hopefully dry out whilst we eat,' Suze reassured him, picking the picnic basket back up, 'which I vote is as soon as we get over on to the beach.'

And then something caught their attention. A sound. A cry.

Theo turned, listened.

Nothing.

It could have been the call of a gull overhead.

But Dylan seemed to have heard it too, as he galloped away from them, up and over the outcrop of rocks they had been clambering over, peering into rock pools like kids on a day out.

Theo followed, climbed over the rocks and down on to the beach to see Dill tearing up it, away from her.

'Dill!' she called, and the dog stopped and turned towards her, wagged his tail furiously, and then, turning away, began to run towards the other end of the beach again, only to stop moments later and look back at her as if to say 'hurry up'.

*

Dylan came flying at him so hard, that he knocked Jonas to the ground, stood on his chest, lay down on his chest, covered his face in wet kisses, jumped off him, jumped back on, barking and wagging his tail like crazy as Jonas clutched at his fur, held him to him, and tried not to cry with relief.

Theo caught up with him moments later, breathless, laughing, apologetic.

Jonas stared up at the stranger who looked so familiar with her dark copper hair and her soft, sweet smile; the stranger who, he saw in amazement, was wearing his scarf and his grandmother's antique pearl earrings, the ones she had worn when she'd got married.

'I am so sorry,' she said.

Holding out her hands and grasping his, she pulled him to his feet, her laughter and her smile lifting him as much as her hands had.

'I don't know what's got into him . . . he's extremely friendly, but he's not usually quite this forward . . . by the way, I'm Theo, and this reprobate is—'

'Dylan,' he said, his face bursting into the hugest of smiles. 'This is Dylan!' And the handsome man with the green eyes full of joy burst into gales of the happiest laughter she had ever heard and then, to her amazement, he threw his arms around her, swept her off her feet and swung her round. Then, planting her back in the sand, he took her face between his hands and kissed her.

Epilogue

It had to be the most unconventional wedding ever seen in Port Ruan.

The bride and groom had shunned the little church and chosen to drag the elderly vicar up to the memorial garden instead, where the marriage ceremony was taking place in the tulip-strewn folly.

The nervous groom had two best men, a handsome young man with laughing green eyes, and a smiling dog in a bow tie.

The bride had walked down the path by the lake to the sound of Michael Bublé being played somewhat erratically by an elderly jazz quartet, one of whom was fast asleep face down on his piano. She was wearing a beautiful white dress set off perfectly by the most amazing pair of Claudio Fratenneli shoes, and was carrying a bouquet of the other two pairs tied together by their heel with ribbon.

The maid of honour had paint in her hair as well a flowers, and the flower girl was a prancing dog in a pin tutu.

The only traditions that had been adhered to were tha of the best man getting off with the maid of honou although they hadn't had the decency to wait until afte the wedding, and the words of the ceremony itself, the most important part of which the elderly vicar, smiling benignly in the September sunshine, had just come to.

'Do you, Suzanne Eva Lord,' he intoned, his voice ringing out across the crowd of villagers who had all gathered to join the celebrations, 'take Geoffrey Hemingway Tarquin Percival Montague De Courcey, Fifth Earl of Whittingshall, to be your lawful wedded husband?'

But he didn't get a reply.

Because, for the very first time in her entire life, at the most inopportune of moments, Suzanne Lord had finally been rendered speechless.

You can buy any of these other
Little Black Dress titles from your
bookshop or *direct from the publisher*.

FREE P&P AND UK DELIVERY
(Overseas and Ireland £3.50 per book)

TO ORDER SIMPLY CALL THIS NUMBER

01235 400 414

or visit our website: www.headline.co.uk

Prices and availability subject to change without notice.